QUEEN'S HEIR

Volume One—The Children of Khetar

QUEEN'S HEIR

BY JOHN E. BOYLE

Volume One—The Children of Khetar

A Fantasy set among the Hittites at the End of the Bronze Age

2016

First Printing: 2016

ISBN: 1532825455

Cover Art: Sirrush on the North Gate of Carchemish
Design: Createspace Design Team

For more information about the Children of Khetar, visit:
www.takeneid.com

For my Parents, Dennis and Marie

"Who set my feet upon the Path of Knowledge and turned my face towards the Light."

Acknowledgments

I would like to thank the following for unlocking the doors of imagination for me, and then doing their dead-level best to jam those doors open:

Greg Stafford, Steve Perrin, Sandy Peterson, Ken St. Andre, Ray Turney

I would also like to thank the members of the PGS group for their even-handed criticism, Master-level sarcasm and thirty years of scurrilous verbal abuse:

Alan Then, Rich Ohlson, Dwayne Pribik, Thad Gutshall, Mark Waterhouse, Keith Kendall, Leon Kirshtein, Scott Watson, John Eckert, Tony Zilz, Harry Kaisarian, Bob Frantz, Rich Frantz, Scott Krepps , Carl Croushore

Table of Contents

PROLOGUE

WE ARE THE CHILDREN OF KHETAR, who the world call the Hittites, and we live in a broken land. Our home is Issuria, the pass between the Pontine Mountains to our north and the Toros Mountains to the south. To the south and west is Thrace and beyond, the Ocean. To the north and west, the river Rhine rises in the Pontines and flows westward and then north to the Cold Sea. To the east is Scythia, westernmost of the lands ruled by the nomads from the boundless steppes; beyond Scythia is the valley of the Euphrates with the cities of Babylon and Assyria gleaming on its banks like threaded pearls. To the south and east are the lands claimed by the Pharoahs of Egypt, who time and again have brought war to our doorstep. In the more than two thousand years since Time as we know it began, our land of Issuria has been fought over again and again, by not just the kingdoms of men but the elder races too (and it said by gods and demons as well).

Perhaps the greatest of the kingdoms of men to rule here was the Dragon Empire, so named because their magic had allowed them to bind all of dragonkind to their service, from the lowest scaled creature to the great Mushusar, the dragons who can scar mountains with their wrath. They came to Issuria from the northwest, following the valley of the Rhine to its source in the Pontine Mountains, and they conquered all who dared to oppose them. Even the massed tribes of the Scythians fell before the Draconic Army, in a titanic battle that lasted two days and devastated the nomads so greatly they have yet to recover from it. For more than three hundred years, the Dragon Emperors ruled Issuria only to have their Empire unravel almost overnight.

We do not know if the Dragon Empire fell because of magic, famine, civil war, plague or some terrible combination of them all; we only know it happened quickly, completely, and to this day none of the dragon kind will serve anyone.

The Breaking of the World

The fall of the Dragon Empire affected tens of thousands of people, but it was not the first nor the last Empire to rise to power and then slide into ruin. Less than a century after the Fall of Dragons, something happened that changed our entire world to such an extent that it is seen to be the boundary between our past and our present. The Thracians use the terms Prin Klao or PK to indicate events that occurred before the Breaking, and

Meta Klao or MK to indicate those that occurred after our world changed. It grows more and more difficult to imagine what our world was like before the earthquakes and the opening of the Rift Valley.

The Dragon Empire had dominated the lands north of the Ocean, and Egypt had ruled those lands to its south, but the Ocean itself had been ruled by the Lords of the Sea, the wizard-kings of the great island nations: Cyprus, Rhodes, Sicily, Sardon, Corsis and silver-spired Crete, Queen of the Waves. Egypt and the Dragons together at their height could not match the fleets of the Sea Lords, and their magical power put them on an even footing with both of those Empires. Trade was the lifeblood of the Sea Lords, and things such as smuggling, piracy and chaos were bad for business and suppressed whenever they reared their ugly heads. When the Dragons fell, the Lords of the Sea naturally began to extend their influence inland to the north; many of their peoples followed, drawn by the promise of lands left empty and fallow by the fall of the old Empire.

Fifty years after the last Draconic army disbanded, the Sea Lords had founded or re-occupied a dozen ports along the northern coasts, from Gadir in Hispania to Eretria on the edge of southern Thrace. Their armies were probing up the river valleys and establishing contacts with any surviving communities, while their agents were said to be sifting through the wreckage left by the Fall, searching for treasure and the magical artifacts the Dragon Empire must have left behind. Then the earthquakes began.

The tremors were light at first, but grew ever stronger. The quakes only struck the islands, so many fled to the mainland and were saved. But at least as many more did not, and thousands died the night when the ocean bed heaved like the back of some great beast. From west to east the earth moved, and smashed the island kingdoms like a child's toys; it then struck the coast south of Arwad and opened a crack in the world hundreds of feet deep and a mile or more wide. This rift ran south east between Baalbek and Kadesh until it finally stopped south of distant Ur. By the time the waves subsided, everything had changed.

The shapes of all the greater islands were different; of the smaller islands, many had disappeared entirely while others were larger. The seas became impassable; the currents of the coastal waters had changed, and new shoals of rocks, whirlpools, geysers and strange beasts turned sea lanes and fishing grounds that had been used for centuries into death traps. The maps of the old world were useless, and outside of protected waters such as the Narrow Sea, people turned the backs on the ocean they dreaded and no longer understood. On land, people fared better, but the changes were still profound. The Great Rift had almost severed Egypt and the entire peninsula of Arabu from the north lands. The seas rushed in to fill the western end of the chasm, and the rest of its length was wracked by landslides and clouds of deadly gases that struck down birds, beasts and men alike. Travel across the Rift was impossible, as was most communication; anyone who found themselves on the side of the Rift Valley opposite their homeland had to find a way to adapt, or they withered and died.

So matters stood for more than five hundred years after the Breaking of the World. Then the Minos raised the first Pharos at the entrance to the Narrow Sea, and the power of that great Lighthouse and the others that were built in other lands has calmed the waters within a hundred miles of each tower such that trade and travel with the lands of the west are possible again.

Now we hear that the Egyptians are nearing completion of the Great Span at Kadesh, and soon we may see the messengers and armies of the Pharoah in the northlands again. From the west we hear that volcanoes such as Aetna and Vesuvius are changing the shape of lands shattered by the Breaking. Slowly the earth renews itself. Slowly we rebuild what were ruins. Slowly we reknit the bonds between the nations sundered by the Breaking. But there is no ignoring the fact that we live in a Broken Land, and it has only just begun to mend.

Look at this sword, Grandchild of mine. This sword was carried by my father and by his fathers before him, since the beginning of Time. My father's name was Danu Queen's Sword, and he was murdered by assassins in the service of the Empire of the White Sun. For that murder, I demanded a blood price from the Empire, and had made it pay that debt several times over before ever I wed your grandmother. How did your great-grandfather die? I will tell you, as it was told to me by one who was there. I believe what he told me; had he lied, the sword he held, THIS sword, would have turned in his hands and struck him down.

This happened in the City of a Thousand Dragons, in the kingdom of Utrigar in the outer provinces of the Empire of the White Sun, in the 600th year since the Breaking of the World. The kingdom of Utrigar is the wildest and least developed of all of the provinces of the Empire of the White Sun. It has only one major population center: the fabled City of 1,000 Dragons, a center of sorcerous learning during the rule of the Draconic Empire, centuries ago. It is not called thus because of the thousands of dragon statues and images that adorn its walls, streets and plazas, but because of its famed Sirrush Legion. This had been composed of one thousand of the fiercest fighters in the Empire, each astride their own sirrush or lesser dragon, each warrior protected by a hauberk of scale armor that matched the scales of their ferocious mounts. The Sirrush Legion had been said to be invincible in battle, but it had vanished more than 600 years ago along with the Empire it served.

Some said that it had fallen when the dragons themselves turned on the Empire and devoured it; others said that the Fall had started as a civil war and ended with famine and plague sweeping away what war had left behind. All of the stories agreed in two respects: first, that the Fall of the Dragon Empire took less than the lifetime of a man, perhaps even less than a decade. Second, that since that time, no one, anywhere, has been able to tame any of the dragon kind to their hands, not even the least of them, let alone the Mushusar, the great dragons that could devastate entire armies. Of all that great Empire: a score of shining cities, half a hundred thriving towns, armies unmatched, wealth and power surpassing even golden Egypt at her zenith, now only a scattered handful of outposts remain, each shrunken and dreaming in out of the way places, remainders of how great the past had been, and of how quickly even Dragons can Fall.

It was night in the City of 1,000 Dragons. In this, the thirtieth year of the reign of Katrin, called the White Empress, this city was the center of a considerable amount of activity, both mercantile and military. As the biggest base of operations for the Imperial troops stationed in the province, this ancient outpost of learning offered not only a large market for those merchants that served the soldiers' needs but safety as well. As a result, the caravans came from all over the Empire and beyond, and the local market was a thriving one. This night, most of the city had gone dark, with the exception of those establishments whose business it was to cater to those abroad in the night for the sake of duty or pleasure.

One such establishment was the White Stallion; a three-storied tavern and hostel favored by those imperial officers with common blood. A cut above the drinking houses favored by mercenaries, to be sure, but still not on the same level as the Scarlet Palace, a drinking and gambling house patronized by officers from the nobility. Othar Inkson strode out onto the north balcony of the White Stallion, and took a deep breath of the cool night's air. Hooking his thumbs in his belt, he rocked back on his heels and hummed to himself with a kind of growling contentment.

"I'm on my way", he thought. "I've got my feet on the steps to power, and only death or my own stupidity can knock me off!".

He stretched and allowed himself to feel the weight of both the sword at his side and the medallion that hung around his neck, an eye-catching sunburst of crimson and white gold. The sword was an officer's saber of spell-wrought iron, and the medallion had been an award from the hand of the Lord of the Eastern Marches himself.

"Recognition and an officer's commission in the auxiliaries; not bad for the last-born son of a temple scribe and a bootmaker." he thought.

Not that it had come easy. The sword, and the commission that went with it, had been bought with ten years of service on the frontiers of the Empire. From the eaves of the Black Forest to the shadow of the God Pillar in Dacia, from the blood-drenched steppes of northern Scythia to the marshes of Rhine-mouth, he had sweated and blistered and bled in the service of the Empress. And killed too. He couldn't remember how many enemies of the Empire he had slain since that first one, a bandit raiding caravans IN Pannonia south of the Rhine. Or how many of his own comrades he had watched die, in battle or due to their own ignorance, an officer's incompetence or just plain bad luck.

"Now the burden of command is mine", he thought, "Now it will be my orders that mean life or death for my soldiers".

Othar clasped the medallion in a clenched fist and swore his own oath to the gods of war:

"It is a soldier's duty to fight and die for his emperor, but no one under my command will die because I couldn't be bothered to learn enough or care enough. At least I won't have that on my conscience when I face the Judges of the Dead."

Now, Luck, that was a different matter. The gods gave good or bad luck as they chose, and a prudent man prepared for the worst and did the best he could with what came to him.

"And if the gods should send a little good luck my way" he thought, "Why, then I'll grab hold with both hands and hang on like a tick to a hound's ear. What was that?"

He had heard something; Othar couldn't place it right away, but it was a sound that didn't belong in this time and place, and he had spent too many years on the frontier to ignore something like that. Those who did, died.

Othar walked over to the balustrade to his right, and leaned over.

"Did you hear something, Kadj?", he called down to the scar-faced man standing by the hitching post in front of the tavern.

Kadj was a broad shouldered man of average height, clad in the bronze and scarlet of a non-commissioned officer of the Imperial Army. He was facing off to the east, with one hand touching his sword hilt.

"Aye, sir. I heard it, and saw something too; it came from over there, towards the Wizard's Quarter. Look, sir, there it is again!".

Othar had already seen it, a streak of silvered light that had flared and then dimmed in the space of an instant. Magic. Othar knew the look and smell of it as well as any soldier, after 10 years with the imperial armies. Well, what did he expect; they didn't call the east section of town the Wizard's Quarter for nothing. Except... that flare of light had come from close to ground level, and the row of shops and warehouses on this side of the Quarter should have blocked any sight of a spell cast near the magicians' guilds. That meant it came from inside or near the east end of the depot and that made it army business, his business to be exact. The army depot in this town was the largest in the province, and the main source of supply for every imperial unit east of Pannonia and west of Dacia.

"No alarms", growled Kadj.

No, and Othar didn't like what that implied, not at all. The depot was warded; nothing fancy, but enough to have reacted to a series of spells cast at or within its boundaries.

"Finish your drink", he said to Kadj, "We are going to take a little walk."

"Yes, Sir!"

"My subordinate sounds a little bored", thought Othar, as he walked down the two flights of stairs to the ground floor to pay his tab. "He knows better than that; boredom in the army meant you were safe, it was when things got exciting that people started dying. Still (grinning tightly to himself as he touched his sword hilt), maybe I'm a little bored too."

Kadj was waiting outside with a shielded lantern; Othar nodded to him and the two of them set off down the lane leading east. Kadj walked a little ahead of his superior and to his left, with the lantern held out to his own left at arm's length. Both men had done enough street fighting to know that a light on a dark street could draw missile fire if there was real trouble ahead. It wasn't that long a walk; two short blocks past the saddler's shop and a stable. Beyond that, the lane met the triple-width road and the six foot high wall that surrounded the Imperial Army depot. Across the road from the mouth of the lane was one of the four entries into the depot; a guard post manned day and night by at least a dozen soldiers.

One glance was all he needed to know something was wrong. The officer on duty was a fresh-faced boy, obviously just out of the academy at Truknow. His second in command was a woman of Othar's age with the eyes of a veteran and the decorations to prove it. The boy was nearly petrified with a mixture of fear and anxiety, but his second made no attempt to hide her relief. Othar knew what that meant, he was too old a soldier not to know when the silver was being passed to him. What was more worrisome was that the depot wards were down; the telltale yellow glow was missing from the sunwheel runes that flanked the gates.

"Who goes there?" came the challenge.

"Othar Inkson, Captain, attached to the Sixth Auxiliaries."

"It is an honor, Captain. I was present at the award ceremony the other day and ..."

In no mood for pleasantaries, Othar tore into the junior officer:

"What in hell is going on here, Watch Officer? I saw magic, what could only be the sign of an intruder on imperial property; and upon arriving here I find the depot's wards down and the officer in charge babbling like an idiot!"

Silence.

"Well?"

"I ccan't tell you, sir", stuttered the young officer, "I..."

It had been a while since anyone had defied him in public; Othar took one step closer to the younger man, his teeth gleaming in a vicious grin, and the watch officer's face went white with fear.

"They ordered me not to, sir.", said the Watch Officer, bracing himself for an explosion.

It never came.

"Damn, damn, damn. Why didn't I stay in that tavern and get stinking drunk, like any sane man?", thought Othar to himself.

Dropping the wards around an army depot and then ordering the army's own guards to keep silence about it had all of the earmarks of a Second Shadow operation. Apparently Kadj agreed. He was ripping off a string of searing curses pungent enough to cause the admiring troopers who were listening to back off a half pace. He ended his outburst by spitting out the phrase "Second Shadow", and making an old peasant gesture to ward off bad luck. Othar had to agree; the Second Shadow was all of that and more.

The Empress's Second Shadow was a covert organization devoted to uncovering subversives, progressives and insurrectionists while encouraging patriotism and loyalty to the Empire by acting as a political cadre. In short they were a pack of arrogant, intrusive busybodies who questioned everyone's loyalty but their own, and who had a penchant for creating a bloody mess that all too often had to be cleaned up by the Imperial Army. Othar had crossed paths with the Second Shadow on half a dozen occasions, and had regretted it more each time. Agents of the Emperor's Second Shadow never thanked you if you helped them, and made you pay if you crossed them; they absolutely hated it when anyone interfered with an on-going operation.

"Which I am almost certainly about to do", thought Othar to himself.

It was too late to back out now; his presence here and now had already been logged by the guards. And if something had gone wrong with the Second Shadow's little plan, it was his duty to see that any damage done was minimized as soon as possible. There just wasn't any way out of it.

"Officer of the Watch, what exactly are your orders?"

"Sir. To maintain watch at this gate and prevent the exit or entrance of any unauthorized personnel. To refuse to divulge any information regarding this operation to anyone who is not a direct superior. To hold my detachment ready to respond to any general alarm or to a specific call for help from my temporary superiors."

Temporary superiors; right. Well, here it was, one last chance to close his eyes and back away from this mess. Ha. His name was already down, and if things went really wrong, he would be on record as having ignored a problem when it might have been small enough to solve. Another thing: the lights he had seen had been an odd silver in color; magic cast by a follower of the White Sun would be white (the color of her aura) or red (the color of her mantle) in color. A magician assigned to the Second Shadow would have access to many different types of magic, but this was still enough to warrant a closer look; it had that kind of feel to it.

"Watch Officer, I am going to investigate a suspected disturbance inside the depot, on my own authority. I am going to amend your orders in only one respect: that you sound a general alarm upon hearing any type of disturbance at all, or in any case in 15 minutes if you have not heard from me. Is that clear?"

"Yes, Sir!"

"I will need the assistance of one of your people, preferably one who is intimately familiar with the layout of the depot."

"Any of my people qualify, sir"

"Then I will take that trooper. You, soldier! Take that lantern, hold it in your left hand, at arm's length, out to your left side. You will follow half a pace behind me and a pace to my left, and answer any questions I have about the depot."

"Yes, sir"

"Can you run?"

"Oh, yes Sir!"

"Pray you won't need to. Carry on, Watch Officer."

Othar returned the salutes of the watch officer and his troops, and motioned Kadj and the lantern bearer to follow him down the east/west lane that crossed the depot from one side to the other. Both Othar and Kadj drew their swords the instant they entered the depot proper. Stretching away on either hand were the serried rows of sheds and warehouses that contained the equipment and supplies that fed, clothed and armed every imperial unit within a hundred miles: Boots and saddles, blankets, cloaks, cordage, tools and tack; baulks of lumber and kegs of nails. Sheaves of arrows and spears, poles hung with helmets and corselets, rack upon rack of sheathed swords and stacked shields. And towering on either side of the lane were the ordered mountains of food: flour, cheese, olives and onions for the troops, hay and grain for their mounts and draft animals; all protected from the elements by tarp and plank, but still readily accessible to the army's teamsters. This depot was the heart of the military province of Utrigar.

"An enemy could damage us horribly here", Othar thought to himself. "All the more reason to be sure that nothing had gone wrong, and to fix anything that had."

"Soldier, is there a guardpost like yours on the east side of the depot?"

"Normally yes, Sir. But not tonight; our temporary superiors dismissed that watch after barricading the east gate. They had some of us carrying lumber for them earlier."

"How far to the gate?"

"Not far, sir. About 100 paces on the other side of this rise."

The lane had begun to slope uphill, climbing the low ridge that divided the depot and indeed the entire city into two portions. "Bad", thought

Othar. "We will be out of sight of the other guard post, and mostly out of hearing as well". They topped the rise then, looking down the lane to the east gate, which was almost completely blocked by a barricade of beams and sand bags, and that is when they caught it: the smell of death.

The body wasn't hard to find; it was cooling on the ground behind its perch, a neatly constructed position on the north side of the road that gave its occupant a commanding view of the east gate. Difficult to spot from the east, this niche was completely open to the west and had been built using a few planks, barrels and sacks of grain and sand. The corpse was that of a thick-bodied man with grizzled hair and the look of a soldier, even in death. He was laying on his back, wide eyes staring up at the stars, with a faint expression of surprise on his face.

Othar flicked one glance at the body and then stopped dead in his tracks. He had expected to find a bow or crossbow and a quiver of missiles in the embrasure, not a siege engine! The dead man had been manning an arbalast; something like a very large, powerful crossbow that required a tripod to brace it. Arbalasts were slow firing but had a range of up to 200 yards or more, and enough killing power to stop a bull. They were normally used in sieges or in the defense of a fortified camp. This one had been set to cover the narrowed opening of the barricaded east gate, and it had been fired.

There was something else, the hint of a scent that was tantalizingly familiar, but which Othar could not place. It seemed to be coming from the arbalast itself. Behind him, Othar could hear Kadj performing a quick search of the body.

"Anything unusual about our friend?", he asked the non-com.

"No wounds of any kind on the body, sir; he had a tattoo: Spade and a badger's head."

That tattoo was a favorite among the imperial field engineers; no wounds on a dead body hinted of death magic and that was very bad...there was that scent again. It reminded Othar of pinetrees, somehow. There was only one bolt left as a reload for the arbalast. That made sense; the dead man had probably expected to get off only one or two shots. If you shoot at someone with an arbalast, either you drop them or they run like hell. There was a small wooden pot next to the engine itself, no larger than the tip of his little finger. Othar leaned over to sniff at it, an impossible idea starting to form in his mind, and then jumped backwards, snapping out a jittery curse. Pinetrees and oranges, the faint but unforgettable smell of *kaymn*. The arbalast bolt had been poisoned!

"He was putting *kaymn* paste on his bolts, Kadj."

"WHAT! Gods, what a filthy way to die."

Kaymn was a poison made and used only by the elves of the Black Forest and then only rarely. To the elven races, the Children of the Forest, it was a rare medicine that was said to heal afflictions of the mind and could induce dreams that might foretell the future. But elves are not human, no matter how much they might look it. For humans, *kaymn* was the deadliest of poisons, bringing its victims insanity, blindness and eventually death in agonizing convulsions. There was no antidote; *kaymn* changed the color and makeup of its victims' blood. Once in the bloodstream, only divine intervention could reverse its effects. But to put *kaymn* on an arbalast bolt made no sense at all. An arbalast could drive an inch-thick bolt completely through a door or through a man in a full suite of plate armor for that matter. You might as well poison a battering ram or an executioner's axe.

"He wanted to be sure; he must have really hated whoever he was shooting at", said Kadj.

"Not hate; fear. He was afraid of his target. If it was hate, he'd have been up close, where he could see his enemy's face. Instead he was back here, and so afraid of who he was shooting at, that he wanted to kill his victim twice over before whoever it was could get close enough to strike back."

Othar look at the dead man again. "But it didn't work, did it? You're still dead, and there is no body in sight down there."

"Second Shadow agents for sure, sir. *Kaymn* is so high on the proscribed substance list that only a ruling House could afford it. I don't even want to think about what they did to get that much *kaymn* in one place; there is enough in that pot to kill a dozen men. One thing is for sure: there will be more of them, sir. Three to five is standard formation for the Second Shadow's field units.", said Kadj.

Field unit? Assassins was more like it; professional hunter/killers who stalked and slew for the Empress, but only a fool would use words like that where anyone could hear, and Kadj was no fool.

"All right then, lets swing south of the road and see what we can find closer to the gate. Trooper, stay close to us."

"With all due respect, sir, I'd ride on your shoulders if you'd let me", was the reply.

Othar grinned at that, glancing once at the soldier behind him. Not even twenty years old, by the look of him; he looked and sounded scared, but the hands holding the scimitar and lantern were rock steady. Othar turned and met Kadj's eyes, both thinking the same thing; "We could make something of this one", they thought. Fifty paces south and and a little east of the first corpse, they found the second body: this one a priestess, dead without any mark on the body.

"Now", thought Othar, "NOW I'm scared".

He and his companions crouched at the points of a triangle, with their backs to each other and the corpse, eyes searching, ears straining for anything, any sign that whatever had struck down a priestess of Hel BlackWitch might still be close enough to kill them.

"Remember, it might be able to fly", he warned.

His companions nodded and strained every nerve in an attempt to penetrate the darkness surrounding them. Nothing; what little sounds that could be heard came from beyond the depot wall, from the town itself. Around them, there was nothing, no hint of movement or life. Othar lowered his saber, and glanced down at the body lying crumpled on its side. The followers of the Black Witch were a nasty lot, as skilled at magic as they were at assassination and subterfuge; any priestess of that cult participating in an ambush would have had every magical protection she could cast or requisition in place before their target ever entered the killing zone. Yet someone or something had punched through those protections to snuff out her life like a man pinching out a candle.

"Looks like they ran into more than they bargained for.", said Othar.

Kadj grunted. "Looks like they ran into more than I'd want to face without a bloody regiment to back me up." He looked around uneasily, "But that isn't all that's bothering me, Sir. There isn't any noise, and I can't see any flames or smell smoke. I mean, sir, if it wasn't an attempt to sabotage the depot, what was all of this about?".

Good question. Unless it was something more subtle than a simple fire: poison. Now there was a nasty thought. Poison some of an army's water or wine casks and you damaged morale out of all proportion to the number of people who might succumb to the poison itself. Putting madweed or elflame in the fodder would do even more harm. An army without supplies couldn't do much more than make a lot of noise. Kill or disable the horses, mules and oxen that pulled the supply wagons and the Imperial units in this area would be nearly paralyzed until replacements were found. The quartermaster and her people were going to have to check every cask and bale in the depot for signs of tampering; it would take a few days, but it was better to be safe.

Kadj agreed, but:

"The quartermaster's boys and girls are just going to love you for this one, Sir."

"Yes, well I'll just have to live with that, <u>if</u> we can warn them. I know when I'm out of my depth; we are going to get some help in here, right now. Trooper, what kind of alarms will the post at the east gate have?"

"A beacon and a horn to be blown, sir."

"We will use them both. Kadj, shield that lantern. I am betting that if anyone is out there, they will expect us to cut back to the west gate for help. Instead, we will try to reach the east gate. We will work our way down to that open area and then make a run for it. What is your name, boy?"

"Sharn, sir."

"Kadj, you'll be on the left, I will be on the right, and you, Sharn, will run like hell for the guard post and sound the alarm. You will not stop for anything, and that includes stopping to help either of us if we go down. Understood?"

"Yes, sir."

"I hope you weren't lying to me about how fast you can run."

"I hope so too, sir."

"Right, let's move."

They began working their way down slope through the rows of crates and casks, to the flat open area just west of the eastern gate. Here is where the wagons and carts were parked when loading or unloading their cargoes. Paved with cobblestones, it was completely without cover, and allowed a clear view of both of the corpses lying in the deep shadows south of the gate.

"Gods, there's two more for the shroud weavers".

"Shut up, Kadj. Ready? All right...Now!"

Up and forward then, like runners off a mark. Swords out; eyes searching the shadows, ears straining to hear an enemy's shout or the tramp of their feet. And all three of them could feel the flesh on their backs crawling in anticipation of the arrow or javelin that would be the first sign that their enemy had outguessed them. There was nothing; no sight or sound of an enemy, no attack of any kind. Othar and Kadj slammed to a halt on either side of the guardpost door and pivoted to face outward. Sharn dove through the door and, dragging a desperate breath into his burning lungs, blew an echoing blast from the brazen trumpet hung by the window.

The first horn call died away into a complete silence that seemed to be the entire city listening. The second blast awakened a distant tumult that seemed to surround the entire depot. Still no sign or sound of an intruder.

"One more time, Sharn and then get that beacon lit."

"Aye, Sir."

"Kadj, is that lantern of yours still lit? Good; let us go take a look at those two bodies".

The two men whose bodies lay sprawled on the cobblestones had worked as part of a team. They had waited here, in the shadows, for the ambush to go off. After the marksman on the arbalast and the priestess had launched their attacks, these two had leapt forward in unison to slay or subdue a foe who had been wounded or distracted by the other members of their unit. It hadn't worked. Their opponent had known where they were and was ready for them. Both men had been wearing plate armor, the first a suit of worn bronze, standard service issue for the heavy infantry regiments.

The other suit of armor was more unusual; it was bronze as well, but had an odd ridged appearance to it. Bending over the body, Othar realized that there was a pattern of snakes writhing across the plates of the armor. The snakes were an odd iridescent green in color, and they seemed to move of themselves. "Magic!", he thought. An enchanted suit of armor, that might bestow unnatural strength or speed or magical protection on its wearer. The price of armor like that was almost unimaginable for someone of Othar's station.

The first man wore the sigils of Hoenir and must have been one of the hard-bitten non-commissioned officers who kept order in the penal battalions of the Imperial forces. He had been wielding a broadsword and a kite shield, the latter a five-foot tear drop of seasoned wood and hammered bronze that would cover most of the average soldier's torso and limbs. It hadn't protected this man much. Whatever had struck him had sheared through the shield like paper, severing the arm that held it and leaving a horrible wound in his left side that must extend clear to the spine. His entrails were bulging through the rent in his armor.

The second man had been wielding a two-handed sword and looked to have been a sworn disciple of Tyr Redhands, the champion of the White Sun and the favored war god of the Imperial military. To reach such a position required a imposing level of expertise in both fighting and magical skills. The Disciples of Tyr went into battle armed and armored by the power of their deity, and were easily the equal of a dozen normal men. Yet, if Othar read the tracks right, this man had been the first to die; whatever had killed him had broken his sword a fingers breadth from the hilt and sent his head bouncing away into the shadows.

"They are going to want that back." thought Othar dazedly, as he touched the man's sword hilt with the toe of his boot. Odd; that sword had to have been of enchanted iron (the hilt was), yet whatever had struck it had cut through the iron as if it were tin, and where was the other part of the blade? Then there were the wounds; damn it, both men had been experienced fighters and well armored, the one superbly so. Yet each man bore only one wound, and each wound had been dealt by a killing blow. Neither man's armor bore the marks of sustained combat. They had been so thoroughly outclassed by their opponent that they might as well have slain themselves. There was blood everywhere, but there was only one line of blood stains that led to or from the east gate.

"Sir! You'd better have a look at this." called Kadj from over by the gate.

Othar strode over to the gate and peered at the gatepost where Kadj was pointing. It was an arbalast bolt, sunk two or three inches into the oaken beam that supported half of the gate; in the lantern light, the blood that dripped from it looked to be as black as ink. The marksman had hit his target after all, and driven the arbalast bolt completely through whoever or whatever came through the gate; and then whatever it was got up and walked away. The gateway itself had been barricaded to the point where only one person at a time could enter or exit, and then only by turning sideways unless they were child-sized.

"There is more, sir. Outside the gate in the lane; you're better than me with tracks, so I thought I should keep my big feet out of them until you could look it over."

"Good work, Kadj. We'll...",

The scream that rang up the street from the south stopped Othar short. It was a death scream and both men knew it. They had heard enough of them in their time.

"Gods, it's gotten out into the city. Listen, Kadj; there has to be at least two of them; the one who killed those two there never got far enough into the depot to kill that marksman with any kind of magic I've ever heard of. He must have some kind of familiar that can fly."

A familiar; that was an unnerving thought in any case; here, in this city, it was terrifying. There were known to be old towers in the Wizard's

Quarter that were off limits by Imperial Edict; mansions abandoned centuries ago, that had their doors and windows barred shut and sealed with silver and cold iron. What if something in one of those towers had gotten *out*?

"Sharn! You stay right there and you don't even think of moving until you are relieved by at least a squad. This whole depot has to be searched and inspected. Where the hell are those reinforcements?"

"There is at least a squad with torches coming over the rise now, sir."

"It's about bloody time. I'll have to give them specific orders; in the meantime, I need to take a look at those tracks."

The tracks came up the lane from the south and lead back that way, interspersed with droplets of blood. Othar wished for the old slinger who had taught him to read sign ten years before. The tribesmen from the delta of the Rhine River could track a mouse across a glacier and see in the dark like cats. The tracks were more than a little confusing until Othar realized that they only lead out through the gate; the intruder had smelled a trap coming in and had climbed over the barricade to enter the depot rather than allow himself to be caught in the narrowed entrance of the gate. That and a look at a clear footprint alongside the depot wall told him something about the killer they had to deal with.

"A hillman?"

"Yes, I don't recognize the tribe though; maybe he's from one of the Pannonian border clans or the Buri. I have no idea what he's doing this far east, but we had better find out before anyone else dies."

The reinforcements arrived then, two full squads under the command of the watch officer they had met at the western gate. That young man skidded to a stop in front of Othar and saluted him in the same motion:

"Sir, my commander is at the west gate and will funnel reinforcements into the depot as they arrive. He is requesting at least two squadrons of cavalry from General Phrales to throw a cordon around this end of the city and has notified the guards at the city gates. They will bar the gates to all traffic until at least sunrise. I and my troops have been placed under your command until further notice. What are your orders?"

Well, at least the local CO sounded competent; then again, he'd probably been expecting something to go wrong ever since the Second Shadow operatives had shown up.

"You will take one of these squads and hold this gate until you are relieved by your CO; I will take the other squad with me. Once more reinforcements arrive, set them to gathering up the bodies of your "temporary superiors"; your man Sharn will show them where the other two bodies are. You will need to send a runner to the Quartermaster; she is to assume that the food, drink and fodder supplies in this depot may have been tampered with and her people must inspect all such supplies. Understood?"

The younger man nodded sharply, his eyes never leaving Othar's face.

"Until further notice, all troops within the depot must move in groups of no less than four troopers at all times. Runners moving along the east/west road should be the only exception. I believe the depot to be clear of intruders at the present time, but there is nothing that says they will not try to return. Questions?"

"No, Sir!"

"Carry on then. You, Sergeant...?

"Cala, sir."

"All right Cala, you and your people will be backing me up on a little hunting expedition. Our quarry is wounded and extremely dangerous. Beyond that I cannot tell you much, except that there is no place for heroics in tonight's work and that I will personally kill the soldier who disobeys one of my orders. Any questions?"

"No, Sir!"

"Good. This is Kadj; get acquainted."

Othar walked over to the guardpost and peered into the supply shed. Pole lanterns, good, he was going to need about four of those. He looked around for the green watch officer; he actually looked a little green now and was shaking a bit with shock after taking a look at those two corpses.

"I'll be taking four of the pole lanterns from that shed. Otherwise, the drill is the same as before: if you hear anything suspicious or if you don't hear from us in 15 minutes, alert your CO. We will be following a trail that leads south, but the only things south of here are warehouses, the Red Spear barracks and a handful of alleys that lead into the Wizard's Quarter. If we can flush him out of the warehouses, we may be able to corner him inside the Quarter, but he could always try to double back on us. Wish us luck, and get a drink of something, it'll help."

After telling Kadj to get four pole lanterns from the shed, Othar had Cala and her squad file into the road outside the east gate. He organized them in three ranks, four soldiers across, with the third rank holding the pole lanterns to provide light for the rest of the unit. Othar stationed Cala at the rear and on the right, but he and Kadj lead the formation, with himself walking point and the non-com two paces behind and on his left side. Normally, one of them would have been stationed on the left to help Cala to close up the files, but there were times where, if you wanted to be a leader, you led. This was one of them. There were two paces between each soldier, this gave him a formation open enough to be flexible (and to block the road) but close enough to provide support for each of his men. Stealth was out of the question; trying to sneak up on a hill barbarian with a dozen troopers, half of them flat-footed city folk, would have been an exercise in futility.

They headed south along the perimeter road, with the depot wall on their right and the blank backwalls of a series of warehouses on their left. After the first twenty paces, they lost the blood trail, but could clearly see their quarry's footprints in the dirt of the road. One hundred paces south of the gate and fifty paces north of the southeastern corner of the depot was the first place where one of the city's streets intersected with the depot's perimeter road. That was where they found the bodies.

Othar waved the others to a halt, then motioned Kadj forward with his lantern to light his reading of the tracks. There was no more blood around the tracks, so their opponent had succeeded in closing his wound, probably by magic. He had been busy, so he hadn't heard the two watchmen running towards the sound of the alarm horn, who ran right around the corner to their deaths. They had been members of the city watch, a pair walking their nightly circuit who had heard the alarm horn sound and came running. They had come west on this road and around the corner, perhaps expecting to help fight a fire, never dreaming that they would be running headlong into death on two feet.

The man on the left had been cut completely in two; the blade had been swung parallel to the ground and caught him in the belly between the pelvis and the ribcage. It had to have been a sword: no axe big enough to do that to a man could be swung horizontally like that, not by anything human, and certainly not without striking the wall to the left of the killer. Both he and his victim had been standing too close to that wall to avoid striking it with a really long weapon. It had to have been one of the two-handed swords favored by the hill tribes. That style was shorter and lighter than the big two-handers preferred by lowland swordsmen, but it was faster and just as deadly as any other sword in the hands of a master. The swordsman had cut the first watchman in half and then completed the swing, pivoting on his right foot. He had brought his blade up, around and down to sever the right arm and gash the leg of the other watchman who would have been starting to turn, staring in shock at his companion's death. It had been the second man's death cry they had heard; he would have lost consciousness in seconds from wounds like that.

But why kill them? Any hillman would have hearing keen enough to hear two puffing townsmen blundering down an alley at night; all he had to do was shrink back against the wall to their right, and the shadows would have hide him from them as they ran by.

"Because he has been poisoned, stupid." Othar thought to himself.

With *kaymn* coursing through his veins, he would have been disoriented, perhaps even delirious by this time. Preoccupied with healing himself, the swordsman wouldn't have noticed the watchmen until it was too late to do anything but react; he had killed them almost as a matter of reflex. His tracks showed that he had barely broken stride passing through the intersection. But how could someone who could sense the locations of assassins hidden in the shadows of the depot never notice the approach of two night watchmen? That is when the answer hit him: because the watchmen had not known he was there, did not even know he existed, and the swordsman could only sense those who threatened him. Death magic that could kill without leaving a mark on the body, sword strokes that clove armor like foil, senses that could pick out an assassin from the deepest shadow: it had to be a follower of Warrunk Atte, the old god of Death and War.

Othar hadn't realized he had spoken out loud until Cala asked him a question:

"I'm sorry, sir, what did you say?"

Othar stood and turned to face his soldiers.

"I believe the wounded man we are hunting is a Disciple of Warrunk Atte."

"The bloody HELL we are!" came one frightened whisper.

"That's enough out of you", snarled Cala. "Or I'll make you pray that you're the first to find him."

The cult of Warrunk Atte was not a popular one in the Empire of the White Sun. There were other gods of war who were more favored by the Empress and her mother, the Sun Goddess who had founded the Empire and who shone so brightly on its fortunes. Tyr Redhands, the White Sun's Champion; Bokar Sha, Auroch Slayer; Sigurd Dragonsbane, Conquering Son. The ancient cult of Warrunk Atte was deemed to be inadequate for meeting the needs of a civilized society. His simplistic code of truth and honor was enough for barbarians no doubt, but the modern life was too complex, too fluid to be constrained by such a limited mindset. Warrunk Atte was one of those gods who time was past, like his brother, Tarhunt who dared to contest the Middle Air with the White Sun. Worship of Warrunk was not proscribed, as was Tarhunt's, but it was considered to be a quaint and backward cult. Time and the world was passing Warrunk by, and soon he would have to give way to a newer, more youthful god of war, one such as Tyr Redhands. Then Warrunk would be out on the dust heap with the other failed deities. But for now, no one dared to laugh at Warrunk; the followers of Death's Master were too damn dangerous.

Well, it could have been worse, Othar thought. It might have been one of Alas Tora's Executioners, or a Blood Drinker of Zarab Adar. Gods! The thought of one of the bloodstained darkling wargod's killers running berzerk in a residential area was enough to put a chill up his spine. Half of the city would have been in flames by now. At least with a Warrunki, the helpless and the civilians were safe. Warrunk's Code forbade threatening their lives or safety. It was only those who attacked him, or those who carried weapons and wore an enemy's uniform who had to fear for their lives. Like us, for example. Unless, of course, the *kaymn* has driven him completely mad, thought Othar with a shiver. That was always a possibility.

"Listen up. This simplifies things. A follower of Warrunk won't set fire to someone's home, attack someone who is unarmed or hold a child hostage. He won't be a threat to the civilians at all, unless they blunder into him like these two did. We are another matter entirely, but if we can bottle him up in a warehouse or between the wards of the Wizard's Quarter, we can wait him out. He's been poisoned, and the effects of the poison will drop him within the hour. But that will not solve the problem of the familiar or whatever it is that is traveling with him. All we know is that it can fly, and it looks like it can cast spells."

"For now, what is most important is getting between any civilians and this hillman. They'll be safe as long as they don't attack him, but right now they don't know that. What I think we can count on is that he won't stab anyone in the back; I believe him to be geased against any kind of ambush. He may very well decide to rush us though, so don't let our superior numbers give any of you a false sense of security; being outnumbered doesn't mean a damn to him. And remember, LOOK UP. He's a hillman; he can scale these walls as easily as you or I can climb a ladder. Now keep your eyes and ears open."

Their quarry had gone right on through the intersection, heading south. They followed, each of them hoping that the poison would kill their opponent before they would ever have to face him. Fifty paces further south the road forked; the righthand or western fork ran along the southern wall of the depot. The lefthand or southern fork began a swing to the east, passing a series of warehouses before ending on the western edge of the Wizard's Quarter. Across the street from the southern wall of the depot was the fortress-like barracks of mercenary company called the Red Spears; the massive wall of the barracks would run along the righthand side of the road as they continued south and east. The Red Spears themselves were currently out of town on contract.

"It's just as well", thought Othar; "they cost too much for me to hire any of them in a pinch like this".

The tracks of the hillman's boots were clear in the dirt of the road before them; this warrior was running right down the middle of the road, never swerving to left or right. This struck Othar as odd until he realized that someone doing so would have the least chance of encountering any type of magical warding on the buildings on either side of the road, something to be considered in a city like this one. As the road continued its swing to the east, it passed two alleys and then ended in a T intersection whose arms curved eastward to meet the avenue known as the Way of the Dragon, the traditional western boundary of the Wizard's Quarter. In between those two arms stood a five-story tall reef of masonry that was all that remained in this district of the old city's original walls; it was more than a thousand old and the tracks that they were following ran right up to it, disappearing 15 feet short of the wall's face.

"He went up that!?", said Cala.

"At a run, from the looks of it", said Kadj. "Sir, if he stays up there, we'll need aerial support to take him down, an air elemental or a griffon at the very least. There are supposed to be rooms in this thing that can be reached only from the top of the wall."

Othar grunted in agreement; he'd been afraid of something like this, but maybe it was for the best. If they could keep him treed up that wall like a raccoon, the *kaymn* in his veins would kill him before anyone else could get hurt. If. Well, it could be worse. What was that noise? Cala was already trotting towards the northern arm of the intersection to investigate. She came running back a moment later, and saluted him.

"Sir, it sounds as if a mob is forming on the Way of the Dragon, and it looks as if there are townspeople with lanterns searching some of the warehouses. If they've heard that we are hunting a wounded fugitive..."

"Some fool vigilante is going to get himself and six or seven of his friends killed confronting this barbarian. So, here is what we'll do..."

"Sir?"

"NOW what?"

"Hoofbeats, sir. Sounds like a single horse coming down the road behind us."

"Hmm. Probably a courier with a message for me. Kadj, Cala, each of you take half of the squad and head up these one of these roads to the Way of the Dragon. Sweep up anyone you find loitering along the way and tell anyone you find on the avenue to go home and get back to bed. Break up any crowd that might be forming and keep them away from this damn wall. This is military business, and unless I miss my guess, that courier is bringing a decree from the garrison commander saying that the city is under martial law until at least sunset tomorrow. You can say that if anyone wants to know why, and if they scream to the city council, I'll take responsibility for it. I'll stay here and wait for that courier. Kadj, you can leave that lantern of yours with me; each of you take two of the pole lanterns."

"Sir, I..."

"Don't worry, Kadj. I promise not to do anything REALLY stupid until you get back. Now get going."

Othar grinned to himself as he watched the half squads trot away up the branch roads. "Bloody nursemaid. Anyone would think he weaned me himself." His grin faded as considered the questions that he hadn't figured out any answers to. What had killed that marksman and the priestess without leaving a mark on the body or touching foot to the ground? What had destroyed that disciple's sword blade? For that matter, why go through the trouble of luring a barbarian follower of an eastern wargod away from his hills to this city just so the Second Shadow could set an ambush for him? Weren't there easier ways to assassinate someone? Although anybody who can take an arbalast bolt through the body and walk away is not someone Othar wanted walking around as an enemy of the Empire. Where the hell was that courier, anyway? He should have been here by now. Cocking an ear, Othar couldn't hear anything, much less the hoofbeats of a trotting horse.

"Idiot. Probably didn't see any lights, so he went back and turned up that side lane where we left those bodies. I had better walk back to the curve so they can see my lantern from the east gate."

Othar bent over to grab the lantern and heard the slightest whisper of a sound behind him, and realized he might have just made his last mistake. Turning, knowing that he would be too late, he raised the saber that he had never sheathed, hearing in his mind his own words of advice to the watch officer:

'...but he could always try to double back on us.'

As he turned, something licked out of the shadows at the base of the wall like a tongue of black flame. At its touch, the enchanted iron of his saber's blade *shattered*, like so much glass. "Well, so much for that question", he thought, backing up with his hands raised as the sword blade slide forward again to tap him lightly on the chest. He heard a grunt, and then the sword flicked at the lantern at his feet, flipping the shutters open to bathe him in light and leave his opponent in darkness.

"So. You are the one.", rasped a quiet voice in a familiar accent.

I'm good with languages and I've heard that accent before, but not around here, thought Othar. He cleared his throat, "Ah, have we met?".

The sword slid forward again to tap him lightly at the exact same spot on his chest.

"Yes, I know." said that voice with the familiar accent.

Othar froze as he realized that the stranger wasn't talking to him.

"Gods, he's got *kaymn* in his blood; he's mad, he could do anything."

The stranger stepped around behind the lantern, and forward into the light so that Othar could see him. He wore no armor, and was not very tall, clad in the leather and homespun common among the hill tribes. He had deeply tanned features, with long, dark curling hair and very dark brown eyes, almost black. He was rather small boned for a hillman, but was heavily muscled and moved on the balls of his feet, almost as if he was walking on tiptoe. The clothing just above his hip on the right side was badly stained, not only by blood, but with a greenish smear of what could only be *kaymn*. Othar felt a thrill of fear run through him and thought:

"Merciful Sif; he must have a triple dose of the poison in his veins. That much poison should have killed him within minutes!"

The arbalast bolt had struck him a glancing blow; almost a miss, but still enough to tear open a wound more than four inches long. It had bled freely until closed by healing magic. Othar looked at the man's clothing carefully and swore, peering at the other man's features and coloring.

"Damn it, you're no Quadi."

"No", grinned the hillman, "Mabirshan".

"Mabirshan? But that's in Khetar!" THAT's where he had heard that accent, when he had been stationed on the eastern borders of Dacia. "What the hell are you..."

"Doing here? Following a dream. Sorry, there is no time for this. My dreams are over, but your's might have just begun. Here, catch.", and he tossed his sword to Othar, flipping it end over end at him.

It was the last thing Othar would have expected; his catch was good, but by reflex and luck, not by any conscious effort. He is mad, thought Othar and he jumped as the warrunki fell suddenly to his knees. The other man seemed to be shivering and Othar flinched when he saw that the *kaymn* had progressed so far that the whites of its victim's eyes were turning blue. He isn't shivering, Othar realized, he is in the convulsive stage of the poison; he should be flopping around like a fish out of water.

"There was enough poison on that bolt to kill three men", he thought, "and this man is holding it off by sheer force of will."

The hillman jerked his head up to glare at Othar, and he had to step back a pace under the impact of the personality behind those eyes.

"Now, swear. Swear an oath; the sword's name is Oathtaker, and she demands a promise from any who would wield her. The more powerful the oath, the more power she can offer you. But break the oath, and you will die, and nothing can shield you from that death, or bring you back once you have died. And never lie while you are holding her; she will cut you down herself if you dare do that."

Madness. A magic sword with a spirit of its own? Ridiculous; the gods and heroes might carry weapons such as that, but a ragged barbarian out of a backcountry kingdom ruled by a tatooed savage? But Othar had seen this same sword shatter his scimitar with a flick of its wielder's wrist. And this man is a warrunki; they avoided lying on principle, some of them even geased themselves against saying anything they knew to be untrue. The man was almost dead; would any follower of Warrunk Atte spend his last moments of life perpetrating a lie?

Oh, what the hell. Othar took another look at the sword; it didn't look like a sword out of the legends. The blade was iron, which in itself made it worth a small fortune, but the sword felt wrong: the balance was off, the blade had the wrong proportions somehow and he couldn't seem to get a good grip on the hilt. He looked again at the man dying on the ground in front of him. My enemy, but a true warrior; if he wants me to swear an oath on his sword before he dies, so be it. Othar remembered the oath he had sworn earlier that evening, less than an hour ago, and repeated it in more formal language:

"This I swear; that no soldier of mine shall die because I did not care enough, or because I did not do my duty when I saw it. I will never fail those who trust me, nor abandon those who need me, nor cause another's death solely for mine own gain. May the Judges of the Dead hear my oath, and measure my life against it, in the moment that I stand in judgement before them."

The dying man in front of him nodded once, satisfied, and as he did, the madness Othar could see lurking behind those dark eyes swelled outward to engulf him. For SOMETHING answered his oath:

"A SOLDIER'S OATH TO MATCH A SOLDIER'S LIFE. WELL MET, OTHAR INKSON; WE ARE AS ONE."

It was a woman's voice that echoed in his mind, ringing like a silver bell and throbbing with ageless power. As it spoke, white fire seemed to run up the nerves in the arm that held the dying man's sword. Silver lightning flickered across his vision and through his mind, seeking and finding every hidden thought and forgotten memory his brain held within it. Then the hilt of the sword he held *shifted* and settled into his hand, fitting it as if each had been made for the other. It no longer seemed unbalanced or oddly proportioned; it seemed the most perfect blade he had ever held. Othar realized that he held in his hands a weapon of the highest order; of the kind that is complete only when it is in use. Then he began to dimly sense the power of the being that lived in that weapon, no, WAS the weapon itself.

"I had been looking for a familiar; some creature with feathers or scales that could kill from a distance; I never dreamed that it was the hillman's *sword* that was the real danger."

The voice spoke again, but softer now, and tinged with amusement:

"Why do you speak as if I am not here, boy? I can hear every thought that crosses your mind, and it is more than a little rude of you to speak of me as if I were a monster."

The whisper of that ringing voice was unnerving; Othar cleared his throat, and haltingly addressed his new companion: "Ah..., you're inside me, Lady?".

"In a sense, yes. You and I will be companions now, until it is time for us to pass on; you, onward through the Veil, and I, on into the hands of the next one who will wield me. Until then, we are linked by a chain that can be broken only by death. Farewell, Dono, son of Robard. I will miss thee, whose like I have not met in long age."

Othar heard those last words, but they were not spoken to him. His attention was drawn away from the sword in his hands by a motion of the man dying in front of him. The hillman was attempting to pull a waterflask from his belt; Othar stooped and held the flask to the other man's lips, the two-handed sword laid across his knees.

"My thanks", said the dying man, licking his lips. He tugged at a heavy gold ring on one of his fingers, its green stone glowing faintly as it left his hand. He reached for the medicine bag hung around his neck, and placed the ring inside with a clink. Holding the bag in his left hand, he held out his right towards Othar:

"My name is Danu Queen's Sword".

Othar took the proffered hand, and the soldier and the warrior gripped wrists; "Othar Inkson".

The warrunki nodded and handed Othar the medicine bag: "This is for you. For your use, until it is time to pass the Sword on to Oathtaker's next wielder."

He grunted suddenly, and arched backwards twisting in a convulsion. It seemed to go on forever; when it finally did pass, Danu was as limp as a wet rag.

"He'll be dead soon", thought Othar. He should be dead now by rights, and Othar didn't know nearly enough of what he needed to. He shook the other man gently. "Danu! Danu, listen to me. Pass the sword on to who? And how will I know when to pass it on?"

Danu's grip on Othar's wrist tightened like a vise, and his eyes seemed covered by a film that glowed with an eerie greenish light. Othar shivered, remembering the stories he had heard when he was stationed in the border of the Black Forest. Of how the elves of that forest would take *kaymn* to induce a trance, in which it was possible to pierce Time's Veil and see a part of the future that might be. The glow faded, and for a moment, Danu's face and eyes were untouched by any magic or poison. His grip was still strong and he winked at Othar with a grin. As he answered Othar's question, the captain realized that this man should have been his friend; the blood-brother he had never known.

"You'll know when it is time", said Danu, "when you see my face again."

Then he died.

The returning soldiers found him there minutes later, kneeling by the body of the friend he had never known. As he stood, he slid a plain-looking iron sword into a sheath he had taken from the dead man, and then he hung the scabbard over his own shoulder.

"It is over", he said to the expectant troopers. "There was only the one intruder. I will make my report to the officer in command of the depot and to the garrison commander. Cala, have four of your people put this body on a shield and carry it back to the main barracks for me. I'll take care of it after I have made my reports."

"Aye, sir!"

"Kadj, could you help me with something later on, after sunrise?".

"Of course, sir. What is it?"

Othar looked at the four soldiers who were carrying the body of Danu Queen's Sword towards the lights at the east gate of the depot.

"I have to dig a grave for one of the Death God's own."

Chapter I: Nesa

Who walks the Path of Kings? Not royalty alone. For every hand that reaches for a crown, there is a faithful, faceless throng who sweat and bleed with every step their master takes. Some are heroes and many are fools, but damnation take the king who forgets those that helped him to his throne and who served with body and blood that their lord might rule.

- Mursilith, King of Khetar

MY NAME IS JOREN, son of Tiranna, and I am one of those who follow the Son of Khetar. There are many of us (although once there were more), and many are the strands in the web that Fate has used to bind us to him. For some it is love, for others it is hate. For some it is a matter of honor; for others, it is the mantle of glory and the weight of gold to be won in his wake. For me, it is some of all of these things, but most of all it is the legacy of my parents (whose faces I cannot remember), and an oath sworn to an old woman dying by the light of a burning barn.

All that I can remember of my childhood was spent in the village of Nesa, in the lands of the Kothmir tribe, not far south of the road to Melid. My aunt Syara was the village crone, and my first clear memory is of her long, strong face in the candle light and the touch of her hands on my brow and cheek.

"So you are the son of my niece." she said. "You look like your father, but you are my own flesh and blood. This is your home, now."

I ate thick soup and black bread, and dozed by the fire after making friends with a brindled wolfhound. While I dozed, my aunt and old Ajax whispered something about a world gone forever, and a long journey on foot along bad roads and through worse weather. I have a vague, jumbled memory of such a journey, but none of anything before that or indeed any clear memory of the man who had shepherded me to my aunt's door, until after she had touched me. An endless grey wall guards the earliest part of my life, and I have never been able to breach it, even in my dreams. I have spoken to many learned sages about this strange blankness, and they have been of three minds regarding it. The first thought is that I have been touched by some great spell or magic; the second thought is that my mind has been threatened by a horrible memory and guards itself by walling that memory away beyond my reach, lest I be damaged by it. The third thought is that I was simply injured by a great blow to the head. The wound had been healed, but not before my memories had leaked out, like honey from a comb. I do not know if any or all of these theories are true, though I favor the last one myself. Having had most of my brains knocked out as a child would explain a great many of my actions since.

The old man whose name I first learned while he sipped cider and spoke with my aunt that night was a part of my life in ways that even now I do not fully understand. Ajax Whitebeard or Ajax the Old was that great rarity among the tribesmen of Khetar: a warrior grown old in constant service to Wurrunk, god of war and death. He was a man somewhat taller than average, with hard, flat muscles and a deftness of hand and foot that were the envy of much younger men. He was quiet, and smiled with his eyes rather than his mouth, and he always seemed to know where I was. Ajax always knew when I was lying, and he had no patience with it. "Don't lie to me, boy.", he would say, "It puts my teeth on edge." He taught me how to fight, and that a man's work is whatever needs to be done, and never to fail a trust. I loved him.

The wolfhound that I made friends with that night was named Kon, and he was my constant companion the rest of his life. He was big, man-tall when he stood on his hind legs, with a thick coat of gold and red-brown fur, and his ears were red. His eyes were an odd silver color, and he never seemed to sleep. Kon and I got along very well together, which you might think strange. Later I learned that he had been a gift to my aunt from my own grandmother, and had been part of our House for a very long time. I think now that he caught some of the scent of home from me and treated me as a member of his pack from the start; once I fed him (and he would accept food from no one but my aunt and I), a bond as old as my family bound us together and we were inseparable. Wherever I went, whatever I did, Kon was there beside me, so that I was never alone. I was lulled to sleep at night by the beat of his heart and the thump of his tail; if I was hurt or frightened, it was the touch of his nose that first comforted me. And when my aunt cradled me in her arms, to sing to me, or to teach me, or just to hold me close, Kon would put his muzzle in her lap where either of us could caress it, and stand motionless in a patient, perfect contentment. It was some time before I realized that he was the only dog in the village, probably the only dog in all of the Kothmir lands. He rarely left the house itself, and never went any further from the house than its yard; none of the village duskcats would enter my aunt's home while he lived.

Kon went to sleep at the end of my second year with my aunt, and was laid to rest in a small house dug into the hillside behind our home. That was when I found how long he had been with my aunt; forty years for a hound is a very long time, and a very full life. Aunt Syara chose not to raise a duskcat afterwards; no kitten could take Kon's place and he had been a last reminder of her own children, who were years dead. She had no desire to reopen any old wounds, and neither did I, so I accepted her decision. It wasn't until after she was dead that I learned that there were no other dogs like Kon; not in Melid or Hattusa, nor anywere else in the lands of the Living.

One more thing I will say of Kon. In another time and place, I was given the war name of Dog. It did not bite me the way that those who named me thought it would, because my first memory of any dog was of Kon. To me, the word spoke of love given without condition, a watchful protectiveness that never faltered, and an enduring faithfulness that neither time nor death could diminish. Kon is why I do not hate dogs as most of our people do. I learned at an early age that not all dogs are killers of kittens and eaters of carrion. I do not forget him.

Ajax stayed with us whenever he could, but he was never in the village more than one week in four. The rest of the time, and whenever Ajax wasn't teaching me, the center of my life was my Aunt Syara; she taught me much, not the least of which was the knowledge and ways of our family, of which she said we were the last. Now, I have said she was the village crone; by that I do not mean that she was a withered hag, but that of the three Earth sisters (maiden, matron, crone), she wore the face of the eldest for our village. Aunt Syara was as tall (and as smart) as any man in the village, with a straight back and a no nonsense manner that she showed to everyone, man or woman, thane or shepherd. She had come to Nesa with her husband Farad, to live in his village and raise their children in his house. Both children and her husband were dead before I came to live with her, but Syara herself had become as much a part of Nesa as its deep, cool well or its grove of walnut trees. Nurse, midwife, herbalist and matchmaker, Aunt Syara headed the Women's Circle of the village and was in charge of the shrine of the Earth Mother. Her tall, brown-cloaked figure might be seen anywhere in or about the village, striding along with her close-stitched pack and her long staff bound and shod with ruddy copper. When I could, I helped her, and I think I filled some of the emptiness of her house, even if I could not banish any of the sad memories that colored its stones and tinted its windows.

Once, when I had lived in my new home a couple of years, I was helping my aunt carry simples to the Women's Hall. I had finished my chores early that day, so that I could take up a strategic position next to the oven; Aunt Syara's honey cakes were almost legendary, and while I had missed the opportunity to lick the mixing bowl, I had decided that the crumbs from the baking pan were mine. I had looked so determined that she smiled and gave me not one, but two cakes for myself. Being a boy, I stuffed them into my face at once, causing my aunt to suggest that I looked like a very large and very strangely dressed chipmunk. After washing my face and hands, I had picked up the baskets and followed my aunt out the door and down the flagged walk to the edge of the hill overlooking the village common. There, I found her looking down at a group of the village's young men and women; she was smiling, and had a far-off look in her eyes.

The men had come in from the fields for the midday meal and had just finished. The older men were stretching and talking quietly before returning to work; the younger men were laughing and teasing the women as they cleaned up after the meal. Below us, partially hidden from the others on the common, were a boy and a girl, just old enough to have become adults that season. It was Kara and Baruth; Kara was a nice girl and a favorite of mine because of her kindness.

Baruth, like the other young men, ignored me (to my relief). I was about to ask my aunt why Baruth was offering Kara a rather sorry-looking bunch of flowers when I realized that Kara was looking at Baruth's face, not the flowers. Baruth himself looked as if someone had just struck him in the head with a mallet. Beside me, my aunt said in a low, dreamy voice: "You would not believe it, my Jo, but once young men looked at me like that". I didn't really understand what was going on, but since I thought that my aunt was a thoroughly estimable woman, I promptly replied "I believe it".

My aunt laughed at that. She cupped my chin in her warm leathery hand and laughed a throaty, velvety laugh that was as much of a caress as the touch of her hand on my face. It was a rather startling sound to come from a bony old woman; it certainly startled Old Simbal and Lanka the Lame. They were two of our village's older and less reputable elements. They appeared to make their living doing odd jobs that came to hand, and spent the rest of their time drinking, embarrassing their relatives and emitting incredibly crude noises at the most inopportune times imaginable. (At the time, I am ashamed to admit of a sneaking admiration

41

for the latter ability.) These two stalwarts had been walking down the hill to the village tavern when they had been shocked to hear such a hearty laugh coming from no one less than Syara the Crone herself. Now, to my aunt, the thought of these two idle men in particular gawking at her in public was absolutely intolerable. She gave them a long stare cold enough to freeze vinegar, and the two old men suddenly remembered a promise to help Korsul Two-Spear castrate one of his hogs. They left forthwith. As did we, after a glance showed us that Kara and Baruth had gone about their chores for the afternoon. I still remember my aunt's laugh; I remember how much I loved to make her laugh, and how much I loved her.

Now, Lanka the Lame was most definitely the least reputable member of our village (and quite possibly of any village between Hattusa and Scythia): he was the village Trickster. Like most followers of Pirwa, Lanka avoided anything resembling honest work with a passion, was often drunk and always knew the crudest jokes and the most colorful language of anyone in the village. He smelled of stale ale and old food (if you were lucky) and Aunt Syara taught me three rules regarding him that have served me well when dealing with any trickster (save one):

Give the trickster food, or better, something to drink.

Don't let the trickster into the house.

Keep your hands and feet away from its mouth.

He was bound to Korsul Two-Spear, our Thane, as he had been bound to my uncle Farad before his death. As such, he was part of our village, and Aunt Syara said he was part of our village's luck. She had an odd relationship with Lanka: she would scold him or poke him rudely with her staff if he crossed her path, but she would often mend his clothing and made sure that he got food if he was sick or goad the menfolk into dragging him indoors if Lanka passed out in cold or inclement weather. Lanka was just another part of our village to us children, but I noticed a few things that made me wonder about him. While we had to guard our livestock from predators large and small like everyone else, no one ever stole from us, and all of the peddlers and tinkers who came our way always seemed to talk to Lanka first. Some turned right around and left after doing so.

Then there was that time when something big came down from the north and hit the herds two nights in a row, taking a calf each time. Everyone who could be spared turned out to hunt it but with no luck; all anyone knew is that it was smart, fast and could probably fly. I heard some say that it might have been a griffin broke loose from the imperial pens in one of the bigger towns; others said it might be a sirrush come east from the old ruins. Whatever it was, it never raided the herds a third time, and no one ever saw trace of it again. I noticed, however, that Lanka did not steal or wheedle food from anyone for a week after the second attack. "Oddly full." was the way he put it. Didn't seem to slow his drinking any though.

Chapter II: The Red Cloaks

SINCE I WAS STILL QUITE YOUNG, and also because our village was off of the main roads, it was some time before I realized that we lived in a conquered land. The villagers of Nesa were of the Kothmir tribe, whose councils were already beginning to be dominated by the warrior woman Shallyra, and which was one of the greatest tribes of the kingdom of Khetar. Khetar was named after the hero who had founded the kingdom by knitting together the nearly two score tribes who inhabited the central portion of Issuria, and who had built the capital city of Hattusa. Hattusa is sometimes called the Eagle's Roost, since it was there that Tarhunt had first come to Issuria atop his great two-headed eagle Akieron.

To the northwest of Issuria lay the lands dominated by the Empire of the White Sun, an immensely powerful nation ruled by a sorcerer queen whose mother was the goddess and founder of that Empire. That goddess is the White Sun that shines over the colder northern lands of her Empire. Our Sun is Arinna, wife of Tarhunt, and it is the warmth of her golden light that blesses our land. The White Sun did not want anyone else to shed light in her domain, and sought to extend that domain farther and over more people every year. To the White Sun, our Arinna is an impostor who must be banished and Tarhunt is just another husband who must be made to bend the knee. Since the White Sun founded her Empire nearly four hundred years ago, her Imperial armies have been on the march, carrying her banner with its white sun wheel on a red field before them. Since only the most powerful among her followers may wear white, the favored color of the Empire is red; in its many hues, this color marks their art, their architecture and their armies. The culture of the Empire is a rich and vibrant one, but it is tainted, as is the White Sun herself. In seeking a place for herself in the world, this White Goddess has made alliance with the enemies of Life itself. In return the White Sun and her followers gained powers, terrible powers that enabled her to force a place for herself, despite the opposition of the old gods. Since its founding, the Empire has continued to expand. Its victories have been many, its defeats few and temporary, until it seems that nothing can withstand the red cloaked armies of the White Sun for long. In many lands, that red cloak marks its wearer as a servant of the White Goddess and it is the object of fear and hatred, as well as stubborn defiance.

In the 602nd year since the Breaking, the year that I came to live with

44

my aunt, a 80 year period of intrigue and proxy wars between the kingdom of Khetar and the White Empire came to an end with the defeat of the Khetarite armies and the sack of Hattusa by the Imperial legions. Suppilmar, king of Khetar, and all of his family were slain. Those men and women of power who survived the fall of Hattusa fled into exile to avoid execution or slavery. On their trails were set the dreaded hunter-killer servants of the Emperor, whose task it is to seek out threats to the Empire and destroy them. Behind them, the people of Khetar were left to face the reality of conquest, to find their feet and somehow deal with the wounds that war had dealt them. And to feel the weight of their new rulers, and the cold, hard grip of the tax collector.

Since the battles had been fought to the north and west, a stranger might think that the village of Nesa had not felt the hand of the war lately past. No buildings were burned, no bodies littered its streets or clogged its well. It would be only after a closer look that one would notice the fields being allowed to fall fallow, the homes boarded and shuttered, the scarcity of men and women of fighting age. War had not burned our village, or crushed it; it had merely bled Nesa white and left it gasping.

When the Imperial tax collectors first came to the village, up the track from the Melid road that King Fasunil built, they did not loot or enslave as sometimes happened elsewhere. They just looked at everything. Everything. Every house, horse, barn, bull, shed, sheep, pen, pig, gourd, goat, shingle and spear in the village. Right down to the nuts in the walnut grove and the nails in the door of the tavern. Then they wrote it all down. When I asked my aunt what the men in the red cloaks were doing with the quills and the parchment, she said

"They tally up our worth so that they will know what tax to demand of us".

I had asked then if being taxed was like being beaten. She gave a dry laugh at that, and said "No, although some might say that it feels like it". She went on to tell me that taxes were not good or bad by themselves, but that it was dependent on what was taxed, how much was taken, and how it was used..

"Roads and bridges do not grow by themselves, Joren; nor are they built by well-wishing or good intentions. They are built by those who govern. We will be governed by the Empire now, like it or not. The Empress can build many things with our taxes: roads, wells, bridges, buildings … or, she can build armies."

As Syara spoke this last, she turned and looked at the soldiers who had accompanied the tax collectors. Twenty soldiers in bright bronze and red wool; twenty men and women who always seemed to have weapons in their hands, and who watched everyone, even the children.

I have said that the tax collectors looked at everything and recorded it with their strange markings; but it was not quite everything. They never saw Ajax or his belongings, nor did anyone speak of him. I could find no trace of the old warrior when I sought to ask him questions about the soldiers and I did not see him again until the afternoon sun was winking off of the soldiers' armor as they topped the low hill to the north, headed for the Melid road. Ajax was standing on the slope above the village common, arms folded, and with a cold, grey cast to his features that frightened me. It frightened my aunt also, I think, because she touched his arm and looked a question at him.

He turned to her, and shook his head, saying "No, not yet. I have a promise to keep, don't I, lad".

He rumpled my hair with a gentle hand, and turned to look a last time at the imperial troops disappearing over the hill in the distance.

"But one day I will join my family again, and nothing will stop me".

He turned then, and picked up his pack, his swords and his armor, and went back to our house. My aunt followed slowly, deep in thought, but I was close on his heels, almost skipping with excitement. For Ajax had allowed me to carry his helm, and I thrilled to the touch of the bright, cold iron and traced the engraved sigil that was the mark of the god Wurrunk, Lord of Swords and War, Death's Master.

In the battle for Hattusa, before the Imperial invaders could slay King Suppilmar and his family, they first had to slay every last member of the Household of Death, a band of Wurrunki loyalists who had sworn to defend the king and Khetar until death, and after. Not all of the worshippers of Wurrunk in Hattusa were members of the Household of Death, but all Wurrunki were proud of their loyalty and their courage, and considered them to be kinsmen. Long years after, I learned that Ajax had known and even taught many of that Household, and that he and I had guested there in the House of Death. Before the last assault, Ajax had wrapped me in a cloak and somehow passed thru the besiegers' lines and past the detachments guarding the eastern pass, and so east to my aunt's village. Rather than die with those he counted as kin, as his heart ached to do, he had let a promise made to my father years before bind him as securely as an Oath to Wurrunk.

Not all debts can be paid with blood or gold.

Chapter III: The Children of Darkness

ILEARNED THE LANGUAGE OF THE DARKNESS PEOPLES at an early age, and it has served me well in the years since. I learned the speech of the Darklings, or Sidhe, as they call themselves, partly because Ajax and Syara thought it would be a smart thing to do, but mainly because I wanted to know something my father had known, to touch him in a distant way, and build a place for him in my memories. I also wanted to know some kind of secret the other children my age did not. It can be hard being a stranger among other children, especially in a small village. Because I was a stranger, with an odd manner of speech and an odd lack of memory, I was a bit of an outcast to the other children, some of whom would bully me.

Once I was old enough (or I should say, well enough), I was tested to see where I could help our village best. I learned to take my turn at the plow and the scythe like everyone else, but children can make good hunters, too. Times were hard, and everyone did what they could to make ends meet and keep food in our bellies. I was taken into the hills one morning by Sora, our huntress, whose husband had also followed the way of Rundar (but he had been lost in the war). When we returned that afternoon with a brace of hares and half a dozen squirrels, she seemed well pleased with me.

"He's very good in the woods, Syara. He knows where to put his feet, and he doesn't fidget when he has to be still. Joren's good with a knife, no surprise there, but he's got a good eye too, and hits what he throws at. And," she said, bringing out a carefully padded pouch and laying it gently on my aunt's table, "He can climb like a duskcat kit."

The pouch held a handful of fresh eggs, and my aunt was delighted; I was delighted too, because fresh eggs meant something was going to be baked.

"He takes after his mother in that; she loved to hunt, either mountain slope or forest glade.", said my aunt. I turned to her at that:

"Like my mother, Aunt Syara?"

"Yes, dear. Just like your mother."

This pleased me very much. I drew my knees up and hugged them, wondering (as I often did) about my mother. I knew I looked like my father; both Ajax and my aunt had said so more than once. But I didn't know that much about my mother. I knew that she was tall, taller than my

Queen's Heir

father, and had had grey eyes and long red hair, and that she loved me very much. Aunt Syara said so. But I couldn't remember her or my father, at all. While I was thinking of my mother, Sora was looking at me, and wondering some questions of her own.

"He's a very quiet boy, Syara, and he doesn't miss much with those eyes of his. Those eyes, I've never seen anyone with eyes such a bright green, like sunlight on grass. Where did he get those eyes? His father?

"No. His father's eyes were dark; and I've never heard of anyone in my family with eyes so green. They're all his own.", touching my face with a fond hand.

Sora waited expectantly, but my aunt didn't say anything else. She shrugged, and turned to me:

"You're fit enough to hunt for the village, Joren. I'll tell our thane as much, and I'll tell your aunt when I want you to help me."

"Thank you, Huntress."

Sora placed the big hare I'd knocked over with a rock on our table, and went on her way. She would distribute the rest of the game to others in the village, as needed. As we watched her walk down the path to the village common, I asked my aunt the question that I had been turning over in my mind:

"Aunt Syara?"

"Yes, Joren?" She went over to the pot over the fire and stirred it, filling the air with a delightful aroma. The hare would be for tomorrow; tonight, we would have stew. I couldn't wait.

"When my mother went hunting, what weapons did she use?"

"Your mother was a fair shot with a bow, but she preferred the javelin. She was quite good with a thrown spear."

"Then I will use a javelin too."

"Just like your mother?"

"Just like my mother."

My aunt caught me up in a quick, fierce hug, and said:

"I think your mother would have liked that, very much."

She put me down, and gave me a nudge towards the back room.

"Now, go wash up before dinner. Everything! Hands, neck, face and ears!"

"Yes, Aunt Syara."

My mother had been good with a javelin, and so would I. That decision affected many things, on down the road of my life.

What Sora had said about me climbing like a duskcat was true; I was

48

good at climbing and since high places never bothered me, I would often climb a tree or up onto a rock outcrop to get some privacy (and so I could spot any of the other children who might be trying to sneak up on me). I liked it up there; it gave me a feeling of accomplishment, and gave me a little bit of solitude when I needed to think. Sometimes, I would just sit up on a high place and enjoy the view and the feel of the wind, but often, I would look at the clouds or the horizon and yearn for…something. Something to do, to be, so I wouldn't always be just the strange boy who was Syara's fosterling. You know, like the heroes in the stories that are told around the table when the evening meal is done. I wanted to do some great thing, to be someone special, but like all children, I had no idea of what that could cost me, or those I cared for.

Now, I've said that I have always been good at climbing and high places, and I am; I've never had a fall while climbing. It has gotten me into trouble though, just not from falling. Like other children, the young ones of our village would have arguments: who was taller, who was stronger, who could throw the farthest…you know. We would wager against one another; but not with money (because we didn't have any) nor with our possessions, since we didn't have many and more often than not, they belonged to our family. When we bet, the loser would have to do something stupid, some dumb trick the winner would come up with. These wouldn't be dangerous, (that would have gotten everyone involved a good strapping) but they might be painful and they were always embarrassing.

My first lost wager resulted in me being perched on the roof beam of our house early one morning, and crowing like a rooster when the sun came up. The other children thought that this was hilarious; the village menfolk were rather amused as well. My aunt was not. Soon after, I informed my playmates that I would not be climbing for bets anymore. That afternoon, in fact; right after the seat of my trews cooled off.

The first time I ever met a darkling, I had just been thoroughly thrashed by an older and larger boy. We had fought in the Grove, beneath the branches of the crowding walnut trees, where we often played our games and fought our fights. I know, walnuts trees don't grow in groves; their roots sweat a poison that keeps other trees at a distance. The trees in our grove did, growing close together almost like pines, until their branches had interwoven to form a roof that kept a cool, dim twilight even in the hottest, brightest day of summer. At the time, I did not wonder why this was so, just as I did not wonder why people did not enter the

49

Grove after they became adults unless they were sworn to the goddess.

I had washed my bruises and my face in the cold little spring that sprang from a split rock in the Grove, and then walked home. I don't remember why Little Sim and I had fought, but I do remember thinking about what I would have done to him if I had been bigger and what I was going to do to him when I WAS bigger.

I entered the long shed behind my aunt's house the back way, under the loose board near the chimney, and was walking towards the back door when I saw the darkling. He was a fomorian, one of the big warrior breed of darkling, and he sat with his back against the wall of our house, his head pillowed by a heavy grey cloak. I remember that he was laughing. His head was shaven (as is common amongst darklings who mingle with our people) and he was clad in black and dark grey, with two swords belted at his waist and a greatsword in a well-worn scabbard set against the wall beside him. He was seated across the shed from Ajax, who was putting an edge on my aunt's kitchen knives, and his shoulders were as broad and as muscular as those of a bull. His teeth were long and sharp and seemed to gleam in the shadows.

I remember thinking:

"If I had teeth like that, I'd have ripped Little Sim open from navel to chin!" What bloodthirsty little brat I was as a child. While I was admiring the darkling's teeth, he and Ajax had noticed me. As Ajax quirked an eyebrow at me, the darkling motioned me forward, rumbling

"Come closer, Small Bite, and let me measure your growth against my sword".

Reassured by Ajax's ease with the man of darkness, I had trotted the dozen paces to my teacher's knee before I realized the darkling spoke as if he had seen me before, as indeed he had. And so I met Kak Bonesplitter, born in the Darkling Woods that nestle against the spine of the Thunderhead Mountains, to the south and west in Lycia. Kak, like Ajax, was a follower of the way of Wurrunk, Lord of Swords and War. Later, I learned how unusual such a thing was amongst the Sidhe; most darklings take Zarab Adar as their war god, and the bloodstained god of slaughter and pillage is Wurrunk's deadly foe. I sat by Ajax and listened to them talk; the old man with his quick, sure fingers, and the hulking darkling with scarred arms and a laugh like thunder, throughout the remaining hour before the last meal of the day, and after dinner, on into the night. As they spoke, I learned that Kak had been my father's friend, had indeed been pupils with him under Ajax's tutelage in the Great Temple of Wurrunk in

50

Byzantium, the greatest city of the southlands.

Kak told me how hard Ajax would pummel a student who was lazy or inattentive (I myself can attest to the truth of this), and how my father Danu had taught him the use of the bow. He had in turn taught my sire the speech and songs of the Children of Nyx, the mother goddess of all the darkling races. As dusk turned into evening, Ajax began to stretch and yawn but Kak seemed to become more alert and a bit restless. When Ajax stood up, I knew it was time for me to go, so I gathered my courage, stepped forward half a pace and begged a favor of my father's friend.

"Dark One, I beg of you a gift, the same gift you gave my father. Will you teach me the speech of your people?".

Both warriors fell silent, and when Ajax laid his hand on my shoulder, I could feel that he was pleased with me. Kak bent his head and looked me in the eyes, and then he did a strange thing. He placed the knuckles of his right hand against my forehead and said:

"In memory of my sword brother, I will teach you what I taught him, and I swear this, son of Tiranna, that I will stand before the throne of my queen and speak for you in an uncle's place, that she will know your history, your name and your face ".

In this way, I gained another teacher and a friend, and the people of Nesa gained a potent night watchman while he was about, although most would had a seizure had they learned of him right then. Aunt Syara also approved of these lessons, and apparently of Kak as well; she treated him much as she would any man of our village who was a proven warrior. For his part, Kak showed my aunt the same wary respect and obedience he would have given a woman of power among his own people. Since my aunt was the center of my life, this seemed only right and proper; it was not until years afterward that I would realize how strange this relationship was.

The second time I met any of the Children of Darkness was a year or so afterwards, in 605. There had been news of war; the armies of the Empire had been massing for more than a season and were finally loosed in a two-pronged assault on the land of Thrace. The White Empress and her advisors sought to gain an outlet to the Ocean, and so made war upon our neighbors to the south and west. The great kingdom of Thrace was a joining of many nations under the leadership of the Minos and was often called the Blessed Country.

The Minos had long been an ally of Khetar, and indeed, many of our ancestors had originally come from Thrace, as had Khetar himself, before he walked the path of prophecy and forged a nation from a pack of squabbling tribes. We did not know exactly how the war was going, as there were wild rumors of both victory and defeat. Some said that the eastern prong of the invasion, into the hills of Lycia was a glorious success. Others said that the main thrust into Thrace proper had failed due to the tremendous power of the Minos, who had released a magic so terrible that soldiers from both armies had been killed when the mountains themselves had moved beneath their feet.

While we waited to hear how the war went, our own lives went on. The harvest had been good that year, and after getting the crops in, most of the able-bodied adults had gone west to help the next village over with their harvest, as they had suffered more from the war than had Nesa. The rest had gone south to help work on the road, as Roic the Fat, Military Governor of Khetar, had decreed that a levy of workers from each village would help keep the kingdom's roads in repair. There were only a handful of grown-ups and we children in the village when the darkling war band topped the tallest of the three hills to the southwest and came down through the pastures towards the walnut grove.

My friend Tarla was the first to see them, then her mother, the tanner's wife. Elnossa was both quick and cool-headed; she grabbed Tarla, their cloaks and a skin of water and was out the door and half way to the Women's House before the rest of us children could make any sense of her daughter's shouts about giants in black robes and armor. The Women's House, like the Men's House across the street, was sturdily built with an eye towards defense, but was a bit smaller and had one less door to defend. It also happened to be where my aunt was tending Grandma Gori and Yrsa, who was expecting twins and had just started labor that morning. Aunt Syara said that it looked like it could be a long labor, it being Yrsa's first pregnancy. Grandma Gori wasn't pregnant, but she was laid up from a bad fall; neither of them could move fast enough to get away from any darkling interested in catching them. Within minutes, everyone left in the village was inside the Women's Hall, bolting the doors, gabbling like a flock of geese and trying to make sense out of what seemed to be a nightmare coming to life. There had been no darkling raids in this area in more than a century, since before King Padmar's time. In any case, darklings did not raid in daylight; darkness was too great an advantage for any darkling to willingly forfeit it.

It took even my aunt several minutes to bring order to that frightened mob of mothers, infants and children, and more than one person got a good shaking or a smack on the rump with my aunt's staff. Finally, everyone calmed down long enough for Syara to get a full telling of what Elnossa and Tarla had seen. That tale seemed to both daunt and puzzle my Aunt.

"Seven darklings, and two of them the giant warrior breed? What about the lesser darklings, the goblins who are their slaves? None at all? Elnossa, are you sure? What colors did you see, what armor do they wear?".

The answers just seemed to puzzle my aunt more and more until she finally slammed the butt of her staff against the flagstones and shouted:

"Enough! None of this makes sense, least of all that we have not been attacked here, nor can we hear the livestock being killed nor anyone breaking into the houses around us. There must be a reason, and I will find it. I am going out; watch the doors but no shooting at anything that you are not sure is an enemy. Joren, stay here."

That was the first time I ever disobeyed a direct order from my aunt.

When Syara turned and strode to the front door, I darted to the table and grabbed her pack. Five or six women crowded after her, and before Karissa could clear the mob away from the door and bolt it behind my aunt, I had squeezing through the crowd and slipped out the door. I followed Syara down the street, and when my aunt heard my feet pattering after her, she spun about, ready to blister me with words or her hand, but stopped at the look on my face. Behind her, what I had thought was a shadow moved and stood up. A darkling had been waiting in the shadows under the white oak by the well, and now she strode forward with one hand grasping a black spear and the other held open, palm outward.

This fomorian woman was imposing enough to make any warrior of our village think twice about crossing her; she towered inches over six feet and was robed and hooded in an inky black fabric that seemed to drink the light. The haft of her spear was a dense grey wood that rang like stone on the cobbles and the head was razor-edged obsidian. She stopped twenty paces from us and pulled her robes aside to show black markings on a bronze breastplate as big as a warrior's shield. The sigil her armor bore was that of Arma Arn, Son of Eresh, the goddess whose stately dance with the Arinna orders our lives with Night and Day. Kak had taught me that Arma Arn's followers served as ambassadors and merchants among his people, as well as warriors. The spear is Arma Arn's sign, and he is greatly revered among the darklings of Thrace; before Time began, he won a great victory there and drove back the forces of Evil. He founded the Kingdom of Night and championed the Earth and her people as well as the Children of Darkness who followed him, and the Earth Mother bore him a child. This sets Arma Arn apart from his kin, since Darkness and Earth are traditional foes. As these thoughts flashed through my mind, the darkling nodded to my aunt and spoke words that bore the intonations of ritual:

"In the name of the One who has come and gone, I ask a Mother's aid for those who serve her Son".

Syara started at these words; they obviously meant much to her, although nothing to me. I hadn't much interest in the rituals of the Earth Mother; the ways of warriors had called to me for as long as I could remember. After a moment, my aunt spoke in return:

"What aid would you have of me, and with what will you balance the scales?"

The darkling's reply was "Healing, and my heart itself will balance the scales."

My aunt gave me an odd look, and then nodded to the darkling, whose name I later learned was Azzhka. "Lead on, then.", she said, and motioned me to follow them.

As we followed our guide across the village common towards the walnut grove, I heard my aunt wonder aloud, "Why did I fill my pack this morning, and what made you bring it with you, when you have never disobeyed me before?". I was thinking much the same thing, and wondering if I wasn't just a little touched in the head after all.

As we neared the grove, I slowed in amazement at what awaited us in the shadows beneath the walnut trees. It is one thing to hear legends told around a fire at night; it is another thing entirely to see them walking the green earth in the light of day. There were six more darklings waiting for us in the grove: two wounded or ill lying on spread cloaks, two tending to the wounded, and two more on guard. The two standing guard were enough to make anyone stare; they were huge, Sidhedo, lesser giants looming more than 8 feet high and wide enough to fill a barn door. They each bore notched greatswords and were clad in nicked and dinted plate armor, either suit worth more than enough to buy every head of livestock our village possessed. All of the other darklings were Aos Si, fomorians like Kak. They are nobility amongst the darklings and lead the goblins who make up the bulk of the darkling armies. I was startled to see that the two tending the wounded were very young, little older than myself, and frightened. I began to realize how wrong all of this was: a group of darklings traveling cross-country in broad daylight, obviously wealthy but all of whom were stiff with wounds and fatigue. Perhaps strangest of all was the absence of any goblins, or lesser sidhe; they are weak and puny compared to the fomorians, but much more common. There should have been at least two goblin guards or servants for every fomorian we saw, and there were none, none at all.

The two resting on the ground were the highest in rank of the darkling party. The male fomor wore not much more than a chainmail hauberk that seemed rent in half a dozen places, and who was so weak from his wounds that he was barely conscious enough to grate out a curse on seeing my aunt. He refused any help, and said he would die rather than accept healing from an earth witch. Syara ignored him and went immediately to his companion, who was not only grievously wounded but feverish. By her clothing and ornaments, she was a matron of her clan, a woman to be reckoned with among her people. All of the other darklings wore badges that marked them as her kin and therefore her subordinates, as darkling society is matriarchal, with the mothers and grandmothers holding the positions of authority among the clans.

As my aunt examined the darkling matron, her face went pale and lost all expression. A cursory look at the wounds of the others was enough to confirm her first impression: their wounds were not scratches, but not crippling either. It was the darkling dying at her feet that had her worried, and quite frankly, terrified me. If such a one was to die in my aunt's care, a blood feud against the village was the least that could be expected. Of more immediate import was the fact that if these darklings even suspected that we had no warriors in the village, there was no way we could keep the two giants from breaking in the door of the Women's House. That brought to mind what I had learned from Kak about the old wives' tales about darklings; they are not just stories, they are the truth. There are those among the darkling races who can and will eat anything that will fit between their jaws.

Syara looked at the darkling blood staining her hands, and then into Azzhka's eyes. "What I can do, I will do", she said, "but nothing is certain." Azzhka took her mother's hand in her own, and nodded, "Nothing is certain." My aunt bade them lay both of the wounded on bare ground, so that their flesh touched the earth, and each of the other darklings to lay a bare palm flat against the ground. At a nod from Azzhka, they obeyed, the male dark darkling snarling curses until he touched the ground with an out-flung hand. He jerked, and fell unconscious, out like a blown candle flame.

My aunt beckoned to me, and I went to her side, kicking the shoes off of my feet when I saw that she was doing the same. She smiled at me and placed her right hand on my head, raising her staff in her left hand, and began a low chant that gradually changed to a song. I could not understand the words, but it sounded somewhat like one of the songs sung in the spring after the seeds have been sown; a song to draw the gift of life from the living earth and into the waiting crops and cattle. Aunt Syara's voice rose to fill the ending of the song, but it sounded different somehow, with a questioning note to it. Then something warm struck the soles of my feet; the world twisted, and I was in another Place.

I was still in the Grove, in a way, it was just that everything looked different. The sky had gone grey and the Sun was very pale; all the light seemed to be coming from the trees and the ground itself, green and gold pulsing like a heartbeat, and the Grove was much more crowded than I had thought. There were other giants guarding the Grove; made all of twisted rock and earth and thick roots, four of them at each point of the compass. They frightened me, but paid my aunt and I no mind, as their attention was for the darklings that they surrounded. There were more darklings in the group before us than I remembered; a half dozen or more, all of whom clustered about the darkling matron and seemed in some way to resemble her. They seemed pale silver shadows of real darklings and they radiated fear as they attempted to aid their kinswoman, whom I saw bled from her spirit as well as her body. I realized that I could see every spot where the wounded darklings had bled on the ground of the Grove, and that the earth was soaking up the blood, almost as if it drank it. I realized too, that the darklings had more to fear than we did; when they found our village, they had instinctively sought the darkest, most shadowed place in sight, which was the thick grove of walnut trees. They could not know that they were placing themselves in the hand of the earth goddess herself.

As I thought this, I was shocked to see that I had somehow attracted the attention of the shadow darklings; first one, then the others turned their faces towards me, and then the greatest of them spoke in an echoing whisper:

"We know thee, Queen's Heir."

Before I could say or do anything, the pulsing lights that flowed from the ground into the trees flared into bright life; I felt something flow out of me, and then I fainted. When I came to, I was face down in a pile of walnuts. This was a little embarrassing, as the juice of a walnut will stain cloth or skin a yellowish brown that must wear off. I was going to look pretty stupid for the next season or so. These thoughts vanished when I saw my aunt; she was down on one knee, leaning heavily on her staff, and I was stunned to see that her hair had turned completely white. I ran to Aunt Syara and took her arm; she trembled with fatigue as I helped her to her feet, but her eyes glittered in triumph. I followed her gaze to the darklings stumbling forward to touch their clan mother in wonder and relief; her eyes were open, and although obviously weak, her wounds had been healed. The other darklings had been healed also, even the snarling ill-mannered noble, although he did not regain consciousness until after the darklings left our village.

My aunt waited until the darklings had quieted and turned their heads towards her; "You must rest here until Arinna sets. Eat nothing save those nuts which lie on the ground, drink nothing save the water of the spring."

"But the nuts are bitter, and stain our hands" said the youngest of the darkling youths, a boy.

"They will not taste bitter now." my aunt replied with a smile. I noticed she said nothing about the nut's juice not staining. The darkling noblewoman raised a hand and spoke:

"It shall be done as you say; the Earth Mother speaks through thy mouth, and we as her guests will obey. Take this, with my thanks."

As she spoke this, the darkling matriarch pulled from her bull neck a necklace of thick hammered plates; it was only when my aunt nearly dropped it that I realized that it was made of gold! Real gold, more gold than our village would normally see in a decade. I was fascinated with it and almost missed the look both darkling women fixed on me. Azzhka rose and went to my aunt and spoke:

"I swore to balance the scales with my heart itself; take this then, in return for the gift you have given to me."

As she spoke, Azzhka took from her own neck an amulet strung on a cord of woven hair; a medallion of worn bronze that had sea serpents circling a small piece of grey crystal. If the gold necklace had startled my aunt, this stunned her and completely mystified me. After all, bronze we see every day; this seemed to me to be no more than a good luck charm that almost any warrior might have, with the sea serpents the only interesting feature the amulet possessed. I would learn better, later. My aunt placed the amulet in her bodice and I promptly forgot about it. After exchanging a few low sentences with Azzhka, Aunt Syara and I returned to the village and left the darklings to their rest. My aunt spent a hectic half hour calming people down and explaining the presence of our strange guests: they were fugitives from a battle in Lycia, where the war was going very bad indeed for the Empress's enemies. Her general there was Fafnir Redblade, a Dacian and a warlord of some reputation, who was proving to be unbeatable.

This process was repeated when the men and women of fighting age returned that evening. Our village thane, Korsul Two-Spear, was more than ready for a fight until Syara told him that the darklings were in the hand of the goddess, and if they meant us ill, She would know it and deal with the problem Herself. While Korsul mulled this over, Syara told him that he had other things to worry about, such as how to exchange the gold necklace for the goods our village needed without the Imperial tax collectors finding out. By the time the evening meal was finished, night had fallen, and the darklings had vanished.

As might be expected for a small village, these events were the topic of conversation for quite some time afterwards. After the last snow of that winter, just as talk was starting to die down, Nesa received a reminder: Kak returned, this time openly, and with a strange gift. It was a small female statue carved from a black rock, no taller than the length of a man's arm. The statue was unusual because it had obviously been carved from solid rock and then polished smooth as glass, and because the darklings had deliberately given it a square base (the square is the sign of the Earth) and they had marked its flat back with a carving of a spear topped by a crown. Kak said that this was one of the sigils of Kasku the Wise, the son of Arma Arn and Mother Earth, who had ruled Thrace for more than 1,000 years before the Breaking. The statue (which Kak called a Nyxlith) was set on the rise east of the Grove, facing north.

With Ajax as his friend, the people of Nesa came to accept Kak's occasional visits, even if they never became comfortable with him. We didn't have any problems with darklings after that, but then we hadn't had any problems with darklings before that either. No one would have thought much about the nyxlith and it would been forgotten (or more likely, eventually broken up and buried), except the presents began to appear. They would be found lying against the west side of the nyxlith, facing the Grove, at very irregular intervals but always at dawn. One time, it was a packet of strange (but tasty) mushrooms. Other times, it was exotic candies or aromatic resins; one time, it was an odd packet that unwrapped to reveal a black flower petal as big as a bed quilt. My aunt was delighted and made from it a fragrant oil that was used from then on in all of the village weddings. Our village (and my aunt Syara) had earned someone's good will, and the people of Nesa took it as a sign of future good luck.

My aunt never recovered from the miracle in the Grove that day. It was if she had sacrificed not just a moment's strength , but part of her life itself in order to heal those darklings and by extension, prevent any blood vengeance being taken upon the people of our village. Although her reputation grew immensely after that day, Aunt Syara became somewhat of a recluse, and physically at least, grew to resemble the image of the Crone that adorned the stone altar in the temple of the Earth Mother. I complained bitterly of this, until my aunt stopped me.

"For all things there is a price, Joren.", she said after a tearful outburst of mine. "Some do not think so, but make no mistake, there is always a price and it must be paid. For what I asked and for what I gained, I am content with the price I paid. It would be easier for me, child, if you could be content also."

For her peace of mind, I closed my mouth and kept it shut. I feared that I would have her with me for too short a time as it was, and did not want to do anything to make my aunt unhappy. My aunt was not the only one affected by the events of that day; Korsul Two-Spear spent the better part of two days deep in thought after the visit by the darklings, and came to a decision. He spoke to all of the parents in the village first, and then gathered all of the children big enough to hold a spear on the village common one night after the evening meal. We huddled together, not knowing what to expect and more than a little afraid of our village's thane. It wasn't just his height or his gaunt, grim face; Korsul was the one who lead the village fighters, the one whose final judgement was accepted by all without argument (even my aunt, after they had argued before the judgement was made), and the one who lit the fires of our Holy Days and who spoke for us all before Tarhunt, king of the gods. Formidable was a good word to describe Korsul. But then he began to speak, and all thought of fear left our minds: he was going to TEACH us all the ways of spear fighting that he knew. Now, Korsul was a master of fighting with a spear in more ways than one, and we had known that, but weaponmasters don't go around teaching children how to fight. They teach warriors with enough skill and enough promise (and enough silver) to make it worth their time. Children are taught to fight by a member of their family or a family friend, such as Ajax. Having someone with Korsul's skill and reputation tutor us was like having a pail of coins dumped into each of our laps. He tested us all, with a master's eye, and after grouping us according to ability, he set us to our lessons and to practice. In the years after, he poured a lifetime's worth of tricks and techniques into us, and we drank it in like fresh rainwater.

Korsul had been badly shocked by the incident with the darklings, I think. It could have so easily ended in disaster and death for the entire village, and that would have meant he had failed the trust we had in him as our thane. The lessons he gave us were a way of trying to make us ready for any other threats we might face, and also, his one last chance at revenge. He had begun to believe that he would not live to see Khetar rise up against the Empire, and if he could not strike against the imperials who had slain his children, then he would ready us so that we could do so for him. He never doubted that Khetar would eventually revolt, and when that time came, he wanted us to succeed (and to kill as many of the Imperials as we could). That thought goaded him into action at first, but then the teacher in him awoke as well, and he began to change. I heard my aunt say that he seemed fully awake for the first time since the war, and while we never heard him laugh, he would smile now and then when we caught on to whatever maneuver he was trying to teach us. He was easier to talk to, and we began to get a glimpse of the man he had been before the war changed everything.

Korsul knew that I had been getting sword lessons from Ajax, so he often used me as a tool to teach the other students how to fight a swordsman. This in turn taught me how to fight with a sword against spearmen. I learned a great deal, and was very pleased to find myself in the top rank when it came to the javelin. After testing our reflexes, Korsul taught us a couple of tricks I had only heard of, the trick of catching a thrown spear and of throwing two spears at once, one with each hand. I was the best of us all at spear catching, and Korsul managed to teach three of us the knack of catching the javelin and then throwing it back, all in the same motion. That sort of thing tends to take people by surprise.

By my aunt's reckoning, I was 11 years old in 605, the year we began to prepare for the war that would break the White Empire's grip on the kingdom of Khetar. That war was 20 years in coming, 20 long years or more until we were free and had a freely choosen king or queen of our own. And when that war came, nothing and no one was ever the same again.

Chapter IV: The God of Endings

Hear my prayer, O Wurrunk,
And craft thou my spirit
As does a smith a sword in a forge.
Let me show Courage with Honor,
Temper Justice with Mercy,
Balance Privilege with Duty,
Guide Power with the hand of Conscience,
And let me fail you not, before Death or after.

- A prayer heard among the Tarhunti Wurrunk worshippers of eastern and northern Issuria

I WAS BORN ON WURRUNK'S FEAST DAY, and looking back now, from the end of my road, I can see that the God of Death has always been a part of my life. Even that part of my life that I cannot remember, for I was marked as an infant by one who served Wurrunk, and from the hour that my memories awakened until I came to manhood, Ajax was never far from my sight or my mind. He was a warrior, a teacher and master of more than one weapon; what and how he taught me has helped to shape my life ever since. I know now that he inspired fear and awe in many, but he was like a grandfather to me, and he loved me as if I was his own flesh and blood. Ajax never spoke of any children of his own; he did say that he was proud that my father had entrusted my teaching to him. My own sire had first been sworn to the service of Tarhunt, and did not take oath to Wurrunk until several years after I was born; a need to prepare for the war he saw coming lead my father into the death god's service. Need, dire need in a desperate time, drove me to take that same oath in my own turn.

Now, I learned my lessons and bowed to Tarhunt just as all of the boys in the village did; Tarhunt is the king of the gods, and his strictures bring order to our lives. But Ajax taught me that Wurrunk is Tarhunt's faithful sword thane and is a part of that life too. Wurrunk's way is that of Death and Truth. The followers of Wurrunk are sworn to fight, to kill and to die in the defense of life, but Ajax taught me the importance of Truth as well. To him, the Truth did not change from one place to another, or because this rich man had ten cows and that old woman had one. He felt that he had sworn himself to the defense of Truth, and of Justice, which is Truth's flickering shadow. To seek the Truth, to defend the cause of the Just, man or woman, farmer or king; for those reasons, Ajax was willing to kill and to die. It took me a while, but I have come to believe these things myself.

As a child, I was drawn to the way of the sword to be like my father and to follow in his footsteps. Because of a promise made to my parents when I was born, in their absence it was Ajax who helped to raise me, and who stood tall in my life as an example of what men should be and of how a follower of Wurrunk should act. In his lessons, and by his example, he taught me these things:

Death comes to everyone.

Do not lie, or others will never be able to depend on you or believe you if you carry important news.

Do not swear oaths lightly, and never break a sworn oath. Such an oath is bound by your own breath, your own life; to break it is to betray your own honor, insult the gods and damage the world itself.

Do not draw a sword (or indeed, any weapon) against anyone unless you are willing to kill them or die in the attempt. Swords are not toys, nor are they used to chop wood or hunt deer.

If you kill, kill cleanly and quickly. There is no excuse for cruelty.

Be prepared to fight for those who love you, for those who trust you and for freedom itself. The alternative is to live meanly and die badly.

Those who have sworn themselves to Wurrunk have sworn themselves to Death, and are prepared to kill or to die at any waking moment.

Since my childhood, I have traveled to many lands and met many followers of Wurrunk, men and women, in both war and peace. One thing I learned in that time, and this you must never forget: there many different kinds of Wurrunki, but all Wurrunki are killers.

As am I.

Ajax, my teacher and guardian, was a Attar of Wurrunk. This meant that he was, in a very real sense, both eyes and hands for Wurrunk in the waking world; it also meant that I could not have asked for a better tutor in the ways of weapons and war. At first, his lessons were stories, full of monsters and heroes and of course, swords. I learned of Dragonbane, the triple bladed sword of Tarhunt, of Sigurd and his sword Gram, of Shieldslayer, the royal heirloom of the Quadi tribesmen, and of Unbinder, the sword forged to fight slavery. He told me about the lost sword of the Iconi tribe, and of Oathtaker, called by some the sword of Truth, and of other weapons out of legend. And he told me tales of what he had seen

62

and done in a long life on the warrior's path, each with their own point.

As I grew older, these lessons became more formal, in both content and structure. I learned my letters; both that of Khetar and the common tongue of the merchants who link the nations of our world. Heraldry and history, battles, tactics, strategy and the laws of my people, all filled my waking hours whenever Ajax pitched his sleeping roll in our shed. I learned something of Wurrunk's followers, and he taught me how to fight with the swords that are the symbol of Wurrunk. I learned to strike with the edge, the point, even the pommel of a sword, and to parry with the flat of the blade and to never, EVER throw my sword. I learned how to use the dagger of the common man and the shortsword of the soldier, the rapier of the Thracian noble and the broadsword of the Tarhunti thane; and I also learned the use of the greatsword or longsword as some call it. This was the two-handed sword of the highlands, not the longer, heavier pike-breaking blade of the lowland armies. The shorter, lighter highland sword is faster than other two-handed blades, but still heavy enough to shear through the best armor; in the hands of a master, it is a truly devastating weapon. I had a natural aptitude for all of these weapons, but I excelled with the greatsword. Ajax was more than content with this odd preference of mine; and allowed me to practice with his own bronze two-hander, rather than my practice blades of wood. Soon after Ajax began to tutor me in weapons, the older boys stopped bullying me.

One other thing Ajax taught me about weapons, and it is a lesson I have had drilled into me again and again throughout my life. Axes, spears, bows, clubs, even swords are really just tools when used to kill. An axe will not walk down a street and slay somone on its own, it must be wielded; but a man or woman can kill with their bare hands, even their teeth. He once said to me:

"The craftsmanship of the sword, training, even magic must all be taken into account, but when it comes right down to it, it is YOU who are the weapon."

When Korsul decided to tutor us all in the way of spears, Ajax heard, and when he found out that I was being taught to catch spears, his eyes lit up. "Show me.", he said.

We went out back, and he began to test me and what I had learned; first with green branches cut from an ash tree, then with a broom stick, then finally, when I didn't expect it, with a thrown knife still in its sheath. I caught them all, and then spoiled the effect by dropping the knife on my foot. Ajax didn't mind at all, in fact, he seemed quite pleased. He came up to me, and clasped me by the shoulders and said:

"Tomorrow, tomorrow I will teach you something new. I will teach you how to cut arrows. Your father learned to do it; I think you can learn too."

I was stunned. Arrow Cutting? Ajax would teach me how to cut arrows from the air? That was the kind of thing that heroes did. And my father had known how to do this? Then he had been a great swordsman. I swelled with pride and, after kissing my aunt good night, went to bed and tried to sleep. I failed miserably. Which is why I was awake to hear my aunt and Ajax talking about me. I know eavesdropping is rude, but I couldn't HELP it. I was so excited that I could not sleep at all, and my hearing has always been good. Apparently, Ajax had been pacing, lost in thought, because I heard my aunt's voice first:

"What is wrong, Ajax?", and I could hear the worry, the concern for me in her voice.

"Nothing. Nothing at all is wrong."

There was something odd about the old man's voice, but I didn't realize what it was until he gave a low laugh. He must have knelt to take her hands, to reassure her, because his voice sounded a bit hollow. He had dropped his voice a bit, and was speaking to Aunt Syara in her chair and the echoes were bouncing off the walls in the corner behind her.

"He is good, Syara; he is very good. He has more than made up for the time he lost and he picks up everything I try to teach him."

"Well, he ought to be good; Ajax, it is all that he does. ALL that he does, aside from chores and hunting. Where the other boys fish or ride or sing, he practices. Where some think of clothing or food, he thinks of swords and spears; where other boys are starting to think of girls, he sharpens knives and shears, or spearheads and axe-blades! Ajax, that is not all there is to life!"

"I know, Syara. But, all things considered, don't you think that this might be for the best? For now?"

I heard my aunt sigh.

"I guess you're right. You usually are. And Korsul did say that Joren is one of his best pupils."

"Did he now? I will talk to Korsul tomorrow. I think this idea of his to teach the youngsters what he knows is good of him, and good for him as well. He seemed more like his old self, today."

"Yes, I think so. But I wonder...the children he teaches..."

"What is it, old woman? What has upset you?"

"Ajax, what kind of world will they make for themselves?"

"We can only do our best, Syara. If we can give them the chance to make their own way, our job will be finished. What kind of world they make will be their responsibility."

I fell asleep about then.

After Ajax began teaching me about battles and history, I began to have strange dreams. I would sometimes climb to a favorite perch and sit there looking out over the village towards the Melid road (because everyone knows roads lead to adventure), and...wish. For what, I really didn't know; I think now that I wanted a reason for my life, a purpose. Then, I had different daydreams of quests and battles and magic and treasure, pretty much like most boys do. I wanted something to happen, something that would set me a goal I could win to, so I could be somebody that my aunt and Ajax and my parents could be proud of. Silly, really. It took me the better part of a lifetime to realize that parents are as proud of the little things their children accomplish, as much or more as the great things. Unfortunately for me, the whole time I was wishing, Someone had been listening.

In 607, two years after the failed invasion of Thrace, war came again to Issuria, twice. That year saw the Roxolani horse people mauled in a battle with an alliance of Scythian nomads. This was ill news; the Roxolani were friends and kinsmen as well as neighbors. Many men and women of the Kothmir and Bastarnae tribes had joined their ranks through the years since old Tasius had first led his people out onto the plains of Scythia. They were also the only buffer we possessed against the raids of the savage nomads to the east. The Imperial governor was also concerned; enough so that he ordered a preemptive strike against the nomads, and he placed in command of this force an officer by the name of Diophantus the Bold. Diophantus had served under Fafnir Redblade, and was noted for his diplomatic skills as well as his ability on the field of battle. His expedition was a success, not only in forestalling a major nomad uprising, but in providing the Empire with its first accurate maps of the Scythian plains.

The other outbreak was the culmination of a long-standing feud between two Khetarite tribes, the Lupaku and the Mabirshar. The Lupaku are the wolf-people; savage primitives who hold the wolves of the forest to be their brethren. They are fanatically loyal to the Khetar royal family, perhaps because the only security they have known has been when the royal house was strong. The Mabirshar were neighbors to the Lupaku; under their old queen Tiresthranna, their border with the Lupaku had been a fence of swords, and the wolf people had raided the herds of other tribes. Upon the death of the queen and her children in a fire in 600, her younger brother Ketilranda took the throne, defying the tradition that a Daughter of Mabirh must sit upon the Black Oak throne.

Ketilranda broke tradition in other ways as well, adopting a conciliatory stance towards the Imperials and openly receiving their priests in his hall. When the war came in 602, Ketilranda kept the Mabirshar spear levy within their own borders, breaking the sacred compact that bound the tribes to the king, and winning the favor of the Empire after the war ended. Many of the other tribes blamed the Mabirshar for the defeat and cursed the Mabirshar king. While the Mabirshar warriors did not number more than most of the other tribes, some said that this breach weakened Khetar as a whole, and enabled the magic of the White Sun to overwhelm the kingdom. This action also shamed many of the tribe's best fighters, most of whom left rather than serve Ketilanda or were killed in the incessant feuds and border skirmishes that plagued Khetar after the end of the war.

The Lupaku neither forgave nor forgot this treachery; by 607, they had recovered enough of their losses to act, and their Warwolves lead an attack that destroyed the core of the Mabirshar tribe. They razed most of the royal steading at Oak Rest to the ground; the Queenshall was left open to the wind and rain, and the Black Oak throne was stained with blood. The White Empire could not afford to allow the destruction of an ally go unpunished; an imperial officer by the name of Othar Inkson led a mixed force of Imperial peltasts and Khetarite tribesmen in a whirlwind campaign that brought the elusive Lupaku to bay, and battered them into submission. Othar gained the battle name of Wolfhound for his deeds, as well as the best of the old Mabirshar lands. The Lupaku lost lands and hostages, and were forced to outlaw a number of their own warriors. Since war was going to be part of my life, Ajax made a point of examining both campaigns in detail with me. He rated both Othar Wolfhound and Diophantus the Bold very highly as field officers, saying that both had displayed three traits that are invaluable in organizing and leading an army: planning, persistence and flexibility.

"Getting lucky or playing a hunch is good enough for a back-alley brawl or a cattle raid," he said, "But you need more than that to build and lead an army. There is more to command than shouting 'Follow me' and 'Charge'. You must plan for bad luck and mistakes, persist in spite of them and be flexible enough to get around obstacles or overcome them if they cannot be avoided. Water and food, for both beasts and troops, have to be found or carried with you".

Ajax made note of the fact that Diophantus had managed to hire mercenaries from two Scythian tribes, the Auchatae and the Skula, to act as scouts and light cavalry. While no one had been able to unite all of the tribes of Scythia in a thousand years, it had been hundreds of years since any outsider had gotten one tribe to fight another. While I looked at the map of Scythia that Ajax had drawn (with the path of Diophantus's expedition traced upon it), I noticed that Ajax paid special attention to a written account of Othar Inkson's personal deeds of valor against the Lupaku. When he had finished, he nodded once and muttered to himself: "The sword has come south". My aunt did not say much about either expedition, in fact, she said little about anything after hearing about the attack on the Mabirshar, drawing into herself for such a long period of time that I began to fear for her health. I couldn't blame her: the stories bandied about regarding the manner in which the Lupaku shamans had killed the Mabirshar king were horrifying.

Even so, when Ajax had explained to me the penalties imposed upon the Lupaku, I had felt a chill run through me. Some of the most capable fighters and people of power the Lupaku possessed had been outlawed by their own flesh and blood. I could not imagine a worse fate then, but I can now. But I would still rather die than live as an outlaw. I do not mean as one of those warriors hounded by the Imperials because they would not put their necks in the Empire's yolk; I mean as a renegade proscribed by both their tribe and their own clan. To never again see the faces of your kin, or hear their voices, or feel the soil of your own land beneath your feet, that is more than punishment enough for most men. But outlaws never know a moment of rest, for all men's hands are raised against those who live beyond the law. Anyone can kill an outlaw without fear of penalty or retribution, and none may offer an outlaw even salt or fire, lest they become outlaws as well. Thus outlaws flee from family and friends, lest they damn those they love to share their fate. What is a man or woman without their own people to love and to be cared for? Nothing, even less than nothing: a shameless appetite, lead by pride and driven by spite to be a threat to all around them. To me, to be made outlaw would be like having my heart dug out with a dull blade, and then be made to live on without it. Each breath would be a cutting knife, each day a leaden burden, until life itself was a torment. Few outlaws live more than a year from the day they are proscribed. In a year, Outlawry will break the strongest warrior, drain power from the greatest shaman, or so I thought then. I would soon learn differently.

When we were finished discussing the imperial campaign against the Lupaku, I asked Ajax what had become of the survivors of the Mabirshar. Surely, the Lupaku had not killed every living man, woman and child?

"No, a number of them survived. To their regret, I think. All of those who survived the attack by the Lupaku are now slaves in their own lands. The Empire attached their bodies and their possessions to help pay for the punishment dealt out to the Lupaku. Armies do not pay for themselves, and the imperials decided that it was only fair that the remnants of the Mabirshar pay for the vengeance wrought in their name. All of them were given to Othar Inkson, to work the lands now his in reward for his service."

Free-born men and women, taken and given as slaves. Yet another debt the Empire owed Khetar. As I grew older, and approached adulthood, Ajax and I would sometimes speak of other things. Looking back now, I realize that he was testing me, to see if what he and my aunt had been trying to teach me had sunk in and taken root. I think both of them understood how dangerous someone like me could become, and they did their best to give me guidelines so that I would know right from wrong, and in Ajax's case, a good, hard shove in the right direction. I owe them more than I can say. Once, Ajax asked me this question:

"Consider this: What if you had taken on a debt from a man in another village, but before you can pay it, illness strikes and many in your village fall ill. This man to whom you owe the debt hears that you and many in your village have died of this sickness, and to avoid it, he takes his family and goes to move to Thrace, where he has kin. But you are not dead; you recover and when you go to his village to repay him, you learn that he and his family are two days on the road to another country and they do not plan to return. What would you do?"

I said "I'll follow him and pay off the debt. I can move faster than he can on the road, and I should be able to catch up without much trouble".

Then Ajax asked me: "Why? He thinks you are dead, and he is leaving, never to return. Also, he did not seek to have the debt repaid by your kin, so it obviously means little to him."

I thought about this for a time, not because I am slow-thinking; well, not just because I am slow-thinking, but because I had never really thought about WHY in quite that way. After a time, I looked up at Ajax and said:

"Because, he did not promise that I would repay him, I did."

Ajax seemed pleased enough with this answer, and said:

"So, your promise means something to you, eh? Good, then it means something to me, too."

Another time, he asked me this:

"What does a man or woman who leads owe to those who follow them? Consider this, you are the youngest son of the thane of a village; when you reach manhood, you travel to see other lands, and over the years, you win gold and honor fighting there. One day, word comes from your homeland that a blood feud exploded into all-out war between three tribes and your father and all of your kin are dead, as are many in your village. What would you do?"

"Am I bound by obligations to anyone in the land where I hear of this?", I said.

"No, none that would prevent you from at least traveling home to see your family's graves."

I thought about this for a bit, and said:

"I would go back to my village and help as I could. If they needed a thane, then I would offer to take my father's place, if the village ring would accept me."

Then Ajax said that word again: "Why?"

I groped for the right words:

"Those people would have trusted my father to lead them in peace and in war, and to speak for them before the other tribes and before the king. That trust would be something…" I couldn't think of the right word: duty, honor, burden, gift, treasure…? All of them combined?

"Something not to be taken lightly. If my father had taken on such responsibility, then it would fall to me as his heir to see it through. Until or unless those same people choose someone else to be their thane." Their lives, their choice.

Ajax nodded at me to go on.

"If the village had found someone else they wanted more as thane, then I would give what help they would accept and see that my kin were buried properly."

I looked Ajax in the eyes and said: "Then, I would find the ones who had killed my kinfolk, and I would kill them."

He stroked his beard and said: "What if the feud was ended?"

"If I'm still alive, then the feud can't end unless they kill me or I accept a blood price, and money or cattle wouldn't be enough."

"Your vengeance would mean that much to you?"

I just looked at him.

Ajax strode over to me and placed his hands on my shoulders; his eyes bored into mine and I could feel the effort he put into his words, so I would hear and remember them:

"Listen to me, boy. I cannot say to you: 'Do not ever avenge a wrong.' Evil must be opposed, the enemies of life must be destroyed, and you must stand up to those who are your enemies or no man will ever rely on you. I have seen the desire for vengeance give men and women the strength to overcome great odds, but... revenge always costs more than you think. More often than not, it is the innocent who pay the greater part of that cost, not the avenger and his foe."

He gave me a gentle shake.

"Joren, if you only remember one thing I tell you, remember this: If you ever find that you have chosen a course of action solely for the sake of vengeance, then you will have made the wrong choice."

Then he nodded to me and left the room, to give me some time to think things through. I did hear what he said to me, and I've never forgotten his advice, although I have chosen not to follow it once or twice. I do remember that I had no intention of following it then and there. I'm not stupid; I've made a fool of myself more times than I can count, and men have called me madman to my face, but I'm not stupid. I had figured out that Ajax had brought me to my aunt's house to be hidden. From what? My father had been a warrior, and I think, a great one. My mother had been a woman of some influence and now and again I had overheard Ajax and Aunt Syara talking when they thought I wouldn't hear: I had had a sister, maybe more than one. And now I had nothing of them at all; I couldn't even remember what they looked like, or the sound of their voices or the touch of their hands. Someday, I was going to find out who had taken my family from me; I would find them, and then I would kill every single one of them.

Chapter V: The Hall of Tarhunt

IT MAY SOUND STRANGE, but it is true, that although I lived within 20 miles of Melid for almost eight years, I only visited that city once in all that time. This was on the occasion of my coming of age and of my taking oath to Tarhunt. It was at the end of the year, in 609, that I made the journey with Ajax to Melid. My journey began with a pleasant surprise: my aunt gave me a sword as my Oathing gift. Not just any sword, but her husband's, that would have gone to the eldest of their children, had any lived. It was a princely gift, given from the heart, and it stopped the words in my mouth and brought tears to my eyes. I gave her a kiss and a tight hug instead, and she told me to stop my nonsense and get moving, or Ajax would leave me behind. I laughed and ducked my head, and left with Ajax. She watched us, from the hill there above the common, until we topped the hill to the north.

I will not bore you with the tale of that journey and of my testing in the courtyard of Tarhunt's temple. It was so ordinary as to be meaningless to anyone but me, but I remember everything quite clearly and will do so until I die. I did well in the testing of my skills, not as well as some, but better than most, and received a grin from Ajax in congratulations. I went with the others then, into the cool wide hall before the altar and bound myself to the service of the King of the Gods. Afterwards, the new adults filed out into the courtyard with their bright swords, and their new hard-edged pride, to be fussed over by their families. I was at the rear, and I took the opportunity to pay my respects at the shrine to Wurrunk (for my father's sake), which was in an alcove off to one side on the north end of the temple. It was being tended to by an old warrior, one who had lost most of one arm, who was dusting the shrine with a soft cloth. He had been one of the witnesses during the rite, and he gave me a friendly nod as I went to one knee. I drew my new sword, and as I bent my head I asked:

"Hail Wurrunk, Lord of Swords. Help me to be worthy of my aunt's gift."

The blade of the sword flared with reflected light and all the shadows were driven from the shrine. I staggered back onto my heels to see that the candles on either side of the shrine were tipped with silver fire, the flames rising three feet or more from the wick without flickering or smoking. The Wurrunki tending the shrine was motionless, caught in mid-gesture as he snapped his cloth one-handed to free it of dust. Time had stopped and then a voice spoke to me, a deep, quiet voice that sounded a bit tired:

"*Hello, Joren. I feel that your aunt's sword will serve both of you well. I have a gift for you on this occasion, the same gift I gave your father when he was your age. Would you have it of me?*"

I looked around; there was no one in sight, and I was numb with shock. But...the same gift my father had been given? THAT I wanted.

"Y-Yes, Lord." I stammered.

"*There is no price for this, it is a gift. I only ask that you not dishonor it.*"

"You honor me, Lord. I will treasure such a gift."

"*So be it. We will speak again one day.*"

The sword in my hands grew cold for a moment, and a cool wind blew into my sweating face; a breath of the North Wind, with just the barest hint of snow. Then the lights went out and everything fell to the floor: me, my sword, the old man and his dust cloth. That's where Ajax found us when he came into the alcove just a moment later, called by the sound of his god's voice. I got up on my knees and started to shake my head to clear it; I was shivering a little, and every hair on my head was standing on end. The junior priest of Tarhunt had come running to see what had happened; he helped me to my feet, and I remember that his hands were shaking. Ajax had checked to see if I was all right then gone to tend the old initiate, who was only just regaining consciousness. The room felt cold and...clean. The candles were gone, wick and wax consumed right down to the brass candlesticks, but there was neither smoke nor soot left in the room to mark such a burning. Ajax helped the custodian of the shrine to his feet, both them staring at me the whole time. Neither of them said a word. After an awkward silence, the Tarhunt's priest asked tentatively:

"Is there anything wrong, Attar?"

Ajax nodded at him politely. "No, there is nothing wrong. Thank you."

The priest gaped at each of us in turn, then firmly closed his mouth and retreated to the inner part of the temple, muttering to himself. The old man tending the shrine threw his cloth over his left shoulder, clapped me on the arm and sat heavily on a bench, breathing deeply. There were rays of silver light peeking from his sword and knife, where the hilts met the lip of their scabbards, Ajax's too. These rays faded as I watched, and I wondered about the words the...Voice? had said to me. A gift? What kind of gift? And he had said that this was my aunt's sword, not my uncle's...it even felt different, like it had its own pulse, but that had to be my own blood pounding in my head and my hands. I looked up at Ajax; he was looking back at me with narrowed eyes. He shook his head once and said to me:

"You get more like your father every day."

That was about as much fussing as Ajax was capable of handling. We left the temple and returned to the tavern where Ajax had taken a room, and he bought me my first draft of ale as a man. When Ajax stepped over to the next table to talk to a friend of his, I fell to talking with a young woman of the Bastarnae tribe who had taken oath at the same time as me. She said her name was Belkara, and she was very easy to talk with. She was what my Aunt would have called "Dragon-kissed"; one of those descended from warriors who had served the Dragon Empire hundreds of years ago. Such men and women were taller and stronger than most folk, but did not live as long as most people, and often found it difficult to have children. We were getting along so well that it was several minutes before we realized that we were no longer alone. A young man, several years older than us, had come up and set two packs on the end of our table. We were as thin-skinned as most new men and women are, and were ready to take offense at the intrusion, but he soothed our feathers with an infectious grin and congratulated us on our coming of age. He wasn't mocking or condescending, and soon we found ourselves deep in conversation with him. He said his name was Silmurth.

As we spoke, I noticed the obvious resemblance between him and the broadshouldered man speaking to Ajax, whose name was Valarl. They looked to be of the Galatian tribe. The two older men stood up and clasped arms.

"A clean wind behind you and a straight path before you" said Ajax.

"And to you, lord. I will see that she gets your message" was Valarl's reply. He turned, and nodding to us, said

"Time we were on our way, Silmurth" to our new companion. We exchanged farewells and the two Galatians shouldered their packs and headed off towards the West Gate.

Bel and I fell to talking about what a pleasant fellow this Silmurth was, and what the lands of the Galatians were like, and how long it would take to get there, when we realized that we were walking down the road behind Silmurth and his kinsman. The temple was already a hundred paces behind us and Valarl was turning around, thinking we might have a message for him. We stopped in our tracks and just stood there, gaping like a couple of fish. It was Silmurth who first realized what had happened. He barked a cheerful laugh at us and said:

"Well? Are you coming to Hattusa with us? Or do you just enjoy kicking my shadow?"

We mumbled a repeat of our farewell and fled up the street, our faces hotter than the door of a furnace. Ajax gave us an odd look, but said nothing; Bel and I were grateful for his silence. We heard more about Silmurth Sharpspear later that day from some of the Wurrunki of the Kothmir tribe. I felt like a fool then, but looking back over the long years, it seems only fitting that we should have begun to follow Mursilith as soon as we were old enough to carry our swords.

We shared our evening meal with warriors of the Kothmir and Bastarnae clans, who had come to Melid to see their newest members sworn to Tarhunt; with them were many of the Wurrunki of both tribes. They all knew Ajax and treated him with a profound respect that was warmed by surprising fondness. The respect I understood; you don't grow old in the service of the god of death by being ordinary. But the fondness surprised me. I loved Ajax, but he had helped raise me; the second clear memory I have is that of his face lit by a lamp he was holding as he tucked a blanket around me. None of the warriors in that hall were blood kin of his, yet he knew them all by name, and they treated him as if he was everyone's grandfather. That is, if your grandfather was a bundle of iron springs and whalebone that could take you outside and whip you like a tub of butter with any blade you cared to draw.

That meal was one of the events in my life that I will never forget. It was not only the first meal that I had ever had in a real tavern, in a real town, but I heard stories from men and women who had served in the war, fought blood feuds and battled with nomads and bandits from one end of Issuria to the other. And I got to sit next to Bel all evening and talk to her as much as I wanted. Pretty thrilling stuff for an orphan boy from a village back in the hills. I felt a bit overwhelmed at first, but as the evening went on, I began to feel something else. For the first time that I can remember, I began to feel that I belonged. It wasn't that I had been outcast amongst the people of Nesa; on the contrary, I was formally accepted as a fosterling, and foster children are well-cared for not only because that tradition demands it, but because of the very practical benefits of fostering children from other clans and tribes. It forges bonds between clans and tribes that can prevent the start of feuds or even outright war. But normally a foster child knows where they have come from and where they are going to; until recently I had known neither of these things, and even now I could not remember anything of my early past or see more than vaguely where I was headed.

None of that mattered here; we were all bound to the same way of life and the same gods, and even if we one day faced each other in battle (for the tribes had warred upon each other before, and the followers of Tarhunt and Wurrunk are always in the forefront of any fight), we would always understand each other better than any outsider would understand us. So I sat there and ate my first meal as a man amid the song and laughter of my brothers and sisters of the sword, and held the hand of my first great love under the eyes of the only father I would ever know, and I will never, ever forget it.

What? You don't think the Wurrunki ever sing or laugh or love? We do, and although we probably do all of these things less than you, they mean that much more to us because of that. At the end of that bright, glorious evening, Bel told me that she and her tribesmen would be leaving the next day before sun up, as they had farther to go than we. I suddenly felt very lonely and must have looked it, because Bel laughed and said:

"Brighten up, Big Eyes; I'll see you soon".

"Promise?"

"You can bet on it", she laughed, and with a hug and a KISS, she bade me good night.

I somehow staggered back to my room alone and was floating around in a daze when I came to a couple of conclusions:

1. I had better get down from this headboard, because if I broke the bed, Ajax would take it out of my hide.
2. I definitely needed to work on this kissing thing. I mean, Bel just hadn't give me enough warning, and I know I didn't do it right. Next time I would do better, but we were going to have to do a lot of practicing. I always need a lot of practice before I get something down the way I want. That is, IF Bel wanted to practice with ME.

A thought struck me while I was cleaning my teeth, and I had a question for Ajax when he came in, whistling some kind of Thracian tune.

"Ajax?"

"Yes, Joren?"

"Are my eyes too big?"

He turned and looked at me; and after a moment or two, said:

"Have you gone blind in one of them?"

"Well, no…"

"Have you grown a third one while your aunt and I weren't looking?"

"Of course not!"

"Then I would say that your eyes are fine, Joren. Now, go to sleep."

"Yes, Ajax".

At least the old man had the decency to wait until the lights were out before he started snickering.

Chapter VI: The Scarred Man

THE NEXT MORNING, Ajax sent me to the market to purchase a number of things requested by my aunt, while he made preparations for our departure. The list was simple enough to fill: herbs and spices, needles and thread; common enough for a townsman, but rather hard to come by back in the hills. I had just finished when my eyes were drawn to an old Lupaku whose kinsmen were trading some very fine furs that day. He looked to be drunk or dozing, draped in his deer hide cloak, but what drew my eyes was his scar. Now, everyone gets scars, but not like this one. It ran from the corner of his right eye, down his cheek, under his ear, across his neck and shoulder, down his ribs to his pelvis. It looked like a sword scar, but what sword stroke would mark a man like a knife laid against wood turned on a lathe? I decided I must be mistaken, and hurried to back to the temple. I arrived just as Ajax was laying out his Oath gift to me: a hauberk of bronze ring mail! It was beautiful, and the sight of it drove the memory of the scarred man clean out of my head; our journey home was uneventful, and with nothing to recall the old Lupaku to mind, I forgot about him.

We were pleasantly surprised to find Kak bunking in our shed on our return home; a trader of the Hermetic Order had dropped him off on his way to Roaring Springs and he had accepted my aunt's offer of hospitality until he could get about again. He was recovering from a fight with a minion of Zarab Adar, and his left arm and leg were useless for a while. The followers of that god can gain the power to enchant their weapons so that the wounds dealt with them can only be healed with time, not magic. I hung upon every word as he recounted to us the tale of that battle; as he spoke, Kak hefted the trophies of his duel: a flanged mace of an odd design and a large oval shield faced with a death sigil. The mace would hang in his family's Hall of Memory, but the shield he gave to me as an Oath gift. I felt it to be quite an honor and was more pleased than I could say with Kak's gift.

The seasons spun past to the end of the year and the start of the ceremonies dedicated to the gods. Although of course I had participated in these ceremonies before, this was the first time I would do so as an adult. It felt different, somehow. Everyone has their place in these ceremonies; Ajax's was to the north, facing outward, as befitted a champion of the war god. Mine was in the center with the other new-born adults, as was Kak's place as an invalid. Our task was to keep the bonfire burning, and to support Aunt Syara and Korsul as they worked the ritual that would renew our part in the mystical scheme whose magic holds the world together. It was then, moments before the ceremony began, that the attack came.

They were Lupaku renegades striking for food and loot, from the north of the village. Outlaws have done such to other villages before, not caring what damage was done to a village or to the life of the land itself; what we did not know was that this was a feint to draw attention away from a more deadly attack. It cost them more than they had thought to pay though, for they had not known that Ajax was there. He had felt them coming, and instead of surprising a handful of bewildered villagers, the Lupaku were met by a volley of spears and the deadly whirlwind of iron that was an Attar of Wurrunk aglow with the power of his god. The outlaws broke and ran, before they could do more than fire the barn that served as a stable for the village inn. But they did succeed in one thing; drawn by the sounds of combat and the need to fight a spreading fire, the rest of the village, both adults and children, moved north away from the ritual circle.

We were left behind; Korsul and Aunt Syara because their lives were bound to the circle lest the ceremony be completely ruined, and me. For the first time, I felt the icy grip of Wurrunk's gift and it rooted me to the spot.

"Death" it whispered, "Death comes from behind you".

"From the South!", I shouted, as I turned to face the enemies who had followed silently behind the villagers who had been on guard to the south.

They strode forward then, into the torchlight, two savage old men paced by grey wolves as big as bull calves. They were kinsmen, one with the plumed spear of a warrior, the other with the bone necklace of a shaman. The latter was the scarred man I had seen in Melid; he had a club foot and he flashed me a knife-edge smile at my surprise. Warrior and wolf glided forward together and Korsul leapt to meet them. Korsul had lost all of his children in the war with the Empire; I think only his sense of duty to his village had kept him alive since then. For the first time in my life, I heard him laugh as a hard-thrown spear took the wolf in the throat and dropped it. Before Korsul could shift his other spear to a 2-handed stance, his foe thrust and I winced as I saw the spear point come out our thane's back. But Korsul wanted to die; such people can be as dangerous as any berserker. He gripped his killer's hand, pinning it to his spear, and forced himself up the shaft. His own blow struck the Lupaku warrior at the base of the throat, and both fell dead.

The shaman snarled when he saw his brother fall, and spreading his arms wide, he barked up at the stars:

"A warrior's death at last!"

Then lowering his head, he showed his teeth to us:

"The same as I shall give you, old woman."

My aunt straightened, a tight, cold smile on her face;

"So, you still live, cripple.", she said, and her voice bit like a lash.

"If you call this life, then yes, witch, I still live", growled the lame Lupaku. He nodded once at the bodies tangled in death before him, and turned towards us, his eyes burning red in the firelight.

"I should have known I would find you here, Syara. We have been enemies since our youth, and I would not want to leave without settling my score with you. Not for us a lingering sickness or a seat by the fire doddering witlessly; there is no honor in that. I will have a warrior's death too", said the shaman, "The same as my brothers, and the same as I will give to you, witch. Your life ends here, now."

"Oh no, Kerchak, not today", said my aunt, gently swinging her copper-shod staff and watching the old Lupaku like a cat watches a fat partridge. There was no fear in her at all, at least not for herself. I think now that she meant to keep him talking, or at least occupy, even wound him, until Ajax could reach us and deal with this savage old man.

"Oh yes, Syara. First you, then Bane's puppy. I will have my revenge, and the blood line of the Traitor will be wiped from the face of the world. Guard yourself, witch."

He snarled again and began to change, and I suddenly realized how someone could get a scar that flowed the length of his body from a single sword blow: he had not been a man when he was wounded. He was a werewolf, and he was here to kill us. But even though fear was tying my guts in a knot, part of me wondered what kind of magic could be forged into a sword to enable it to scar a werewolf for life.

I know, I know; I wasn't thinking. I knew wolves hunted in packs, but I had let myself become distracted when the werewolf began to shift shape. Legends are one thing; actually seeing a shifter change his skin has a horrible fascination to it. The only thing that saved me was my new shield; a flicker from the corner of my eye was all the warning I had, and the shaman's wolf brother was in under my sword. Jaws that could crush the shoulder blade of a bull clamped shut on my shield and twisted, snapping the worn straps that held it to my arm and sending me sprawling. The wolf lunged at me: burning eyes, hot breath, a thicket of teeth in a gaping maw and ... and the Night itself reared up and slammed the wolf to the ground. I had forgotten about Kak.

The Lupaku had used an old raider's trick: attack from two opposite directions at once, across the wind so that the livestock don't catch your scent. It had worked, but it had prevented them from catching the scent of a darkling where none should be. Kak had waited until the last moment to stake his life and mine on one desperate leap, and won. With only one good arm and leg, he used surprise and his greater weight to pin the wolf to the ground for the seconds he needed to close his jaws on his foe's back behind the shoulders. I saw the terribly strong muscles in the neck and jaw bulge and heard the snap as he broke the wolf's spine and tore it in two.

Despite what many people say, the Lupaku tribe is more than a band of stone-age savages with well-trained pets. The bond between a tribesman and his or her wolf sibling goes deeper than training or even common interest. It is a tie of blood that lasts beyond the grave. The werewolf felt his wolf brother die, and screamed in anguish. When I had shouted my warning, I had unknowingly saved both my life and Kak's; Ajax heard my voice behind him and had turned to come to our aid, his feet winged with magic. He leapt into the circle with a sword in either hand, exactly two steps too late to save my aunt. Kerchak leapt forward and batting Syara's staff aside, sank his teeth into the joining of her neck and shoulder. Before I could do more than cry out, he had shook her like a terrier shakes a rat and thrown her against the wall of the nearest house. When the werewolf turned to deal with Kak and I, he found Ajax in front of him, both swords agleam with the blued silver fire that is the touch of Wurrunk. The Lupaku leapt at Ajax, seeming to flicker in the torchlight, but was met by a over-hand slash that knocked him to the ground and choked his snarl with blood. As Kerchak rose to his feet, he took a thrust in the chest from Ajax's shortsword and I heard blood rattle in his lungs. He staggered backwards, coughing reddish foam, and grated out:

"Make an end, Wurrunki".

Ajax's hard, flat swing took the werewolf's head from his shoulders.

I staggered towards Aunt Syara's body, sobbing and telling myself that she was still alive, that there was still time to heal her, that it wasn't too late. The sight of the blood pulsing from her wound shocked me sick, but I set my hands on her shoulder and put every thought, every ounce of strength and will into the words and working of the first spell that every child is taught: Healing. And it worked!

The blood stopped flowing between my hands and I felt the flesh knit itself back together, not completely, but surely enough for Ajax to finish, for a proper healer to complete, for my aunt to go on living ...

"No, Joren". Syara's eyes were on my face, and her quiet steady voice went on.

"No, child. You know that Korsul and I were linked to the circle for the village. With Korsul dead and the circle broken, my life must seal the breach, or our people will have no anchor for the coming year, and our village will begin to die. You know this, Joren. My goddess calls me, and I must obey."

I realized that I was holding my aunt's hand very tightly, straining to hear her voice as it faded, as her life was fading.

"Listen to me, Joren. You are the last of your line, the last of the royal family of the Mabirshar. The Lupaku killed all of the others, down to the last child. To you falls the mantle of your mother. There is a letter, among the things I have left you as my heir...not enough time. Promise me one thing, promise me you won't forget your people. They have no one else but you, now."

"I promise", I stammered through my tears.

She smiled then, and said "Farewell, child of my heart". Then she was gone.

They laid my aunt to rest in her place on the edge of the walnut grove. Before the end of the season, a seedling would break free of her grave and join the other trees of the grove in their guardianship of the goddess's shrine. That first day of the New Year was full of bright sunshine and clear skies, but I'll always remember it as being rather dark; I was too scared, too lonely and too sorry for myself to see it any other way. I sat on the edge of the hill, looking out over the village for what I thought was the last time, my aunt's letter on my lap. She had left the house and its land to her successor as crone, but she had given me a backpack full of warm clothing, a handful of silver and the amulet gifted to her by Aazhka. That, and her love, would see me a long way on the road I would travel. It was the letter that had me scared, for it pointed out the path I must walk and, in a very real way, it contained my soul.

I'd had a family and a home of my own once; they were gone now. My mother had been Tiresthranna, last reigning queen of the Mabirshar; my father had been her consort and warchief, Danu Queen's Sword, called Bane by the Lupaku. Before the last war with the Empire had begun, my father had journeyed north and west, into the Empire itself, seeking the answer to a riddle posed in my mother's dreams. He never returned, but Ajax said that Othar Inkson, conqueror of the Lupaku and lord of the best Mabirshar lands, carried my father's sword. In my father's absence, my uncle Ketilranda had joined with Imperial agents to murder my mother and siblings. I have no idea how I escaped; Kak and Ajax had found me wandering a mile or more from the fire, dirty and blank-faced. Until the Lupaku had attacked our village, they had thought me forgotten by my family's enemies. We knew better now, and I would have to leave before they attacked again. We would load up Ajax's mules and head east to Scythia and perhaps seek our fortunes in the city of Carchemish. We would stop first at the oasis of Roaring Springs, a stronghold of the Roxolani tribe.

So we had chosen the path we would follow from day to day, with Carchemish as our goal. But what path should my life take, and what should be my goal? To spend my life running from my enemies would be cowardice; to spend it seeking only vengeance would be not only pointless, but irresponsible. By right of blood, my oldest daughter (should I live to father one) would be the rightful queen of the Mabirshar. Until then, I was responsible for the Children of Mabirh; the fact that the survivors of my tribe did not know I lived did not lessen that burden even so much as a feathers weight. I thought of the last words of my aunt's letter:

"To keep your tribe from dying, you must walk the Path of Kings".

Simply being a warrior wasn't going to be enough. Before I would be able to gather the remnants of my tribe together, I would have to prove myself as a leader. Before my people could live free in our lands, the grip of the White Empire would have to be broken. Before my tribe could flourish, the other tribes of Khetar must accept them. In order for my people to live again, I would have to walk the Path of Kings to find the true heir to the throne of Khetar, and by my service help him to that throne. For only by the favor of the king of Khetar would my people find their place again.

I sat there stunned by the immensity of the task in front of me, until I realized that this was what I had always wanted. I had prayed as a child for my life to have purpose, for a great task to accomplish, for a prize to win, and my prayers had been answered.

Served me right.

I took a deep breath and stood up. Turning to Ajax, I said:
"How do I find the Path of Kings?"
He smiled at me and said: "You have just set your foot upon it."

Chapter VII: My Family

I SAID A LAST FEW FAREWELLS and then, less than an hour after my aunt's burial, we left Nesa behind us. I have been back there since of course, but it was never the same. I spent the first few miles looking back over my shoulder at the only home I could remember. I recall feeling very young and very lost at first, but gradually other emotions began to distract me, a desire for revenge aimed at those who had slain my aunt eventually gaining the upper hand. I turned to find Ajax watching me out of the corner of his eye. When he saw me look at him, he gave me a companionable nod, and waited for me to say what was on my mind.

"So. The Lupaku destroyed my tribe, and they slew my foster-mother, and they tried to kill me. I must assume that they will try again."

"Well, they didn't get all of your people. Several clans kept their distance from the Queenshall after Ketil took his place on the Black Oak throne. They didn't like him or his ties to the imperials; the Lupaku werewolves didn't bother hunting them down because they didn't have any royal blood in them. And in the years after your mother's death and before the Lupaku attacked, more than a few of the tribe's best fighters left the Mabirshar lands entirely, preferring to wander other lands with their families, rather than live under the rule of the Accursed One. No one really knows how many there are left or even where they are, now. But you're right, boy.", Ajax said with a grim smile, "You'll meet the Lupaku again, count on it. You're the son of Danu Queensword and the last living relative of Ketil the Accursed; no Lupaku, outlaw or not, will rest easy while they know you live."

"Well, if I'm going to fight them, I'm going to have to know them. Tell me about the Lupaku, Ajax. Tell me how to fight them, not just sword to spear, but mind to mind. Tell me how they think."

Ajax gave me an approving nod and began at once:

"First thing you must realize is that all of the children of Lupak Wolf-father, both two and four legged, are of the same blood. They are all wolves, boy; never forget that..."

We traveled north and then east, with perfect weather for traveling; bright and clear during the day, with a brief, gentle rain almost every night. Our pace was slow enough to keep from jarring Kak's healing arm and leg, but steady, so we could make as much time as possible while the weather held. Kak was on his way to Gazian, to meet some of his kin, and we would travel there with him, then on to Carchemish. My spirits soon lifted; it was hard to go on feeling sorry for myself with such beautiful weather, and I was buoyed by that odd exhilaration that fills many people when they begin a journey. My companions felt something of the same emotion; Ajax whistled a number of jaunty airs that I later found out were sea chanteys, and even Kak seemed to enjoy the fine weather as long as his hood and cloak kept the sun off of his skin. He insisted on continuing our lessons in the language and ways of his people, and between Kak's persistent tutoring and Ajax's expert instruction in warcraft and swordsmanship, time passed quickly.

I soon realized that Ajax and Kak weren't just teaching me because they had to, or just to pass the time; they were literally pouring the experience of two very eventful lives into my lap. Every trick and skill needed for traveling was soon revealed to me: making and breaking camp, where to camp, how to find water and forage for your animals, how to load pack animals, how to pick a route through strange terrain, and always, always to watch your back trail. They told me of the enemies they had fought, the places they had seen and of the peoples I would meet in the lands that surrounded Khetar. I learned what they knew, not just of the Lupaku tribe, but of the nomads of Scythia, the servants of the White Empress and the followers of the Minos. I soon felt full to bursting with the knowledge that they sought to pass on to me, but I always had room for anything either Ajax or Kak could tell me of my family.

For a short time after each evening meal, both warriors would sit and tell me a little of my parents and of my sisters, and answer one or two of my questions as completely as possible. Never too much at once, because what I learned caused pain and aroused anger, but I was kept busy enough with my chores and lessons that I didn't brood, much. I remember noticing that Ajax watched me closely at these times; I think now that he and my aunt spent a great deal of time and effort preparing me for a life that would need immense amounts of both control and direction, and he wanted to see if it had taken hold. The permanent loss of my early memories had left me with a gaping hole in the treasury of information that everyone uses to guide their actions and to make decisions. The values and ideas that Ajax and Syara taught me have given me the structure I needed in my life to keep from going mad, but there were some wounds they couldn't heal. I have never had much of a sense of humor; and I have never been able to wholly banish either the aching loneliness my family's death left in me, or the cold, unrelenting fury directed at those who did this to me and mine.

The damage done to me as a child has had far reaching effects, and I know now that I am less than I could have been. I finally learned so much of what had been a mystery to me for so long. I learned of my ancestors, and of tribe of the Mabirshar, the "Children of Mabirh" and of my mother's parents. I learned of my uncle, Ketil the Accursed, the Betrayer of Khetar; of how he died and of the doom he had brought to my tribe and the kingdom of Khetar itself.

I learned of my sisters: Tirwin and Loriel, of how they had loved their baby brother and how they were murdered by their uncle and the imperial agents of the Second Shadow. And finally, piece by piece and through the eyes of others, I began to see my mother's face. She had been Tiresthranna, last reigning queen of the Mabirshar and its last legitimate ruler. "She was tall; a head taller than your father when they stood back to back", said Ajax, "with long dark red hair, and steady clear grey eyes. She was a quiet one; never laughed much until she met your father. You've got your father's face and coloring, but you get your bones from her, as she got it from her grandfather, old Morkalranda. She got her force of will from him too, and had a good sharp mind of her own. She was a good fighter and an even better queen; your people did well under her rule. Had she lived, things would have gone differently when the Empire invaded".

That was the great might-have-been of our kingdom's loss to the Empire of the White Sun. What if the usurper Ketil and the Mabirshar spear levy had joined the other tribes in the defense of the kingdom, instead of holding back, never even leaving their tribal lands? Granted, the additional troops would not have given Khetar a significant advantage in numbers, but the presence of hundreds of experienced fighters might have made a difference at any one of the dozen or so engagements that lead up to the final battle at Hattusa. A small defeat that is changed to a draw or a small victory can change the outcome of an entire campaign.

What had been worse was the damage done to morale and to the covenant that bound the individual tribes into the whole that was the kingdom of Khetar. The anger and hatred felt by those tribes who had fought the imperials towards the Mabirshar would last for decades and deservedly so; treason is treason, no matter what the excuse. How would you feel if your friends and neighbors left you to fight and die alone? And I shuddered to think what the effect had been on the Compact itself. When Khetar the Wanderer came to Issuria, he found a diverse collection of unruly, feuding tribes; when he left this world, he left behind him one nation. That nation was bound together not only by treaties and common interest, but by the will and power of its peoples. The king is the focus of that power and is supported by it. When Suppilmar fought the White Empress at the storming of Hattusa, he needed the full support of all of his subjects; because of Mabirshar treachery, he didn't have it. It must have been like fighting with a hole in his belly. Think: a hand or a foot doesn't weigh much compared to the body as a whole, but what would you do if one was taken from you, suddenly, when you most needed it?

"I wonder when your uncle changed"; mused Ajax. "I never knew him well, and never saw him at all for at least five years before you were born. Perhaps it was when he met those imperial scholars, although I don't believe he ever actually entered the Empire itself. I do know he had a falling out with your father, before your sister Loriel was born, and kept very much to his own lands afterwards. Little wonder about that; had your father sensed that he was a threat to your mother or his children, he'd have cut Ketil down without hesitation. Tiresth, now... she wouldn't have believed anything that bad about her own brother, but Danu never took any risks he didn't have to, not where his family was concerned. Your uncle didn't die an easy death, but it was less than he deserved."

I thought about that for a while, as we sat digesting our dinner, the firelight flickering across our faces. We were still in settled lands, within the borders of the Bastarnae tribe, so it was safe enough to keep a fire lit. We had our mules too; treated like pets by us, they would be quick to sense any intruders and let us know about it. Why not horses? We were planning on entering Scythia, and the tribes of Scythia call themselves "the People of the Horse". When in Scythia, all horses belong to the Scythians, and if the nomads find anyone riding a horse who isn't a member of one of the tribes, they will put the strangers on foot, or worse. None of the tribes care a hoot about mules though, except to eat them if game is scarce.

A branch popped and flared amid the campfire, and I asked:

"Tell me about my sisters".

"Ah. Well, Tirwen was the oldest and the most like your mother. Loriel was the darling, so beautiful and so sweet she stole even Kak's heart"

"She would ride on my back and call me Horse", Kak rumbled from his shadow over by our bedrolls.

"And they loved you dearly, never doubt it. Tirwen had just come of age and Loriel was almost ten, when Ketil struck. Your sisters were the pride of your tribe, Joren; they excelled at almost everything they did, and they were born leaders, everyone could see it in them. With your parents as tutors, the Mabirshar would have been well served indeed when all three of you reached your full potential". He stopped then; I had buried my face in my hands, and I wouldn't have heard a word he said if he had gone on.

Chapter VIII: Ketil the Accursed

THE NEXT NIGHT, they told me more of what they knew of my people. Ajax spoke first of my uncle:

"I think that's what drove Ketil to his crimes: he realized that he hadn't a chance at any real power as long as your parents or any of you children were alive. And that burned him, for by that time his lust for the Black Oak throne and the power that went with it filled his mind to the exclusion of all else. The imperials saw that in him, perhaps many years ago. The Empire is very patient, boy, never forget that. Its servants can wait a long time for what they want, for their plans to come to fruition. I think an agent of the Empire saw this hunger in your uncle, his desire for the throne he felt should have been his, and that imperial agent or another fed the flames of your uncle's ambition until they consumed whatever honor he had. Ketil forsook love and loyalty, and chose a path that lead first to murder, then treason, and finally to his own death and the destruction of the Mabirshar tribe itself."

I spoke then, for the first time since the night before, and said:

"He helped kill my father too, didn't he?"

Ajax's eyes narrowed as he glanced at me, but it was Kak who answered:

"A shrewd guess, youngling, and one I think touches the truth. Your sire went north and west, into the Empire's lands to seek an answer to a riddle posed in your mother's dreams. I think the Betrayer had a hand in planting this dream in your mother's sleep: Ketil was a man of power in his own right, and who knows what magic he might have obtained from the Imperials? I do know this: when your father left the Mabirshar lands, someone sent word ahead of him to the Temple of Hel Black Witch in Aquincum. They knew he was coming before he ever crossed the border."

Ajax continued when Kak stopped:

"Kak and I were in the south then, in the Minos's country, but your father didn't go alone. He took five companions with him: Rall Wolfscar, Torbild Bluehand, Rokas the Silent, Three Tailed Orthan and Horusa Longknife; good, steady fighters all. Rall and Torbild were your father's swordbrothers and Horusa was your mother's foster sister; none would have left your father's side short of death. They were a formidable group of warriors and it cost the Empire dear to pull them down."

"When word reached Kak of your father's death, he slipped across the border to investigate, while I tied up some loose ends in Byzantium. He spoke with others of his people, who have ways of knowing things, and found that the day after your father left the Queenshall, seven Second Shadow agents left Aquincum to intercept your father. And the day after that, fourteen more left the administrative center at Carnuntum to link up with the first seven. Better than three to one odds against your father's band... the Second Shadow didn't want to take any chances with your father; he had made too many enemies inside the Empire, after the battle at Novae." Ajax sighed deeply and stirred the fire with a long stick.

"We're not sure of what happened after that. Later, I found a report of a cavalry patrol that spotted what sounds like your father and Orthan near a small village on the north bank of the Rhine near Vindibona. Both were said to have been wounded. The hunt was up for them; every garrison in Dacia had been called out by then and there was no clear road back to Khetar. I don't know what was in your father's mind at that point; I do know that, when he finally reached the City of a Thousand Dragons, all five warriors that had left Khetar with him were dead, and of the 21 imperial assassins sent to kill them, only five were still alive. The Second Shadow agents reached the city before your father, and four of them set a trap for him. Danu spotted their trap and sprang it; he killed all four of them and then died himself."

"How?", I asked.

It was Kak who answered. "I'm not sure; there were at least a dozen rumors. Everything from a poisoned arrow to a duel to the death between Danu and Othar Inkson."

"But it is Othar who now carries my father's sword, Oathtaker."

"Yes, and I heard that he spoke with your father before his death. I do know that Othar Wolfhound buried your father himself, and later brought Oathtaker south with him in the Empress's service." Kak shifted his weight forward, propping his arms on his knees as he absently whetted the edge of his shortsword. It was a good blade, more than a foot long and three inches across, but it looked like a belt knife in his broad, thick-fingered hands.

Kak was as tall as most men, but inhumanly wide through the shoulders and thick through the chest. He kept his head shaved, as did most darklings when among humans; and his skin was mostly grey in color: dark grey on his shoulders and back, shading to a light grey/white on his belly. He had sharp, white fangs that were uncommonly thick, and a collection of scars that would have done any warrior proud, but it is his laugh and his eyes that I remember best. Kak's laugh was a ready, comforting rumble, so low in timbre that it was felt as much as heard. His eyes were a dark brown, and glinted with a keen wit that missed little, and a quick and surprisingly gentle humor, for a darkling.

He went on: "What I had learned in the Empire troubled me; I sent a warning to your mother and then went south again to meet Ajax at Tomis. I do not know if the Queen your mother ever received the message. I have never met anyone who remembers seeing the courier I sent; it seems likely that Ketil forsaw that someone might try to warn your mother. He would have had the time and the resources to ensure that any such messenger was intercepted and silenced. And who would suspect the Queen's own brother of acting against her? I curse his name and his spirit: may the first never know respect, and may the second never know peace."

Ajax spoke up, then. "We saw the smoke from five miles off, and we could feel that something was wrong. We ran the rest of the way to Oak Rest, and came in from the west, through the woods as quiet as we could. I didn't want us to be seen by anyone until we knew how matters stood. That turned out better than I could have planned; night was falling when Kak found you shivering under that red-bud bush. You looked a fright, boy. Your eyes were wide and blank, your face stained with soot and your tunic soaked with blood not your own. I bundled you up in my cloak and we got you the hell out of there. I waited with you in a shepherd's lean-to the next valley over, while Kak went in to scout things out while it was dark. He tried to backtrack you, but had to give it up. There were too many people out beating the woods for the assassins, and too many of those near to where we found you were strangers".

"Strange to the eye, the nose and the ear," said Kak. "Not Mabirshar, not even Khetar folk, I think. I have never been able to place them, though I do know that, although not tribesmen, they later became the Accursed One's personal guards. They died with him when the Lupaku came. That night, we decided to hide the fact that you still lived. Ajax took you south to Hattusa, while I wiped out our tracks and then laid a false trail that lead west towards the God Pillar. In the dark, I can get very close to your people without them knowing it. I overheard some of the searchers say that your mother and sisters were dead, though they never did find Tirwen's body. They assumed that both of you had been consumed by the fire that destroyed half the Queenshall; and so we let them think, while Ajax kept you safe in the House of Death in Hattusa. But every winter since that fire, the North Wind that blows through the valley of Oak Rest blows stronger there than anywhere else in Khetar, stronger than at any time anyone can remember, even among the Children of the Dark Mother. It gusts strongly enough to pull limbs from the trees and cloaks from the unlucky; it is said that every building in the valley loses something to the wind each winter: a shutter torn from a window or thatch plucked from the roof. It is as if the wind is searching for something, or someone. The Accursed One hated the North Wind; he would never go out if it was blowing, but would stay close in the Queenshall, with all of the rushes lit. Whatever has enraged the North Wind so, it wasn't after Ketil; it has continued to blow just as strongly in the years since his death."

Ajax grunted: "I haven't been back there since your family passed through the Door, but there is something about the way the wind blows in that valley that bothers me. I didn't have time for it then, I was in Hattusa trying to find out what had happened to you. I had you looked at by the King's own healer, Joren. She said that she had never seen anything like what had been done to you and your memory, though she did know that the priests of the White Sun possess magic that can damage the mind of their enemies." Ajax rubbed his chin, remembering.

"We kept you there, safe in the King's own city for nearly two years, until war came. When the Empire's legions encircled the city, I took you and fled east to the Kothmir lands."

"To Aunt Syara", I said, remembering her face and her last words to me. Her last words... The letter she had left to me had spoken of things that only our family should know, and only one of our blood could ever use. Syara had been my maternal grandmother's sister; she had known secrets that no one outside our blood kin could know. Two of those secrets hinted at how someone could have carried me from our burning home. I would have to see for myself someday.

"Did the Lupaku leave anything standing when they took their vengeance?", I asked.

"Not much. The Queenshall itself was set left standing; every other building, and the walls of the royal enclosure itself were pulled down. I don't know why they didn't chop the Royal Oak itself down. Maybe there is some kind of magic left in the Black Oak throne that prevented them, or maybe they were just leaving it to last and had to abandon it when the Imperial relief column was spotted. What they really wanted was blood, and there they drank their fill. The Lupaku took the clans that made up the bulk of your tribe by complete surprise and wiped them out. They killed everyone: man or woman, from the sickbed to the cradle. They had Ketil to thank for that."

"In your mother's day, the Queenshall housed a half dozen or more Oath hounds, like your dog Kon, who was the last of the breed. The tales handed down by your mother's family say that the Oath hounds first served Mabirh Longstride, the first queen of the Mabirshar, and were not whelped by any mortal bitch. I believe it; those dogs never slept, they feared nothing and could smell magic and see the wind. They never left the Queenshall until Kon left with your aunt; that was the first time that any Oath Hound had left Oak Rest in living memory. Those hounds lived to protect the ruling queen; they would have died defending your mother and set up such a howling racket while they fought that they would have alerted half of your tribe. Anyone who sought the life of the queen in secret would need to first silence the hounds who guarded her."

I started feeling sick to my stomach, as I saw where this was leading.

"If an assassin would kill in silence and in secret, he would probably use…"

"Poison. I cannot prove it, because Ketil made sure that the hounds' bodies were taken by the fire, but I think he poisoned them himself. They would accept food only from the hand of one of the royal blood; and why would anyone suspect Ketil? He was not only the queen's brother, he would have been known to all of the hounds from childhood. I do know this: from the time of your mother's death until the attack by the Lupaku, Ketil and all who followed him lived under the curse of Canis, Father of Dogs. No dog, no matter what the breed, would live in Oak Rest or in the steading of anyone who called Ketil their king. If left loose, they would run away; if kept chained, they would starve themselves to death. And because those who followed Ketil chose also to follow the White Sun, there were no duskcats in any of the steadings; the children of Sarrumas will never serve the White Goddess or her people."

"Ketil and those who followed him relied on their status as imperial clients to keep them safe, believing that fear of the Empire would deter anyone from attacking them. They were wrong. When the wolf people attacked, there were neither hound nor duskcat to sound an alarm, and Ketil and his tribesmen were taken completely by surprise; the report of the Imperial relief column said there was no organized defense at all. The Lupaku struck, killed, took what loot and livestock that struck their fancy, and then left the Queenshall standing open to the wind and rain after leveling everything else. The wolf people didn't put anything to the torch; they don't much like fire, and there is too great a chance of a fire spreading into the woods. Later, after the Empire had the Lupaku punished, they gave the best of the empty Mabirshar lands to Othar Wolfhound as a reward. They built the Watchful Fort on top of the ruins inside of Oak Rest, and Othar himself had his manor built onto the remains of the Queenshall. It contains within it the Black Oak Throne of the Mabirshar."

Ajax folded his arms and waited, both his eyes and Kak's on my face.

I was still feeling sick. Ketil had poisoned those who had trusted him, the way Kon had loved and trusted me. Dogs or no, they had deserved better. Damn him. I found myself staring at my hands; they were clenched tight into white-knuckled fists.

"I have to know how and why my family was destroyed", I said. Both warriors nodded at that; it was only right and proper that I follow that trail, and take vengeance on my family's enemies when I had done so.

"Of all of those involved in my family's deaths, Othar Inkson is the only one I know to be alive. And he has Oathtaker, my father's sword."

"Even so. He wielded it against the Lupaku, when he led the force that broke them."

"Tell me about Oathtaker. Are all of the stories about it true?"

Ajax scratched at his chin. "Well, I don't think I know all of the stories about that sword, Joren. It's been around for a very long time, and I'm sure there are stories that have never been heard by anyone who is still alive. But what I do know about it is strange enough. In form, it is a two handed sword, but not as long or as heavy as some of the pike-breaking swords you see in the lowlands. It's lighter than it looks, and very sharp. There is nothing inscribed on the blade, and there are no gems inlaid in it; in fact, with the exception of the hilt, it is completely unadorned. The hilt..." He paused briefly.

"The hilt is formed in the shape of a woman, whose arms and hair twine together and run into the sword's guard. The pommel of the sword has been shaped so that a woman's face looks out from the end of the sword hilt instead of a pommel stone. The face is beautiful, but it isn't a...human beauty."

"Elven?" I asked.

"No, not elven. Different from anything I've ever seen. The sword's design is simple, but the magic enchanted into it when it was made is anything but simple. It is bound to Truth. If you lie while holding the sword sheathed, it will twist itself out of your grasp. If you lie while the sword is drawn, it will turn in your hands and strike at you. And there is a deeper power in it: it is a matrix for Warrunk's oath magic. Anyone who swears an oath while holding the sword will die within minutes if they break the oath. Not even the Lords of the Sea could find a way around this spell; that is why they called it 'The Shackle'."

Ajax paused and nodded at me. "Remember that, Joren. For when the sword passes from one wielder to another, the new owner must swear an oath or the powers of the sword will not work for them."

"Powers? What kind of powers?" I asked.

"They seemed to change from one person to the next. Sometimes Oathtaker could slay the spell that enchanted iron for its user, and break iron weapons like glass. Other times, it would enhance the senses, or increase the range or duration of magic someone already possessed. Your father told me once that the tighter you bound yourself to the sword, the more power it offered you. Hmm."

Ajax looked at me and smiled, his eyes crinkling.

"You wouldn't remember, but from what happened that one time I visited your parents, I would say that you have had a closer look at Oathtaker than I've ever had."

Huh? I couldn't remember anything of my childhood up until the moment Aunt Syara had first touched my face, but from the way both Ajax and Kak were grinning...

"What did I do?"

"Your father and I had walked into the other room while talking about something, I forget exactly what. Your mother had gone into the kitchen to see if dinner was ready to be served, and you were left in the East Room with a couple of the Oath hounds and Oathtaker. Your father had secured the blade with thong so it wouldn't slide out of the sheath, and I remember that he had left it leaning away from you, against one of the chairs. Yet when we walked back into the room, the sword had somehow managed to tilt the other way and slide the length of the table so that it fell hilt first into your cradle. I don't know whether a servant had moved it or if one of the hounds had brushed against it, but we could hear you babbling away as if you were talking to someone. By the time we had reached your cradle, you had braced both of your feet on the cross guard, wrapped both hands around the hilt and were gnawing on the face in the pommel."

I stood up and grabbed my hair in both hands. "Aaaaagh!!!"

"That sword is more than a thousand years old, it has slain monsters and kings, led armies into battle...and the stories say it glows with its own magic! Even if it wasn't magic, it would still be worth a fortune because it is wrought iron, and you're telling me I used it as a TEETHING RING?"

"Well, yes."

"Ajax, that's just...WRONG." They both started laughing at me.

Kak spoke up then:

"I wouldn't let it bother you; your father said:

'She didn't mind, she just wanted to get a good, close look at him.'.

I stopped at that. "She? Oathtaker is a she?"

He nodded. "My swordbrother always spoke of Oathtaker as 'she', 'her' or 'The Lady'. Never 'It'. Othar Wolfhound may know more; the power of the sword is awake for him."

So, somehow there was a spirit bound into the sword. That was said of other swords of legend too.

"Well, since he is the one who has Oathtaker now, I think I'll go and talk to Othar Wolfhound myself. Before I take my father's sword from him", I said as I met Ajax's eyes.

I saw Kak nod, but Ajax just looked at me and said: "Not yet, boy. I'm not done teaching you yet."

I lay awake for some time that night before falling asleep. For as long as I could remember, I've had a mark on my tongue; I can't see it clearly, but I've been told that to some, it looks like the outline of a face. The sword Oathtaker had marked me as an infant in the cradle; I had to wonder what else she might have done to me. I also thought about what Ajax had said about not being done teaching me; I agreed with him, but that night I prayed that fate would let Othar Wolfhound live long enough for me to talk to him myself. I had strange dreams that night, filled with the flash of blades, the smell of blood, and tinted with a cold, sick anger that filled my soul even after I awakened. I found out later that Fate had heard the words of my prayer, and would wait more than a decade before ramming them down my throat.

Chapter IX: Bel

THE NEXT DAY FOUND MY MIND FILLED with thoughts of revenge for my family, to the exclusion of all else. I performed my chores mechanically; I don't really remember doing them, or even seeing the countryside we passed through for the first few hours we traveled that day. Now, revenge can be like a disease, or a poison: you have to get hold of an antidote fairly quickly or it can damage you forever. I didn't know it, but we were riding right towards the antidote for the icy thirst for vengeance that was eating away at me. I mentioned before that we were in the lands of the Bastarnae tribe at this time; they were the easternmost of the tribes of Khetar. Beyond their lands lay the plains of Scythia, and beyond that, the ruined city of Carchemish that sits on the edge of the world, or so I thought then. The Bastarnae are allies with the Roxolani tribe of Scythia, who are a buffer between Khetar and the fierce nomads that call Scythia their home. The Bastarnae share a number of characteristics with the Roxolani: they make good allies and bad enemies, and are ferocious warriors as well as superb horsemen. A man could do worse than to have one as a friend.

I had been slouching along in the saddle all morning, not paying much attention to my surroundings, when we crested the brow of a long, low hill overlooking a small steading. It was a very nice piece of land with plenty of water and a corral near the main house into which a small herd of horses were just being driven. The drovers were a grey bearded man of average height, and a girl who topped him by inches. Both waved when they spotted us, but it was the clear, ringing shout that the girl voiced that jerked me out of my funk. It was Bel! We had met only for that one day the previous season, the day we both made our oaths to Tarhunt, but I had felt a bond with her, a sense of rightness that I had never had with anyone else. Besides, she was beautiful, and now she was here, spurring her horse towards us at a gallop. My mind was immediately filled with thoughts that had nothing to do with vengeance.

She rode up to us and saluted Kak, who answered:

"I hear you, Heron Girl. Aren't you finished growing, yet?"

Then she kissed Ajax on the cheek and punched me in the shoulder.

"Took you long enough" she said, blasting me with that smile that seemed to carry with it the warmth of the sun. My response was a smooth, suave:

97

"Huh?"

Ajax turned to me, and said:

"Your aunt and I had planned this trip last year; but now, we travel the same road for a different reason."

Bel listened to this, and then searched me with a look from those deep brown eyes.

"Oh", she said, and taking my right hand in her left, rode along beside me without any other words. The touch of her hand spread a wave of warmth up my arm and into my chest and heart. It drove back the cold sickness that had been eating at me for the past few days; it didn't drive it out of me completely, nothing ever has. But it did seem to push it back into a small dark room inside of me, that I could lock and turn away from, as long as she was with me.

Later that night, after we had our evening meal and spread our bedrolls near the corral, Bel told me of her own parents; they had died in the year Hattusa fell, leaving her to be raised by her uncle Barlan. Barlan was her grey-bearded companion and her closest living relative; at first glance he appeared rather non-descript: average height, average build, just another Bastarnae tribesman who raised horses. But I soon noticed that his eyes were very steady and didn't seem to miss anything; his hands were immensely strong and he didn't make any wasted motions. It turned out he had blood brothers among the Roxolani and had traveled extensively in southwestern Scythia. Barlan was familiar with both the city of Carchemish and Gazian, and he and Ajax talked long into the night. The next morning, they spoke briefly again, and then turned to us.

"We are going to change our plans a bit", Ajax said. "Belkara, you will come to Gazian with us; we will go from there to The Needles, where we will meet up with your uncle." Belkara was Bel's full name; in the dialect of Lycia, it was Bel Karra, the great grey heron that stalks the shallows and tidal flats of the Narrow Sea.

Barlan scratched his chin, and mused aloud, "I think the Empire is up to something". He turned to Bel and went on:

"We will take the herd to Ateas's Cist for the tribe's gathering; that should be finished in three weeks' time, and then we will drive the market herd to Hattusa for sale. You four go by mule from the Cist to Gazian, and I'll see what I can find out from my brothers among the Bright Alans. Let us meet at The Needles in two weeks' time; that will give us a week to get back to the Cist in time for the drive to market".

It sounded good to me. It would give me plenty of time to practice.

The trip to Ateas's Cist didn't take more than a couple of days; we were herding horses, not sheep. I did get to practice; my horseback riding (our mules weren't up to riding herd on their cousins) and kissing too (when time permitted). Mainly it was work from sunup to sundown, and then more lessons around the fire at night, and then bed. Barlan was almost as bad as Ajax was for cramming information into you when you weren't working, but it made sense. Bel and I were new adults, and we had a great deal of responsibility to our families, our cult and our tribes. We needed to know a great deal to fulfill those responsibilities and to make the decisions that were part of an adult's place in our world. Those decisions could mean life or death, especially where we were going.

We had been getting rain almost every night, and it was starting to have an effect: the hills around us were starting to green up nicely as the trees, shrubs and grasses began their yearly race to see which would get the most sunlight and water. They began to flower too, and soon the hillsides were splashed with color. This made the change from hills to the flat lands of Scythia even more noticeable. It wasn't that Scythia is barren, far from it. It is just that the plants that grow in the soil of Scythia are different from the trees and shrubs of Issuria; what makes an even greater impression is the abrupt change from wooded hills to grasslands. Scythia is battle land; it was fought over by the gods before Time began, and by men, monsters and heroes ever since. That kind of conflict has an effect, and the change over from hills to plain is as sharp as if it were a line cut in soft clay with a sharp knife.

Chapter X: Ateas's Cist

THERE HAS NEVER BEEN A TOWN or even a village at Ateas's Cist, but everyone in Issuria and Scythia knows where it is nonetheless. The barrow that contains the cist-faen (or stone crypt) of Ateas Whitemane was raised atop the tallest of the ridges that border Scythia, but it is not in Scythia itself. In the centuries since, the prevailing winds from Scythia have added sand and soil to the barrow, year by year, so that now the Cist is the largest by far of all the local landmarks, and is visible for miles out on the plains. When the White Sun Empire conquered Khetar in 602, they unknowingly entered an area where myth and history are so intertwined that they cannot be easily separated, if at all. So it is with Ateas's Cist.

Ateas had been the greatest of the kings of Old Scythia, and the last king to unite all of the nomad tribes under one banner. He had ruled more than a thousand years ago, and had dared to challenge the Empire of the Dragon rather than kneel before the Dragon Emperor. Still hale at the age of 90, Ateas had led the massed tribes against the imperial forces led by Philip Wyrmrider, one of that Empire's greatest generals. They had clashed just to the east of the Cist, in a titanic battle that lasted two days. The losses on both sides were measured in the tens of thousands; Philip himself was wounded, and lost an eye as well as the draconic mount that gave him his war name. But the Scythians had been crushed, their survivors so scattered and few in number that it was said that it took two hundred years for them to regain their strength. Ateas and all of the tribal chieftains fell in battle, the sacred talismans of each tribe were looted or lost, and the royal regalia of the Scythian kings were laid at the feet of the Dragon Emperor. To ensure that the tribes never forgot their defeat, the imperial magicians raised a barrow for Ateas on the highest hilltop overseeing the battle field. There, they set his remains in a stone box marked with draconic runes and wound about with spells of inhuman power. They set the heads of the scythian warriors slain in the battle and the heads of all of their dead horses on the slopes of the barrow and that hilltop, and then they set the entire hill aflame with dragon fire. It burned for a year with an eerie green flame that could be seen for miles.

The tribes never challenged the Dragon again.

Even after they nomads regained their numbers, they stayed away from imperial territory, so for four hundred years there was peace within the

100

Shadow of the Dragon, and it held all of the lands from the edge of the Cold Seas to the southern grazelands of Scythia in the grip of a fierce golden peace that brooked neither dissent nor opposition. There was conflict outside the Empires' borders, especially with the Lords of the Islands to the south. But within the Empire itself, there was peace, until the Fall.

After the Fall, dragon magic of all kinds failed; there began to be some very strange things seen and heard on and around the barrow that holds Ateas's Cist. Sensible people stayed away from it if at all possible, and even the tribes steered clear of the area unless they were raiding into Issuria. When the imperials first heard of Ateas's Cist, they didn't pay much attention to it; there are legends found in every land, and they had enough on their plate absorbing Khetar and planning to invade Thrace. It wasn't until 604 that the Imperial Governor took official notice of Ateas's Barrow. In that year, a group of imperial veterans, recently discharged from regular service, decided to try their hand at grave robbing. After buying the appropriate permit from the Governor's office, they made their camp just south of the Cist, and climbed up its south face, taking borings and measurements in an attempt to place the location of the treasure room that is supposed to lie somewhere beneath Ateas's burial chamber. They disappeared in broad daylight, in full view of an entire troop of Imperial cavalry. No trace of them was ever found, but if you stand in the right place, it is said that you can still hear them screaming.

Since then, the Imperials have been a little more cautious, especially since the first magical investigation revealed the presence of literally hundreds of ghosts on the barrow itself, apparently standing watch. Further investigations caused one sage from the imperial Rhineland duchies to postulate that the barrow is an open portal or gateway to the Spirit world, since the number and identity of the ghosts standing guard changes constantly. Legend says that the Ateas's burial mound is guarded from interlopers by the spirits of every nomad who died following him into battle against the Dragon Empire. The Imperials seem to be willing to accept that legend on face value: the barrow at Ateas's Cist is forbidden to all but the highest ranking Imperial officials, the approaches to the barrow have been fortified with triple-strength walls of stone and magic, and a detachment of 300 imperial regulars was posted to keep watch over both the barrow and the plains to the east. Ajax said that the nomads he had spoken to seemed to regard the imperial defenses at Ateas's Cist with a certain amount of amusement, but the presence of 300 well paid soldiers had provided the Bastarnae with a commercial opportunity that the tribe had not been slow in taking advantage of.

The imperial troops at Ateas's Cist were literally the last outpost of the Empire; although the Cist itself wasn't in Scythia, and was surrounded by scattered forest and well-watered meadows, there were no permanent posts between the Cist and the Bright Sea to the south, the limitless steppes to the east or the Pontine Mountains to the north. No matter how well paid, silver doesn't do a soldier much good if there is nothing to spend it on, and Bel's people had moved quickly to give those troops something to buy. To break the monotony of military rations, the Bastarnae provided fresh mutton and pork, wheat and rye for the camp ovens and a variety of the supplies that every military camp needs, and never has enough of: honey and salt, ink and soap, seasoned timber and wool blankets, leather for boots, belts, saddles and tack, and every kind of potable they could get their hands on. This was everything from weak beer to the best ales, deep red wine to our own golden mead, and the surprisingly potent drink some tribes made by freezing cider and skimming the ice off of it. The imperial military had ferocious punishments for any soldier caught drunk on duty, but did not forbid drink off duty. It wouldn't have stopped the drinking and probably would have started a mutiny.

Bel's people had taken to gathering the tribe's produce at Ateas's Cist before driving their herds west to Hattusa for the Great Market. This way they had the added protection offered by the presence of 300 imperial soldiers and the imperials benefitted by getting first pick of the tribe's wares, including fresh horses for the officers and cavalry and teams of mules and oxen for drayage. Besides, it gave the Imperials a chance to collect their taxes at the source, which cut down on the smuggling traffic. As we rode down to the pens just west of the Imperial camp, we could see that we were almost the first to reach the gather; there could not have been more than 2 dozen head of horses and barely a hundred mules and other stock present. We made camp while Barlan rode over to register with the imperial watch commander; the next day, the wares we had escorted to the Cist would be tallied up and assessed. Although Barlan would pay a toll for the use of the springs dug by the imperials, it would be the tribe itself that would pay taxes that would be based in part on the total value of the goods gathered here by the Bastarnae. Whether or not the tribe actually sold the goods and cattle gathered here meant nothing to the Empire, it was the increase in tribal wealth that the tax was based on.

That evening, as the sun dropped below the peaks of Khetar's Toros mountains to the west, I went to look at the immense barrow that the winds of Scythia had helped to build for Ateas's rest. I was surprised to see wisps of fog floating above the upper slopes of the hill; it had looked to be our first clear night all week. That was when I realized that the only fog in sight for miles around was on the Cist, and that it was getting thicker by the minute. When the sun had dropped out of sight to the west, the fog began to pour down the sides of the barrow and within two or three minutes had covered the entire surface of the hilltop in a thick gray sheet that shifted and flickered with a life of its own. Shapes began to take form out of the mist, the shapes of riders and mounts of the tribes of Scythia: Sakae and Dahae, Kushan and Sogdian, Auchatae and Traspians, even the Great Golden Auroches that can be ridden only by the Paralatae (the Royal Scythians), and there were other things in the fog as well. I saw swords that gleamed like silver under water, and lances that rose in pale, deadly thickets; and in the distance I heard horns blowing whose only echo came from within the barrow itself.

I started at the sound of a step at my side, and turned to see Ajax standing beside me, arms crossed, motionless. The only movement came when his eyes moved and the ghostly light streaming from the Barrow caused them to flicker. Beyond him I could see the other Bastarnae drovers standing open-mouthed in awe and beyond them, the entire Imperial garrison, both the armed patrols and the off-duty troopers, standing motionless in terrified fascination as an army of the dead took form on the hill above them. Even at a glance, it was obvious that the ghosts on the Cist outnumbered the imperial garrison by at least ten to one. If Ateas appeared now and launched his phantom guards against us, we were all dead, and everyone knew it.

"This doesn't happen often, does it?" I asked.

"No", Ajax replied. "Only when great things happen to the tribes do the Barrow guards stir like this. It could mean that the white bull calf whose birth has been foretold for centuries has finally come, or that one of the tribes has suffered a great defeat or won a great victory or a great magic has been made or found. It doesn't necessarily mean we will ever see or hear of it though. Remember boy, the steppes are the true home of the nomads; what we call Scythia is just their front porch. No man or woman alive knows the boundaries of the steppes, let alone everything contained within it."

Less than an hour after sunset, the light from the ghostly army on the

Barrow began to fade, and soon only a thick patch of fog remained, although it stubbornly clung to the top of the Cist and refused to shift or dissipate. There was no other sign that anything unusual had happened: the livestock were quiet and the sounds made by the insects and animals of the night were normal in every respect. The rest of that night passed without incident and when not on watch, we all slept soundly. By dawn, the details of the spectral army guarding Ateas's barrow had taken on an almost dream-like quality, but we all knew it had not been a dream. The next morning, Barlan arranged for some fellow tribesmen (a woman by the name of Vanioth and her three sons) to look after his family's livestock for the three or four weeks we expected to be gone. In return, Bel would do a little trading for them in Gazian, and Barlan promised to cook Vanioth her favorite meal. Bel made a point of telling me later that women appreciate it when men cook for them (probably because they think there are so few of us who can be trusted near an open flame).

By mid-morning we had finished the task of saddling up our mules, and we set off on the separate legs of our journey; Barlan southeast through the Roxolani territory to the oasis at Roaring Springs, and from there northeast to The Needles. The four of us (Ajax, Bel, Kak and I) would travel northeast to the town of Gazian in the foothills of the Pontic Mountains, and from there southeast to The Needles to meet up with Barlan. Bel gave her uncle a tight hug and a kiss; she hated being left behind for any reason (exactly how much so I was to find out for myself), but she knew that Barlan would travel faster, and learn more from his contacts among the tribesmen, if he went alone. So, with a firm handclasp and a last wave of our hands, we were off: Barlan with four mules so he could travel at speed, and the four of us with an even dozen mules for riding and as pack animals. Barlan was soon lost to sight, and although he survived the events of the next season, I never met him again. He was a good man, and I was more than a little pleased when Bel later told me that he had approved of me.

Chapter XI: Gazian

WE SET OUT TOWARDS THE NORTHEAST with clear weather to favor us, and we made good time. Kak's leg had healed to the point where he could sit his mule, so the travois carried trade goods instead of a darkling warrior. He was still careful with the arm he sometimes carried in a sling, but he was able to do more around the camp and take a more active role in training Bel and I. He was as excited as I had ever seen him, and the first night out from Ateas's Cist, he told us why. He was going home.

Kak had been born into the darklings of the Thunderhead Mountains to the south of Khetar, but had left his birth place to wander farther than is common for his people. He traveled the length of Thrace from the coast of Lycia in the east to the border marches of the Illyrian tribes; and in the company of Ajax and my father, he went from the Minos's capital of Byzantium to the northern hills of Dacia. He had climbed the lower slopes of the Godpillar and walked the Dragon's Road from Aquincum in Dacia to the city of Carchemish which sits at the edge of the steppes on the banks of the Euphrates River. He was uncommon too, in his choice of patrons (Warrunk is not commonly worshipped among the Children of Darkness) and friends, Ajax for one, and my father for another. The only family he had left was an older sister, Xakjota, who had also possessed a wandering foot; she had eventually married into a darkling clan in the southern Pontic Mountains, near Gazian. Now she was a matriarch with her own children to raise and her adopted clan to guide, and she found herself in need of a strong right arm and a ready blade that she could trust. So she had sent word south to her little brother to stop his wandering ways and come settle down where he would do some good.

Among men or darklings, family is family; Kak had not even considered NOT answering his sister's summons. Apparently, now that he had had a chance to think it over, he was a bit excited about it. Kak was more than just an experienced warrior; he had commanded troops in the army of Minos and done well at it. He could speak, read and write in a half a dozen languages and had dealt with almost every foe imaginable in the length and breadth of Issuria. After more than two decades in faithful service to Warrunk, his magical abilities and his skill at arms were impressive, and last, but not least, he had a certain amount of wealth. All of his swords were of the finest quality, and he carried with him his ransom of 100 gold eagles (although a warrior's ransom would normally be kept safe by his temple or regiment). Half of our party's mules were his and they were stuffed with the gifts he was bringing for his sister and his in-laws.

But the most obvious indication of his wealth was his armor: a full suite of bronze plate. It bore, in black enamel, the sigils of Warrunk and was engraved with the mark of the Minos's armorers and throbbed with their magic. Moreover, it had been hammered and fitted to the massive dimensions of Kak's frame. Now, suites of metal armor in Kak's size are just not very common in any of the human lands; suites of fine plate in his size are almost unheard of and incredibly expensive. Kak's armor had to be worth at least 10 times the amount of gold he carried as his ransom; it had been given to him by the command of the Minos himself, in reward for my friend's outstanding service suppressing bandits in the western marches of Thrace. Now that Kak was feeling more like himself, Ajax began to twit him about what a catch he would make for some lucky darkling maiden; Kak just brushed off his teacher's comments with a remark to the effect that he was sure that his sister had someone suitable lined up for him. I think now however, that at least part of Kak's anticipation was due to the impression he intended to make on both the men and women of his sister's clan when he arrived. He knew what he was doing; first impressions are lasting ones.

So we rode on to Gazian. Our route took us northeast, out of Issuria and into Scythia proper. We past the peak called the Watcher, where the Dragon Empire had built a watchtower. Although it was said to offer a splendid view of the lands around it, the tower was in ruins and said to be haunted. More to the point, the road that led up the hill to the tower had been washed out years ago and now there was no safe way to reach the top. We had no time to waste, so we skirted the Watcher and rode on until we struck the Way of the Dragon. That road is nearly a thousand years old, but still in good shape; we should be able to travel at a swift pace from there to Gazian. It is an eerie place, in the shadow of the Watcher; you always seem to feel the eyes of someone on you, and the wind blows unceasingly. There are no ranches or settlements nearby, and it is a lonely place, but I wasn't lonely, then. My memories of that ride are still bright and clear: the broad-shouldered darkling with his laugh like thunder, the quiet old man who loved us all and who always had something else to teach us, and Bel, with her eyes like stars and her own laugh that was like a musical spell. Those memories are dear to me, and old habits die hard; I am loth to share these memories, even with you.

The town of Gazian lies to the west and north of Carchemish, near to the foothills of the Pontine Mountains. It has stood there, they say, since before Time began. In the 600 years since the Fall, Gazian has been ruled by assyrian warlords, darkling queens, nomad khans and the local robber chieftains, who pass themselves off as nobility when the pickings get lean. Despite having been sacked a number of times in its history, Gazian remains a thriving market. It is the center of the trade that flows between the nomads of Scythia, the darkling queendom of Stygia, the kingdom of Khetar and the lands ruled by Babylon and Nineveh.

Gazian is divided into three sections. One is the Open or Nomad Quarter, where you would find the slave block, the outer corrals and the camps that hold whatever nomad clans happen to be in town. The Nomad Quarter has no permanent population. Another is the Darkling or Night's Quarter, where you will find the homes and temples of the darkling tribe who dominate this part of the Pontine foothills, as well as the ever-shifting hovels of their goblin shanty town. The Night's Quarter is located between the ruins of an old wall and the New or Walled Quarter, and may reach a size as large as 2,000 (if there hasn't been a nomad raid recently), but only three out of every ten is Aos Si, fomor warriors like Kak or one of the nobility; the rest of the population consists of goblins, who rarely reach man height.

It is the Walled Quarter that most visitors to Gazian think of as Gazian itself. It sits within a reinforced stockade that protects the non-nomadic, mostly human inhabitants of Gazian. There aren't much more than 300 or 400 people who live here year-round, although the caravans might swell the town's temporary population by several thousand people at the height of the busy season. It is in the Walled Quarter that you will find the Temple and Market of Nabu, the shrines and homes of the people who make Gazian their home year round, and the different taverns and inns that service both the locals and the merchant trade. The largest and best of the inns in Gazian is the Traveller's Rest; both it and the tavern attached to it (the Cup and Sword) are owned by the Kinbi family, and have been since Khetar PeaceMaker came to Issuria.

The Flat Purse is a tavern favored by caravan guards, mercenaries and the occasional small group of travellers, like ourselves. The Tipping Bowl was the tavern frequented by the locals, and the Broken Bottle was the clapboard dive that served two different kinds of hooch to the riffraff that no other place in town would let in their front door. There is a fourth Quarter to Gazian, but only the locals speak of it, and then, not very often. The Fourth or Lost Quarter of Gazian hasn't existed in 1000 years; it is the term used to refer to the old walled city that was destroyed by the nomads when Ateas's horde stormed Gazian before his defeat. The only visible remnant left of the old city is the crumbling wall that is the outer boundary of the Darkling Quarter; although there are rumors of tunnels and old basements beneath the town that can be entered through passageways in the darkling temples or the older buildings in the Walled Quarter.

We reached Gazian a few hours before sunset one day, but we didn't ride right on in. Gazian was a rough town in those days, and Ajax and Kak didn't want to take any unnecessary chances, so Ajax decided to take steps to ensure that we made the right impression when we entered town.

"I wouldn't want anyone to get the wrong idea about us", he said.

So we stopped a couple of miles from the town gates, and while looking over each other's shoulders, we changed into full armor and loosened our blades in our sheathes. We rode into Gazian as if we were riding into a fight, and everyone who looked at us knew exactly what we were. Now, that place has changed quite a bit in the years since my first visit; the Imperial patrols made life difficult for bandits who might interfere with their tax revenues, and Mursilith himself made quite an impression on both the town and its people. But one thing hasn't changed; whenever I go to Gazian, I follow old Ajax's example: I wear armor and I keep at least one blade loose in its sheath. I've killed too many people there not to. I don't like Gazian: whenever I'm there, my back itches, right between my shoulders.

We rode up to the Front Gate at Gazian an hour before sunset and we drew a crowd, or I should say that Kak and Ajax did. Even swathed in the cloak he wore to keep the sun off, there was no hiding what Kak was, not in Gazian. A big darkling traveling in daylight, armored in plate and wearing the swords and mark of Warrunk was enough to make anyone stop and look. But what made them follow after us muttering and calling to one another was Ajax. He had put aside his traveling clothes and his armor of leather and ringmail, and girded himself for war. His armor, three of his swords and his shield were all of enchanted iron, each tied to Warrunk's service by a piece of Ajax's own spirit, and they glittered as the light of the setting sun sparked silver fire off of the sigils that marked his arms and armor as that of an Attar of Warrunk.

108

We rode up to the half-open gate in fan formation, Ajax on the left and Kak on the right, with Bel and I riding between them and two mule lengths behind. There were five guards at the gate, the watch commander and two others on the left and two more on the right, all five carrying spears, but with at least two more guards in the gate tower with bows or crossbows. The watch commander was the one with the scale hauberk, and Ajax rode right up to him. Leaning down from his saddle, he looked the guardsman in the eye and, speaking slowly and very clearly, as if to someone slow of wit:

"We are here for trade. What is the toll?"

Everyone who traded at Gazian paid a "toll", which was a tax on trade levied by whoever was running the place at the time. The amount of the toll would vary depending on who was standing guard and just how gullible or wealthy a trading party looked. The unfortunate guard coughed to clear his throat and said,

"Ah..., one silver per trader, my lord and 5 coppers per mount." Not too unreasonable.

Ajax grunted and then nodded to me, and I moved forward to count out the toll from the leather purse of small coins he had given me at our last stop. On the other side of the gate, Kak had put his back to the sun, and with the light out of his face, was amusing himself by yawning himself fully awake. Kak had a respectable set of fangs, even among darklings, and those two guards found themselves staring down his throat with a sort of horrible fascination. Our seniors had made such an impression that none of these swag-bellied thugs had thought to ogle Bel, until she drew their attention. She had been watching with a certain professional interest as Kak proceeded to intimidate two armed men without saying a word or drawing a weapon, and then she turned to look at me; the flash of her eyes and her smile in her open-faced helm drew their attention like sunlight off a mirror. One of the ones in front of me leered at her and pursed his lips to make the kissing noise that some men consider such a complement, when Ajax spoke to the watch officer, without so much as flickeri

"You look at one of us, you look at all of us; and I don't like the way you look."

The watch commander jerked himself erect and slammed the butt of his spear onto the booted foot of the leering pig in front of me. That man staggered back against the gate, his face red, sputtering curses until he realized that his both of his companions were staring at him and not us. The blood drained out of his face and he limped back a couple of steps and shut up. I remember thinking that his actions seemed a little strange. The watch commander was looking a little pale as well, as he tried to head off the possibility of any violence:

"Please accept my apologies, lord. My men and I don't want any trouble."

Ajax started to turn his horse towards the open side of the gate, and said mildly;

"Your apology is accepted, commander. But if you should change your mind, look me up. I have more trouble than you or your men will ever need."

Then we rode on through the gate.

We took rooms in the Flat Purse, one for Kak and Bel, one for Ajax and I. Normally, we would have counted ourselves lucky to get one good room for the four of us, but there was an unseasonable lull in the caravan traffic. No one knew (or was saying) why, but the nomad encampment in the Open Quarter was almost empty, and the few nomads left looked to be leaving in a day or so. Also, there were no caravans from the Empire; the only caravans that were in town were a small pack train from Carchemish, a couple of small caravans from southern Khetar and three or four larger caravans from Thrace. As a result, we had more elbow room and a much greater choice of goods than was typical in Gazian at that time of year. After Kak paid a visit to the Night's Quarter after sunset of our first day in town, we settled into what worked out to be a convenient arrangement for everyone: Kak was slept most of the day while we shopped and bartered, and we slept and kept watch during the night hours when Kak would be up and about. This meant Kak guarded all of our belongings while awaiting his kinsmen's arrival and we examined the wares of the Gazian market. At night, we in turn guarded the baggage while Kak strode the alleys and lanes of the Walled and Darkling Quarters, searching for a last few gifts and listening for whatever information rumor and gossip might bring him. He also managed to pick up some healing from his own people, since after the third day, his arm didn't bother him anymore.

The next morning, we went shopping. Although the market did not exactly bustle with activity, we did get a glimpse of the bewildering array of merchandise that passed through the Gazian market. From the darkling lands of Stygia came luxurious furs and strange perfumes, amber and ivory, mushrooms and pine seeds, tubs of pure thick wax and jars of strangely colored honey from the fairy bee hives of the Shadowed Vale, urns of strange, bitter incense and garments made of priceless spider silk.

From the plains of Scythia came other, different furs, and hides of every description: sirrush, deer, bison, horse and auroch. Superbly carved implements and weapons made from horn and stone, eagle, condor and griffin feathers, semiprecious stones and strange dyes, and finely tanned leather boots, saddles, cloaks and tack that would fit any need and any mount drew the eye and excited the imagination. From Khetar, Thrace and the lands beyond came thick blankets and long bolts of the warmest fabrics and the finest cloth in every color of the rainbow, pots and pans of sturdy bronze, knife and sword blades, axe and spear heads, all ready to be honed to a keen edge. There were barrels of salted fish (a great delicacy), strings of sea shells and chunks of coral, and fine tools for delicate work: needles, awls, chisels and hammers. From Carchemish and the East came ivory, incense, jewels, silk and spices. Last, but certainly not least, there was every container you could imagine of every drink you had ever heard of: wood kegs, leaden tuns, clay amphorae, leather bottles and hammered hogsheads of Khetar ales, the strange darkling beers and their intoxicating mushroom wine, blood red Thracian wines and the deep gold of the finest mead.

It was all a bit much for a country boy fresh from the hills, so I kept my mouth shut and my eyes and ears open while I carried everything that Bel bought or bartered for. Bel bargained well; she had a knack for it that I have never developed, and not even the most devious merchant in Gazian cared to try to swindle her with a Attar of Warrunk looking over her shoulder. With me along to carry the packages, we moved through the market fairly fast. Bel knew exactly what she wanted as she had a list drawn up by her fellow clansmen and women, and the expensive items (like amber or the spider silk that was more precious than gold) were out of her reach, so they never got a second glance. At least from me. I was paying attention to other things, like the three young men who seemed to be following us from one merchant to another, always at the same distance. They smelled of stale beer and onions, and there was something else: they felt...cold. I realized that Warrunk's Gift had awakened, and I could feel them, knew where they were even when I wasn't looking their way. They were a threat, but not to me; it was Belkara they wanted and the coins they knew she carried. Bel was looking at needles, thread and some very fine, very soft leather when they began to make their move. A merchant who spoke of sword sheathes and whetstones pulled Ajax off to his booth and they saw their chance. The short one swung wide through the crowd to come in on my right from the rear, and I felt something begin to change.

I swung around to face them and everything began to slow around me; then it felt like a door opened up deep inside me, and someone walked through that door and peered out through my eyes and spoke to me in my own voice:

"One step further, and you can kill them all."

This wasn't the voice of a deity or of Ajax, this was my voice, part of me, and I knew how I would kill them. The short one was the fast one, the cutpurse, so I would kill him first. I had dropped the packages in my left hand to the ground and it would be easy to pull my shortsword (on my right side) and strike him in the throat, he was looking at Bel, not at me. I would drop the sack in my right hand as I turned to my left and draw my broadsword, so I would have two blades out when I leapt at the one in the middle with the beer belly.

He looked to be the smart one, and since the big one was behind him and to his left, if I forced him to back up, they might foul each other and then both would be easy meat. The smart one was bigger than me, but fatter and a bit of a slob. His weapons were not well cared for, and there were at least four different places where his armor of boiled leather wasn't covering his blubber. His balance probably wasn't very good, so I would feint at his eyes, and when he raised his guard, I would bring the other sword down across his belly from the lowest right rib to his left thigh, and I would disembowel him. That would cause enough of a mess that I would have a good chance at a clean strike at the neck or eyes of the big one, who carried a studded mace. I looked into the eyes of the smart one in the middle, their leader; he would give the signal to strike, and when he did, I would start to kill them. He had been looking at me, not Bel, and as he looked into my eyes while I decided how I would kill him, the predatory grin faded and the blood drained out of his face. The cutpurse hesitated, waiting for his signal, and the big man shuffled his feet once and went still. Now all three of them were looking at me, and I looked back, and that is when we started to draw attention.

In the woods or on the plains, it is movement that draws the eye; in the busy places of men, it is often the lack of motion that alerts people that something is wrong. People were starting to step wide of our tense little confrontation, and since no thief wants to attract attention (unless they're a decoy) this particular thief decided that this wasn't the right time or place, and gave an odd whistle, of breath drawn IN through pursed lips. He began to slowly back away from me; three steps later, all three turned and faded into the crowd. I heard a faint choking noise come from my left across the way, and turned to see Ajax holding the merchant who had sought his attention by the throat with one hand, while he watched me deal with the would-be thieves. Bel had turned to back me up when she heard that strange whistle, and now she was growling at me:

"You weren't going to get into a fight and NOT give me some, were you?"

"No, Belkara."

"Good, because that would make me unhappy and you don't want that, do you?"

"No, Belkara."

I loved it when she growled at me.

Ajax let that merchant go once he was satisfied that the man's sales pitch had been seen as an opportunity by the thieves, and had not been part of the trap itself. I picked up the sack and the parcels and we finished our business in the marketplace without further incident. Later, Ajax asked me what I had done to make those thieves back off like that. I shrugged and said:

"I just looked at them, and thought about how I would kill them if they came a step closer."

Ajax grunted and said: "Has anything like this ever happened before?"

I was silent for a moment; I had never really thought about killing anyone in Nesa, but I have a habit of staring at people if they say something to me that I don't understand. Being the strange boy in the village, I was always wary of being baited by the other children, or of just not knowing enough to answer any question asked by one of the adults. My hearing has always been very good, and I often heard things not meant for my ears. So I just said: "Some of the women in the village told Aunt Syara that I had cold eyes." They said other things as well, but I didn't want to talk about it.

Ajax nodded once, and said:

"Huh, I'll just bet they did. Listen to me, Joren, you are not a bastard, a changeling or some witch's child born to bring bad luck into the world."

It seemed like Ajax had overheard the same conversations I had.

"You're a bit different from most people, but it is just that you don't fool around and you don't back up worth a damn. And you don't let anything distract you, which is very useful in our way of life. Now, as for the way you look at people... That could wind up being a useful talent, boy, but be careful who you look at that way".

I nodded at him:

"I know. 'Try not to stare at people, and when you get angry, don't aim your look at friends, children, small animals or women you like. Everybody else is on their own'. Aunt Syara told me."

Ajax burst out laughing, and when he had stopped, he ruffled my hair and said: "You miss your Aunt, I know. So do I".

I thought about that encounter of mine later that night. I realized that the thought of killing all three of those men didn't bother me at all. They were threatening Belkara, and I would not allow that. As it turned out, I did kill all three of those thieves, but not until the next time I came to Gazian.

The biggest temple in Gazian is that of Nabu, god of trade, heralds and travelers, and it's high priest is the one of the most influential in the entire town. This isn't surprising, considering the amount of commerce passing through the three Quarters. There is no temple to Warrunk in Gazian, only a shrine kept up by donations from the caravan guards or the occasional band of mercenaries or warriors that might pass through. This was enough for a small community like this; it had no need and no way to support anything more. Major repairs and religious services are the responsibility of those followers of Warrunk who pass through Gazian, and it was to the shrine that Ajax first went when we entered the Walled Quarter. It was near the cluster of shrines around the temple of Tarhunt, but separate, and it faced north. It wasn't in that bad a shape; it needed sweeping and dusting, and a new coat of paint, but nothing that couldn't be taken care of in less than a day. As in any small community, word spread fast through Gazian that there was an Attar of Warrunk in town, and that services for anyone who cared to pay their respects to the god of death and swords would take place just before sunset of the second day after we hit town. After we had settled in at the Flat Purse that first night, another Warrunki came to pay his respects to Ajax: Dargo Longarm, a bounty hunter and caravan guard from Carchemish, and his nephew Corlan. Corlan was a gangling youngster of my own age who hadn't fleshed out enough to match the height his last growth spurt had given him, and is one of the most obnoxiously cheerful people I have ever met. He is also one of the few people in the world who thinks I'm funny, so we get along.

Ajax spoke briefly with Dargo, and by the end of our second morning in Gazian (with Dargo's aid and direction) Corlan, Bel and I had the shrine prepared with enough time left over for a little sightseeing. Bel said she would pass on the opportunity; she wanted to check over the merchandise she had picked up that day, before she packed it for transport. So we dropped her off at the Flat Purse, said hello to Kak and then Ajax, Dargo, Corlan and I made the rounds of Gazian, checking every inn, tavern, bar and flophouse to make sure that everyone in town who followed the Death god knew services would be before sunset.

It was an education for me, and I think that is why Ajax went about it the way he did. I still had a number of illusions regarding city life, but they didn't survive that little trip. I got a good look at just how vicious, dirty and self-centered life can be when too many people live too close together with no hope and no concern for one another. I learned a lot that day, but not enough to dampen my spirits for long, I was too young and too stupid. After the second stop, I overheard Ajax mutter something to Dargo:

"What is going on here? NOBODY will talk to us. Nobody wants to hire us for anything, no one wants to sell us anything, and not even the prostitutes will look us in the face while we talk to them. Come to think of it, the guards at the gate charged us less than usual".

Dargo's eyes were constantly shifting as he answered:

"I'm not sure, lord, but it's been like this ever since me and Corlan came into town two days ago. The only thing that might explain it was something I heard back in Carchemish: there was a rumor running around Backside that there was new underlord in Gazian."

Ajax grunted at that; underlord or boss was a term sometimes used to designate the man or woman who was the most powerful member of the local underworld. They might just be the most powerful faction in a city's underworld of gambling, theft, smuggling and prostitution, but in a small town like Gazian, they might actually run the place. The thing was, unless they jumped us, we had no reason and no time to stay in Gazian just to dig around looking for the source of some rumors.

The Tipping Bowl is a tavern that served the local people of Gazian; as opposed to the places that catered to the trade brought in by the caravans, like the Flat Purse or the Cup & Sword. It was smaller, quieter and it didn't have nearly as wide a selection of entertainment the more popular establishments had. That is not to say things couldn't get lively. The younger crowd in town could be just as rowdy and at least as stupid as youngsters in any other place I've seen. The tavern got its name from a large wooden bowl set atop the tavern's sign; that bowl was weighted and hinged so that if the bracing rope was cut, the bowl would tip over and douse anyone standing beneath it with whatever had accumulated in the bowl since the last time it was washed. This might be anything from rainwater to nightsoil, and the tavern help were more than happy to fill the bowl from the roof with whatever the local wag might want, for the right price.

The brace for the bowl ran from over the door across the front of the tavern, over a beam bracing the roof and around the corner, to be snugged at a hook by the owner's bedroom window. A series of nails set into the corner of the building let the owner change the height of the rope, so as to add a little variety to the jest, and to keep the village idiots from cutting a new window into his place of business. It wasn't considered sporting to cut the rope anywhere but where it crossed the beam. As a result, the length of wood in question was marked with all kinds of gashes and cuts everywhere from knee height to more than 12 feet off of the ground. Last time I was there, my cut was deeper than any other at that height or above, which just goes to show that you don't have to be from Gazian to be an idiot.

It was that nitwit Corlan who started it, but the fault was mine. No one can MAKE you do anything; at one point or another, it is your decision, and no one else's. He had been needling me constantly for the last two stops, calling me a shallow-stomached yokel just because I had puked my guts out after leaving a reeking den called the Callow Youth (which had to be the filthiest brothel between the God Pillar and Carchemish). I couldn't help myself; they just don't have places that smell like that back in the hills. When we reached the Tipping Bowl, Dargo suggested I wait outside, since I was still looking a little green. Ajax nodded agreement and then lead the way inside.

I was moping a bit next to the water trough when an idea struck me. Corlan had told me all about the rope holding the bowl in place, so I raced around the corner of the tavern to check its height; it was high, a good four yards off of the ground and looked like it had been there a while. I thought I could do it though. I went back to the front door of the tavern, and stepped inside, stood to the right of the door and squinted around to find Corlan. Ajax and Dargo spotted me first, but seeing that it wasn't an emergency, returned their attention to the group of merchants at the big table in the back of the main room. When Corlan spotted me, I gave him the high sign and stepped back outside. I raced around the corner to the spot I had paced off, and stood listening for Corlan's voice while I watched the door. I heard the door open, and Corlan call my name, and then I ran

116

forward three steps and jumped upwards with everything I had in me, swinging the bright length of my broadsword as hard as I could. I hadn't gotten this hitch in my step then, and like any young man, I could put an incredible amount of effort into the most ridiculous stunt imaginable. I made the jump, and my sword cut the rope like it was thread, and as I dropped back to the ground, I landed on both feet and one hand, listening for the sound of .....nothing. Not a sound, no yelling, cursing, nothing. Then my stomach hit my boots when I heard AJAX call my name.

I sheathed my sword and marched right around the corner, no use in trying to escape this. I was dead; no, I was going to WISH that I was dead... I stopped short, stunned by the scene under the sign of the Tipping Bowl. Ajax, his arms folded and his face a grim mask, was untouched. As was Dargo, whose face had gone completely blank, and Corlan (the jerk) who was as pale as fine linen. It was the man who was with them who had caught every last bit of what had been in that damn tipping bowl. I had managed to drop two rotten eggs, a fist full of feathers and straw and about a pound of bird shit on the high priest of Nabu, the richest man in Gazian.

At first, all I could do was stare at the man and think: "He will take every silver I have as an insult debt, and then Ajax... I will be scrubbing every pot, digging every latrine, washing every single piece of clothing in our party FOREVER....", when my eyes were drawn to his face. I expected to see anger and embarrassment, and it was there: his face was red with it. But it was being tamped down and controlled by something else: Fear. This was a man of wealth, who possessed prestige and real power: his magic would be a major defense of the town if attacked. And there were already catcalls and jokes being yelled at his expense, from within the tavern and down the street from passersby, his loss of face was going to be considerable, but instead of an explosion of righteous anger, there was the desperate silence of a frightened man who had a lot to lose. As I stood there, I actually watched him as he grasped his emotions with an iron hand and literally pulled them off of his face. In seconds, the anger and the fear were gone, and what remained was a stout well-dressed man of middle years who somehow managed to look dignified while wearing a bird's nest.

Ajax, Dargo and Corlan all saw this as well, and then I remembered what I had overheard the two older men speak of earlier that day. Someone or something didn't want us to stay in Gazian any longer than we had to, and that someone had ordered the entire town to see that we had no reason to stay longer than we planned. Anyone who could scare both the decent merchants AND the cutthroats and gutter scum of Gazian that badly had to be someone to be reckoned with, and that meant we (and everyone we spoke to) was being watched. As I thought this thru, I realized that I probably wasn't going to be punished (at least not as much as I deserved) for my act of thoughtless foolishness. If this merchant, as the injured party, refused to make anything of this, then Ajax in fairness would not either. At least not much; I still wasn't going to have much spare time for the next season. But that didn't mean that I did not owe this man a debt; I had bruised his pride (always a dangerous thing to do to the wealthy and powerful) and I had damaged his communal dignity, his reputation, and that could cost him real money. I stepped forward and bowed to him, while touching my sword hilt.

"My apologies, sir. I owe you a debt", I murmured in a low voice.

Ajax stiffened and immediately spoke on the heels of my words; "I witness this". Dargo chimed in right after Ajax: "I witness this". The merchant froze in the act of reaching for his ruined hat, and turned to look first at Ajax and Dargo, and then at me. His eyes narrowed as he looked me over, and I could almost hear him mentally ticking over the implications of what I had said, and what I was. He turned back to Ajax, and ruefully began to try to clean his hat and his hair.

"Your pupil?", He asked.

Ajax gave him a bland smile while he dusted the merchant's shoulder of feathers and bird refuse. "MY pupil" he replied, making sure the man heard the emphasis, and then began walking down the street away from the tavern. The priest of Nabu thought this over as he absently followed Ajax; Dargo gave the merchant's cloak to Corlan to dunk in the horse trough and I followed at the man's shoulder. Without looking at me, he spoke in a quiet voice:

"But I have no need of someone of your skills at this time…"

I replied in a voice equally quiet:

"I understand, but time will not lessen my debt to you. If you should send word to me, no matter where it reaches me, whether it is Khetar or Carchemish or elsewhere, I will find you and make my amends. I swear this."

Those last three words are not ones that anyone speaks lightly in the presence of an Attar of Warrunk, least of all by someone who had already been touched by the god of Death and Truth. He turned and looked me in the eyes: "I accept your apologies, young man.", and his voice held a certain satisfaction. I bowed to him again, and dropped back a few paces. Dargo retrieved the hastily scrubbed cloak from Corlan and draping it around its owner's shoulders, dropped back a step as the old warrior and the master merchant spoke a few pleasantries and then parted ways: the merchant to his home to bathe and change, and the warrior (and us) to our lodgings at the Flat Purse.

Ajax never said anything to me of my asinine stunt at the Tipping Bowl, but I did catch him looking at me oddly, almost as if I had reminded him of something or someone. Both Bel and Kak had a lot to say about it, and laughed at me for a good hour over it (and Corlan's way of telling it). That was all right; I loved to make Bel laugh.

On our second night in Gazian, Kak had received word that some of his sister's clan (her husband and oldest son, in fact) would arrive in Gazian on the next night, to escort Kak to his new home. The next morning, I asked him what he thought of his brother-in-law, only to find that he had never met any of his sister's family.

"Distance and events have kept us from meeting. That ends tomorrow; my sister's clan will judge me according to a demanding standard: that of their own survival. The first impression they have of me will be a lasting one. Will you help me make it a good one, Small Bite?".

I said of course I would, and after talking with him a moment, I took the silver coins he gave me and went to the market to pick out some livestock. Of the six mules that Kak owned, four had already been sold to Ajax, and would stay with our own small herd; considering how well Bel had bargained, we would need them. The two mules who remained were the oldest of the lot, but because of our pampering were also the fattest, since at the end of Kak's journey, they were going to be someone's meal. Since the rest of Kak's belongings were going to be carried by goblin porters, what did he need any other head of stock for? Now, darklings think a lot about meals; it may sound surprising, considering that they can eat almost anything from a beached whale to a block of granite (given enough time, and with perhaps an old boot thrown in for flavoring. I am NOT joking about this), but they do. Since darklings like pig, Kak wanted me to go and buy the two biggest pigs in Gazian and I wasn't going to let him down. Naturally, I asked Corlan to come along and help me.

We toddled on over to the livestock pen on the east side of the Market, and started looking around. It didn't take us long; pigs have that certain smell about them and the market just wasn't that busy. As we got closer, I spotted a likely purchase: a white and black sow that was dozing in the afternoon heat. She looked mean enough to have some wild boar in her blood and had to weigh at least 500 lbs. I walked over to the pig herder and prepared to dicker. He was leaning on a railing and seemed to muttering to himself until I realized he was conversing with one of his pigs.

"...gotta sell soon, or I'm going to have to let you go for dirt to the taverns; I'll barely make the toll, and I won't have a damn thing..."

"Hey, you. I want to buy one of your pigs".

I had decided on the direct approach. The pigherder jerked upright, his mouth dropping and his eyes widening as he took in my swords and my armor.

"You want to buy some pigs?", he said.

Hmmm. I hadn't thought he'd counter with that particular tactic.

"I want to buy that pig", jerking a thumb at the sow.

"You want to buy that pig?"

"The big sow"

"The big sow?"

Damn, that was getting annoying; I hadn't thought he'd be a master bargainer, but his ingenious replies to my questions had backed me into a corner.

"I have silver", I said, giving him a peek at some of Kak's coins.

"You have SILVER?!", he blurted.

All right, he had me. I gave up and decided to follow a piece of advice my Aunt Syara gave me: "When all else fails, try being rude."

"Do I stutter? I want to buy that damn sow, now are you going to sell me that damn sow, or are you going to keep that damn sow and marry her off to one of the locals?"

"I'm going to sell you that damn sow right now. How much do you want for her?"

Wait a minute; wasn't that supposed to be MY question? By this time, the sound of our voices had unsettled the livestock, and the pig in question woke up and moved a bit closer to see if all of this shouting was a prelude to a meal. It was at that point that I realized that what I had thought was the sow's shadow was actually the blackest, ugliest and meanest-looking boar I had ever seen in my life. It had to have wild blood in it AND it was the second biggest pig in the pen; perfect.

"I want the boar, too."

"You want the boar too?"

"WILL you stop that? Yes, I want the damn boar too."

Corlan cut in: "Joren, are you out of your mind? Half of that brute's weight has to be scars, gristle and tusks! What kind of meal would he make?"

"Corlan, I'm buying for a darkling. It isn't like I'm buying for the Minos's personal larder; pig is pig."

"Now, which boar are you interested in, young sir?"

"That one, the black, butt-ugly mean one..."

"I think he heard you, Joren", warned Corlan.

"Shut up Corlan. I want THAT boar, he is fairly easy to spot since he IS the only full-grown boar in sight. Now are you gonna make this sale, or..."

"There will be no 'OR' necessary, young sir. The pigs are yours and for a very reasonable price...."

I didn't want to wait around and let this sharper clean me out entirely; I shoved a fistful of coins at him (he was babbling something about 'Bless you, bless you'), and told him that I would take possession of my purchase after sunset. I then fled with my bill of sale, my smart-mouthed companion and what little dignity I had left. After I was out of sight of the stock pens, I slowed to a walk and thought about the other item on Kak's list. I turned to Corlan: "I need to buy some rock candy".

"Oh, good. I could just go for something sweet myself."

"Not for us, you ass. I need to buy every piece of rock candy I can find for Kak."

"Joren, that's insane. We have no idea how much rock candy is in Gazian! What does he need all that for, anyway?"

"It doesn't matter: his money, his candy. Although, if there is a lot, I doubt he'd begrudge us a piece or two each. Now, where do we go?"

"Well, alright. We can try Lubro's; he had some the last time I was in town."

We cleaned out Lubro's and then had a stroke of luck: an Thracian merchant who had just arrived had gambled on selling candy to the nomads, and was now looking at a loss because the nomads had all but cleared out of Gazian. We picked up his entire stock of rock candy for a song...well, maybe a few songs. Then we headed back to the Flat Purse.

"You sure know how to cut a damn bargain, I'll say that for you."

"Shut up, Corlan. Or don't you want that other piece of candy?"

Bel was waiting for us on the porch of the inn; after looking us and our packs (185 lbs of rock candy can be a bit bulky) over, she closed her eyes and asked: "Do I want to know what you paid for that?"

"No.", we chorused.

"Alright, put those packs upstairs and then go wash up. It's almost meal time."

She didn't have to tell us twice. Shopping is hungry work.

After our evening meal, I gave Kak his change, his candy and his bill of sale for his pigs. He tasted the candy and approved; after a visit to the livestock pens to look over his new pigs, he returned laughing, and agreed with me that they were perfect. I still wasn't sure what he was up to, but I couldn't wait to find out. The services at the Warrunk shrine that evening were only sparsely attended, but none of us were surprised, and we didn't have enough time to dig around Gazian: Kak was leaving later that night, and we would be off tomorrow to The Needles, as were Dargo and Corlan. I learned later that Dargo's guess was correct: there was a new underlord of Gazian, a outlaw of the Sakae called Skonai Bigspear, who had wanted no part of an Attar of Wurrunk, and who had made our stay in Gazian as smooth and as uneventful as he could, so as to get us the hell out of town as soon as possible. After our evening meal, I sat a while and pondered the promise I had made to the priest of Nabu, whose name I had learned was Priennus. It was the first oath I sworn in any god's name since becoming a man, and I had meant every word of it. It was good thing I did; Priennus did not forget me or my promise. It would be his message that would draw me back to Gazian, and when next I saw this town, my presence would set off a chain of events that would leave more than a score of men and women dead, and that in turn, would lead me to Mursilith and his service.

All of this was years in the future, but I already was thinking that it might be a bad idea to underestimate the merchants of the world, the men and women who sit and count. They have a cunning all their own, and a type of cold courage completely different from that of the battlefield. I would have to think about this; Aunt Syara and Ajax were right; you can make friends and enemies in the strangest places.

Chapter XII: Kak's Farewell

THAT NIGHT, WE SAID OUR FAREWELLS to Kak Bonesplitter. Dargo and Corlan didn't attend; they have a great deal against darklings, in Carchemish. We would see them in the morning. Each of us spoke to Kak alone. I don't know what he said to Ajax and Bel, it wasn't any of my business and I didn't ask. I do know he gave a shortsword to Bel, along with a great deal of advice that made her laugh. He and Ajax had discussed many things during the course of our trip, so they spoke just briefly, but clasped arms for a long moment and then parted. (Ajax was not wearing any iron save a sheathed sword; flaunting iron near darkling dwellings is a quick way to start a war.)

Kak spoke to me last, and spoke only after he had looked me in the face for a long moment:

"My sword brother would be proud of his son, Queen's Heir. May it always be so."

"I will do my best to remain so, Man of Darkness. And I will strive to remember all that you have taught me. Thank you."

He clasped arms with me, as one warrior to another, and then asked me to go with him when he met his nephew and brother-in-law. I was happy to oblige. Kak had been making good use of his nights; he was by now fairly familiar with the ins and outs of the Night's Quarter of Gazian, which is just starting to awaken when Arrina sets in the west. He had paid his respects to almost all of the darkling shrines and temples, and had made some useful contacts (well bribed).

He knew from them not only what night his kinsmen would arrive, but roughly what time as well. So when his brother-in-law Rogkob and his son Xiorog entered town just after midnight, word reached Kak in minutes and we made ready. Rogkob was a merchant-priest of Arma Arn, the darkling god of trade, whose sign is a spear and whose priests are often found in command of the regiments of goblin spearmen and skirmishers who make up the bulk of any darkling army. As expected, when Rogkob came into town, he went to pay his respects at the temple of Arma Arn first. That is when we made our move. Since Arma Arn's followers are usually in charge of dealing with humans, his temple was the closest of the darkling temples to the Walled Quarter, with the temple gates facing the main gate of Gazian. This enabled us to approach Rogkob's goblin followers without having to stumble around in the goblin slums that make up most of the Night's Quarter.

I was leading the sow and the mules; all of which had been given a mild drug, so the strong goblin scent wouldn't panic them. Kak lead the way, with the hog-tied (how else?) boar under one arm and the packs of rock candy over his other shoulder, and headed straight for the unruly mob of goblins huddled in front of the temple. There were twenty of them, half spearmen, half porters, and they parted before him like sheep. Kak strode up to the two darklings standing on the temple steps and bowed to the eldest. This was a full priestess of Brighid the Serene, the darkling goddess of healing and midwives, and I realized, my friend's source of information within the Darkling Quarter. No wonder he knew so much so quickly. The priestesses of Brighid are healers who aren't afraid to fight for those who need their healing magic, and they are greatly valued by darkling society in general; from the goblins for whom they are the only source of pity or kindness, the healers of Brighid receive something approaching blind adoration. Raise a hand against one of Brighid's healers in a darkling community, and you had better pray you were dead before they caught you. Healers of this cult often know everything that goes on in a darkling community, since they hear gossip from everyone, from the dreaded nobility to the lowest goblin.

Kak greeted this healer warmly and pressed a hefty package of rock candy into her hands. As the priestess sat down to enjoy her sweets and the show, Kak turned and gave a much smaller package of candy to the Arma Arn initiate, and spoke to him briefly. This was Rogkob's apprentice, and it was he who was in charge of the goblins in their master's absence. Having temporarily bought the apprentice's silence, Kak then turned to the goblin mob gaping at him, and began sorting them out. Rogkob's guards got a mouthful of candy and were set down by the scruff of the neck exactly where Kak wanted them to be. Rogkob's porters got a mouthful of candy and were placed in a line near the mules. Anyone else got thrown into the gathering crowd. Then Kak began unloading the four mules that he had sold to Ajax; pack after pack flying unerringly at each of the waiting porters, one after another. One hapless goblin was distracted by the crowd and was flattened by a bundle made up of Kak's bedroll and some of his best tunics and cloaks (he always was a sharp dresser). It lay there squealing, pinned beneath a package nigh as tall as itself, until two of its fellows could come to its aid. The mules were unloaded in minutes and I ground hitched them off to one side, while Kak and his sack of rock candy made the rounds of all of the goblin again. This time he broke open two of his packs and then gave them very specific (if simple) orders, and the goblin did exactly as they were told, bemused by this novel combination of strength, discipline and generosity.

When Rogkob and his son stepped out of the temple a short while later, they stopped in wordless fascination at the sight of a towering darkling warrior clad in bronze plate standing at attention before an ordered formation of goblins, THEIR goblins, clad in coarse black tunics marked with the sign of their clan, each goblin standing ready with pack or spear, each sucking in unison on a piece of candy the size of my fist. Kak took advantage of their surprise and strode forward to meet them, leading one pig on a leash and carrying the other (tightly bound) under one arm. Xiorog was a year or two younger than me, but already big enough to look his uncle in the face, eye to eye. Kak handed him the sow's leash and said:

"THIS is for your mother", and then as his nephew sniffed appreciatively at this snuffling delicacy, surprized him further by slinging a baldric and sheathe across Xiorog's shoulder.

"THIS is for you".

It was a finely crafted shortsword, and the black leather of its harness was adorned by pieces of coral and obsidian set in intricate patterns; and the darkling youth huffed with pleasure as he ran his fingers across the stones and leather of his gift. Rogkob had not moved an inch since first seeing Kak, and he seemed to be fascinated by this new in-law of his. Rogkob (his honor name, translated from the darkling language was something like 'He who counts his sheaves', that is, one who takes nothing for granted and is hard to swindle) was well-dressed enough, for a merchant who was well off, but not what you might call rich. Like most merchants, although he aimed for trade, he was ready for war: the torchlight from the town gate reflected off of a chainmail hauberk worn under his thick cloak, and in addition to the long spear he was using as a staff, a heavy mace swung from his belt. As this darkling merchant's gaze swung from the sight of his goblins (HIS goblins?) clad with their new tunics and standing in ordered lines (possibly for the first time in their lives), to the packs and laden mules (carrying what was obviously a fair amount of wealth) to Kak's gleaming suit of plate armor (a fortune in itself) to gifts bestowed on his wife and son, and finally to Kak himself, a slow smile spread across his face.

Kak turned to his sister's husband at last, and without further ado, slapped the hog-tied boar into his brother-in-law's arms. The boar, enraged by the scent of so many predators, finally began to wriggle free of its bonds and Rogkob broke its back with an absent-minded gesture. Kak put his hands on his hips and leaning forward demanded:

"Well, my brother, am I QUITE what you were expecting?"

Rogkob just stood there and shook his head, his smile having completely taken over his face:

"Oh brother, you are so much more than I had hoped for. Welcome!"

"It has been years since I have heard my sister's voice, when can we leave?"

"Now, if you like. My messages and cargo have been delivered, the goblins have been watered, and we can snack on the way!", he said, shaking the boar's carcass.

"Then shall we be off? Ah, one thing first." Kak gestured to me:

"Joren, son of Tiresth, Danu's child, this is Xiorog, son of Xakjota, Rogkob's child."

I bowed to the merchant and nodded to his son: "I will know you again", I said.

Rogkob nodded back politely, his gaze flickering from me to the figures of Ajax and Bel waiting at the Walled Quarter's gates. Xiorog nodded and said "And I will know you."

Kak rubbed his chin with a certain amount of satisfaction: "You will meet again."

He waved once at Ajax and Bel, and roared "Remember!" in a voice that must have carried for a mile.

They waved in reply; I said: "Always.", and with one last clasp of my shoulder, he was gone, he and his family disappearing into the shadows of the Night's Quarter on their way north into the Pontine Mountains. I did meet Xiorog again, but that story and how we dealt with the enemies of his clan is for another time. That was the last I saw of Kak Bonesplitter, sword brother of my father, my friend and my teacher. I heard later that he served his new family well, that he married, and that when his time came, he cut a bloody swathe through his clan's enemies and in the end, it took more than one of them to drag him down. I honor his memory.

There are some who say that all darklings are monsters; in the West, they call them "night demons" and "devils". Now, I have met some darklings who were murderous killers and a threat to everything and everyone around them, but I've known men and women who met that description too. Remember that darklings are NOT human, but keep this in mind: Kak never lied to me, never failed a trust or broke a promise. Because of an oath sworn to my father before my birth, Kak gave to me, a child of another race, the same care and protection he would have given his own brother's child.

His advice, his teachings and his training helped to make me who and what I am, and saved my life more than once. Most importantly for me, the memories he recalled of his youth brought my father to life for me. Now, if love and trust, mutual support and honesty are part of what we call humanity, I have known a thousand men and women who were LESS human than Kak was.

What does that say about us?

Chapter XIII: The Needles

WE LEFT GAZIAN THE NEXT MORNING, and headed south towards the marshy pond known as Lake Xir, where we would turn east and south towards The Needles of Ishara. I wasn't sorry to leave Gazian behind me, but then, I never have been. It's just that something always seems to come up and I wind up going back there. Corlan says the same thing.

Our route skirted the foothills of the Pontine Mountains, which thrust a tall arm south at this point. As we rode past Lake Xir and turned towards The Needles, the snowclad peaks of the mountains called the Nine Titans rose up on our left, beyond the foothills. Off to our right stretched the western edge of the Scythian plains. It was an uneventful trip, and that seemed to disturb Ajax. We didn't meet any nomads, and both Ajax and Dargo said that was unusual. We saw some game, but none of the herds of horses that the nomads tend and none of the great herds of wisent and wild auroches that they hunt; that seemed strange, even to me. There had been nothing wrong with the rains this year, and the grass seemed to coming in pretty thick; the herds should have been following the grass. Ajax and Dargo talked it over for a bit, and then shrugged, saying that we would learn more at The Needles, where we were to meet with Barlan.

It isn't that far from Gazian to The Needles of Ishara; a week maybe if you travel with a pack train, depending on the weather. Less, if you push it. We made good time, rounding the last of the Nine Titans (the peak called Sokar) and then passing south of Giant's Arm Hill, we came up on The Needles from the west. The Needles itself isn't a town or commercial center, although it is a convenient stopping place for the caravans moving between Gazian and Carchemish; it has water year round and some decent grazing. The reason why it is important, and why you might find people there at any time of the year, is because it is a shrine, a holy place to Ishara, goddess of oaths and of love. It is also sacred to Tarhunt, King of the Gods, and a place of power for all of the children of the wind and air. The holy place itself is atop a low, conical hill, and is marked by two standing stones that are so weathered that they appear to be natural and tower more than 40 feet into the air. The stones lean towards each other slightly, and are made of a pale blue stone that is not to be found for hundreds of miles in any direction.

There were a number of people at the Needles, but Barlan was not among them. We were right on time, but Ajax and Barlan had allowed for some leeway in our plans, so we made camp and settled in for a few day's wait. Dargo and Corlan made camp with us, but would continue on to Carchemish the next day. After we set up camp, we made the acquaintance of the other groups who were there. There was a small caravan from Carchemish that was headed for Gazian, groups of Tarhunti from the Navari and Carpi tribes, as well as some of Bel's people, the Bastarnae. But with one exception, there were no nomads, and that was unusual. Although the tribes honor Tuhus as the god of chieftains, there are Tarhunt worshippers in almost every tribe in Scythia; some of them stop by the The Needles whenever they are in the area. And even if there were no Tarhunti nearby, often one or more of the followers of Tillar, the Bull would ride in to pay their respects to their god's brother, or recruit for a warband to hunt their enemies. But there were no nomads in sight, and from the droppings, none had been near the shrine in at least four days.

The one exception was an old Tillari of the Traspian tribe, who seemed to spend most of his time drunk. The Traspians are unusual even among the Scythians in that many of them actually ride and herd wisents or bison. The old man didn't speak much; all he did was stare at me blearily out of blood-shot grey eyes when I offered him the wineskin Ajax told me to give to him. I remember that he had a thick braid of white hair the length of my arm, and good half dozen knives in his belt or boots. The most that anyone could get out of him was that he had followed a dream that lead him here, to the The Needles of Ishara. The dream had said that there would be a sign given here, a sign of the coming of the White Bull, and he would know it when it came. So he waited, he and his enormous mount. This was the first bison I had ever seen up close, and it was difficult to get used to just how big it was, more than twice the size of a horse, but built different. Now, the war mounts of the Scythiaian nomads are trained to fight for their masters. The thought of having to fight both the mount and its rider gave me pause; it wouldn't be easy to do.

Each group that came into The Needles would pay their respects at the shrine and perhaps hold a ceremony, to ask for luck, or to obtain an answer to a question that troubled their clan or tribe, or to initiate new members into Tarhunt's cult or to raise one of their members up to the status of Disciple or Priest, although that was typically done on a day holy to Tarhunt. When they were finished, each group would leave and go on their way. The day after we arrived, Dargo and Corlan bade us farewell and left for Carchemish. We wished them well, they were good people and both Bel and I would meet them again. The next day, the caravan and the Navari tribesmen left and a group of Abasgi warriors came in from the east, having served for a while as mercenaries in the Carchemish city guard. No one came in from the west, which had Ajax frowning a bit.

The Carpi tribesmen were set to leave the next day; Bel's tribesmen were expecting another group of her people to return soon from Carchemish, and then all of them were heading to Ateas's Cist. This was the group that Barlan had planned on meeting up with, and there was no sign of him. All of this had Bel a bit upset; her uncle had been the center of her life since her parents died, and although she knew he could take care of himself, she was still badly worried. That day, after the evening meal, we took a walk and I tried to cheer her up.

Ajax was having a talk with the Abasgi warriors; it seems he knew some of them and some of the warriors they had served with in Carchemish. Soon they were trading information and stories over some more of that wine Ajax had picked up in Gazian. This left me alone with Bel, really alone, for the first time since we had met. I was glad for the opportunity; there was an awful lot I wanted to say to her. We walked in the general direction of the standing stones, not really saying much, just walking side by side. Bel was worried about her uncle, and my attempts at conversation, either to amuse or distract, were failing miserably. As night fell, we kind of stumbled to a halt, Bel moping with her back against a tall stone, me pacing back and forth in front of her, dithering. She was falling deeper and deeper in dejection and I was getting a bit frantic; finally, in desperation, I grabbed her hand and called her by her full name to get her attention:

"Belkara!"

Her head came up, and just like that, I was struck dumb: the fall of her hair, the lines of her face and throat, the curve of her lips and the deep, glowing stars of her eyes, and I just couldn't remember what I was about to say. I stood there for an endless moment, completely bereft of anything resembling coherent thought, until somehow I stuttered out the only thought my mind could form:

"Uh... I love you."

Oh, THAT was smooth. Well, if what I wanted to do was to distract and amuse her, that pretty much ought to do it. I just stood there, waiting for a laugh, a slap or a blistering insult, when I was jolted to see Bel's brilliant, beautiful smile grow and take over her face. Then she had me by the shoulders and was kissing me. When we came up for air a few minutes later, Bel's eyes were burning and she was growling at me; me, I wasn't capable of that level of speech, so I just concentrated on breathing. We were holding each other so tight, we couldn't both breathe at the same time, so we backed up so that we were holding each other at arm's length, and a small, cold wind seemed to swirl around us. I suddenly felt a chill run down my spine: What was I thinking? We were no more than teenagers; we had no wealth, no property; we hadn't even earned our honor names yet. If things went on tonight as it felt it would, we could be parents in a year. A child? Now? The thought staggered me; I had oaths to keep, and vengeance against those responsible for my family's deaths was a responsibility I simply could not shirk. To do so would mean that I would have no honor at all, and what kind of family, life or future can a man build without honor? Not to mention the fact that the duties of a father scared me spitless, and what kind of a father and husband would I be if I abandoned my wife and child to walk the road that my oaths demanded?

From the look on Bel's face, I could see that many of the same thoughts were running through her mind. We looked at each other, nodded, and we both seemed to sag with disappointment.

"We could just cuddle for a while", I said hopefully.

Bel looked at me, and smiled wanly, "If you want".

Boy, did I want. But we wound our arms and cloaks around us and settled into the lee of a tall stone, and just sat for a while. The wind died down, and after a bit, we weren't cold anymore. Have you ever just sat and held someone you loved in your arms? The scent and feel of her skin, the sound of her breathing, the beat of her heart against mine, all of this was more precious to me than words can say. And what did we say to one another, as we held each other that starlit night? None of your business.

After a while, somewhere between a promise and a kiss, we slept.

That night, we both had strange dreams, if they were dreams. Bel told me later that she remembers speaking to both of her parents, and someone else, a voice that asked her a question. My dreams were at first were a jumble of shifting shapes with glowing eyes and deep rolling laughter that was NOT human. Then everything became very quiet and I felt a warm wind blow from the south, and it seemed to carry a voice that asked me a question:

"Who would you serve?"

Well, I was already sworn to Tarhunt, and Warrunk had apparently taken an interest in me as well, but I felt that this was not what the voice was asking. Warrunk is different things to different peoples, but in Khetar, Warrunk is Tarhunt's faithful weapon thane and champion. The only way I could meet the responsibilities that were given to me by birth, and demanded of me by honor, was to find and serve the king of our people. Only the king of Khetar would be able to help me reestablish my tribe, and such a favor could only be gained by faithful service to that king. So be it.

"I would serve the rightful King of Khetar", I answered, but the voice did not reply.

Then the wind veered and shifted around so that it blew from the north, carrying with it a burst of snowflakes; out of that wintry blast stepped a figure that at first was unfamiliar to me. He was a dark-haired warrior with very broad shoulders; not tall, but muscled like a panther. Although he wore no armor, being clad only in the buckskins and homespun of any Khetarite hillman, the broadsword at his side was iron, and his brow and hands bore the sigils of Warrunk. Then his eyes met mine, and I realized I wore his face. He spoke, and even ten years dead, the force of his will jolted me:

"Grow strong, boy. Live, learn everything you can and gather as much power as you may. Because I can't find your mother and your sisters, HE hid them too deep, and that means YOU must find them for me."

His voice was thick with a terrible anger, not at me, but at my uncle Ketil whose lust for power had destroyed our family.

"I will, Father. I swear it!"

He rubbed one hand across his face:

"No time, no time to teach you, no time to tell you even the first thing you need to know...You seem to have pretty good judgement where women are concerned, so I can skip that lecture. But try not to give Ajax a seizure, son, he's earned an honorable death in battle. And Joren?

"Yes, Father?"

"I love you".

A wound I never knew I had healed over inside me. Then he was gone, but I remembered everything he had said, the look in his eyes and the sound of his voice. Later, when I had a chance to think over that dream, I realized why the winter winds struck so savagely at the old Mabirshan lands: it was my father's raging spirit driving the winds before him, ever searching for the family that he had lost.

Bel and I awoke the next morning at the same time, just as the eastern sky was beginning to lighten. We hugged each other for a moment, and then Bel spoke:

"I dreamed last night..."

"So did I."

Then I froze; towering above us on either side were The Needles of Ishara themselves. We had fallen asleep in the space between them, right in the heart of Tarhunt's holy place. No wonder we had the dreams that we did; I was surprised that our hair hadn't fallen out or our skin turned blue for our temerity. We waited for lightning to strike or a whirlwind to descend upon us, but nothing did. After a few minutes, Bel took a deep breath, and said: "Things like this happen for a reason."

I agreed; and while I was admiring her profile (she looked beautiful in the morning) something occurred to me. As usual, I didn't stop to think it through, I just went ahead and did it. I touched her face, and when she turned those glorious eyes to mine, I said:

"I meant everything I said last night, and I want to prove that to you."

I kissed her and stood up, pulling her to her feet. There are a number of stories about the Needles, and I had been thinking about one of them since the day we arrived. The tale told of two lovers who had bound themselves to each other with an oath sworn on these two stones, and of how that oath had created a link between their spirits that had enabled them to find one another across the width of Scythia and the chaos of a war.

I stepped over to the northern blue pillar and placed my left hand palm flat on its surface; it felt smooth and cool to the touch. I held out my other hand to Bel and waited, with my stomach tied in a knot and my lungs refusing to work. She knew the same story I did, and if she felt the same way I did, she would know what to do next. If she refused, then I would crawl back into my shell and wait for another tall, beautiful, intelligent woman with a smooth backhand cut to find me attractive. My chances weren't really that bad, if I lived for three or four centuries.

Bel grinned at me and putting her left palm on the southern pillar, stretched her right arm out to me. Our hands met, with our fingers just touching each other's palms, and we began to recite the old poem that every Khetarite child knows: "I to thee...", just as the rays of the dawning sun lit the tops of the Needles of Ishara, goddess of oaths and love.

The instant the first words left our mouths, we could feel something begin to happen. The birds stopped singing their morning songs, and we heard a deep humming that seemed to come from the stones on either side of us. The stone beneath my hand grew cold, and I seemed to be able to feel it pulling at me; we could no longer feel any wind on our faces, but we could see that the wind was blowing around the shrine, widdershins, raising a curtain of dust about the stones. Our voices grew thin with fear, but neither one of us stopped; we could feel a tension growing within us and around us, and as it filled us to the point where our hair began to stand up on our heads, we spoke the last words of our promise just as the morning sunlight touched the base of the pillars.

I felt something burst and surge out of me, and into Bel's hand, and at the same instant a warm wave of energy flowed out of her fingers and into me, to slam down the length of my left arm and into the pillar of stone beneath my left hand. Then the twin pillars of the The Needles rang like struck bells. Bel and I staggered into each other's arms, barely able to see, and then we stumbled down the northern slope of the hill that the shrine sits atop. Luckily, this was the side that faced away from the encampment. We were both felt dizzy and completely drained, and we held tightly onto each other's hands, white-faced with shock at what we had done. We tottered away from the hill and began to circle around to the camp, where I knew Ajax was probably skirting apoplexy, and where I was going to have to come up with some kind of explanation for all of this. I had just realized how inadequate words were going to be for that, when Bel squeezed my hand and said: "Boy, I'll say this for you: you sure know how to show a girl a good time". I felt better right away.

When we came in sight of the camps, we stopped dead in our tracks. Everyone, including the drunken nomad and his bison, were at the base of the hill and staring at the stones, which were glimmering faintly in the morning light. They were still reverberating slightly, but other than that there was no outward sign that we had done anything.

It was the old white haired tribesman who broke the silence:

"It is the sign! The White Bull is come to Scythia, and nothing will be the same again!"

He leaped astride his mount with surprising agility for someone of his age and condition, and galloped off to break his camp. Everyone else burst into excited conversation. One of the Abasgi said that he actually SAW the sound of the stone's ringing spreading outward from the shrine, like waves rippling outward from a stone thrown into a pond. A priest of Tarhunt of the Carpi said that it was a warning from Tarhunt, a sign of both a beginning and an ending. Others had other things to say, but everyone agreed that it WAS a sign of some kind. Everyone but Ajax. He was standing off to one side, looking at me with that expression on his face again. Well, there was no avoiding him. I walked over to him, and began:

"Ajax, I..."

He interrupted me with a raised hand.

"You get more like your father every damn day, and it's starting to worry me, boy. When he was your age, I had to get him into a war to calm him down."

There were times that Ajax was so foresighted, he scared the hell out of me.

Anything else anyone was about to say was cut short by a warning cry from a Bastarnae lookout:

"Dust cloud!".

We were going to have company.

Those in camp who were leaving that day started loading up their pack animals, while the rest of us kept an eye on the approaching dust cloud just in case the sounding of the The Needles HAD been a warning from Tarhunt of danger coming near. Before long, we could see that a small party of mule riders were heading our way from the southeast; not galloping, but making good time. They were Bastarnae traders, those whose arrival had been expected; but by this time, we could see that there was not one dust trail, but THREE. The second cloud came from what looked to be a very large group of people moving east to west on the Dragon's Road from Carchemish. But the third cloud was immense; it was so much dust being raised, it looked like a forest had caught fire. Someone wondered aloud what could possibly cause that much dust and Ajax replied:

"A nation that moves. It would take one of the great tribes of Scythia to do that, all of the clans moving together; either that, or all of the tribes have united and are sending an army to raid Issuria. That is why we haven't seen any nomads in a week; they have all been called up by their tribe's Khan. In any case, it means that war has come to Scythia, and that you had better start heading home."

Although we had hoped that Barlan would be with the Bastarnae traders coming from Carchemish, he was nowhere to be seen. Their leader, a lean man with a scarred nose named Heteorl, agreed with Ajax's conclusion regarding the nomads, although he hadn't actually seen any of them. What he had seen was the ordered columns of spearmen marching west on the road.

"That is what is causing that smaller dust trail; the Spears of Sekhmet are on the march. Not just the Temple Guards either, some of those I saw were militia spearmen; Nomarch Pen-Seti must have called a muster of every spear in his Nome and whoever isn't guarding the Temple of Sekhmet itself must be down there on that road. I've never seen anything like it."

"No one has seen anything like that, not in the last 400 years anyway. The last time the Spears of Sekhmet fought outside the boundaries of their Nome during a full muster was when the city of Harran fell in 200 MK. Who is rich enough or powerful enough to persuade them to do this, now?" Ajax's question was a rhetorical one; we all knew its answer: the Empire of the White Sun.

The Spears of Sekhmet were the descendants of an Egyptian regiment that had been stranded by the Breaking. Their Leader of a Thousand had been offered land by a canny lord of Carchemish, and he had accepted, founding the Nome of the Raging Lioness. Since then, the Spears of Sekhmet had served as allies of the city of Carchemish and as occasional mercenaries for the other cities that gleamed like pearls on the strand that was the Euphrates River. Mostly, they kept to themselves within the boundaries of their nome.

"That is why we haven't seen anyone coming from the west; the imperials will let anyone coming from the east pass, but they would have closed the border to all travellers headed our way. We must have left Ateas's Cist just in time, and if we don't all leave here now, we'll have to deal with the outriders of not one, but two different armies, and neither with any love for us."

The Carpi priest of Tarhunt, whose name was Lelwyn Spearbreaker, agreed:

"Our clans are depending on us; our news, the fruits of our trading and our good sword arms, are all vital to our people. I agree with Ajax: Pack and leave for home, right away."

There was a murmur of general agreement, and everyone in camp began hurriedly gathering their belongings and loading their pack animals. Ajax motioned me over, and told me to cut out five mules: our mounts, two remounts and a good pack beast, and load them for a long ride on trail rations. I nodded and went about it. In the meantime, Bel had gone to Heteorl and was pleading with him to do something about her uncle. Heteorl's face set into a grim mask;

"I know he is your only kin, child, but we can't sacrifice everyone and everything we have in the off-hand chance of finding a needle in that haystack.", gesturing towards the plains to the south with one hand.

"It bites at me to leave one of our tribe behind, but..."

"You won't.", interrupted Ajax.

"We'll find Barlan". Bel's face rose at once. "Your clan is depending on you, Heron Girl, so you go with your people and head on home. If Barlan is out there, we'll find him, and bring him back. Count on it. Vanioth would never forgive us if we didn't."

Bel threw her arms around his neck almost hard enough to knock him off his feet.

"I love you, Ajax. Thank you."

"Huh. Go on, those mules won't pack themselves now, will they?"

Heteorl clasped arms with Ajax and said:

"Our thanks, Attar. We won't forget this."

"Thank us when this is done. In the meantime, get yourself home safe. Best to clear the board, before the Empire starts its game."

We broke camp as quickly as we could, and as was demanded by custom, made sure that the spring was clear and that there was some firewood set aside in the lee of The Needles before we left. There would be others coming here to worship, and there was no need to be rude. As we tightened our cinches and mounted up, Lelwyn and Heteorl rode over to Ajax for a last word before leaving. Seeing her opportunity, Bel rode over to me.

"We'll bring him back," I said. "I promise."

Bel only said "Shutup", grabbed me by the arms and kissed me. I kissed her back and we put everything we felt and wanted to say into it. It was the longest, greatest kiss of my life, and it's a good thing too, because that one kiss had to last me for more than seven long years. By the time we had finished, the women were laughing at me, the men were pounding their shields and hooting, and Heteorl was beside himself.

"YOU!" He roared. "Who are you to put your hands on a Bastarnae woman?"

I was feeling a bit dizzy and seeing spots in front of my eyes, but I yelled back at him: "I am Joren, son of Tiranna, and the next time you see me, I'll be talking to your clan about marrying that Bastarnae woman!"

"Well ...well, just see that you do it soon; our women are nothing to trifle with. Good luck, Attar. The wind at your back..."

"And a clear road before you. Good luck to all of you. Come on, boy, let's ride."

I looked at Bel one last time. I couldn't think of anything to say, but she growled at me:

"Remember, you belong to me now. Be sure you bring yourself back too."

"I will, love. Just as soon as I can."

That turned out to have been a very poor choice of words. Bel remembered every last word I spoke to her when we parted. When I finally made my way back to her, the only thing that kept her from making a real issue of them was the fact that there was a city on fire around us. We went our separate ways then with one last wave of our hands; Bel, her fellow tribesmen and the other Khetarites rode west, and Ajax and I galloped south. We aimed to cut the road well ahead of Sekhmet's followers, and then head south by southwest.

Our path would skirt the edge of the Red Grasses and by hitting every seep and waterhole Ajax knew of, we would see if we could find some trace of Barlan or of his passing. The trail would take us towards Dwarf Hill, and eventually to the oasis of Roaring Springs, if there was no sign of Bel's uncle before then. We went riding to find a friend gone missing; what we rode into was the greatest battle Scythia would see in a generation. Well, if Ajax was trying to get me to focus on my sword lessons, it worked.

Chapter XIV: Roaring Springs

WE MADE GOOD TIME, and cut the road well before the Spears of Sekhmet came into sight. We concentrated on speed, not stealth; Ajax said that Sekhmet's people were fine infantry, but would spend little effort to track down anyone who fled their approach. They didn't have the time or the inclination. The nomads following after them were another matter entirely; their scouts would be too numerous and too skilled at tracking for us to hope they wouldn't spot our tracks. When they did, we had better be as far away from them as possible, just in case a few of them decided to trail us in hopes of scalps and loot.

I asked Ajax if he thought Dargo and Corlan would be alright; they would have been heading right into the path of the armies we could see on the road. He said that he thought they would be safe enough; Dargo was no fool, and they would have ridden for Carchemish as quickly as possible. They might even have gotten past those armies before they moved onto the road. Corlan told me years later that the two of them had had swung north to visit some friends of Dargo, and had been well out of the way of both armies. As for us, Ajax thought moving fast was a good idea, so we traveled as lightly as possible, staying off the ridgetops and making cold camps away from the water, once we and our mounts had drunk our fill. On our first night south of the road, I realized something: I could FEEL Belkara, where she was and how she was feeling, although not how far away she was. This had to be a result of our swearing our promise to one another at the Needles. I could actually close my eyes, and get a feel for her emotions; right then, it was mainly worry, and her temper was starting to slip. Hmmm.... This new ability could be even more useful than I had thought. Maybe I was better off where I was, for now. I was scrapping the plates after dinner when Ajax caught me looking preoccupied and asked me what was wrong:

"You look like you're thinking of bringing up that meal, and I know I'm not THAT bad a cook, so it must be something else. What's wrong, boy? Lonely?"

"Uhm.., not really." So I told him. He grunted, and crouching so as to shield the light from any prying eyes, cast a spell: for a second, Ajax's eyes gleamed with an eerie light. He then straightened and turned towards me; and after a moment:

"Well... There's something you don't see every day."

"What?" He was needling me; and maybe I deserved it, but that didn't mean I had to like it.

"See WHAT?"

"Your life bond, you idiot."

"Life Bond? Me? With Bel? Like in the stories?"

"Yes, like in the stories. In fact, just like in the stories; I haven't seen one this strong in ... a long time. Just what did you and Bel DO back there, boy?"

So I told him. Everything: my dreams, how Bel and I felt towards one another and the oath we had sworn. He pondered it all for a few moments, and then:

"It is nice to know your father's concern for my welfare: I really would like to die with a sword in my hand, and not face down in a platter of beets because your table manners gave me a stroke. We will continue with your lessons, too; it sounds as if you've quite a row to hoe, boy. Just one thing: why use THOSE words for your oath? Nowadays, they are remembered only in nursery rhymes."

"They were the only words we knew."

"Huh. Perhaps the two of you have done better than you know. The life bond between the two of you is very strong, maybe as strong as any I've seen. It is going to have certain ... effects. It is going to be very difficult for anyone to persuade either of you to do anything you don't want to do; you may even be able to resist certain types of spells, but you will never really be happy with anyone else but each other."

"Suits me."

"I thought it might. But if one of you dies before the other, it will leave an aching wound that will never really heal."

I just looked at him.

"Yes. I think that might be why this bond is very strong; all it is doing is reinforcing something that already exists. Let us see just how strong it is."

He went to his pack and pulled out a small brazen bowl. Placing it before me, he poured some water into it, just enough to cover the bottom of the bowl itself.

"A mirror is best for this, but almost any liquid or reflective surface will do: water, wine, even a knife blade, just as long as it's clean. A pool of still liquid is good, but a film spread across a good blade will do as well. Now, think of Bel and breathe into the bowl, then look at the reflection from the surface of the water."

"There isn't much light for this." I said.

"More than enough; starlight is best, but candlelight or a low fire will do. You're not really looking with your eyes, you know."

Ah; with my heart then. I leaned over the bowl, and clasping it in my hands, breathed on the water's surface, and thought of my love. The reflection of the stars above me became very clear; "Bel!" I called softly, and suddenly she was there. She was asleep, or trying to; she was wrapped in a cloak, with her head pillowed on her pack and I could see the flickering shadows of a fire behind her, and the frown on her face. "Bel!" I called again.

Her eyes snapped open; I could see her lips move and knew she spoke my name. Closing my eyes, I thought of her, and how much I loved and missed her, and said "Dear One."

Then I heard her answer me: "Joren?", her voice whispered. "Where...".

I jerked in surprise, and the water slopped in the bowl, nearly spilling; all that it showed now was my shadow and the fading stars above. The vision of her was gone, but the feel of her was just as strong as ever. Bel didn't seem angry now; she seemed oddly content, and I could feel her falling asleep. I turned wide eyes to Ajax, and said:

"I heard her."

He seemed startled for an instant:

"You heard her voice? The bond is very strong then, stronger than I had thought. Enough for one night, get some sleep. We will be on the move tomorrow".

I had one question though: "Ajax?"

"Yes?"

"Why was there no answer to my request to serve the rightful King?"

"You were answered; you're still alive, aren't you?"

"Huh?"

"You slept in the lap of the King of the Gods and swore an oath to span a life time. If Tarhunt had not approved of your desire to serve the King of Khetar, all that we would have found of you would have looked like a piece of bacon that had been left in a hot pan too long."

"oh"

"Yes, 'oh'. Now go to sleep."

The next morning was a cloudy one, which was just fine with us; no direct sunlight meant less chance of a glint reflected from a weapon or harness that might give us away to an enemy. We saw no one, and very little wildlife for the first few days, as we made our way from one waterhole to another: Broken Cup, Seven Horns, and Black Eye Hole, right on the northwestern edge of the near desert that is the Red Grasses. All of these are seasonal watering holes: seeps or tanks that hold the rain of winter and spring, but usually go dry in the heat of summer. We found no sign of Barlan at any of them, or indeed, of anyone. Every now and then, Ajax's eyes would stray to the north, and the two dust clouds that were traveling from east to west along the road from Carchemish to Khetar.

"I don't like it, boy. The nomads and the Spears aren't friends; sometimes the Spearmen will hire out to a nomad tribe if the price is right, or if the Nomarch of the Raging Lioness Nome is in the mood, but for the most part, they're unfriends. There have been too many raids on the farmers of that nome over the centuries for it to be any other way. But here, here we've got a horde of nomads that can SEE the dust trail the Spearmen are raising, can read their tracks, and yet, they stay the same distance behind over days' of travel. It's almost like they're screening for each other."

It felt wrong, even I could sense it.

With no sign of Barlan up until then, Ajax decided to swing west-southwest, towards Dwarf Hill. We hit the waterholes at Mourningbird Wells and at Copperfeather Creek (which isn't a creek, just a ravine), but we didn't find anything until we got to Shortman's Walls, the last waterhole before Dwarf Hill itself. The waterhole was clean, but hadn't seen any use by anyone except the local wildlife in days. We searched the area protected by the low, oddly-uniform drystone walls, but hadn't found anything until Ajax called me over to the waterhole itself. What had caught Ajax's eye was something I would have passed by without a second glance; a handful of long grass had been loosely twisted together to form a length of crude twine, and then tied in an odd little knot around the stem of a yellow bud bush, close to the water's edge. It was right where someone might squat down to wait while their water bags filled, and looked to be the kind of thing one might do absentmindedly to pass the time. I couldn't see why Ajax had picked it out until he tapped the knot with a finger and said: "That's a sailor's knot". Well, that left out the nomads.

Ajax rubbed his chin and mused aloud

"You left me a sailor's knot as a message, Barlan. Why?"

Then we both turned and looked at the waterhole itself. I spotted it a split second before Ajax did: one of the flat stones in the waterhole had been wiped clean of mud and algae. We fished it out and turned it over, to find that two words had been scratched into its surface.

"Teufeln Plateau? That's no place I've ever heard of."; I wasn't well traveled then, but I had a good memory for names and places.

"No reason why you should, boy. The Teufeln Plateau is deep inside the Empire; it's a rugged, barren sort of place, like Scythia in some ways. It is where the Empire recruits its Red Sakar Lancers." He looked up at me and waited to see if I caught it. It took a bit.

"SAKAR Lancers? From a place like Scythia... You mean like the SAKAE tribesmen of Scythia?!"

"Exactly like the Sakae. Diophantus is a planner and a thinker; he lead the first invasion of Scythia a few years ago, and when he saw the Sakae tribesmen, he came up with an idea: bring in the Red Sakar Lancers and see if he couldn't split the nomads, set one against the other. It looks like it worked; that kind of trick has worked for the Empire more than once before this."

"If the imperials have the Sakae, then that explains how those Spearmen could march the length of the Carchemish Road with a nomad tribe behind them and not sweat it. The Spears of Sekhmet, the entire Sakae Tribe... Ajax, this is big!"

"Too damn big; we've got to get the hell out of here. If the Imperial army enters Scythia, the tribes will know it and ride to war. The last place you, me and Barlan want to be is between two armies looking for a fight. Mount up; we're going to circle the waterhole; if we find tracks that could be Barlan's, we'll follow them. If not, well, with our water bags full, we've got more than enough water to let us strike straight for Roaring Springs."

"Roaring Springs?" I'd heard stories of that oasis, who had not? The best water on the Carchemish road, not to mention its famous hotsprings and geysers that erupted every seven days. It was considered to be a holy place by many peoples as well; to the gods of the forges such as our own Hasemeli and Hephaestus (whom the Thracians call Father of Volcanoes), and to Arma Arn because of the geysers that seemed attuned to his cycle.

"Aye." Ajax nodded; "The Roxolani control it last I heard, and Barlan has friends among them. If he's alive, odds are he's there, or at least news of him is. Let's go."

We circled Shortman's Walls, but found nothing; hoping for the best, we turned west and headed for the oasis of Roaring Springs, bypassing Dwarf Hill and its legendary copper mine, and the strange statues that stand guard on its slag piles. As it happened, Barlan wasn't at the oasis. I learned later that he had encountered some old enemies of his from the Dahae tribe, just after he had seen a troop of Red Sakar Lancers near Dwarf Hill. After losing two of his mules (and two of his enemies) in a running fight, he had managed to evade his foes and strike out across the plains with some water, a little food and a wounded mule. A week after the battle, he staggered into the camp at Ateas Cist on foot, more than half dead, after a journey that would have killed most men. Bel and Vanioth nursed him back to health, and marriage respectively, and he gave his blessing to our own marriage, but I never saw him again. He had been dead a year before I saw the Bastarnae lands once more.

The oasis of Roaring Springs is one of the best in Scythia: it has a pure and reliable water supply, plentiful fruit trees (date palms and pomegranate, apricot and olive), lush grazing and the fabled geysers that give the place its name. Of course, I didn't actually see the inside of the oasis until years after the battle, but you can see why people wanted the place. The tribe of the Roxolani controlled Roaring Springs in 610 MK and had built a small fort on the high ground to cement that control.

When Diophantus the Bold lead the second imperial invasion of Scythia, he made use of the maps and information he had gathered on his first trip, and he chose the oasis as his staging area. All of the elements of his army: the Imperial Heartland regiments, the Dacian levies, his mercenaries and his nomad allies, they all came to Roaring Springs.

The first regiments to arrive were the Imperial regulars: legions of heavy infantry from the lands surrounding the Imperial Capital, and phalanxes of Helvetian spearmen, supported by peltasts and slingers. Next came the Dacians, with some mercenary foot soldiers and then Auchatae and Skula mercenaries as outriders. They evicted the few score Roxolani that were garrisoning the oasis and set up camp. Next to arrive were the Spears of Sekhmet, and then the Sakae nomads at the last. As they arrived, each was set into their place by Diophantus, and then he waited for the tribes of Scythia to come to him. The nomad tribes did come, in their thousands, and we came right along with them.

We had pushed hard after leaving Dwarf Hill, with the aim of getting to Roaring Springs as soon as possible, so we could get some kind of lead on Barlan or at least his path of travel. Almost immediately, we realized we were following, not one or two but a dozen or more different nomad war parties, all headed in the same direction as us. Before long, we started to feel as if something was coming up behind us as well; we didn't know who, but something was making the mules skittish, so we decided to go on as best we could. We made good time, and although it served to get us into a battle we had not planned on getting caught up in, it also served to keep us out of the path of the last element of the nomad army to arrive at Roaring Springs, the most savage fighters of them all. I now think that there was no way to avoid that battle, no matter what we did. Battles are often like whirlpools of violence that tend to draw all around them into their surging current of destruction. Roaring Springs was like that.

Ajax had decided to avoid approaching the oasis from the north or east, to minimize the chance we would encounter any imperial or nomad patrols. He directed our path south and west, so that when we turned towards the oasis, we were approaching it from almost due south. This meant that we ran right into the last band of Roxolani tribesmen to reach the battle field; they were from the tribal lands farthest to the south, around the Roxolani stronghold that we in Khetar call Aleppo. There were some Warrunki amongst the Roxolani, and a few of them recognized Ajax:

"Heya, Old Man with a Sword, are you coming to the Springs? You are! Then travel with us and give us some of your luck."

We saw other Khetarites with them, fighters from the eastern tribes of Issuria, who were come to Scythia in search of glory and treasure, or just to strike a blow against the empire where they could. Together we rode to Roaring Springs and to war.

Our arrival with the last of the Roxolani tribesmen brought us right into the left rear of the nomad army. From the vantage point of a low rise, we could see the entire force mustered against the Imperial units; it was an impressive array, especially to my inexperienced eyes. The skirmishers that guarded either flank of the nomad horde were primarily made up of riders from the Dahae tribe; shorter in stature than the other tribes, they rode into battle naked armed with only knives and bows, depending on the speed of their agile mounts to keep them out of the melee while their bows kept up a deadly fire on their opponents.

The Dahae are the most numerous of the Scythian tribes, and their war bands swarmed around either flank like ever-shifting flocks of birds. There were other bands of warriors aiding the Dahae with their task of skirmishing; on the left flank where we sat they were aided by Jarrian horse archers from Carchemish, who were adept with both sword and bow, and who traced their lineage back to the defenders of the city of Old Carchemish, in the days of the Draconic Empire. The center of the nomad army consisted of two groups: the front rank of heavy cavalry backed up by a second rank of infantry. The van of the nomad army was made up riders from the Kushan tribe, with the Roxolani on the left and the Traspians on the right. They were backed up by a second rank consisting of various bands of nomads on foot, many of them not even human: the fierce Sandasi, children of the Lion god, and the Mitas Huwarni, the Red Hunters, red-skinned spearmen who towered over the other nomads. There was a band of minotaurs, descended from Tillar the Bull himself, and there were slingers and spearmen from the tribes that lived along the banks of the Euphrates below Carchemish. But as imposing as this horde was, even I could see that there were some tribes missing. Ajax had seen it right off and was more than a little worried.

"Neither the Sogdians nor the Catiaroi tribes are here, and there is no sign of the Paralatae at all; the nomads have less than half their strength in warriors and magic to throw against the imperials!"

I realized he was right; more than half of all the nomads in Scythia and the steppes beyond are members of the Five Great Tribes: the Sakae, the Dahae, the Kushan, the Sogdians and Paralatae (or Royal Scythians). The Sogidians have a reputation for cruelty, but are not afraid to fight on foot; they often lead the fighters that some of the smaller towns provide the Scythians as tribute, and provide the anchor that the other tribes move around when the massed tribes go into battle. The Paralatae are considered by many to be the most powerful of the Five Great Tribes, and have not only have some of the finest heavy cavalry on the plains but also possess a great deal of influence with the other tribes because of their magic. They are often referred to as the Royal Scythians because their chieftains can claim Ateas Whitemane as their ancestor and because many of their warriors ride auroch bulls into battle.

If the Sogdians and the Paralatae were not here now, they weren't coming to the party at all, and with the Sakae gone over to the Empire, the nomads were going to be at a crippling disadvantage when facing the discipline of the imperial army and its imposing magical support. There had to be something we hadn't seen yet, some kind of equalizer the nomads had gotten hold of, to offset the advantages Diophantus had gathered for his army. Because I didn't doubt for a moment that the imperial general had planned almost all of this, although I had no idea what trick he had used to sow such dissension amongst the Scythian tribes. I can see using the Red Sakar Lancers to recruit their kinsmen, but what trick had he used to infuriate some of the largest tribes to the point where they would refuse to join the others to face an invader?

We were watching the army gather from a vantage point behind the left rear of the Roxolani warriors, just to the left of the Red Hunters. There were a couple of hundred riders grouped there: wanderers, adventurers, Khetarite tribesmen and Scythian outlaws; some were there by choice, goaded by hatred or vengeance, some (like Ajax and I) were there by chance, but we were all caught up in the same war. We could all die in it too, just like everyone else on this battlefield. Ajax and I had dismounted, and I was watching the old man pace back and forth, snarling to himself; he didn't like it, and I now knew enough to see why. It was then I noticed that one of the tall spearmen of the Red Hunters had set his long spear point first into the ground, and was watching Ajax's every move. He looked to be a spirit talker, a shaman, from what I could see of the bone ornaments that hung from his neck, and just for a moment, I thought I saw something perched on his left shoulder. But then the cowl of his headdress shifted, and I saw it was a trick of the light.

The Red Hunters are what we call them; they call themselves the Children of Horus, and are another of the Egyptian forces that were stranded here on the north side of the Great Rift at the Breaking. They have leathery skin that is the dark red of a ripe apple, hawk-like features and eyes like those of a bird of prey, which can look at the Sun without blinking. Their eyes fascinated me; they range from a tawny yellow to gold to orange to a bright blood red in color, striking in a people so dark of skin. They are hunters (not herders) of beasts, and tower head and shoulders over the other nomad peoples. They are not entirely human, at least not any more. They do not feel heat or thirst as other men do, and can run down anything that walks. It is a point of pride that none of their people will ever ride when they are still hale enough to travel on their own two feet. This shaman was staring at Ajax with blood red eyes that seemed to see more than mere flesh and metal. Suddenly, he dropped to his haunches, and taking the contents of a pouch from his belt, he spread his hands in a casting motion, and I heard the click and clatter of falling bones. He must be a sort of seer then, and was casting the runes to try to peer into a future. The shaman stared at them for a moment, and standing, called out to Ajax in a deep voice:

"What do you see, Messenger of Death?"

Ajax jerked to a stop, and turned to face the eyes of every spearmen in the Red Hunter phalanx. They stood there, motionless and unblinking in the bright sun, but even the eyes of their commander (marked by the red stripes in his sphinx headcloth) had turned towards Ajax. He opened his mouth to reply, and the wind shifted from the south to the east, and we all caught the stench of the last contingent to join the nomad army at Roaring Springs. It struck at our senses like a blow, and I could hear men gagging. The mounts, whether horse, mule or whatever, didn't like it any better than we did, and began to fret and dance. Ajax paled, and looking to the east, to the right flank of the nomad army, raised his voice in a roaring shout:

"No! NO! You go too far! Nothing is worth THAT!", pointing to the brazen chariots that had topped a ridge to the southeast and were pouring down to take their place on the far right flank of the nomad horde. Assyrians!

The thought that an Assyrian army might have penetrated this far west without being spotted was unnerving, but there were only a dozen or so chariots in this force, backed by several hundred spearmen and an equal number of bowmen. A dozen was enough; instead of the 2 man chariots used by the Egyptians, the Assyrian battle wains carried 3 or 4 men into combat and their wheels were bladed to cut down enemy infantry. They were pulled by the fabled Asshuran steeds, horses so strong and enduring they could wear armor and still pull the armored chariots of their masters. But even without the chariots, we would have known them as Assyrian, even in the darkest night: Assyrian magic was blood magic, and the stench of it could not be hidden. The armies of Nineveh had slaughtered entire towns to fuel their dreaded magic, and the smell of old blood marked them. The chariots flew pennants that were a strange twist of black and red, and their infantry marched ahead of a banner that was a black blot on a blood red field. Behind the banner rode a single figure robed in red and black on a bone white horse; the outlines of both horse and rider were indistinct, as if wrapped about with a shimmering haze. I blinked and realized that I didn't want to look at that rider for any length of time; it took an effort of will to not look away from it.

"Erra.", I heard Ajax say quietly. I turned to look at him, and found him looking not at the Assyrians, but at me.

"The Black Goat's Head on a Red field is the banner of Erra, who commands the Ilu Sebbutu, the seven demons that serve Nergal, the Assyrian god of pestilence, war and the underworld. Only a wizard steeped in the black arts of of Assyria would even think of flying that banner in the broad light of day. This is no place for you."

But Erra's name had sparked a memory of Ajax's history lessons.

"Wasn't it an Assyrian legion flying Erra's banner that destroyed Harron?"

That would explain why the Spears of Sekhmet marched with the empire's forces and not against them. Four hundred years ago, the city of Harron had hired them, paid them in full with gold bars and coins to aid in the war with Assyria, and the Spears had marched. But they had come too late, and found only smoking ruins and the bodies of the dead, an entire city butchered as a warning to those who would dare resist the armies of Assyria, and to fuel the magic that helped make them so deadly. The Spears of Sekhmet had returned to their nome, and never again sent their full muster to any battle. It was said that the gold of Harron sat unspent in their coffers; it had not been earned and there was no one left alive to return it to. But now they had a chance to make good on their word. Even though 400 years had passed, the Spears of Sekhmet had marched hundreds of miles for a chance at a fight with this enemy. I did not think that any of the followers of Erra or Sekhmet would leave this battlefield while the others lived. I did wonder what the Scythians had offered the Assyrian wizard to bring him this far west. Or was there something here that he wanted?

I heard the clatter of bones behind us; we had forgotten about the shaman of the Red Hunters. He dropped the bones he had scattered back into the pouch that hung from his belt and spoke to Ajax again:

"You do not know all, Killer. The shamans of the tribes have accepted the aid this Assyrian sorcerer offered against the invaders, these servants of the White Sun. The walls of the world shall be broken open, and a great spirit called. Gibil the Devourer is to be loosed upon these Red Cloaks, to feed as he will. Now tell me, what do you see, Messenger of Death?"

The shaman repeated his question without changing position or expression; Ajax's face might have been the only thing in the world for him. The old man's features set in lines as harsh as stone.

"Gibil", he said, nodding.

Gibil? But Gibil was the spirit of the wildfire, not a simple fire elemental; his power would be immense. Still, while Gibil's power was great, it came at a cost and a risk; you cannot expect a living forest fire to just come when you whistle, and when it does come, it could burn you as well as your enemies. Would the shamans of the tribes be willing to pay that price and take that risk? My eyes turned to the Assyrian battle wains formed up on the other end of the nomad line, backed by spearmen and foot archers clad in hobnailed boots and scale armor. They would.

149

Somewhere to the south of us, behind the nomad line, there was a drum beating; at first, it was more felt than heard, but it kept getting louder and louder.

Ajax had turned to look at the oasis; it had a link to Hephaestus, Father to Volcanoes and to Gibil himself. Gibil's power would be strong here. Then his gaze wandered over the imperial army across from us, and settled on the ranks of the Helvetian hoplites; their banners were crimson and gold and seemed to glow in the sun's light. He turned to face the shaman and the phalanx of tall warriors that stood behind him:

"What do I see? That this whole battlefield is a trap, and we are in it. Before the Sun sets again, the minions of the White Sun will strip the bodies of your dead, and leave them for the hyenas."

And that damn drum kept on beating.

The shaman nodded once, and turned to speak with his commander. Ajax turned to face me, his eyes burning and said: "Get the mules, we're leaving."

I stared at him, my mouth hanging open. This was my first chance to fight in a battle, to wage war against the enemies of our people, to strike at those ultimately responsible for my family's death...

"What? Ajax, this is my first chance to...".

The old man grabbed my reins and silenced me with a look.

"Listen to me, boy. My word is not straw. I swore an oath to your father that I would do my best to teach you what I could, and see you as far along the path you have to take as I am allowed. It would not be in keeping with that oath to let you be buried in a mass grave here today, on the site of an imperial victory. Not until you know better, and can make the choice yourself."

"But, Ajax, what will everyone say? They'll call us cowards." I could see some of the others looking at us out of the corner of their eyes and whispering.

"Feh. If those idiots stay here, they won't live long enough for anyone to hear what they have to say. Besides, do you want to fight on the same side as THAT?", he said, pointing to the Assyrian banners of red and black. I imagined I could catch the scent of old blood from where I stood.

"No."

It just wasn't the way I had pictured my first battle, and against the enemy who had occupied our kingdom; and since I was young, what the others thought of us DID matter to me. Ajax could sense this.

"Don't worry boy. There will be other battles for you, count on it. As for me, a thousand men can call me coward, if it means an oath I swore is kept. Once you keep the oath, you can always go back and see if any of those thousand men want to argue with you about it."

He had a point there.

"Right. I'll go ready our mules." I headed over to the area behind the lines where the pack animals were being kept, either ground hitched or in a rope corral. I dismounted and gathered the reins of our mules; they were a bit jumpy because of that damned drumming. Behind me, Ajax strode up to the others, and I heard him cut across their questions with two short, sharp sentences.

"This place is a trap. We're leaving; I suggest you do the same." Then he turned and left them sputtering.

Cries of "Coward!" and other, less flattering names began to be heard. I could feel my ears and face getting red; being as young as I was, I felt that it just wasn't fair of Fate to go ahead and cheat me out of a good fight. It also occurred to me that it was going to take an awful long time to live this down. Both of these thoughts were driven from my mind by what may have been the opening volley of the entire battle.

Scythia is often thought of as a flat limitless plain, broken only by the occasional oasis or ruin; in reality, it is quite rugged, being cut by any number of low ridges or ravines and hollows. A band of Sakae braves had decided to try for the honor of First Blood, and using every feature of the terrain and every trick of stealth they knew, had managed to sneak in past the Dahae skirmishers. These tribesmen were armed with composite bows, short curving bows made from layered wood and horn, which had surprising power and range. When they had gotten in close enough to risk a shot, they waited until most people were looking the other way, and made their move. They nocked their arrows, rose and loosed as one and then mounted up and rode like hell out of there. They aimed high, so their arrows would come down from above, and at the largest target that would produce the greatest amount of confusion: the pack herds.

The nomads had been making war since time began; they knew you don't treat it as if it were a night's raid: hit, grab and run for home. You have to plan for the long haul: food, water, first aid supplies and most of all, ammunition. Arrows don't grow on trees in Scythia, you have to bring them with you; warriors like the Dahae packed their reload arrows in bushel baskets. Our mules were over by the Roxolani cattle herd (the horse herd was farther south), in a rope corral that held hundreds of animals, mainly steers, who were both pack beasts and food animals for their masters. I was over between the mules and the edge of the cattle herd, double-checking the packs, when someone spotted the Sakae archers. I heard the shout of "Arrows!" and I dropped to a crouch and dragged out my broadsword, while I tried to catch a glimpse of the nervy bastards who had gotten this close without being turned into a Dahae's pincushion. That is when I heard the meaty thunking sound of arrows hitting flesh, behind me, followed by a pain-filled bawl from a wounded steer. That was enough; already fretful from the tension in the air before a battle, by the stench of blood and magic coming from the Assyrians, and by the beating of that damn drum, the herd tried to stampede.

The Roxolani had herdsmen watching their cattle and soon brought it under control (this wasn't the first time that trick had ever been tried), but I was oblivious to that and everything else that happened for a while. One of the Sakae rider arrows had caught a steer behind me just in front of the shoulders; the arrow struck the beast in the spine and dropped it, on me. All I remember is something hitting me from behind, and two snapping noises, (which were my left arm and leg breaking) and I was out like the proverbial light.

I dreamed that I was in a dark place, and I could hear a drum beating, louder and louder; and around the sound of the drum, the sound of thousands of hooves thundering against the earth. I remember feeling not pain, but heat, and seeing a red light that flared brighter and brighter as two great voices roared in a language I did not understand, one voice in command and the other in anger. And I seemed to hear people and animals screaming. Then a great weight seemed to be lifted off of me, and I heard Ajax's voice calling my name, and then, I felt pain. I could see again, and the pain ebbed away to just memories everywhere except my left leg, where settled into a dull ache. I could still hear the screaming though, and it was HOT.

Ajax helped me to my feet; I felt sticky and realized that I was covered in blood, not my own, but that of the steer that fell on me. Ajax had gotten me out from under its carcass by dismembering it to the point where he could pull me free. He had spent prodigiously of his magic to keep me alive after the steer had fallen on me (I think I had been trampled as well, in the stampede) while he butchered the steer and to set and heal my limbs. The only reminder I have of that battle is a slight limp, caused by a muscle that stretched wrong when he set my leg; it doesn't really bother me, just gives this little hitch in my step. It could have been worse; the screaming I still heard came from the warriors and mounts wounded in the battle lines to the north of us. Around us were the bodies of a few animals; of our five mules, only two had not stampeded with the Roxolani cattle: Ajax's mount and one of the pack mules. Ajax didn't waste any time accepting my thanks or sightseeing; he practically threw me onto his mount, hopped onto the pack mule and yelled "Ride, damn it!". We rode south as fast as we could.

Behind us we left a battlefield that was more than just a blood-soaked stretch of ground strewn with the bodies of men and animals; it also held the wreckage of any nomad hopes of controlling western Scythia. After their victory at Roaring Springs, the White Sun Empire and its Sakae allies would control all of Scythia from Issuria to the steppes and from Gazian in the north to the southern edge of the Red Grasses in the south; even the city of Carchemish capitulated after a day's siege. A generation would pass before the nomads would gather again in the numbers they had in 610 Meta Klao. Now, the way the imperial historians tell it, the battle at Roaring Springs seems to have been a near bloodless victory: the charge of the nomad heavy cavalry failed, the Dahae riders were scattered, the nomad infantry was crushed and Gibil turned on the shamans who summoned him and savaged them. There was more to it than that, but any words I can use will still fall short of the bloody truth, because the battle of Roaring Springs was anything but bloodless.

Diophantus the Bold planned that battle well, and earned the title Count of Scythia that the White Empress gave him. He used all of the information that he had gathered on his previous foray into Scythia, as well as the news his Sakae allies had brought him; thanks to them, he knew exactly what the nomads had to throw at him, both militarily and magically, and he could plan accordingly. His greatest problem was how to deal with the charge of the nomad heavy cavalry, especially the Kushan and Traspian riders; he solved it by making the nomads fight on ground of his choosing, and he prepared that ground by seeding it with a carpet of caltrops, 3 cornered spikes that will bring a charging mount to its knees or madden it with pain. On seeing the Traspian rider and his mount at The Needles, I had wondered how one would fight a nomad warrior and his war mount; Diophantus's solution was to drop the mount and then deal with the rider. It worked, but not without cost. Even when put afoot, many of the nomads still fought and couldn't be ignored, especially the followers of Tillar, the Bull. The Tillari live to fight and they fight just as fiercely mounted or on foot; when in the grip of their god's berzerk fury, they feel nothing: neither shock nor pain nor fear. In order to stop them,

153

you must literally cut them to pieces. Many years later, I spoke to a woman who had served in a mercenary company at Roaring Springs; she said she saw a berzerk Tillar khan push himself up the 12 foot length of a pike just so he could tear out the throat of the man who killed him.

The willingness of some of the nomads to fight took many of the imperial troops by surprise. The Spears of Sekhmet had been fighting the nomads for more than 600 years, so they knew what to expect, and came out of the battle relatively unscathed. But many of the imperial troops were unprepared for what the nomads could throw at them, despite the warnings of their new allies. It was the Tillari of the Kushan tribe that slew Arintheus of Truknow and half of his regiment, when they were too slow in closing ranks after the nomad cavalry stumbled to a halt short of the imperial lines. The raging warriors of the Lion people and the tall spearmen of the Red Hunters chewed two Dacian regiments from Aquincum to pieces, but it was too little, too late. The phalanxes of the Helvetians and the Imperial Satrapies ground forward and slew or drove off all that they faced.

On the right flank of the imperial army, the Sakae riders drove the Dahae and Jarrian riders they faced from the field, but not before their arrows took a heavy toll, especially of Sakae mounts. On the Imperial left, the mercenary cavalry of Autchatae and Skula took casualties dispersing the nomads they faced, but then the Autchatae were called back to deal with a potential disaster. The charge of the Assyrian chariots took a regiment of mercenary hoplites from Utrigar by surprise, and the Red Spears were obliterated. This demoralized the mercenary infantry and isolated the Spears of Sekhmet who nonetheless held the Assyrians at bay until the Auchatae returned from their pursuit of the Dahaes. The arrows of the nomad horse archers tore holes in the ranks of the Assyrian infantry and drove them back. Unsupported, the Assyrian chariots could not break the Spears' tight formation and were fought to a standstill, then driven back as their horses were slain. Cut off by the nomad cavalry, the Assyrians had to face the Spears of Sekhmet supported by the imperial regulars and were wiped out.

Only the horse carrying the Assyrian sorcerer escaped unseen by friend and foe alike; all of the other Assyrian troops died fighting, and the four hundred year old debt owed by the Spears of Sekhmet to the people of Harron was finally paid. This action allowed a number of nomads to flee to the southeast, that otherwise might not have escaped, since the Skula did not push the pursuit on the eastern side of the battle as hard as they might have.

On the western flank of the battlefield, the Sakae riders and their Red Sakar kindred did not have this problem, and proceeded to throw themselves into a relentless pursuit that would turn the next few days into a nightmare for everyone who survived it. For those days, the sound of hoof beats never seemed to fade, and that is what I remember most about the battle of Roaring Springs. To this day, the sound of distant hoof beats will wake me from a sound sleep, sweating, as I remember that battle and the pursuit that came after.

Was I at the battle of Roaring Springs? Yes. It was a great battle and a great defeat; we lost, I ran away, and a cow fell on me. Any other questions?

Chapter XV: The Long Road South

WE STARTED RUNNING, and we knew we were in trouble; neither of our mounts were rested, and we had lost half of our food and water on the mules that had stampeded. The loss of the food was bad enough, but that of the water might kill us. It was hot and getting hotter, with a dry heat that cracked your lips and sucked the moisture from exposed skin. The cause of the heat was east of us, where the spirit drum of the nomad shamans had finally stopped beating. The shamans of the Kushan and Dahae tribes had succeeded: they had broken open the walls of the world and let in Gibil, Devourer of Forests, the spirit of the wildfires that burn where they will once lit by malice or accident or lightning. Once they had summoned this great spirit of Fire, the shamans then loosed it against the Imperial forces, only to have it turn and savage them with a fury that left most of its victims' charred cinders.

The shamans had either forgotten or else never knew that Gibil is a servant of Hephaestus, Father of Volcanos, who is worshipped by the common people of the lands within the empire. There, Hephaestus is the patron of farmers and spearmen; and many of the hoplites in Diophantus's army had made sacrifice to him before the battle. Warned by his Sakae allies, Diophantus had the imperial priests supporting his army prepare a ceremony to beg the favor of Hephaestus; it worked, so that when the shamans summoned Gibil, the fire spirit found his intended prey under the protection of his own lord. Cheated of the kindling he had been promised, Gibil had then turned on his summoners and destroyed them. The destruction of the shamans' power allowed Gibil to fade out of the world, but not before he left his mark on this part of Scythia.

No one I have ever spoken to managed to get a clear look at the Fire spirit; the glare and the heat haze was too intense. But the heat caused by just Gibil's presence was incredible. Imagine the heat from a furnace 100 yards high and more than half a mile wide, with the door jammed open. It killed men and beasts, it dropped birds from the sky, cracked leather, scorched plants and even began to change the direction the winds were blowing, because heated air rises, and cooler air will rush in to replace it, often fanning the flames. The battle of Roaring Springs took place in the wettest part of spring, but for everyone within a dozen kilometers of the battlefield, it might just as well as been in the heart of the hottest summer.

We rode south, and pushed our mules to a killing pace. We had to get as far away from the battlefield as we could before the Imperial cavalry regrouped and swung in, to cutoff retreat. We also had to get as far away from the scorching heat of Gibil's presence and try to reach water before it was drunk dry by other survivors fleeing the battle; fighting (and bleeding) makes you thirsty. Food wasn't nearly as important as water; if push came to shove, we could eat the mules.

All about us lay the wreckage and residue of battle: abandoned bedrolls, broken weapons, a scattering of fallen arrows and the bodies of men and animals, already swelling in the heat and swarming with flies. We rode around the first water we came to; it had been a wide, though shallow pond that morning: now it little more than a mud flat ringed with the bodies of dead and dying nomads and their animals. From atop my mule, I could see that what little water there was left was an odd pink in color, from the blood. So we rode on.

We passed places where Sakae riders had been caught by a shower of arrows before they could come to grips with their Dahae opponents, where both riders and mounts lay in a loosely grouped formation, feathered by the shafts that had slain them. We passed places where the Dahaes had been caught between two groups of their enemies, or penned in a gully or pinned against a dune by Sakae riders, and the smaller nomads and their diminutive mounts had been slaughtered without downing even one of their enemies. A knife won't take you very far against an enemy twice your size armed with lance and saber. That is why typical Dahae tactics was to scatter and avoid melee with heavier opponents, taking a shot or two over their shoulders at their pursuers. But the Dahaes, although more numerous than their Sakae enemies, had to split their forces to cover both flanks. This gave the Sakae riders a local superiority in numbers, which they made the most of. After driving the Dahae tribesmen from the field, those Sakae riders still able to fight regrouped and began slashing at the flanks of the nomads fleeing the battlefield. Their pursuit was persistent and lethal; superbly mounted, ably led by their own chiefs, they were held to the mark and critically bear-led by a sprinkling of Imperial officers, often from the Red Sakar Lancers. There are blood feuds in Scythia older than most nations; scores of those feuds were settled, and others started, in the three days of pursuit that spattered the soil of Scythia with blood from Roaring Springs to the Scarred Place.

The second waterhole we found had a number of refugees like ourselves, scattered in twos and threes around its muddy margin. Ajax wanted to talk to the largest group (four men and women, some who looked to be Khetarite tribesmen); he threw the reins of his mule to me, and told me to get our water bags filled first, then let the mules drink. They were in pretty bad shape, and wouldn't last us nearly as long as we would need. I walked over to a likely spot near two men who were lying prone at the water's edge; when I got close, I realized it was really just one man, since his companion was staring sightlessly up at the sky with dead eyes. They weren't nomads; they wore the non-descript clothing and leather armor common to mercenaries and adventurers in many lands. Both men's clothes were stained with blood, and the one who was still breathing had the broken stub of an arrow protruding over his belt, just to the left of the buckle. A belly wound was never something to laugh at; here, now, it meant death, barring a miracle. He heard me coming, and jerked around, half drawing a greatsword from its sheath; both the hilt and the sheath had seen a lot of wear, but the blade was well cared for.

"Who's there", he barked, and then bit back a groan as the motion jarred the arrow in his gut. He blinked and squinted at me; that wasn't good. His color was bad, and if he was having trouble seeing, he wasn't going to be waiting on this side of the Veil much longer.

"Steady. Just someone who wants water; I can go somewhere else."

"Wait, please." His voice stopped me. Aunt Syara had taught me that the wishes of those about to die should be respected as much as possible. Besides, my words to him had been in the common tongue, but his response had been in the language of Khetar; that meant he recognized my accent.

"You want water? Take mine, you'll need it. And take this", holding out his sword to me, "you will need this too. Forged it myself, at my father's anvil, and no one's hand but mine has ever swung it. Be damned if I'll let a nomad or some imperial scum get it. Take it, boy."

I kneeled in front of him, speechless, and took the sword from his hands. The gift of three full waterbags was priceless at a time like this, but it was the gift of the sword that dazed me. It is one thing to buy a sword, or to even take one as spoil of battle; there are even times when robbing the dead is the only recourse open to you. But to receive a sword from the hands of a warrior before he dies, that has a certain meaning to it for those who follow Tarhunt. It is, in a sense, a gesture of trust. For me, a boy who had yet to draw blade in battle, it was both an honor and a burden.

"Thank you. I... I won't let your blade be dishonored", I stammered.

He fell back as soon as I took the sword, and began to spit blood. I clasped his shoulder to steady him, and he turned to look me in the face.

His eyes were starting to film over, but they widened. "I know you! You....". Then he died.

I walked the mules over to Ajax and the people he was speaking to when I had finished watering the mules. They weren't going to last much longer, but there was no need to be cruel to them. I was introduced to those who we would be traveling with from then on. Two of them were from Khetar, and the others were a Roxolani woman and a Jarrian warrior who had both lost their mounts. Vargast and his son Donal were of the Abasgi tribe, at least originally. I got the impression that the Imperial authorities were interested in both of them. Donal wasn't that much older than me and very clever, but had a sour disposition; understandable considering his heavily bandaged knee. His father Vargast didn't say much and seemed to spend most of his time worrying. The Roxolani warrior was Leera, she pulled her own weight, but kept her own counsel, and rarely spoke. The Jarrian said his name was Adadniril, but to call him Niril. Since I never heard him say more than a few score other words during the time we traveled together, I can't tell you much more about him. He was good with a sword, better with a bow, and his weapons and armor were well cared for; and he never faltered in a fight. I've seen worse epitaphs.

One other companion joined us at that time. Not far from us, a lone wisent was hitched to a travois, with a badly wounded nomad tied into it. Astride the bison was a second nomad, a warrior of middle years with his shield arm in a sling, and he was arguing with a third member of his tribe, a big man armed with sword and axe. The big one didn't seem to be paying attention to anything the other was saying; he finished checking the wounded man in the travois, the saddle bags and straps and finally rubbed the bison's face good bye with a surprisingly gentle gesture; all without saying a word or changing expression. The mounted nomad gave up talking and just stared at the other in frustration, and then suddenly he leaned from the saddle and ruffled the big man's hair, and I realized that they were kin. After saying something in a low voice, the warrior on the bison turned his mound and rode away to the southeast, and the big man slung a pack over his shoulder and strode over to us. Neither nomad wasted time looking after the other, but I knew what I had seen: three nomads, all from one family, and only one mount. The strongest had given the wounded the only mount so they would have the best chance of getting away, while he took his chances on foot. Well, there weren't enough mounts to go around as it was, and we would all be on foot soon anyway.

I saw that I had misjudged his age because of his size; up close he wasn't any older than me, but he certainly was big, the kind of big that looks fat and sleepy, but can be full of surprises. His weapons were well cared for and he bore the sigils of Tillar, the Bull who rules the desert winds; when he came up to us, the others looked at him doubtfully, but Ajax only said:

"So, you'll be traveling our way for a while?"

The bison rider touched his sword hilt and said "Yes, Lord.". Ajax nodded and turned away to lead his mule to the south. That was good enough for me. I nodded at him and said:

"My name's Joren; I'm from a village near Melid, in Issuria."

He looked me over and said "You have not been given a battle name yet?".

I realized I was still covered with dried steer blood, and that I must look to be older and more experienced than I was. I shook my head and said:

"This isn't the blood of my enemies; it's the blood of something that fell on me. I have not killed yet." It wouldn't do to start off with a lie; that tends to lead to complications.

His eyes widened a bit, he hesitated and then said:

"I have not killed yet either; my name is Evar, of the Blood Skull clan."

I nodded at him and said: "You want to carry some of this water?"

He straightened at that; in Scythia, you don't give any of your water to someone who is just tagging along.

"Yes. Nice sword."

"Thanks."

That was how I met Evar Redcap, the Khan with the Red Hat, who the Sakae Queen would curse with her dying breath, and for whom the Empire of the White Sun would one day offer a reward of 20,000 pieces of silver. Later, Ajax asked me about the greatsword and the extra waterbags. When I told what had happened, he thought a while and then spoke:

"And he knew your face, your father's face. What did he look like?"

"Nothing out of the ordinary, for a mercenary. He had the arms of a blacksmith, and plenty of scars. Blue eyes, red hair going grey; not much past early middle age, and he had a short sword and 3 knives: belt, boot and another in a sheath down his back."

"Hmm. Let's have a look at its maker's mark." Every sword bears the mark of the smith who wrought it, and I had to unwind the leather wrappings on the hilt to find the sign etched into the tang of the greatsword. When I did, it sent a chill through me. It was the outline of a hare's head, under the shape of a spreading oak, the sign of the Mabirshan tribe, MY tribe.

"Mabirshan, Silver Hare clan. I didn't know that clan's warriors very well; he must have been one of those who left after your father's death, either because he displeased Ketil or because he refused to serve him."

The Silver Hares had been one of the clans wiped out by the Lupakui raid that slew my uncle Ketil. I could feel the hair standing up on my arms and the back of my neck: a sword that was the gift of a dying warrior with no name, from a clan that was dead, from a tribe that was no longer thought to exist, except by me and Ajax.

"You were meant to have that sword, boy. That means you're going to need it."

It was a fine weapon: it took a keen edge, and had a well-tempered blade just over a yard in length; the balance was nigh perfect. Turned out Ajax was right, I did need it. We pushed on through that night, which was only a little cooler than the day; we could see the heat sucking the life out of our mules while we watched. The sky to the north of us was lit by a dozen red glows, and even as far south as we were, the wind brought the smell of burnt meat. The Empire was burning its dead; the dead of its enemies were stripped of anything of value and left for the carrion eaters. From time to time, we heard shouts or screams from the north or west of us, but we were not attacked. An hour before dawn, our mules gave out and we killed and butchered them. After sharing out the meat, we continued south for a few hours and then laid up in a draw to rest.

Except for our lookouts, we spent that first day trying to get as much sleep as possible. It wasn't easy; a half a dozen times the appearance of a band of Sakae riders would cause a lookout's hiss to jerk us awake, gripping our weapons and blinking the sleep out of our eyes in preparation for a fight. The first watch was kept by Ajax, who seemed to be made of iron, but we all took our turn. My turn came in mid-afternoon; I relieved Leera, who stopped me before she headed back to her blanket roll.

"There is something out there; something that watches. I don't know if it's watching for us, but it's out there. No birds will fly over this place, and nothing larger than a beetle will show itself."

I took a look around, careful not to expose any more of myself than I had to while I scanned the surrounding area. It seemed pretty empty to me: grasses bleached by the heat, some dying thorn bushes, some wilted flowers. Then, without any kind of sound to warn me, a spearman of the Red Hunters stood up, no more than 60 yards east of us. He just stood there, arms folded, waiting. Evar had awakened about the same time as me, and was wolfing down a snack of mule meat and bison cheese on bread (it tastes better than it sounds), when he heard my breath hiss between my teeth. He picked up his axe and made his way over to me, taking care not to step on anyone.

"Something wrong?", he asked.

"There's a Red Hunter loitering out there, waiting to be noticed."

"Hmm. I'll watch; you go get the Old Man with a Sword."

"Right".

I tiptoed over to where Ajax was sleeping, and squatted on my haunches next to him. That was enough to awaken him; he looked a question at me.

"Company. A warrior of the Mitas Hwarni; I think he was with the regiment at the battle, but I'm not sure. He's just standing out there, waiting."

"Ah." He sat up, rubbing his face, and took a swig from his water bag. After looking at the sky and around the camp, he said:

"What is Evar eating?"

"Mule and bison cheese on bread"

"Sounds good. Get some for me and put some garlic on it. I need to wake up."

He splashed a handful of water on his face, and then rinsed his mouth with another, grimacing at the taste. Well, if you eat garlic with your mule, you had better be prepared for a sour mouth when you wake up. I prefer onion, myself. The Red Hunter's name was Kakaw Longtrail, and he was the leader of a group of spearmen who had been sent away from the phalanx at Roaring Springs before the battle engulfed them. The captain of the Red Hunters and their shaman had taken Ajax's words to heart, and had selected those warriors who bore heirlooms or where the last of their clan's fighters, and sent them south in a bid for safety. They had been ordered to return to their tribe, so that something might be saved from the disaster that they had foreseen. So they had come south to this place, running at a pace that would have killed any horse of mortal birth, to wait for us.

"Wait for us?". That took even Ajax by surprise.

"Yes. Our shaman, The Twisted One, told us that to reach our families, we would go where the living do not walk, and one who was marked by Wurrunk would lead the way."

Ajax was silent for a moment. "All right. We'll travel together."

This brought our numbers up over 100; we were safer in one way and in more danger in another: the smaller war bands might seek easier prey, but would alert others to our passage. Sooner or later, we were going to attract the wrong kind of attention, from an enemy force big enough destroy us. We just had to make sure we were out of their reach before they tracked us down. Ajax said we would have a better idea where we stood after taking stock at the next waterhole. Long Ear Springs had a year-round supply of good water, and even some fruit trees gone wild. If the spring was unoccupied, we would stock up on water and whatever was edible and then head south. If there were other survivors of the nomad army there, we would get water and news of the battle and its aftermath, and then head south.

If there were Imperial troops there, we would fight them for the water. It was that simple; there was no place farther south that could be reached with what little water we now had. If the Empire or its Sakae nomad allies held the waterhole, we would have to kill them and take the water. There were no other options.

Chapter XVI: Long Ear Springs

IT TURNED OUT THAT THE SPRING was indeed occupied, but not by our enemies. It held a disorganized mob of refugees from the battle, a few from almost every human tribe who had sent warriors to the disaster at Roaring Springs. We had started moving at dusk, and reached the springs a couple of hours after midnight; after careful scouting, we had identified ourselves as allies and not enemies, and moved in. Our entry into this poor man's oasis caused a bit of an uproar; there was only just enough to go around amongst eight score fighters. Nomads are a touchy bunch at the best of times; throw in the facts that they had just lost a battle and were being hunted like animals, and you can see why it almost came to a fight a dozen times before Ajax managed to calm everyone down and get them all pulling in the same direction. It helped that the Red Hunters don't need as much water as other people, and that our group outnumbered everyone else two to one. A damn good thing, too, because the Sakae hit us at dawn.

We hadn't been expecting them, exactly. Which was only fair, because they weren't expecting us, at least not so many of us. The Sakae riders had scouted the springs and its mob of refugees at sunset the day before; they had missed our arrival later that night. So when they attacked at sunrise, instead of forty or fifty disorganized, demoralized losers, they ran into more than twice their own number of fighters who had just been put in their places by an Attar of Warrunk, and more than 100 of them were the best spearmen in Scythia. What had started almost as a hunting party attempting to flush out two-legged game turned instantly into a desperate fight on both sides: theirs to disengage and sound the alarm for reinforcements, ours to kill every last Sakae attacker in order to delay the inevitable pursuit.

When the attack came off, I had just finished washing, by popular request. I had spent nearly a full day coated with dried blood and the cloud of flies buzzing around me had started to cast a shadow. They were the only ones who could stand being that close to me; I smelled so bad that Ajax had me walk downwind of everyone else and I couldn't blame him. A few hours before, once everyone had calmed down, the first order of business was to see that every container that could carry water was full.

Once that was done, we could bathe, being careful not to foul the tank that held the spring itself. Of course, the youngest, and those unproven as warriors got to go last; that included me, Evar and half a dozen others. Evar had finished first and went to get something to eat; I had just finished putting on my armor when the fighting started.

The pool we had bathed in was the last one and the lowest in elevation; a path lead up through the bushes to the level area where most of us slept and where the few mounts still alive were penned. That was where the main attack hit; when the alarm sounded, and the shouts and the screams began, the four of us left grabbed our weapons and ran up the path to the fight, me dead last because of this hitch in my step. That is probably why I survived the fight.

The main camp was a surging tangle of friends and foes. Those enemies nearest me were fighting in a 3 cornered knot, each covering the others' backs, two on foot and the other on horseback. The fighter still mounted was a nomad armed with saber and shield, who fought as if he and his mount were one creature armed with hooves, teeth and a blade. One of the dismounted fighters was a big woman with a two-handed axe hacking at a Red Hunter named Mahu Fourcrows, who was wounded and down on one knee parrying with a spear. The other was a woman who bore the sigils of a priestess of Bokar Sha, and whose saber glowed white and red with magic. Leera had dropped the priestess's mount, and paid for it with her life; the big woman had dismounted to guard her lady. Then we came up the path from the spring; the four of us ran at the priestess, and she started to kill us.

I rubbed the focus of the spell taught to me when I had sworn myself to Tarhunt, and I felt something run out of me and into my greatsword and set it thrumming in my hands. As I did, the priestess threw a dart winged with magic that took the Dahae tribesmen in front of me in the throat and dropped him. I leapt over the body as the first of us, a mercenary from Carchemish, reached our foe and swung at her with a mace and missed. Before he could recover, she hacked him down with a blow that sheared through his leather armor and sent him spinning to his knees, one hand trying to hold in the blue ropes of his entrails. The third of us to attack her was a Roxolani using his lance like a two-handed spear; I saw the priestess's empty left hand clench and then open as she raised it above her head. It was engulfed by a brilliant white orb that she threw into the face of the Roxolani before his weapon could reach her, and the nomad dropped to his knees, screaming and clawing out his own eyes. I came up last, and as she shifted stance to face me, the priestess slipped in Leera's blood and feel to her knees and one hand. Her face came up, her eyes widened as she looked into my face and we both knew she was already dead.

As I swung my sword back behind me for a strike at the priestess, the world seemed to slow and almost stop around me. My movements slowed as well, but I seemed to have all of the time in the world to consider my actions. I realized that I was not facing one opponent, but four: the priestess, her guardian, the nomad and his mount, who was helping to keep two warriors at bay with his hooves and teeth. The best position to attack the four of them was from within their formation, so I leapt past the priestess and pivoted as I swung my greatsword from the waist; the edge caught her underneath the chin and I pulled it *through*. I felt her blood scald me, and then I was past her body and behind the other imperial fighters. In a continuation of the same swing, I slashed at the left haunch of the nomad mount to my right and heard it scream as I hamstrung it.

I pulled the blade from the horse and swung again, right to left; as I did, I heard a second scream as the animal fell on its rider and broke his leg, pinning him to the ground. I put my weight behind my sword as I swung at the woman with the axe; she was just now realizing that her companion was dead, and was starting to turn to face me when my blade caught her in the back of the neck, beneath the tail of her helm. Head and helmet flew off, and I pivoted again, to bring my sword down on the neck of the Sakae warrior, and then I swung again to split the skull of his mount which was screaming in agony. The world speeded up again to its normal pace, and I heard someone sobbing as if his heart would break, and I realized that it was me.

Part of me seemed to step back and wonder: "This is what you have been waiting for? To slay your enemies in battle? To earn honor and respect from these other warriors? To take the revenge that is rightfully yours? Then why is it that all you feel is sick?"

The other part of me kept moving. I stooped so that Mahu could get his hand on my shoulder, and then straightened as he heaved himself up onto his one good leg. A Sakae brave ran at us with an axe, howling through a mask of blood. I parried the axe, and Mahu drove his spear into the nomad's mouth, and then tugged it free of the corpse as it fell. We were startled by a thunderous uproar to the northeast, and yet a third group joined the fight at Long Ear Springs: more than 200 warriors on foot, the last of the Sandasi and Red Hunters to survive the battle at Roaring Springs had come up behind the Sakae riders and lit into them with a fury driven by desperation and a thirst for revenge.

Every Sakae still mounted and not locked in melee turned and rode like hell for the south and west. A hail of javelins dropped most of their mounts, but some would have gotten away if Niril hadn't managed to fight his way to his bow and quiver. He stuck his sword into the ground and after stringing his bow in a single movement, sent a steady stream of arrows into the handful of the mounted nomads attempting to flee the springs, until the ravine to the southwest was choked with the bodies of kicking and screaming horses and their riders. But one almost got away. One rider had spurred his mount straight up hill and had almost reached the crest of the rise to the south. He was out of javelin range, and as Niril drew a feathered shaft to his ear, one last Sakae brave burst free of the melee to the north. He was armed with a lance and he bore down on Niril from behind, determined to kill the archer or draw his fire away from the one Sakae tribesman who might get away to summon the rest of his tribe's warriors for a vengeful pursuit. Half a dozen of the Sandasi lion people bounded after the nomad, clawing at his mount's heels, but they were too late.

A score of us yelled a warning, and Niril heard us, I'm sure of it. He knew what might happen if he did not drop to the ground or dodge away from the threat coming at him from behind. He also knew what would happen to all of us if this last Sakae rider got over the hill and away to summon the other Sakae bands we knew to be in the area. So he chose a chance for life for all of us, over a chance for life for just himself, and made his last shot count. His last arrow struck the Sakae antelope on the crest of the southern hill just behind the rib cage, and went on into the heart; it reared up and fell backwards, rolling over its rider twice and both bodies slid into the ravine below. An instant after his shaft cleared his bow, his killer's lance tore through his back and out his chest; then we were on his slayer.

The biggest of the Sandasi warriors leapt onto the hindquarters of the Sakae's mount just as I cut its forelegs out from underneath it. It slammed nose first into the ground, pitching its rider over its head and right into Evar's lap. The nomad was trying to lunge to his feet, on hand on his sabre's hilt, when Evar split his skull with a blow of his axe. I went to stand by Niril's body, and Evar came over to join me.

"What was his name again? His full name?"

"Adadniril"

"I'll remember."

We killed the last of the Sakae riders, and buried our dead.

After he had checked to see if I was still breathing, Ajax oversaw the redistribution of water and supplies and the rest of us stripped anything of value from our enemies' bodies. I was a bit hesitant to touch the bodies of those I had killed, but they had food and water we needed, and they might have valuables and magic that would help me further along the road I had chosen. Not to mention the fact that my enemies would do the same to me, and if I didn't loot the bodies of the people I killed, someone else would. I found silver and even some gold, and a good shortsword, along with two matrices for spells, which I would have looked at later. The nomad's armor was no better than my own, and that of the priestess and her bodyguard wouldn't fit me, but I found something around the neck of the priestess that raised the hair on the back of my neck: an iron amulet set with a yellow stone half the size of my fist, and the stone glowed of its own light. I had picked up the amulet with the end of a knife and was wondering what Ajax would think of it when a shout behind me just about scared me out of my breeches.

"AHUUU!" It was Mahu Fourcrows, and he was standing (his wounded leg healed with magic) with his spear raised in both hands over his head.

"AHUUU!" Every one of his fellow tribesmen had turned to look at him and hear what he had to say, as did everyone else in sight. Ahuuu means roughly 'Hear my words', and is a formal request for attention. Mahu lowered his spear in one hand and pointed with the other at me:

"I see you, Warrior, Swordsman, Chopper of Necks, *N'kopje!* "

N'kopje means "Beheader" in the speech of the Red Hunters. Those of his tribe who had seen me fight shouted "Vov! N'kopje!" in witness. All of those who had seen their first fight here and lived to tell of it were also named and saluted as fellow warriors. And last I heard Ajax's voice:

"You! I see you, Warrior, Bull's Servant, His helm runs red with the blood of his enemies!"

Ajax had stepped forward to name Evar as a warrior and give him his battle name; it was a bit long, but fair. In Scythian, it almost sounds poetic. Ajax took my amulet and a shimmering red scimitar he had taken from the body of his opponent, a captain of the Red Sakar Lancers who had been riding with his Sakae cousins. Laying them on a flat rock, he pounded them into powder and broken shards using another rock and the pommel of his sword. Turning to those of us watching, he explained:

"They could have tracked us more easily with those, but make no mistake: they will track us down eventually no matter what we do, as long as we stay where they can reach us. We have to move, now, if we are to have any chance of evading those who pursue us. We are probably the largest group of fighters left this close to Roaring Springs, and that means we will draw our enemies to us like a gutted deer draws flies."

One of the Sandasi spoke up:

"Go where, Old Man? There are dust clouds the length of the Vulture's Trail to our west and as far east as Dwarf Hill. We are caught between two horns, and they are closing fast, faster than we can move on foot."

"Then we go where the horns cannot close on us. We go through the Scarred Place."

There was complete silence.

"Is there any other choice?"

No one could come up with one, so we packed and left Long Ear Springs behind us. We weren't very cheerful about it; only the mad, the desperate and the outlawed entered the Scarred Place. But since we were all at least two of the three by that time, we moved right along. We numbered about 360 all told at that point; 250 or so of the Red Hunters, three score Sandasi and the rest a collection of Khetarite adventurers and survivors of the other tribes who had fought at Roaring Springs. Most of the latter were mounted, on a collection of horses and mules, one of which Ajax rode, since its rider had not survived the fight at the springs. That was all that was left in northern Scythia of the nomad horde that had gathered at Roaring Springs two days before.

We headed southeast, with Ajax in the lead; he seemed to know his way around this part of Scythia, but then he seemed to know his way around pretty much every place I ever went with him. I began to wonder, for the first time in my life, just how old Ajax was. I still don't know for sure. I walked at his side; he was silent at first, but then he spoke to me quietly:

"Do you remember what Kakaw said, back there yesterday, when they first joined us?"

"Yes, sir. Something about going where the living do not walk, and one marked by Warrunk would guide them."

"That's right. Except that we are both marked by Warrunk, and the one their shaman spoke of could just as easily be you as me."

"Me!? What do I know about the Scarred Place? I've never even seen it!"

"Stop babbling and listen to me, boy. It's easy enough, at least to know, it might be a little bit harder to actually do it, but that's the way life is. Now, look where I'm pointing, look right down the length of my arm. Do you see that mountain down that away, that peak that looks like a bear sleeping on his side?"

"Yes." More like a bull than a bear, but yes, I saw it.

"That's the mountain some call the Guardian; it is the westernmost of the mountains in Inara's Garden, and it is on the other side of the narrowest part of the Scarred Place. If something happens to me, or we get separated, you head for that mountain. If I'm alive, I'll see you somewhere between the Scarred Place and that peak. We'll be safe enough once we get to Inara's Garden; it would cost the empire more than the lot of us are worth to send an army there, and we have those among the tribes who will vouch for us, now. At least as guests, anyway. But listen to me Joren: once you enter the Scarred Place, no delays, no detours, you just go straight on through as fast as you can. Do you understand me, boy? People who dawdle or get lost in that place do not come out."

"Yes, sir. I'll remember."

We moved as fast as we could, and all around us we saw signs that the Empire and its Sakae allies were drawing their net tight in an attempt to catch every fish they could. For the Sakaes, this was just the way war was fought: those you killed, you looted; those you captured, you sold or ransomed. For the Empire of the White Sun, it was more a matter of nits make lice; kill your enemies while they're small, and you won't have to worry about them when they're big. We changed that; we were so big a target, we couldn't be missed, but we were too big for most war bands to deal with. They had to join up with other bands and troops of riders in order to coordinate an attack, and in doing so, other fugitives were able to slip through the net.

By mid-morning, we knew we had been spotted. By mid-day, we knew that we had at least two cavalry forces coming up behind us, each at least as big as our own group, as well as two or three small bands on our flanks. We stopped a mile or so short of the northern edge of the Scarred Place for a mouthful of meat or bread and two mouthfuls of water to wash it down, while some of the best hunters went to scout ahead. They soon returned, with word of a holding force already in place ahead of us. I heard Mahu report to Ajax:

"No more than five or six tens in number, the ugly ones who stink and who ride under the totem of the big pigs. They have made a cold camp and have three of their pigs with them, but they don't seem to be expecting us. A trap, maybe?"

"Skula. Hmm, maybe a trap, but I think it may be that either they've gotten sloppy because they think anyone that they'll face has already been beaten, or they just haven't been told yet. Skula are no one's favorites; they might just be last in line to hear of us, or someone might want them to take a beating, they are that unpleasant."

"Are the pigs good eating?" queried a woman not more than 2 or 3 years my senior, but who was at least 2 meters tall, with the golden eyes of an angry hawk.

"Not bad, but they've got a lot of gristle", Ajax replied.

"Heh, a heh" laughed the woman, whose name was Galazi. "We might as well charge them now then, because everyone knows that Mahu can't walk past any animal he hasn't tasted yet."

"And why not?", preened Mahu. "Hunting, and eating what you hunt, is one of the three things that make life worth-while." I asked him what the other two were, and he replied "Your mate, and the children they give you."

That made me think of Bel; I could still feel our link and her feelings: worry for me, and a growing resentment of what was keeping us apart: the White Sun Empire. That was good; I'd heard that every couple should share one great passion. Ajax decided to move in and then charge the Skula ahead of us when we got to within bow range. We began to spread out as we moved forward, but about half of a mile short of our target, some of our flankers came in to report: there was a newer and bigger mounted force coming up behind us and to the west, and the first two groups we had spotted before were picking up speed. Ajax called a halt:

"We're going to change our plans. I think the Imperials are using the Skula as unwitting bait in a trap. They expect us to get caught up with crushing their mercenaries, and then they plan on hitting us in the rear while we're disorganized. Here is what we'll do: Our main force will run right over the Skula; no prisoners, no pursuit, just go straight through them and into the Scarred Place. Anyone else on foot who doesn't want to risk the Scarred Place can try cutting out to the east, and everyone who is mounted will come with me; we are going to create a diversion for that cavalry to deal with. Any questions? No? Then let's get to it."

Ajax gripped my shoulder in farewell and told me: "Remember."

171

"Good luck and good hunting", was all I could get out, and then we split up.

Our force of about 300 or so spread out into a long, shallow crescent and we came up over a swell in the ground about 100 yards from the three score Skula in our path. Right away, we could see they hadn't been expecting that many of us. There was a moment of indecision and then they tried to make a run for it, half bolting to the west and the others making a run to the east. That moment of indecision cost them, for when we caught sight of our enemies, the Sandasi and the Red Hunters readied their javelins and began to run, and for the first time, I realized how much the rest of us had slowed them down.

The Sandasi are the children of the Lion god, said to have been slain before Time began, and although they have been bound in servitude to the nomads of Scythia ever since, the blood of lions still runs in their veins. A Sandasi warrior thinks nothing of jumping 6 or 7 meters in a single leap, or of bounding 3 or 4 meters into the air. They formed the outer horns of our crescent, and I could hear some of them roaring as they closed in for the kill. The Red Hunters are the descendants of an army of spearmen who have fought in Horus's name since before the Pyramids were built, and they scorn the thought of going anywhere on anything but their own two feet. They split into two lines, one lead by Kakaw to the left and the other by Mahu on the right, and they leapt ahead of us, each man and woman in their own place, their measured strides like the beating of a heron's wings. By the time they were within throwing range, they had matched steps, and a hail of javelins dropped half of the Skula, horses and riders. The Red Hunters locked shields and charged the Skula in formation, moving almost as fast as a horse could run. They swept over their foes in a thrusting, stabbing tide and the Empire's mercenaries never had a chance.

I had slowed to a walk, and was watching this with my mouth hanging open, when Evar nudged me in the shoulder:

"If you're going to be leading THEM anywhere, shouldn't you start to pick up the pace?"

"Huh? Oh, right. Let's go, then."

By the time we caught up with the rest of our group, the Sandasi had stripped what they wanted from those they had killed, and were grouped together. The tallest of them nodded to me, and said to Kakaw:

"We go now, east to where our prides wait. THAT place has no luck for us; we will go east and lie low in the tall grass, until the Red Ones who fight for the White Sun and the Sakaes pass us by and seek other prey. If we live, we will hunt together again, for the Red Ones and their spears will not forget that we strove against them. I think we will seek each other's blood until the world changes around us."

"I think you see both far and straight, Ssuegar. Good Hunting."

We saluted them, and they loped off to the east without a backward glance. I looked over the men and women stripping the enemy dead of anything of value, and a thought came to me, something about the unclean habits of the Skula, who were rumored to be cannibals. Mahu came up then; he had been scouting out the lay of the land to the west of us by the simple trick of standing on the shoulders of two of his fellow tribesmen. From this vantage point, a good 4 meters above the ground, he had seen something of interest to us all.

"The Old Man with a Sword is playing tricks with the Sakaes", he grinned. "It looks like he had every warrior tie a bush or branch to a rope or length of rawhide, and drag it behind their mounts. They raised a dust cloud big enough for a thousand riders, and he lead them due west. The Sakaes know it is some kind of trick, but they pulled all of their riders into one group to deal with any real threat they might run into. Then, he stopped dragging bushes and lit a brush fire, just to further confuse the issue. Now it looks as if the Old Man is starting to move off to the south, daring the Sakaes to a race the length of the Vulture's Trail."

"Buying us time."

Kakaw turned to me, as did everyone in earshot. "So, You Who Has Been Marked by Warrunk, do you have anything to say before you lead us to safety?"

I could understand the sarcasm under the circumstances: a proven warrior of more than twice my years needing MY help to survive in the land he was born in? Sometimes shamans can be extremely irritating, even when they're dead.

"Yes. Check every canteen, every waterbag and every bottle you stripped from these bodies. The Skula mix blood with their water and their ale." I had remembered that from one of Ajax's lessons; it is a filthy habit.

"Blood? You mean blood from their herds, the way the other riders do, sometimes?", asked Galazi.

"No. They drink the blood of those they torture, and I have heard they eat the flesh of those they kill that way."

Fully half of the supplies taken from the Skula was fouled in some way.

173

We discarded them, and then everyone still with us formed up around me, where I stood with my arms folded, thinking.

"I'm not going to make a secret of this, so listen up. The Old Man with a Sword told me that the peak he called the Guardian marks the narrowest part of the Scarred Place. That is where we're heading. If I go down, or if we get separated, go straight for the Guardian, no waiting, no side trips. Any questions? Then let's go."

Then I turned and set my foot in the Scarred Place.

Chapter XVII: The Scarred Place

LONG AGO, BEFORE TIME BEGAN, the gods fought their enemies (and each other) for possession of the world before men were born, and much of our world was broken, destroyed or lost. In some places, the signs of that titanic struggle are still visible; the Scarred Place is one such sign. It is irregular in shape, and 40 miles or so across, depending on where you enter it. It is uneven, broken land and something terrible happened there to drain it of all life. The earth in the Scarred Place is lifeless, without power or magic of any kind. Spells will not work there; indeed magic of any kind dies in the Scarred Place, if you stay there long enough. Enchantments and charms will fade, and the souls of the living weaken little by little, day by day, as if something in that place is leaching it from them. It is said that even the elves and darklings will become mortal, should they enter the Scarred Place, that some western wizards call the Lair of the Abhorrent.

When I set foot in the Scarred Place, it was if I had set foot in another world, and the line between Scythia and that world is sharply drawn. The soil of Scythia is thin and dry stuff, but still fertile enough to support the grasses that the herds feed off of. The soil of the Scarred Place is not much more than blasted ash and gravel drifted between ridges of sharp-edged rock; what few plants grow there are found only around its edges and are poisonous to the taste or touch. There are no animals in the Scarred Place; birds will not fly over it, nor will even insects dwell there. Wild animals will turn and fight a hunter before crossing its boundary, and even domesticated animals must be whipped or spurred before they will enter it.

The only place in this barren waste that is not leached of all life is within the ruins of the old ring fort known as Khipa's Crown, right on the eastern edge of the Scarred Place. I had heard that it was a palace or a prison (maybe both) before time began, but was abandoned after the disaster that blighted this area. So it is possible to find water and even grazing there, just outside the borders of the Scarred Place, but we would avoid it. It would be the first place the imperial troops would search, and probably even garrison. The fringes of the Scarred Place were known to be the hiding places of the most desperate renegades and outlaws in Scythia, and Khipa's Crown would be the logical base for patrols in this area.

Moving into the network of sharp-edged gullies and crack-floored ravines of the Scarred Place, we were soon out of sight of the Skula encampment. The peak of the mountain called the Watcher was clearly visible at first, and we moved as quickly as possible. On open ground, in normal weather, we could have covered the distance from one side of the Scarred Place to the other in less than a day and a night, it is only about 25 miles or so.

It took us four days. The ground wasn't open, and the weather wasn't close to being normal. Even the wind seems to die in the Scarred Place; any kind of movement kicks up a fine alkaline dust that just seems to hang there, and it gets into everything. It burns the eyes and the mouth, cracks lips, and cuts at the lungs and the sinuses. By nightfall of the first day, we all had blood in our spit. The land itself was a barrier; a maze of gullies and ravines lined with rocks sharp enough to cut leather, without paths or game trails. Often we had to climb over, up or down shelves of rock and small cliffs.

Normally, we would have pushed on a bit under the cover of darkness, but here we had to make camp at sunset. Some of those cliffs were high enough to reward a misstep with death or maiming, and we had noticed that those who were nursing wounds were not healing right. And over it all was the feeling that the place itself was draining us, sucking at our spirits, eroding our power, our magic and our lives bit by bit, day by day. I had felt it the first instant my boot touched the soil of this wasteland, and so had some of the others; by the middle of the second day, everyone could feel it. That was when we ran into the first trap. We were moving through a particularly nasty little maze of twisting fissures, when I realized no one was behind me. I turned around and saw that everyone else had stopped a dozen paces back, and were standing as if listening.

"What is it?", I asked Kakaw.

"Can't you hear it? It sounds like a child's voice; over there.", he said, pointing to our left, to the northeast.

"Not a child, a woman", said one.

"No, a young girl", said another spearman, as he and several others slid their packs from their shoulders and prepared to go searching for whoever owned the voice they heard.

A voice that I could not hear at all.

"Hold, let me listen", and I held my breath and waited. Nothing, except off in the distance, I heard what might have been the ringing of a single silver bell. From the northeast, in the direction of Khipa's Crown. That is when I felt it: the cold whisper of Warrunk's gift to me.

"Death" it said. "Death comes in the chiming of a silver bell."

"There it is again"; this was from Evar.

"What do you hear?" I asked him.

"I hear...something." He seemed reluctant to say, and I think what they heard was different for each man and woman.

"Hold!" roared Kakaw, and his tribesmen stopped in their tracks. He turned to me. "But you hear nothing", he said.

"I hear the ringing of a single bell, from the direction of Khipa's Crown. It is a trap, an Imperial trick of some kind. That place is the most likely one for the Imperials to garrison, and I think that they have brought a magic there, perhaps a person, perhaps just a thing, and its sound is madness. Remember, they don't have to strike us with sword or shaft in this waste. All they have to do is confuse us, delay us or get us lost, and the Scarred Place will kill us for them."

"How is it that you hear this bell and not the voice?" Galazi asked.

"The one who raised me was a woman of power; she and the Old Man with a Sword thought that the imperial magic that almost killed me as a child, broke something inside of me. I think...it is what was broken that the magic of that bell speaks to, and I am deaf to it."

I think also, that the lifebond that I shared with Bel shielded me from this magic as well, or at least in part. But I would not speak of Bel, or our gift in this place. I could not feel Bel all of the time, not since we entered the Scarred Place. I was beginning to fear our bond was breaking.

Kakaw nodded once when he heard my explanation.

"The Twisted One saw this. He saw you would lead us through this trap. Lead now, and we follow." He turned to the others in line behind us.

"Let each tie their right hand to harness of the warrior in front of them, and grip them tight. We move now, and will not stop again until we hear these voices no more."

Kakaw tied his hand to my baldric, and then we pushed on, slowing sometimes as someone would lose their footing and be dragged. It was two hours before we were out of range of that bell's magic and could stop; when we did, many were in tears or were swearing horribly and spitting blood from bitten lips. When we counted heads that night, we found we were short an even score of warriors. Two were Red Hunters, the others had been almost everyone else in our column who was not a member of Kakaw's tribe. That left only me, Evar, a woman from Carchemish called Hamsha and a Thracian who called himself Joppar the Pick who were not

Red Hunters. No one suggested going back, and I didn't blame them. Our tracks were clear enough; if they came to their senses soon enough, they could trail us out. But none of them made it.

The third day dawned through an odd kind of haze that persisted throughout the day. We found that we had to periodically stand someone on another's shoulders to get a bearing on the peak of the Watcher. It didn't seem to be getting any closer, and a look at our back trail didn't seem to show any changes either. We seemed to spend that entire day moving through a pain-filled dream that just went on and on. We finally stopped that night, and I had never been that tired before in my life. I was leaning against flat rock at the top of a ridge we were climbing, taking a drink. Mahu walked up to me and said:

"We must leave this place by sunset tomorrow, Young Walker, or we won't make it at all."

"We'll be out of water by then, won't we."

Not to mention the will to go on. Young Walker? When did they start calling me that?

"Just so. Remember to get something to eat before you sleep."

Food didn't sound all that appetizing just then. It might have if everything didn't seem to have the same gritty alkaline taste to it. Oh well. I braced myself against the corner of the boulder I was leaning on....corner? Rocks don't have corners, unless of course they are the stone lid on a ...TOMB? I backed away from it, shivering. A tomb? Here in the Scarred Place? I felt the hair on my neck start to rise. "Mahu! Get some torches!"

After a few moments, we all gathered around it, staring. It was set square to the four directions, with one side facing to the north, south, east and west. From the south side lead what could only be a by gods' ROAD, that lead spear straight off into the darkness. There were no symbols or sigils cut into the face of the tomb, just a massive bar of lead and a lock of a kind I had never seen before. Joppar had climbed up on one knee to examine the lock with an odd kind of professional interest, with Hamsha holding a torch to give him light. The Red Hunters were a bit uneasy and I was growing more and more afraid by the minute. Something told me to get away from this place, now.

"We go by the road tomorrow?", asked Evar.

"I'd say no." said Mahu. Kakaw and I agreed: south meant going the length of the Scarred Place, and there was no guarantee that what the road had been built to lead to was still there.

178

"Can you do it?" I heard Hamsha say to Joppar.

"Sure." he said.

"Do what?" I asked.

"Look kid, I realize your people sometimes have a problem with this sort of thing, but in Old Carchemish, we've been jumping ruins like this for years. Joppar says he can crack that lock; we open it up, take a look inside, grab anything that looks valuable and be on our way tomorrow. If you don't want any part of the loot, don't sweat it; you won't have to take any of the risk."

I was a little stunned by how dense they were, but I didn't have much of a handle on how greed and curiosity can twist some people's judgement, then. I could see where the nomads' wouldn't see it, they didn't have doors. But Hamsha and Joppar should have known better. All I said was:

"Think. If you wanted to keep someone OUT, what side of the door would the bar be on?"

I left it at that, and I shouldn't have. I should have set guards on the tomb, or kept moving or ...something. I wasn't thinking clearly, none of us were.

I didn't sleep well that night, even as tired as I was. I kept on having dreams of being locked in a dark place, and of hearing a thin piping sound, always repeated three times. I awoke at dawn in a bad mood, grumbling at Evar's tap on my boot until I got a good look at his face: he was afraid, and it takes a lot to scare a worshipper of the Bull. I looked to where he pointed, and choked back a panicky curse. None of us had slept close to the rise where the tomb was, but we could see that the lid of the tomb had been slid to one side. Joppar and Hamsha were nowhere in sight, but their bedrolls were, and a coil of rope had been tied to a rock outcrop, with its other end slung into the tomb. If that rope was Joppar's then it was about 50 meters long, and just then I heard three piping sounds and something tugged on the rope. A half dozen of us rushed the tomb. I had my sword out without realizing I had drawn it; I called out:

"Joppar? Hamsha?"

The only response I heard was something that sounded like a tittering laugh, and then three notes sounded on what might be reed pipes. From within the tomb.

I slashed the rope as the others threw their weight against the stone lid of the tomb. I heard that piping sound again, and caught a whiff of something very old and very rotten, and then the lid slid into place. We almost hurt ourselves slamming the lead bar back into place, but we couldn't figure out how to reset the lock. We didn't waste any more time than that. I sheathed my sword, Evar threw me my pack and we ran out of that place as if the entire Imperial army was chasing us. When we spoke later, we realized we had all had the same dreams the night before. I didn't hear those piping sounds again, and although the rearguard kept treading on everyone else's heels, neither did anyone else, so I guess the bar held. We never saw Joppar or Hamsha again, though.

The rest of that day is just one long blur of putting one foot ahead of the other. An hour or so before sunset, we came to the top of a long, rocky slope, and suddenly, we could feel the wind in our faces. Two more steps and we were in Scythia again, and our spirits were free of the draining pull of the Scarred Place. The lot of us fell face down in the dirt. I didn't rouse until I heard Mahu shout:

"Heya, Old Man!"

Between us and the mountain called the Guardian, I saw the light of the setting sun glint off a raised sword in the hand of an old man wearing grey, standing next to half a dozen mules and steers loaded with food and water. Ajax always did keep his word.

We parted ways with all but one of the Red Hunters there. They were to travel to the sacred grounds of Inara's Garden to meet with their people, and a sad tale they would carry with them. A thousand spears had their tribe sent against the Empire of the White Sun at Roaring Springs; only one in four would return. Before Kakaw lead his people away, he touched both Evar and I on the shoulders and said:

"May I see you again, Young Walkers".

He saluted Ajax with raised spear and rejoined his tribesmen; they saluted us with raised hands, and loped off to the southeast. One of them remained with us; his name was Ankubi, and I had seen him in conversation with Evar from time to time. He was a bit unusual for a Red Hunter in that he too was a follower of Tillar the Bull. He saluted Ajax and I with a raised spear, and asked if he could walk a ways with us, since he had no kin left and was curious to see the stone and wooden tents of the Roxolani. Ajax had no objections and I certainly didn't mind, so the four of us set out. Evar told me later that Ankubi has something of a reputation of being both a loner and a ferocious fighter. We got along well together, and made good time.

Later that night, Evar and I recounted our tale of the crossing of the Scarred Place to Ajax. He sighed when we told him of the tomb and loss of

Hamsha and Joppar, but said nothing. What Kakaw had called us had drawn his attention though.

"Young Walkers? When did they start calling you two that?" asked Ajax.

"After the second day", replied Evar.

"It is what they call their own children, the ones who are ready to pass the test to adulthood. It means that should either of you wish to be adopted into their tribe, anyone who has called you by that name is willing to be your sponsor. They are a proud people, and do not offer that honor lightly."

Evar and I looked at one another, slightly stunned. "Huh" was all either of us could manage.

We were going to the oasis at Three Altars, and Evar was coming with us. There is a Warrunki holy place there, and a good chance Evar would find some of his fellow tribesmen, sooner or later. Then he would be returning to his own people, but we wouldn't forget one another; something told both of us that we would meet again, and we did, many times. As for myself and Ajax, we were going to leave Scythia entirely. Ajax needed to speak to a few people first, farther south, and then we were going to Aleppo, the stronghold of the Roxolani. Ajax said he knew of a backway into Khetar from there, and we could go get Bel. I really didn't want to go anyplace without her; once we had Belkara with us, we would aim south.

"It is time you saw the land were your father was born, Joren, and where he grew up. And if she still lives, your father's sister."

I had an aunt on my father's side? Family? We would go to Thrace then, where the Minos ruled; I was starting to look forward to it. When we had gone about 9 or 10 miles to the southeast, Ajax said we were almost due west of Inara's Garden, which is the beating heart of Scythia. We could see the edge of the lands sacred to all Scythians, and it was so lush with green grass and thick brush that you would have thought it was a mirage, another world. Yet Ajax said that once, all of Scythia had been so green, with standing forests, before Time began. Then the gods made war upon each other; that had changed everything.

Our way did not lead to the Garden, so we turned southwest, and that is when I first noticed the storm clouds. We could see the trees that marked the oasis at Three Altars and behind them towered a mass of swirling clouds that stayed in the same place, yet were never still. I was about to call attention to this oddity, when Ankubi spoke:

"The Anvil wears a thick cloak indeed this day. They say it is often so when great battles are fought."

It wasn't just a storm I was looking at, but one of the wonders of the world: The Anvil (called by some The Anvil of The Gods). As we drew closer, I could make out the outlines of the Anvil through the storm clouds that eddied about it, and I felt something go very quiet inside me as I realized just how big it really was. The Anvil is more than a mile high, and about 3 tenths of a mile wide and nearly a mile long; it juts upward from the Scythian plains just as it has since the beginning of Time. Our legends say that the first iron swords were gods who fell from the sky, and the Anvil is where they were forged. It is also a place of power for Tillar the Bull and all who follow him. That is one of the reasons why the Anvil is guarded by bands of roaming nomads or minotaurs, and why they will kill anyone they catch who has come to the Anvil uninvited.

And come they do, from lands near and far, for the the Anvil is made of stone that is found nowhere else in the world. Godquartz is said to be magic in solid form, and is an imperial purple in color, shot through with shifting bands and clouds of gold. It cannot be worked with normal tools, and the only way to obtain it is to gather shards of it that are scattered around the base, or use magic to cut stone from the Anvil itself. This is taboo for any nomad, and is another reason why Tillar's Children slay outsiders found near the Anvil. This does not stop the outsiders from coming; I have since found that the Anvil has other names in other lands, and their sages know different stories about its origin and purpose.

As we traveled, we could see the storm clouds enshrouding the Anvil begin to peel away and move to the west, towards the southern branch of the Toros range, which we called the Thunderhead Mountains. The clouds almost seemed to be tied to the surface of the Anvil by flickering waves of lightning bolts that struck it over and over again, accompanied by thunder that we could clearly hear miles way. Eventually, the thunder and lightning died away, and the clouds moved some distance off to the west, leaving the Anvil standing alone. By the time we reached Three Altars, just before dusk, we could see that the angular shape of the Anvil was unobscured and as dark as any thunderhead. Three Altars has been a holy place for those who follow Warrunk for centuries, but it has no temple. Aside from the good water of the oasis itself and the palm and date trees that surround it, there is just the altar and a small natural amphitheater (at least it looked natural) that served as a dueling ground. The tales of lore that Ajax had taught me said that this place had seen challenges (both Trial by Combat and personal disagreements) issued and answered at least since Time began.

Normally, Warrunk's followers would see each other in this place only in passing, and never in large numbers. But Ajax said we could expect to see more in the aftermath of a battle such as Roaring Springs, and we did. There were Warrunki from what seemed to be every tribe in Scythia present, all seeking news of the recent battle and in particular, of the casualties suffered by the nomads. Those from tribes that did not send forces to the battle, such as the Royal Scythians, were eager to hear what any could tell them of the battle, and seemed not at all happy to hear of the Imperial victory. Those who had been present at the battle were engaged in something more somber and more important than passing news along; they were gathering what information they could about those who had fallen in the battle. It was often the duty of those who follow the god of death to bring the news of a warrior's death to his or her family, and the tally of the dead at Roaring Springs was high indeed.

There were a number of Traspian tribesmen there, and after speaking with them, Evar found that he and they had friends in common, though they were not of the same clan. Since they had a spare mount, Evar decided to join them and return to his people in their company. Ajax made sure his fellow tribesmen heard of Evar's deeds in the journey south from Roaring Springs and of how he had gotten his war name. They were quite pleased with Evar and soon began referring to him as Evar Red Helm or Bloodhelm. Evar didn't seem to mind. He thanked Ajax and then said good bye to me and Ankubi. He wished us good hunting, and told us we would see him again. He left the next morning, but he was right; when I returned to Scythia years later, I did see him again. We rode together against our common enemies more than once in the years that followed. By then, the Imperials wished they had killed us all at Roaring Springs several times over.

After seeing Evar on his way, we made the acquaintance of a one-eared Warrunki of the Roxolani tribe, by the name of Alton Whiteaxe. He was from Aleppo, and since our way would lead past the chief stronghold of the Roxolani, we had some questions for him. The most important being: Would we be welcome there? Losing friends and family tends to put people on edge. As it happened, word had spread of the fight at Long Ear Springs and of the Sakae pursuit and Alton thought we would be quite welcome.

"Might have some work for you, if you're a mind to work with cattle", he added.

Not so much herding, as keeping off the predators from what he said. This sounded interesting enough, but we weren't going to hanging around long enough for that. Nice of him to offer, though. We settled in for the night, planning on an early start, when we noticed that the stars were dimming. There was an odd purple light coming from the southwest, and every face in the oasis turned to its source: the light was coming from the Anvil. It waxed brighter and soon we could see quite clearly even though the Sun had set an hour before. I looked a question at Ajax, and he shrugged:

"Only the gods know why the Anvil does what it does."

I have never seen anything quite like it in the years since. The only thing that I can compare it to is the golden light that sometimes sheathes the Great Monuments of Egypt; but even then, it was different. The Anvil not only shed light, it seemed to contain swirls and clouds of light within it, all in constant movement. We were all practically entranced by the sight, until we heard the thunder of hooves approaching. A half dozen heavily armed and armored riders rode into the oasis, mounted on beasts from every scythian tribe; their leader rode a magnificent golden auroch and it was his voice that rang out in the silence:

"To all of those who fought at Roaring Springs, and who bear the mark and favor of their god: Hear yea the Voice of Tillar and come to the Anvil! Yea are summoned to both take counsel and to give counsel, for the World has changed around us and we must give thought to what we must do to face the old threat that these new invaders have brought to Scythia. Come to the Anvil, before the Sun sets again."

He struck the heel of his lance against the ground, once, and then twice in quick succession, and at this signal, all six riders wheeled their mounts and rode into the night, in the direction of the Anvil. Voice of Tillar? I turned to ask Ajax a question and saw that Ajax and a number of others were gathering their belongings and loading their mounts.

"You're leaving? Right now?"

"Yes. One does not ignore the summons of the Bull in his own backyard."

I gave him a hand, and when we were done, he turned to me:

"Listen, Joren, I've been to some of these gatherings before, and it could take a day or it could take a score of days. Why don't you talk to Arton about that offer he made; you might as well keep yourself busy while I'm occupied at the Anvil."

We found Arton and spoke to him about his offer; it was still open and he seemed glad enough to take us on. The Roxolani had lost far too many fighters in the past few years to be able to brush off the men and women lost at Roaring Springs. They could use our help and I could use the experience. Ankubi just wanted to see a town actually looked like with his own eyes; that and possibility of earning some hard money and getting in some good hunting was enough for him. We said good bye to Ajax for now, and traveled south and west alongside Arton Whiteaxe and two other Warrunki of the Roxolani tribe. Two days later, we sighted Aleppo.

Chapter XVIII: The Scent of a Wolf

A FEW WEEKS LATER, I had picked up some of the finer points of herding cattle and had become somewhat familiar with the fortress town of Aleppo, which the Roxolani had controlled for centuries. Since I had no idea how long it would be until Ajax finished his business at the Anvil, I was making myself useful by keeping cattle from wandering off and by putting down any of the local predators that tried to sneak in and pick off any of the calves born that season. Ajax would join me at Aleppo as soon as he could manage; he knew of a trail through the Thunderheads we could use to sneak back into Khetar and get Belkara, before we headed for Byzantium.

Aleppo is located in the foothills of the Thunderhead Mountains, south of Tuhus's river. It is the stronghold of the Roxolani tribe and the center of the cattle trade in Scythia. Because of the caravans that come in from Carchemish and because of its location near the borders of both occupied Khetar and to Lycia, which owes its allegiance to the Minos, Aleppo has a large and thriving market. The walled town lies uphill from a sprawling shantytown consisting of taverns, caravansaries, warehouses, brothels and barns. The walled town is well-defended and has never fallen to either attack or treachery. The shantytown, on the other hand, has been burned to the ground at least a half dozen times.

The other nomad tribes call the Roxolani the "Bastards" because they are the descendants of a band of Bastarnae and Carpi adventurers who came to the rescue of a scythian clan whose menfolk had been killed during the troubled times after the Breaking. Even though they had proven themselves to be capable warriors and thrived in the harsh conditions that faced every Scythian for the past 500 years, they were still seen as outsiders. Every once in a while, one or more of the other tribes raid Aleppo to remind the Roxolani just how unwelcome they are.

Those Scythians who do not herd animals tend to be a bit less judgmental than the five great tribes, and often will work for the Roxolani, outsiders or not. I was working with two such warriors at that time: Ankubi, whom I had been travelling with since Roaring Springs and whose honor name I had learned was Sirrush Stalker, and an old Sandasi named Kithgar One-arm. We spread our bedrolls in a small barn on the northern outskirts of the shantytown, and got to know each other over the course of those few weeks. Kithgar didn't say much, at least not until he got to know you. One bright morning, when the whole town seemed to be taking its time in waking up, Kithgar decided that he knew us well enough to ask us to tell him what we knew of the battle at the oasis of Roaring Springs. He had missed the battle because he was too old and lacked his left arm from the elbow down, not because he lacked the will to fight. I think he dreaded dying of old age, and had wanted one last chance to go through the Veil fighting, but he had been left behind by the Roxolani. He listened closely to our recounting of what we had seen at the battle, and was greatly agitated by the time we finished.

"Outsiders" hissed Kithgar, "This Empire has no love for us; our cubs, our hunting grounds, our lives mean nothing to them. Curse the Sakaes for siding with them, and curse those tribes that did not fight at all for the short-sighted fools that they are."

The old Sandasi's anger seemed to awaken an answering fury in Ankubi, who began pacing the length of the barn we were quartered in, the materials he had gathered for his new spear forgotten, his fists clenching as his anger deepened. I watched him closely; he was a follower of Tillar the Bull and I already knew not to go drinking with him. He didn't indulge often, but when he did, he liked to break things. Buildings, for example.

"How did these Imperials treat the bodies of our dead kin?", asked Kithgar.

I spread my hands and said:

"I didn't see with my own eyes, but if they treated them as they treated their slain enemies in Khetar, the bodies were stripped of anything of value and then thrown into a common grave."

Or they may have been left to rot, food for the jackals and hyenas, but I decided not to bring that up. He snarled at that, and Ankubi answered with one of his own. They were interrupted by a banging on the barn door. We heard a voice say: "They're in there.", and then someone slipped into the barn through the half-open door and walked towards us, hands spread to show his intent was peaceful. He was tall, certainly taller than me, but short of Ankubi's more than two meters height. His armor was chainmail of good quality, and he carried a spear slung over his shoulder, and two swords in well-used scabbards; when he spoke I realized that I knew him! It was Silmurth Sharpspear, who Bel and I had met the day we were initiated into Tarhunt's cult, in Melid only a few seasons ago.

"Well met! I do not mean to disturb you, but I was told that the best tracker in town could be found here. I have some business... Ha! Joren? Is that you?"

"Hello, Silmurth", I said.

I wondered what he was doing here. He seemed equally and pleasantly surprised to see me. We clasped arms and he said:

"Well, I know you can't be the one I'm looking for, you can't be much better at tracking than I am. Are you the one I need to talk to, Spearman?"

"I'll talk to you, if you are a friend of N'kopje, but if you want the best tracker in this end of Scythia, you want him." Ankubi said, pointing with his thumb at Kithgar, who had risen when the newcomer entered the barn, and stood leaning on his spear, looking Silmurth over intently.

Kithgar One-arm was the oldest Sandasi I'd ever meet, and one of the toughest. He was nearly as tall as me, which is tall for a child of the Lion god, with a ruff of thick white hair that fell half way down his back. He was almost as fast a runner as Ankubi and could outjump both of us with ease, and he was very good with that spear of his. Kithgar had sworn his life in service to Davin Whiteaxe, founder of the Whiteaxe clan of the Roxolani; now that Davin and his children were dead, Davin's grandchildren didn't seem to think Old Kithgar was anything more than a senile Sandasi who taught children how to read sign. They were wrong.

Kithgar nodded once at Silmurth and said: "I listen, Sharpspear"

Silmurth blinked at that; I had not introduced him by his full name, which meant Kithgar knew him. Silmurth didn't waste any time.

"There are imperials in the hills above Aleppo." he said. Well, if he wanted our full attention, he had it with that one sentence.

"Not many, just a small band of eight or nine, who were seen near the place called the Three Tall Sisters. But I need to know what they are doing here, and if necessary, I may need to stop them from getting back to Khetar to make their report. I need help in finding them; I may need help in killing them as well."

"You speak plainly, more plainly than I expected."

"I don't have the time to be persuasive and a warpath that is walked because of a lie is doomed from the start. I need to leave within the hour; what do you say?"

Kithgar nodded once and replied: "I will go with you. My mate and my cubs are long dead, but these outlanders have slain those of my kin, and I will see a blood price taken from them."

I looked at Ankubi. "This comes at a good time: the herds have been gathered in from all of the outer pastures for the calving tally, and that pack of bladefoot we just put down was the last group of predators in 20 miles."

He nodded. "They do not need us here, now. And these lovers of the White Sun, they owe me blood debt as well: only one out of four of my people who fought at Roaring Springs ever saw our tribe again. I fought them there, and I will fight them here, now. I will run with you, Sharpspear, to hunt and to war."

I turned to Silmurth. "That makes four of us. Will it be enough?"

"It will have to be. Meet me at the North Pens in ten minutes, and thanks."

We gathered our weapons and packs, and went to speak to Lorn Whiteaxe, old Davin's grandson. He had lost a son and a daughter at Roaring Springs, and had the look of a man going without much sleep. Lorn had no objections to us going on a hunt:

"You three go ahead. You've done your share here; maybe by the time you get back, we'll have gotten back on our feet, and won't be acting like a horse someone has hit in the head with a mallet. Good Hunting, Old One."

We saluted him and left. We found Silmurth alone with a brace of pack animals, 2 horses and 2 mules, plus his own mount, a sleek chestnut gelding. Kithgar snorted in amusement:

"Leave them. They will be safe here, and on the paths I know that lead to the Three Tall Sisters, they would only slow us down."

Silmurth nodded at that. We helped him stable his animals, and after grabbing his own weapons and pack, he loped off with us. We made good time, reaching the brush-clad slopes of the mountains proper before our midday meal. We ate that meal near a spring which had a pure, sweet taste, and I remember that day was a particularly fine one, almost perfect. Silmurth sat next to me while we ate.

"I'd expected to get more of the Roxolani to come with us." he said after a time.

"The loss at Roaring Springs was a bad shock; they've lost hundreds of fighters over the past three or four years, and now they have to come to grips with the fact that if the Empire pushes south along the mountains, the whole tribe has to either pack up and run for Lycia, or stay and live with the imperial boot on their necks. The Kushan and Dahae peoples are moving their herds east of the Euphrates or northeast, into the steppes. That choice is not open to the Roxolani, and they have to do some thinking. If you came back in a few days or a week, things might be different. You might get twenty or thirty to ride with you, just for fun."

"I don't have a few days; it was a pixie I know who spotted them. She had urgent business to attend to, so she left word with me and flew on home. She will bring others to back us up if she can, but there was no guarantee they would get here in time, so I had to find someone else. Aleppo was the closest place where I could hope to find anyone, and I got lucky with you three. We have to find these imperials, Joren, and find out what they're doing this far south and east. They aren't anywhere near any kind of trade route, and there is only one reason I know of that will cause the Empire to send a small party like this across unmapped wilderness: they are advance scouts for the Imperial Army."

"You think they're looking for an eastern route into Lycia?", I said.

"That's my guess. The memory of the battle at Falling Mountains doesn't sit well with the Imperial Command; they don't like losing, and they want a rematch. When we find them, we have to find out what they're up to, and either stop or delay them long enough for any help the pixie could find to get here. Then we can harry them to the Doors of the Underworld. By the way, where's Belkara? And what does N'kopje mean?"

"She's back with her clan in the Bastarnae lands; we got seperated before Roaring Springs, and I'm trying to get back to her without running into any Imperial officials who might want to know where I was at the time of the battle. N'kopje means Beheader."

"Ah. Nice sword."

"Thanks."

It clouded up soon after that, and there looked to be a heavy overcast the next couple of days. Kithgar took us up into the Thunderhead Mountains along a path that only he knew, taking us in almost a straight line that avoided the valley of Tuhus's River entirely. That was how we found them; they had been traveling on foot, both two feet and four feet, avoiding the known paths in an attempt to reach Aleppo undetected. It had failed horribly, as we saw when we found their last camp. Not the camp of the imperials, the camp of their victims.

It was the smell that lead us to them; there were no carrion birds about, which seemed strange to me, but Kithgar said that magic will sometimes keep the birds off for a while. The smell of a battlefield is something you never forget, especially in the heat. It smells an awful lot like a slaughterhouse, and for a moment, I couldn't tell which one this was. The glade where the camp had been set was masked on three sides by thick brush to the north, east, and south; the camp had been ransacked and the debris burned, so that now the only things in the glade where three graves, a dozen bodies and more blood than I could comprehend at first. It was fresh blood; this had been done today, this morning. There was blood, and flies, everywhere, even on the undersides of the branches and leaves overhanging the clearing. The bodies looked odd until I realized that they had been flayed, with the skin and the heads removed, and most of them weren't human. The hides were nowhere in sight, but eleven bloody heads grinned at us from atop stakes set into the ground around the twelfth body, lying spread-eagled on the blood-soaked ground. The light was strange too, as the clearing was dimly lit by a pink glow that flickered in an odd rhythm, a glow that came from a piece of red stone laid on the still moving chest of the body in the center of the clearing.

"One of them is still alive?!"

We had come into the clearing from two different directions, Silmurth and I from the north, Kithgar and Ankubi from the south, crosswise to the wind. The two of us were young enough that this horror stunned us silent. We just stood there while Kithgar began making a circuit of the clearing to check for tracks leading into and out of the clearing, Ankubi started checking the graves. Both Silmurth and I were feeling sick, but something else was bothering me: this scene had a terrifying sense of familiarity about it, as if I had been told of something like this before. I walked further into the clearing, and got a better look at the last body, the one which was only half flayed, and which still lived.

It was that of an old man, I thought at first, and then I saw the shape of his skull and the grey fur on the flaps of skin that had been peeled away from his chest and abdomen, and I realized that he was a werewolf, a Lupaku, and why all of this seemed so familiar. I knew then what had been done to him, but I looked anyway with a sick fascination. He had been blinded and castrated, and then his eye teeth had been ripped out and the tendons of his legs and arms cut. Then because he was a shapeshifter, they had pinned him to the ground with silver knives while they had half flayed him. The piece of red glowing stone had to be a white sunstone covered by blood, and its magic was keeping him in were-form, and would keep him alive in terrible agony until someone or something released him from his torment. Also I think it was there as a reminder as well, to the werewolf himself:

"Cross those who follow the White Sun, and you will pay, no matter how long it

takes, no matter how far you run".

This entire clearing was not just an execution, it was a message to anyone who might find it, as well. Then the spread-eagled body in front of me stirred. My footsteps had roused the werewolf from his delirium of pain and he spoke:

"Who is it? Who's there?" and he began snuffling at the air to catch our scents.

Silmurth's voice was harsh with disgust: "How long did some imperial pervert toy with this idea before he came up with..."

I interrupted him:

"No imperial, the Lupaku themselves came up with this. This is a reenactment, not some imperial ritual, except for the magic of the sunstone. This is how the imperial relief column found the body of Ketil, the last king of the Mabirshan, after the Lupaku had wiped out the core clans of the Mabirshan. Except the Lupaku used stakes made of oak wood, instead of silver."

I looked at the pitiful wreck of the Lupaku's body, and I realized something else:

"You were there weren't you, Wolf? That's why they killed you this way. You were one of those who slew him, so they ordered that you suffer the same fate."

Silmurth shot me glance in surprise, and spoke:

"Ketil? Ketil the Accursed? The Betrayer of Khetar? The coward who left his friends and neighbors to face the imperial armies without him and the Mabirshan spear levy?"

"Betrayer!", howled the mutilated Lupaku, and I could hear rage and hate warring with the terrible pain in his voice. Then his bloody head turned towards me with unnerving accuracy, and he spoke, forcing his words out through his agony and his hate. Those words forced me to confront something I had tried to forget since before the battle at Roaring Springs:

"Treachery and cowardice were the least of his crimes! Shall I name the others? Oathbreaker, Usurper, Kinslayer! Whatever we did to him, he deserved worse, didn't he, Queen's Heir? Kerchak was right! I did not believe him then, but I believe now. I know you, Son of Bane, as I know the sound of your father's voice in yours, and as I know your scent as one of your family and the taste of your kinsman's blood. Tell them, tell ME the Accursed One deserved less than this!"

The black hate that has lurked within me ever since I learned of my family's death swelled out and engulfed me:

"If Ketil had three lives, he deserved to die this way three times over!"

The blinded werewolf's laughter nearly choked him:

"There speaks the blood of the Mabirshan! Your mother's family knew how to hate, boy, but are you only your mother's son? Is there nothing of your father in you at all? Do you follow his path? Or have you chosen another road to power?"

He was up to something; blinded and crippled as he was, he was moving our words where he wanted them to go.

"I am my father's son, and I will follow his path as I may. But do not make the mistake of thinking I am even half the man my father was.", I warned.

Kithgar and Ankubi finished their work and strode over to where we stood, drawn by the voice of the werewolf. Kithgar was expressionless, but Ankubi's lips had drawn back in a snarl and both fists were clenched on his spear's shaft. He was a born fighter, like all the Red Hunters, but he did not understand (and heartily despised) torture. He spoke to Silmruth and I:

"The graves hold the bodies of three imperial soldiers, no armor or weapons."

Kithgar made his own report:

"The tracks in the clearing are too muddled to read clearly, but the trail that leads northwest was made by two mules and seven people on foot. One mule was ridden, the other carried a heavy burden; of the seven on foot, three were soldiers, all wounded, and the last four were children."

"Children?"

He nodded. "Two very young, two nearly grown. In chains."

Silmurth's voice grew harsh: "Children in slave chains."

I looked at the stakes surrounding the old man's body; eleven heads, three men, eight wolves, and eleven flayed bodies left for the crows.

"He made the children watch, didn't he?"

Ankubi jerked as if he had been struck, and Silmurth went as pale as I knew I was, but Kithgar nodded at me once.

"Yes; if I read the signs right, he killed and skinned the pups in front of them, and then the bodies of the dead, and then this", pointing at the tattered body of the old man on the ground. "The one who did this has an appetite for pain."

"Oh he does, does he? We'll see he gets a belly full of it then...".

I think Ankubi and Silmurth were going to be in a race to end that imperial's life. I was distracted by the sobbing of the Lupaku:

"My grandchildren, the last fruit of my mate's love for me, my last hopes, my only dreams...Bane's Son, I will bargain with you."

I realized that I was holding my greatsword in my hands.

"What do I need to bargain for, Old Wolf? I'm going to take your head off to end your pain, and then we're going to hunt down the imperial scum who did this, and end THEM."

Silmurth and Ankubi grunted approval, but Kithgar clucked at us reprovingly.

"Cubs. These servants of the white sun left here no later than mid-morning; it is now no more than an hour before the Sun enters the Gates of Sunset. We cannot catch them today, and with even the stars covered by these clouds, I will not be able to follow a trail in the dark, which means we cannot catch them before tomorrow mid-day, at the earliest."

The werewolf howled in anguish.

"Too late, too late! If you cannot catch them before mid-day, you will not catch them at all. They were led by a sorcerer, a man of power who took me for a weak old man. But I had one last weapon left, hoarded from my travels on the paths of Magic, and I struck him down and took his life before he knew who it was he faced. It was his apprentice who did this to me and mine. The Empire will pay much for this sorcerer of theirs, to be brought back to life and their service. His apprentice boasted that all they need do is get far enough north to be within range of an imperial garrison, and the imperials will send griffins to pick them up, guided by magic."

Griffins. Silmurth and I looked at one another at that. Whatever help that pixie might gather might not be enough if we had to deal with imperial griffins and their riders. I gave the werewolf a drink of water, and waited. He soon went on:

"You do not want this to happen, Bane's Son; this sorcerer is from Semnonia, one of three brothers who hunted and slew for the glory of their White Sun; twenty years ago, two of them hunted your father; Bane slew THEM and threw their heads into a midden. Now the last of these brothers has come to Issuria, and if he lives again, he will seek you. These imperials, they say that we are savages, no more than animals, yet they follow the blood feud just as thirstily as we."

"Me? Why should he seek me? The imperials think me dead along with my mother and sisters."

"No more. One of Kerchak's band spoke of you to an imperial official in hope of mercy, and now there are imperial patrols combing the hills around Melid, seeking an orphan boy named Joren."

That made my blood run cold; if those patrols spilled over into the Bastarnae lands, they might hear about Bel, and then the Empire would have a hold over me. Would I disobey the wishes of the Empire if it would mean Bel's life? I didn't know, and didn't want to think of it. Then Silmurth spoke, in a reasonable tone that started to raise the hair on the back of my neck:

"You know, Joren, you could do quite well out of this. The Mabirshan were the first tribe to accept imperial missionaries; their destruction was a loss of face that the Empire would like to redress. If you played your cards right, you could be very useful to them. All they would have to do is take a clan from this tribe, two from that one, and who knows, you could be a king before...."

I spun and stepped into him, even faster than he had expected. His hands were out at his sides, empty, but his eyes still widened at how quickly I had reached him. We stood there, literally nose to nose, with my sword edge just not touching his belly armor, and I spoke to him in a level voice that surprised all of us with its steadiness:

"You will not ever insult me in that manner again."

He nodded. "No, I will not. But if we're going to walk the same road together, I had to see what kind of man you are. Come now, have you never tested a sword you might have to use in battle?"

"You came damn close to grabbing this sword by the blade instead of the hilt.", I replied.

"Well, I had to see if the sword was balanced."

"Ass."

He laughed at that; Silmurth is like Corlan, he thinks a lot of what I say is funny, though I don't necessarily mean it to be. He just doesn't think enough of his own safety, but then, he never has. I gave the old werewolf another drink of water, and when he had swallowed, I spoke to him:

"You have a plan, don't you, Old Wolf. Well, spit it out."

"A wolf sees with his nose, not his eyes; and the nose doesn't go blind when the skies go dark. For this one night, you could be as a wolf." I jerked away from him as if he had snapped at my hand. He felt me pull away, and he cried out in pain and despair, and played the last tricks in his bag:

"Queen's Heir! I no longer have a name, and where once I was a warrior and a speaker to the spirits (a shaman! I knew it.), now I am less than nothing. I am the last of the Forsaken, the warriors and shamans outlawed by the Children of Lupak at the demand of the White Sun, because we had done what all had wanted to do, but did not dare. Once I had power and honor among my tribe, now I have nothing, not even a tribe, just the promise of a future that my four grandchildren carry within them."

"As my people have forsaken me, so now do I forsake THEM. Know this secret as my gift to you: when we slew the Accursed One, we fed his power and his blood to the spirit wolves that serve Father Lupak, and they went forth and spoke to every Lupaku shaman in the world. In their dreams, every shaman of my people had your family's names spoken into their ears, and the smell of your family's blood breathed into their nostrils. That knowledge will be passed through every generation, so that no matter where you go, no matter what you do, if there are any of the wolf people in that land, sooner or later, they will catch your scent, and hunt you down."

This was a gift?

"One last thing, Son of Bane. Your father was a landless wanderer and the starkest warrior I ever fought. He slew our wolves by the score, yet he never broke a promise, never betrayed a trust, never failed to show mercy when he held the upper hand. You are his son by birth, and the nephew of Ketil the Accursed by blood, but it is up to you to decide which of the two shall have you as his heir."

You know things are bad when your family enemies can play on your emotions like a harp.

Silmurth snapped his fingers to get the Lupaku's attention:

"Why Joren, and not me? Or one of the others?"

"He and I have a bond that I don't have with anyone else: I helped to destroy his tribe, and I was one of those who killed his uncle, tasted his blood and took his power. That bond will be reinforced when he kills me tonight."

"Kills you?" I perked up at that.

"The sunstone on my chest is a trap; should anyone give me the mercy stroke, or remove the rock, I will die and my spirit will be bound to the rock, in service to the White Sun forever. But I have one last magic left to me, one last enchantment: if somone already marked by Death whom my spirit knows should finish what the sorcerer's apprentice began and flay my skin from my body, the Solar spell will be undone, and I will be able to substitute my own. When I die, my spirit will be drawn into my hide....for a time."

"What do you mean 'for a time'?" I knew there was a catch in this somewhere.

"I must not die until the Sun has gone through the gates of Dusk, and we must be finished with our task before she comes again through the gates of Dawn. One night is all that we have; but for that night, you can wear my hide as a cloak, and I will see through your eyes and you will read the wind and the earth with my nose."

"Or what? What will happen if I still carry you when Sun rises in the east?"

"If I am carried by one not of my own blood when the light of the rising Sun touches me, my spirit will fight theirs for possession of their body. The loser will serve the victor for as long as they live."

There was a moment's silence. I looked around and realized that we had only moments until the sun would set. We would have to start as soon as possible after darkness fell. I stooped and put my boot on one of the werewolf's maimed paws; in the same movement, I grabbed the hilt of the silver knife that held it pinned to the ground and wrenched it from his wrist. He howled in agony.

I looked over at Kithgar: "Have you ever skinned a wolf?" He set his spear against a tree, and said: "Yes, more than one."

"Show me how it is done." The werewolf howled again, this time in grim triumph.

We moved through the night at a trot, only slowing to a walk when it grew too dark for Kithgar to see. But dark or light, the trail of those we followed was as plain before me as the Hattusha road. I couldn't bring myself NOT to follow it: the scent of the four children whose faces now haunted my memory was a physical pull I couldn't ignore. I followed their tracks at a lope, with the old Sandasi running at my side and guiding my steps when the path grew rough. Ankubi and Silmurth were tied to me by a length of rope, and we ran blind, trusting to Kithgar to keep us from breaking our necks. We made good time, but so had our quarry; whoever was leading the imperials was pushing them all to the point of exhaustion.

Around us, the night was alive in a way I had never felt it before. Not only could I smell things I couldn't before, but it changed the way familiar scents affected me; it also interacted with my normal senses. I thought that sometimes I could actually SEE the scents of those we followed, shifting along the ground like threads of fog. I caught the scents of rabbit and deer, of grouse and elk, and my stomach rumbled alarmingly. I smelled the scents of pine and oak and I wanted to howl just to hear if anyone answered me, and I felt as if I could run all night. I had tied the forelegs of the Lupaku's fell or hide around my neck; his head had fitted over my helm as if made for it, and his hindlegs were wrapped around my waist of their own accord. His thoughts wove between and around my own, or hovered somewhere in the background, looking at me, at my life, at my soul. His spell had bound him closer to me than my own skin; his senses and his vigor were mine to use and my mind and my spirit were opened to him like a book. My life bond with Bel had given him quite a start:

"What in a titan's tall tale is THAT? A life bond? I've never seen one so strong."

Later, I could hear him murmuring to himself, and with a start I realized he could read some of my memories.

"Killed a priestess of the white sun, have you? Good."

"Did you know that you have a broken place in here? You do? What caused it?"

"I was struck with Imperial magic when my mother and sisters were killed."

"To the lasting regret of the imperials, I think. It looks as if you might be immune to some of their magic, now."

"I like this mate-to-be of yours; she is a fighter, her teeth are very fine, and she smells good too. Brown hair, brown eyes... handsome. I think there must be Lupaku blood in some of the Bastarnae clans..."

"When we get to where we are going, would you like me to throw you into a fire and dance on you?"

"Ah, no, thank you."

"Then shut up. And stop pinching; I tie a good, solid knot; you aren't going to fall off."

"I would rather not take any chances, if you don't mind."

Once, when we stopped to rest, I asked him if he could show me a memory of my father. There was silence, and then I suddenly smelled weapon oil and blood and magic, and there was an image of my father grinning at me on the other side of a flash of bright metal. There was a stinging in my side, and the world spun as I fell for a long way into some very cold water. Then I was back to myself, leaning against a rock with the hide of a flayed werewolf hanging around my shoulders.

"That is my most vivid memory of Bane; he nearly killed me that time, you can still see the scar over my right hip. Bane's Fang sheared right through my spear, and I escaped by throwing myself backwards into a lake."

"He didn't come after you?"

"No, just spent a few moments laughing at me and then went home. Fighting was a joy to your father, not that he was slow about killing either. But he did love to fight."

"Thank you."

"You are welcome, Bane's Son."

We found the camp we were looking for not much more than an hour before daylight. I smelled woodsmoke, bloody bandages, mules, boot leather and armor, burned bread and charred bacon, a fresh corpse and something else. Four scents that seemed to have faces and my (our?) heart leapt in my breast. Four Lupaku children who were the only hope of a dead old man; four children on their way to an imperial slave market, where they would bring a high price as exotics, and who knew what use their buyers would put them to? I caught another scent as well, separate from the others: pigs. I had a thought that drew a low bark of approval from the wolf on my shoulders, and I turned to share it with Kithgar. He liked it as well.

Our plan was simple: Ankubi and Silmurth would sneak up on the camp while Kithgar and I went and found the pigs I had scented. They were upwind of the camp, and we would drive them into it with fire, and the smell of a wolf and a hunting cat. While the pigs distracted the Imperials, we would attack, concentrating first on making sure the children were out of harm's way, and then to make sure our enemies were either slain or driven out of the camp on foot. They wouldn't be able to go far, and we could pick them off one by one tomorrow. It wasn't a bad plan, and it even worked, sort of.

The camp had only one soldier on guard at one time, but more than one type of guard, and it was only by sheer chance that Ankubi and Silmurth spotted the second one. They had begun sneaking up on the camp when something fluttered from a blanket-covered litter over to the only tent in the camp, the one occupied by the sorcerer before his death, and now by his apprentice. This fluttering something looked a lot like a bat, except bats don't have necks half a yard long. Well, when you think about it, have you ever heard of a sorcerer who didn't have a familiar?

This stopped our companions at almost twice the distance we had planned on, since the familiar kept flying from one end of the camp to the other with unnatural vigor. They readied their javelins, but would need the distraction of a swine stampede to get any closer. They got it, and a little bit more. The wild pigs that roam the eastern flanks of the Thunderhead Mountains are much smaller than their giant kin that roam the Pontine Mountains, but are very tough and just as mean. By the time we moved into position east of the herd, they had caught our scent; they were all awake and milling around the scarred boar that led the herd. The sows and piglets could smell two types of predator from us, and they didn't like one bit. But that boar didn't smell or look afraid, in fact he seemed to be working himself into a rage.

When we lit the pile of brush at the head of the ravine they were holed up in, that boar let out a squeal of anger and CHARGED west out of the ravine, straight for the imperial camp. I figure that he had caught the scent of fire and wolf from the camp earlier, but had been willing to leave them alone as long as the humans didn't bother him or his mates. There are a few things about pigs that you should know before you trifle with them: they are smarter than most herd animals, they're definitely meaner than most other herd animals and they will eat anything. When we lit our fire, that boar apparently considered it an act of war; those pigs didn't stampede through the imperial camp, they attacked it.

We did have two pieces of luck. First, the Lupaku children could smell and hear the pigs coming and took to the nearest trees, leg shackles and all. Second, Ankubi and Silmurth had begun shifting to the left to sneak closer to the camp and the wild pigs raced right past them. Then all hell broke loose. The boar attacked the nearest mule and hamstrung it with a slash of his tusks; it screamed in agony and collapsed kicking madly. This threw the remaining mule into a panic and it bolted; the pigs then proceeded to wreck the remainder of the camp, scattering and trampling the food and bedding, shredding the tent and then tearing off into the night on the other side of camp. Just about then, I came up over the hill, silhouetted by the fire behind me, at the same time someone with a damn sharp eye spotted Silmurth and sounded the alarm. To top things off, two of the slowest (and fattest) of the pigs found the sorcerer's corpse and decided to have a snack. That sent the familiar into a screaming rage, and magic began to ripple across the clearing.

Once the spells began to be cast, no one seemed to hold anything back. Kithgar gave a full-throated roar and his shape seemed to shift. The sorcerer's familiar was shrieking in a high-pitched voice while it lashed the pigs attacking its master's corpse with white fire. Then a tall figure in yellow robes stepped from the wreckage of the tent with a glowing staff in his hands and began intoning a spell that I could feel 100 yards away. A volley of javelins flew towards me and Silmurth, and I had other things to worry about.

The imperials were using a type of javelin I hadn't seen before: short but very heavy, with a long neck of soft metal that would bend once it had stuck in something, and a weighted socket where the metal sleeve of the spearhead met the wooden shaft. It had a shorter range than some throwing spears, but a tremendous amount of hitting power. Each imperial soldier threw two of them and then waded into melee, and these were regulars, heavy infantry, not a handful of bravos the sorcerer had picked up in some bar.

Mine and Silmurth's shields were useless after that second volley and we dropped them to wield our two-handed swords against the charge of the imperial soldiers. Their leader was a grizzled decurion with a long face seamed with scars, and an iron torc that glowed with a green light. He told off one man each to face me and Kithgar, and then went for Silmurth himself.

The imperials came in slow, eyes peering over their rectangular shields, shortswords held low, point first. Kithgar ignored his foe to focus on the familiar. The old Sandasi put everything he had into a superb cast that caught the familiar thru one wing and pinned it to a tree; the Lupaku children promptly leapt on the creature and tore it limb from limb. As Kithgar turned to face his opponent, the imperial thrust his short sword into the one-armed hunter's side with a practiced roll of his shoulders and then withdrew it, expecting the body to fall to the ground. Instead, he found himself looking into the eyes of a lion-headed warrior who ignored the death wound in his side and nearly ripped the imperial's face off with a snap of his jaws. Kithgar had clothed himself with the power of the Lion god, and ignoring the wound in his side, bit and clawed at his enemy with a fury that drove him back on his heels. I had just enough time to realize that Ankubi had not been spotted, and then I was trading blows with my own opponent.

When I dropped my shield, I had traded my long sword for my greatsword, and I used it to parry my foe's first thrust. Both of our blades were alight with magic and he winced as I hacked at his shield, sending splinters flying. He tried to bull me over backwards with a quick rush behind his shield but I danced backwards and cut at it again, taking one of the corners off of it. He was starting to sweat and thrust at my face; I parried him, and seeing an opening, cut at his shoulder: he couldn't recover in time, and my heavier blade bit through his armor. His arm fell useless, dropping his shield to the ground, and he missed his parry when I slashed at his legs. He went down and my thrust took him just above his collar bone.

Wrenching my blade free, I turned to help Kithgar, but I was too late. The old Sandasi was down, and his foe was racing at me, his sword raised in both hands, shield gone, blood dripping from his face and one arm. I met his attack with one of my own, and hammered him back on his heels. Using the longer reach and greater weight of my greatsword, I forced the imperial backwards step by step towards where Kithgar lay. Sensing a trap, he flicked a glance back to see if Kithgar was going to trip him, and instead of slashing, I thrust, and the point of my blade took him underneath the chin. I pulled my sword free as he went down, and went to help Kithgar. He was still alive, but just barely, sustained only by the power of the divine magic he had invoked.

When the spell ended, so would his life, but he was unconcerned. He was coughing up blood, and I realized he was laughing.

He looked me in the face, faded yellow eyes twinkling, and said:

"Today was a good day, and this was a good fight. I am glad I had the chance to end like this, instead of sick on an old bedroll, in a place no longer my home. Say farewell to Ankubi for me, N'kopje, and each of you take something of mine with you, a lock of hair or a claw. You may need to speak to me again, on the roads you each will walk. Ah...the Sun..." and he died.

I looked over my shoulder and realized that dawn had come, and sunlight would be spilling into this little valley in a matter of minutes. I had to move fast. I turned to see that Silmurth had killed his foe and was nearly at the tent on the other side of the camp, only to find Ankubi there before him. The big spearman had hunted since childhood, like all of his tribe, and had used every inch of cover to move in as close as he could to the camp. This meant that he was within throwing distance when the apprentice began a spell powered by his master's staff that could have been our undoing.

It was a long throw, but Ankubi made it, striking the imperial magician in the arm and spun him around, breaking his concentration and disrupting the spell. This gave the Red Hunter enough time to close with his enemy; arms spread wide to grapple. The magician had struck at Ankubi with the staff while he prepared a spell, but the blow had gone wide and Ankubi had caught his foe by the neck and belt. Lifting the imperial off of the ground, Ankubi then spun and slammed the magician into a tree with enough force to break half of his ribs. Then, muscles straining, roaring Tillar's name, Ankubi had switched one hand to his enemy's thigh and raising him above his head, broke the imperial magician over his raised knee like a child's stick doll. Then he wrung his foe's neck, just to be sure.

As I trotted towards the tent, I passed the stretcher that held the body of the Semnonian sorcerer so highly valued by the Empire of the White Sun. The pigs hadn't really done that much damage, so I hacked off the corpse's head, just to be sure he stayed dead. I began to feel a strange warmth on my back and neck, and then I heard the voice of the Lupaku shaman whisper to me:

"Beware, Bane's Son! The Sun comes and my time is almost gone. Remember your promise!"

I remembered. Silmurth, Ankubi and I strode over to where the four Lupaku children stood, the two oldest in front, armed with a length of firewood and Kithgar's spear, the two youngest behind them. It was to the youngest boy that my gaze was drawn, he had a harelip, and over him, I seemed to see another image, that of a silvery wolf. He was the one the old wolf had chosen as his heir, and I could see why. The other three were staring at me in horror, seeing only the flayed skin of their grandfather. But this boy seemed to see something else. "Apha?", he said. "Grandfather?"

I untied the werewolfskin's forelegs from my neck, and spoke the words the old shaman's ghost had whispered to me, as I twirled the skin over my head three times and threw it into the air over the heads of his grandchildren.

"Blood calls to Blood. Seek now your own!"

A strange wind came from nowhere, and caught the werewolf's skin, so that it fell, not like a sodden blanket, but like a leaf, lightly about the shoulders of the youngest of the Lupaku before us, the little boy who bore the mark of a shaman. The arms of the skin tightened around the old wolf's grandson in a loving hug, and the jaws of his head opened as his voice growled soothingly to his family. The children crowded around in wonderment, to touch the fur of their grandsire, and began to cry, in relief and at last to vent their grief.

The clearing was starting to grow light around us; we didn't have much time, so while I began the ceremony, Silmurth and Ankubi searched the tent and the body of the apprentice, and found what we had hoped for: an small black bowl, made of some kind of fired clay. It was sealed with red wax, and in it was a cupful of the werewolf's blood and those things that had been taken from him: his eyes, his teeth and his manhood.

I drew my sword and lightly clasped the blade, just enough to bring blood; I cut the boy's arm lightly as well, so that his blood as well as mine dripped into the bowl that held the greater part of the old shaman's power. Our blood and our will was what the enchantment needed to be complete. I filled the empty sockets of the wolf's head with that blood, and pressed home the bloody orbs that glowed, and then blinked at me in gratitude, a wolf's eyes once again. As the boy took the last grisly trophy left in the bowl, I set the werewolf's teeth back in his gums, and they reseated themselves, growing sharp and firm again, so that the shaman could defend himself and his family in the Spirit Lands.

Last, the boy held his cupped hands against his grandsire's pelt and whispered some words I did not hear, and the werewolfskin jerked and seemed to come alive as the old one's manhood, the heart of power for most male shamans, was returned to him. Just then the rays of The Sun's light spread into the clearing, seeming to search out each shadow, and the pelt that held the spirit of the Last of the Forsaken raised his head and howled in triumph. He was at home in the arms of his family again. Me, I was just as alone as I had been the day before, and I felt like I'd just spent a long day plowing fields.

We stripped the imperials of anything of value, and salvaged what food and clothing we could from the camp's wreckage. Most of what we recovered we gave to the Lupaku, since they had lost everything when their camp was sacked. It took a while to get the shackles off of them, but a key from the belt of the oldest soldier did the trick. When we had, the four of them clustered together and faced us. The oldest girl held out Kithgar's spear, and asked:

"May I keep this? I would remember the one who died helping to save us."

Ankubi and I looked at each other, and I nodded.

"Yes. His name was Kithgar One-arm, and he was a great hunter and a cunning warrior."

Ankubi stepped over and handed his spear, stained with the blood of the sorcerer's apprentice, to the oldest boy. "Take this, as well. I'll be making some new ones for myself." The boy gripped the spear tightly and swelled with pride; a warrior's weapon, given as a gift by that warrior, was no small thing.

"Where will you go?", Silmurth asked the old wolf.

It should have been a laughable sight, the pelt of a grey wolf hanging on a boy who looked barely old enough to carry its weight. But the boy stood tall, draped in his grandsire's power, and he held himself with a man's dignity. Then the jaws of the wolf's head opened and he spoke aloud:

"West, to Vale of Mist. I have friends among those who dwell there; I will seek counsel with them, and we will plan our future. A future that has nothing in it of the tribe of the Lupaku. Blackmane was right; I didn't want to listen, but he was right. The time of the choosing is upon them, and I think they will choose poorly."

The old werewolf's eyes flicked to each of us in turn, as his grandchildren gathered their packs.

"We will remember you, Ankubi Sirrushtalker, Silmurth Sharpspear and you, Bane's Son. I think we shall meet again, in spirit, if not in body. Now, we go."

They waved once, and then they turned and loped off through the trees to the west.

We gave the soldiers a decent burial, and then sorted through what we had taken from their camp. Of the loot we gathered from the camp, almost all of the gold and silver we had given to the wolf children; we had more than enough for ourselves and they would need whatever they could scrape together for the strange life they would build for themselves. Not that we were shorted by this: we had six sets of bronze scale armor, imperial army issue no less. One of them fitted me, and I took that in place of my own sturdy ringmail. That armor would make for a heavy load on the trail back to Aleppo, but it represented more wealth then Ankubi or I had ever had before. We could build a sled and drag it after us; most of the way home was downhill anyway. We also took four shortswords and a broadsword for sale or barter. The sorcerer's staff, which the apprentice had wielded, we destroyed, and it burst into flames when we broke it. It was Ankubi's idea to treat the bodies of the sorcerer and his minion in the same way:

"N'kopje, could you strike off this spawn's head for me?", asked Ankubi.

"Not a problem", I said.

As I cut the apprentice's head from his body, Ankubi suggested something that appealed to me:

"That old wolf said that your father slew the two brothers of this dead sorcerer, this empty one, and threw their heads in a midden."

"Yes. They had hunted him, and instead of running, he confronted them in a public place and taking them by surprise, slew them both with his sword Oathtaker, the great blade the Lupaku called Bane's Fang."

"I know of a midden in the Camp of Wood; it sits back of the biggest brothel in Aleppo. I think I like your father's sense of humor."

Ankubi had a point: if a midden was good enough for my father, it was good enough for me. That one in Aleppo would do just fine, but we had one last task before we could break our camp. We needed to say farewell to Kithgar. We sought out the branches of the pitch pine and the hickory, so that the flames would come quickly and burn hot, and we built a pyre for our fallen comrade. None of us knew what Kithgar's people did for funerals, but we dared not leave his body where the imperials could find it. If the imperials had found shamans who would do their bidding, then their reach could extend beyond the grave, if only they had some part of an enemy's body in their hands, and none of us cared to see our friend's head and hide taken as trophies, either. Once the pyre had been built, we prepared Kithgar's body as best we could. Since he had given me leave to take one of his claws in memory of him, I gave him one of my claws in return: my best knife and my belt to hold it around his waist. Ankubi laid a bright spear head and a fresh cut pole of white ash on his breast, saying that Kithgar preferred to make his own spears. Silmurth took his own cloak and wrapped the old Sandasi's body with its warm blue wool. We took our places on three sides of the pyre; I to the north, because Warrunk speaks for the North Wind, Ankubi to the east, for the East Wind is the Bull's Wind, and Silmurth to the south, because the south wind is the wind of luck, Tarhunt's Wind. And when the Sun had passed noon and begun his westward journey to the Gates of Sunset, which is an entrance to the Realm of the Dead, we set flames to the wood, and each of us spoke our farewells.

Since I was the youngest and the least in name, I went first:

"You taught me the ways of track and trail, and never to begin a hunt I would not see through to the end. Old Hunter, I will not forget."

Ankubi spoke next:

"You showed me that age is not weakness, and that caution is not cowardice. Good Hunting, Old Lion, in that land where your spirit now walks."

Silmurth spoke last:

"I summoned you to a battle not of your making, and you answered without hesitation or demand of reward. No stride was swifter, no blow was surer than yours. Old Warrior, the honor was mine."

The wind strengthened from the east, and fanned the flames that ate hungrily at the wood we had gathered. Those flames flared high and hot, and before an hour had passed, the pyre and the body we had laid atop it were consumed.

"Maybe we ought to leave this place.", said Silmurth. "Now."

He didn't get an argument. I looked back once, to fix that place in my mind; I could lead you there again, if I had to. Once out of the valley that held the imperial camp, we slowed our pace and took our time. Although luckily none of us bore wounds much bigger than a scratch, we were feeling every one of the miles we had traveled without sleep. We made a cold camp that night, and since the sky had cleared, I took a small bowl from my pack and filled it with spring water. I went off a bit by myself, and sat with the bowl in my lap, so that I could see the stars reflected in the water's surface.

Well, Ajax had said starlight was best, so I cleared my mind of everything but the woman I loved: her eyes, her smile, the way she used her sword...and speaking her name, I breathed on the surface of the water and waited. The water rippled and then stilled and there she was. She looked beautiful, and she was looking right back at me, and seemed a bit surprised. Apparently, I had interupted her while she was washing for the evening meal, and she was staring down at my reflection in her washing basin. I could hear Silmurth's footsteps coming up behind me, but I ignored him, so I could get the first word in.

"Bel, I love you." It worked better than I hoped, it seemed that she could hear me, and I could hear her. She looked incredibly exasperated.

"Joren, where ARE you? I love you too."

"In the south of Scythia; Dear One, listen. You may be in danger because of me. The Imperials know about me, and they are searching the lands around Melid for me. You have to be ready if they come to your tribe's lands. Be careful. If they take you, Belkara, I'll do whatever they want."

She snorted and jerked her chin at me.

"Nonsense. I have three good horses. If the imperials can catch me on my own lands, it will be because I am already thru the Veil." Dead, that is. Well, if she died, I would die soon after, as would every imperial bastard I could get my sword into before they hacked me down.

Silmurth had come up behind me, and must have seen something in the bowl:

"BELKARA?" he stammered.

Bel heard him. Her eyes widened, and she shot a question at me:

"Whose voice was that? Joren, who is there with you?"

"Silmurth Sharpspear"

That jolted Silmurth: "She can HEAR me?"

Bel's temper started to slip.

"Silmurth Sharpspear! You're off somewhere with him, aren't you? You fought in that battle without me, and now you're off on an adventure with Silmurth Sharpspear, WITHOUT ME! You wait until I get my hands on you, boy. I'll..."

Those beautiful hands of hers clenched and she started growling at me. Maybe that old shaman was right, maybe there WAS Lupaku blood in the Bastarnae. I had better make sure she never heard that from me though.

"You make damn sure that none of them are romantic adventures, you jerk, or, or..."

"Hah. As if there was another woman in the world like you, my love."

"Ah. I miss you. Come back soon." Her eyes were filling with tears, as were mine.

"Just as soon as I am able, Dearest One. I miss you."

Bel drove her fist into the wash bowl and broke our link. I hadn't wanted to make her cry.

Silmurth cleared his throat behind me, and apologized for intruding.

"I'm sorry, Joren. I had no idea... What did I just see, anyway?"

"Bel and I have a lifebond, a strong one. Sometimes, we can see and even hear one another through a reflection. Water, under starlight seems to work best, but I managed to do it once with a mirror." She had been asleep, and I had looked at her face for a long time.

Silmurth grinned at me:

"It must be very strong, but that doesn't surprise me. When I first met you two, I could see you were meant for each other. I hope you see her again, soon."

"So do I." Maybe I'd dream of her, tonight.

"Let's get some sleep, Joren. Ankubi said he would take first watch, and we are going to need to push to reach Aleppo tomorrow." Right enough.

We reached Aleppo at sunset the next day. Two days later, Silmurth took his leave of us, saying he had people to talk to in Carchemish. He said farewell to Ankubi and then clasped arms with me:

"I'll see you again, Joren."

"Count on it."

You can learn a great deal about someone when you stand alongside of them with lives in the balance. Silmurth and I knew each other now, better than you might think. We would both need to rely on that knowledge when next we met, more than seven years later. Seven years of learning and looking for the king, and never knowing that I had already found him.

Ajax came into town a week later, and I had a great deal to tell him. We talked it over and decided to change our plans. Instead of going directly back to Khetar, we would wait and let the Empire's interest in the rumor of an heir to the Mabirshan throne fade. We would say farewell to Ankubi and to the stronghold of the Roxolani tribe, and travel south and west, to Drakesfort, the gateway to the lands ruled by the Minos. We would leave Scythia; and go to Thrace, and I would see the place where my father was born, and where he grew to manhood.

I brought something else back from our hunt besides the loot taken from the imperial's camp. Ever since that night when I ran through the darkness guided by a wolf's nose, with the grim fell of a Lupaku shaman draped about my shoulders, my sense of smell has been much keener than that of other men. Not as good as a wolf's, of course, but still very good. Sometimes, I can scent things other than physical odors; sometimes I can smell emotions such as fear or hate, and sometimes I can smell magic, and when I smell pine smoke, I often think of Kithgar, and what he taught me.

"Never set foot to a trail, if you don't intend seeing it through to its end", he once said.

So be it. I had set my foot to a man-made trail, the Path of Kings, for the sake of vengeance and duty and half a score of other reasons, although it would take me years to realize it. I would follow the road I had chosen, right through to the end.

No matter where it would lead me.

Chapter XIX: The Trail to Drake's Fort

IT HAD BEEN A BRIGHT, CLEAR DAY when we made our preparations to go our separate ways. I knew that Ajax had spoken with Ankubi the evening before, so he had heard about our fight with the Imperial troops and of their Lupaku captives, but I was a bit surprised at the look he gave me. I tried to remember where I has seen it before, as I was bidding farewell to our towering Red Hunter friend. He placed a dark, broad hand upon my shoulder and I lifted my face to meet Ankubi's gaze. He had golden eyes, like bright coins, that could indeed look at the Sun on a cloudless day and not blink.

"You travel far, you and the Old Man with a Sword?", he asked. At my nod, he nodded back:

"But I think you will come again to Scythia, N'kopje, and when you do, we will see each other again; we will go hunting: for food or for a fight, or maybe both!"

As it happened, we did just that. We saluted each other and strode away; he towards the barn where his belongings were stacked, me towards Ajax and our mules. Ajax was giving me that look again, kind of like the one he sometimes gave me when I pick up a new technique faster than he expects. But he didn't say anything, as we mounted up and headed south, he just kept on looking at me.

"What? What is it?" I was starting to wonder if my trews were falling down or something equally embarrassing. He laughed.

"It's just that I leave for the Block, and you're a boy. I come back, and you've changed."

"Changed? Changed how?", I asked, wondering how just that little time could make such a difference.

He nodded once at me, and said: "You are a man, now."

I was a bit confused.

"Because I killed two imperial soldiers? But I killed more than that when we were attacked at Long Ear Springs! Why is this different?"

He gave me that look again.

"Not because you killed an enemy, but because you gave your word to an enemy, and you kept it. You might be surprised to find how many would never have even considered keeping their word to an enemy of their tribe."

That is when I realized what that look meant: he was proud of me. I

210

didn't really understand; I made a promise, gave my word and I kept it. It was, after all, MY word, my very breath given as a bond, why ever would I make a promise and deliberately NOT keep it? I suppose that I was then (and am still now in some ways), very naïve. Meanwhile, Ajax was rubbing his chin thoughtfully:

"Since you act like a man, I must treat you like one. There are things I have not told you yet, about your childhood, about your father and his sister. What I tell you might seem strange to you, or hard to bear, but you have a right to hear it, and now, I think you have need to hear it as well. When I took you to Hattusha after the death of your mother and sisters, I took you to the safest, most secret place I could think of: the House of Death, Wurrunk's Temple. I remember carrying you in through the back entrance of the temple, wrapped in my cloak and blinking like an owl. It was after midnight, but something seemed to draw people from their beds almost as if a bell had been rung. There was a bit of an uproar when they saw you and realized you were hurt. Most said that you had no place there in the temple, that you belonged with kin or in the care of the Healers of Kamrusepa."

"I had kept walking, past the kitchen and the assembly hall, up the stairs and into the Outer Ward, where the conference table was. There was a chair set at that table for each of those who spoke for Wurrunk among the tribes of Khetar, and I set you down in the chair your father had sat in, and when I did, the torch above his seat lit by itself. That pretty much ended the arguments that you had no place there. Horfui himself performed the divination asking when you should leave the temple; the Answer was:

'Seven days before this House will fall.'"

"And it was so. When war came, and Hattusha was invested, I saw that the imperial siege lines would not be held back for long, and I fled the city by a secret way, taking you with me. By night I brought you to the House of Death, by night I took you from it. Seven days after we left, Hattusha fell and the temple was leveled, its stones scattered from one end of the city to the other. The king of Khetar was slain, and every member of House of Death still in Hattusha died defending him."

Ajax was silent for a time then.

"We kept your presence, the fact that you even lived, a secret. Outside of the House of Death, only the king knew, and his personal healer, who he sent to tend you. He and your father had thought a great deal of each other, and if you could be healed, he would have tried to see you set in your rightful place."

"But the healer could do nothing for you, saying that only time would tell if you would recover. So we tended to you and waited, hoping. You were no trouble. You would eat and drink if food and water were placed before you and you could keep yourself clean. But you never spoke. We spoke to you as often as we could, in hope that we could provoke you into responding, but to no avail. Sometimes, you would wander off, but after the first week, we always knew where to find you: either in the armory sharpening something, or in the Hall of Silence listening to those who were sick or wounded. They seemed to find comfort talking to you. You would hold their hand and look into their face, and they would talk of their life to you: their families, their friends, what they had done, the things they had seen in different lands. And sometimes, those badly wounded or seriously ill would speak to you of what was in their heart and thoughts just before they died. Do you remember any of this?"

I shook my head; I could remember none of this, nothing at all.

Ajax went on:

"Most of those who knew you then died in the war, but in the Great House of Death in Byzantium where we now go, you may meet those who remember you from that time."

I thought about this for a bit, and then asked: "You mentioned the armory and me sharpening things?"

"Yes. You would often wonder into the armory and just stand and watch. I thought at first it might be your memory trying to pull itself awake: you would often sit and watch your father tend to his blades when you were young. But it never went further than you watching until Askos gave you that old knife and a sharpening stone, more to get you out of the way more than anything else. To his and my surprise, you finished that knife in a few moments, and we found that you would sharpen anything with an edge that we might give you. Tonalang, who was in charge of the armory, said you got to be quite good. He was a good man; I owed him a favor I never got a chance to repay."

Ajax paused for a moment, and then went on:

"Yet, with all of those blades you sharpened, for nigh on to two years, you never once cut yourself. Ever. You never have, cut yourself by accident, I mean."

No, I hadn't. I had not really thought about it, but I always know where sharp things are, and I avoid them. I don't even know I'm doing it.

"That's a handy skill to have, boy. I think you'll need it."

212

He was silent for a time, and then spoke: "There is someone else you will meet in Byzantium: the last of your father's family, his sister Natyr.

"It may be that I am at least partly responsible for the bad feelings between your father and his sister; if so, I never deliberately sought to come between them. It just seemed to be the way things were, and I just happened to be the one who provided an excuse for it to come out."

"Your grandfather, Robard, came to Byzantium from the West; he had been a mercenary captain in Francia and had won a certain amount of fame there. He was quite wealthy, and made an impression on the people in the higher circles of Thracian society. He made more than just an impression on the young Lady Mirani, and after a whirlwind courtship, they were married. They were quite happy by all accounts, despite the disparity in their ages; their marriage was blessed by two children: Natyr, the eldest, most like her father in temperament and Dono, your father. While his physical resemblance to his father was striking, Dono was more like his mother with his easy-going ways and his quick laughter. They were quite happy, until the year of the Coughing Mist and the sickness that took so many of Byzantium's people, including the Lady Mirani. Robard was never the same after that, and three seasons after his wife's death, Robard himself took ill. Or perhaps, began to show a sickness that he may have had for quite some time. It affected his muscles and his reflexes and the thought of spending his last days helpless and twitching did not appeal to the old mercenary at all. So he ordered his affairs and, after speaking in private with his daughter, kissed his children good bye and took a plain bronze broadsword and 20 gold coins to the worst section of the Byzantium wharves in the middle of the night. There, he picked a fight with pack of smugglers and was killed by them."

I thought about this for a moment, and asked:

"He took 20 gold coins with him to make it worth their while?"

Ajax nodded: "From what I was able to gather, your grandfather killed three men and wounded half a dozen more before they pulled him down. I don't know what he said to them while he fought them, but they propped his body up facing east, on the steps of the Customs House, so he was facing the dawn when the harbor watch found him the next morning. It seemed a strange courtesy for smugglers to pay a dead man. They took the gold and the sword though."

I shrugged. "They earned them."

"They did indeed." He was silent for a time after that.

We traveled south, skirting the eastern edge of the Thunderhead

Mountains. We were headed for the outpost at Drake's Fort, near the southern end of the mountain range. Drake's Fort was the easternmost holding of the Marcher Barons who guard the eastern rim of Lycia, itself the most easterly province of Thrace. While we traveled, Ajax continued to teach me, of course. He continued our lessons in weapon handling, but added others in the lore and customs of Thrace, and in magic. Not the spells that anyone might know, but the ceremonies and rituals that are the privilege and the duty of those who speak to and for the gods.

Part of what he began to teach me was based on what I had learned of the lore of Tarhunt, but much of the rest I seemed to already know. It had been part of my Aunt Syara's lessons, in a more simple form. When Ajax realized that he was covering old ground with me, he spent an entire day asking me questions, in order to get a handle on exactly what I had learned from my aunt. When he was done, he rubbed his chin in reflection and then squinted at me:

"Now, I know that when you aren't paying attention, you're just like any other boy your age: what goes in one ear, goes on out the other ear without even slowing down. But when you focus, when you really look at what I'm trying to teach you about an attack or a feint, you remember EVERYTHING. Is that the way it is with other things too?"

"Yes, Ajax."

"Your Aunt Syara's recipes?"

"Yes, Ajax; some of them, at least." My favorites, anyway.

"Can you remember what Kirnar said to you and the other children the night he decided to teach them spear fighting?"

"Yes. He said: "I've made up my mind; I'm going to teach all of you everything I know about fighting with a spear. I think you will all need to know it, and I need to know that my knowledge will not die when I do...""

Ajax stopped me: "Did you know that you were altering your voice? To make it sound like Kirnar's?"

He was right, I HAD been doing just that, only half aware of what I was doing.

"Did I sound like Kirnar?"

"You sounded just like him; you're a natural mimic, boy. But have a care with that: mimicry can be the same as lying, if you put words in someone else's mouth."

I didn't want to be a liar. It went against everything that Ajax and Syara had taught me. But more to the point, a liar could not wield Oathtaker, my father's sword. If you lied while holding that sword, it would turn in your hands and strike you down. Or so it was said. It didn't seem to be the kind of thing I wanted to test.

The weather was good for traveling, although it was getting hotter as we got farther into summer. We didn't see anyone else, and we made good time as we skirted the foothills of the Thunderheads that rose to our right as we rode south. Each night, Ajax would tell me more of my father and my aunt and the city that was our destination: Byzantium, greatest city of Thrace, and one of the greatest cities in the world.

"You are going to see more people than you ever imagined existed, Joren. The lands ruled by the Minos are warmer and more fertile than the slopes of the hills that lie in the Godpillar's shadow. They harvest two crops a year in Thrace; more food means more people and more wealth if they have someplace to sell the surplus. When Mino built his great Lighthouses and opened the seas, trade with other nations brought wealth, strange goods, stranger people and great opportunity to the old ports along the coasts of Thrace. That in turn brought people in from the countryside, to take advantage of the wealth and the opportunities."

"Now, Thrace has sometimes been called the Land of Queens, for it is the women who rule there, not the men. Each city has its own queen who governs on a day-to-day basis and deals with things like taxes and armies, but that is not where the real power lies. The real power in Thrace is the group of matriarchs known as the Council of Crones, which is made up of elders from each of the clans, and which has existed in one form or another since before the beginning of Time. The power of each clan's Crone is absolute within their family line, even to the point of arranging marriages and exiling those who defy a Crone's commands. Never forget that behind the decrees of the Minos and the armies of the Queens sits the Council of Crones, which watches and weighs the world through the eyes of those who guard the interests of their grandchildren."

"The larger families (and those who depend on them) are often called the Great Houses, and are tied to the earth, as befits a people whose toil brings so much wealth from their land. The lands north of Seuthopolis at the crossroads of North Thrace, have been governed by the House of the Brown Earth for more than a thousand years. The queen of that House is called the Brown Earth Queen, and her name is Dilfara the Weaver. She is a very patient and persistent woman; she is not called the Weaver just because of her skill at the loom, but also because of her ability to plan and craft to her will the strands of politics and power that run through Thrace. The house of the Brown Earth lost a great deal of power and wealth in the turmoil that engulfed the region after the Breaking of the World; entire towns in that area were leveled, and it has never fully recovered, despite the proximity to the great crossroads at Seuthopolis. So when the Pharos lighthouses were built and opened the sea lanes, thousands of people from the lands of the Brown Earth flocked to Byzantium in search of work and a better life. Moving from one place to another does not sever the ties of family and blood, so the interest and the influence of the House of the Brown Earth came to Byzantium with its people, as did the other great houses whose people came to swell the population of Byzantium from 20,000 to more than 100,000 people in little more than a generation."

I gaped at him. A hundred thousand people living in one place? My mind couldn't grasp it; I couldn't really imagine that many people, let alone what it would be like having them all together in one city. Without thinking, I said:

"It's going to smell something awful."

Ajax laughed at that, and then told me to get some sleep.

The next night, we spoke of Thrace again, this time, specifically about my aunt Natyr.

"Your grandmother Mirani was of the House of the Brown Earth, and as a child, your aunt became the best of friends with Dilfara. When they both reached adulthood, Dilfara set out to rebuild the fortunes of her House and your aunt Natyr was at her side every step of the way. They made a formidable team, and after Dilfara's marriage to her first husbands, and the birth of her first child, the Crone of her family named her as Queen of their House, the youngest to be crowned in more than six hundred years. In the 30 years since, Dilfara has taken what was a poor clan from the backcountry and built it into one of the three most powerful houses in Northern Thrace, with a seat on the city council of Byzantium and the ear of the Minos himself. In all that time, Joren, your aunt has been Dilfara's strong right hand. In Byzantium, she has been ambassador and street general, mistress of spies and priestess of the Earth, occasional advisor to the Minos and an enchantress of no small repute. Over the past 30 years, Natyr has outwitted, outfought or outlived more enemies that she can remember; there isn't a soul in Byzantium that does not know your aunt's name, and a great many of them fear it. The queens of Thrace wear formal attire in the old way: robed and bearing a crook and a flail. The crook is that of a shepherd who cares for the people under their care, and the flail is the lash of war for their people's enemies. For the past 20 years, your aunt's court title has been 'The Flail of the Brown Earth

Queen'".

I tried to digest this and then asked a few questions.

"You said Dilfara married her first husbands? More than one at once?"

Ajax scratched at his beard a bit.

"Yes. You should know about that. Thracian women sometimes take more than one husband at a time. Dilfara has had seven husbands all told, and borne five children. Her husbands are all dead now though; one fell ill, two were murdered and the other four died protecting her, although Dilfara herself is pretty good with her axe. Politics can be a very final sort of thing in Byzantium."

Then I asked the question that had really started to bother me. I had been looking forward to meeting my father's sister; she was all that was left of family to me.

"You said that there were some bad feelings between my father and my aunt?"

Ajax sighed, and then turn to look me right in the eyes. Uh oh.

"When I first met your father, I was teaching at the Great Temple of Wurrunk in Byzantium. He was the best of my pupils, and it was a pleasure to teach him. He soaked up everything I taught like a sponge, and I did not realize he was drinking in my tales of Issuria and Scythia just as thirstily as he was my instructions in the use of weapons and tactics. I did not mean to drive a wedge between your father and his sister, but that is what happened."

"I did not even see any of this until the moment that Natyr herself told me I was not welcome in her house, not that day or nor any other day that might dawn before the world ended. By then, your father had become friends with Fasunil and Kak; he was filled with a hunger to see the distant places and peoples we had told him so much of. He wanted to travel, to see, to strive and DO something with his life. The very last thing he wanted was to be another piece in the game of politics that your aunt and Dilfara were playing in Byzantium. Or, and this was only a rumor, the next of Dilfara's husbands. He would have been a very valuable piece in that game of politics, if he had been a mind to stay. City life, as you will see, is quite a bit different from what you are familiar with. Dueling is a common method of settling disputes in Byzantium, and your father was a dangerous man in any kind of fight. Due to…personal differences, he killed two men who were famous duelists and his sister meant that he would be the Sword of the Brown Earth in its disputes with the other political powers of Thrace. Your father refused, and did so in a very public place."

When he didn't go on, I asked "Just how public a place?" This sounded even worse than I had feared. I was right.

"Hmm? Oh, um, quite public actually. It was in the Hippodrome, in fact."

The Hippodrome. The great race track built to the Minos's own design, where they could race a dozen chariot teams side by side, in an arena that could seat more than 40,000 people.

"There weren't...a lot of people there, were there?" I had a bad feeling about this.

"Ah, well, it was pretty much full as I remember."

My father had embarrassed my aunt in front of a crowd big enough to hold a half dozen Khetarite tribes. She must have gone into a proper fury.

"There's a rumor the Minos himself was present, in a disguise. He would sometimes do that, to get a feel for what the people in Byzantium were saying and feeling."

My father had humiliated my aunt in front of 40,000 people and the greatest Sea King of them all. Did I say fury? She must have gone off like an erupting volcano.

"That is when she called upon the powers of the Earth to curse your father."

I felt as if Ajax had punched me in the stomach. She had cursed my father, her own brother? The curse of any priestess in a vengeful rage is no small thing.

"What...what words did she use to curse him?" I asked.

"She cursed him with loneliness, so that he would never find anyone to love him. She cursed him with sterility, so that he would never father children. Then she cursed him with wandering, so that he would never know his own place in the world."

I felt sick. That curse was worse than outlawry. It was horrifying in the.... Wait a minute.

"But, but my father met and married my mother!" I stammered.

"He did."

"And she loved him and bore him my sisters and I."

"She did indeed."

"My father was warchief of the Mabirshan, and a friend of the King of Khetar himself. He won and held a place of honor for years...That curse never found my father, did it? It never had any effect on him."

"Not on him, no." said Ajax.

A curse that cannot strike its intended target will often rebound upon the one who voiced the curse in the first place. "And my aunt Natyr?", I asked.

"Your aunt has never married. She has never borne children and it is said that from that day she cursed your father to this, she has never slept in the house that your grandfather Robard built for your grandmother. She has allowed those in service to the Brown Earth Queen to use that house while they are in Byzantium, and it has served as a barracks from time to time when things got lively in the city. Natyr herself either stays at the house of a supporter of the clan or occupies a room at one of the temples of the Earth; as is her right as a priestess of the Earth."

Then it would seem that the curse had struck at my aunt instead of my father. I thought about that for a bit, and then asked Ajax:

"Are you SURE she wants to talk to me?"

"Oh yes. She was very clear about that the last time I was in Byzantium. I remember it quite clearly, since it was the first civil thing she has said to me in more than 20 years. I don't think you have anything to fear from your aunt, Joren. What happened, happened between your father and your aunt. I believe it ended when your father died. "

"In any event, she has every right to want to speak with you: you are her heir after all. More importantly, I think that YOU need to speak with her. There are things that only she knows, and you need to hear them."

All the while, we kept moving, and the miles slipped away behind us. We were following the line of the hills to our west as they curved away to the southwest, towards the oasis at Drake's Fort. This was the last good watering place in this corner of Scythia, and the lords of the lands of Lycia and Thrace had taken and fortified the oasis centuries ago in order to minimize the chance of a nomad raid coming out of Scythia. The garrison at the fort would allow small groups of nomads to pass through, but anytime the nomads showed up in force, they were denied watering rights, and they needed the water if they wanted to get reach Lycia in any shape to fight. More often than not, this meant that the nomads wound up attacking the fort itself, which I'm sure was part of the plan as far as the fort's owner was concerned. Individual braves and small warbands might be able to tough it out and work their way through the hills on either side of the oasis and get into the High Marches behind it, but an army wouldn't be able to make it to the Kyphax River without water. The villages and ranches of the High Marches that lay between Drake's Fort and the Kyphax were well fortified in recognition of the threat posed by such raiders, but a Scythian army couldn't cross the Kyphax into Lycia without taking the fort that commanded the oasis, and the Scythians hadn't managed to do that in centuries. The fort was just that tough a nut to crack.

While we traveled, my lessons continued. At my request, Ajax told me what he knew about the forces that could be fielded by the Empire of the White Sun. Anyone who served the White Empress would be happy to pass word to the imperial authorities that the heir to the tribe of the Mabirshan was still alive, and I had to learn how to recognize and deal with them. As far as I was concerned then, that meant killing them. To me, they were all just enemies, they were all responsible for my family's destruction, and they all had to die. This was a stupid and dangerous way to think, and Ajax called me on it as soon as I was dumb enough to say it.

"Don't be a fool, boy. There are thousands of people in the Empire who know nothing about you and who could care less. They have their own lives to worry about and they have the right to live them, same as your family did. You know what you must do with your life; you know what your obligations are and what you must do to meet them. Focus on that; fight and kill when you have to, but killing people just because of the color of the cloak they wear is a thing unworthy of the son your parents brought into this world."

I didn't want to hear that, but the way he put it made me listen, and now, all these years later, I know he was right. It just took a while to sink in, that's all. He let me brood on it for all of about a minute, then he tapped on his sword hilt until I met his eyes.

"Now, pay attention. You must remember two things about fighting the Empire: it will use both time and every tool available to it against you. Time, because it is not bound to act in any particular season: the imperial army doesn't have to worry about getting home in time to bring in the harvest. People somewhere else in the empire are doing that for them. The imperials will wait seasons or years to gather what resources they need and then strike at you when you can least afford it. These resources might be water and mounts, magic and money, or they might be people." Then he paused to look at me.

"Ketil" I said and nodded at him. I had been thinking about my mother's brother and his crimes for quite some time. Had the rise of my uncle to power and his acceptance of imperial missionaries been one of the last pieces the empire put into place before they invaded Khetar?

"Just so. I think the plan to kill your family and put the Accursed One in your mother's place was formed years before you or your sisters were born. The empire thinks in terms of generations, boy. Remember that."

"Now, as to the tools of the empire and their use in times of war: there are many peoples living under the Gaze of the White Sun. Each of these peoples have their own strengths, and sooner or later, the empire uses them all. Often, there are entire units formed of them and they fight for the White Sun under the command of their own leaders. Do you remember what I have taught you of the Saxon Bearshirts? They are woodsmen, born to the use of the axe and the hunt; the Bearshirts are tireless when set to a trail and they never give up..."

As we traveled, I thought about Bel. Worried about Bel is closer to the truth. I had to get back to her as soon as I could. When I had spoken with my aunt, I'd have to see what Ajax and I could come up with as a plan. I didn't want her within reach of the White Sun Empire for a minute more than was absolutely necessary; I knew that I'd certainly feel much better if she was within my reach every hour of the day. Sometimes, I would catch glimpses of her sleeping, usually in a bowl I would hold in my hands before I went to bed, She seemed to be busy and tired, and more than a little worried about me, but not in any danger herself. Not yet anyway.

As we got closer to Drake's Fort, I began noticing more tracks. We had not seen anyone since we left the vicinity of Aleppo, but now we began to see the tracks of quite a few travelers, some old, some fairly recent. Ajax said it was because the oasis was not only the last good waterhole heading into Lycia from Scythia, it was also the last good watering place for a full two days march for anyone heading into Scythia from Lycia. That made Knight Fort a choke point that funneled the movement of any sizeable body of raiders or troops in this area. Any mount, even the hardy beasts of the Scythian nomads, will always consume more water than its rider, sometimes a great deal more. No wonder the Minos had a full garrison at the fort at all times; if he did not, someone else would, and he was much better off having his own hand around the throat of the water bottle, so to speak.

When I got my first look at the fort itself, I would have mistaken it for a natural rock formation, if not for the colors of the banners that flew from its towers. It loomed above the trees of the oasis on a shelf of native rock, and its walls and towers were made of cut blocks of that same stone, so that the fort and its base seemed from a distance to be all of a piece. And it was only when we entered the oasis proper that I realized how big it was. It could have held an entire steading within it. There were 3 towers, one large tower in the center of the fort and two smaller ones linked to it. Ajax said that the fort was double-walled; beyond the walls we could see there was a moat and then another set of walls that protected the fort proper. There was a well within the fort that had never failed, so that the garrison did not need to draw water from the oasis, and a cistern and storerooms cut into the rock beneath the fort itself. A group of determined fighters could hold such a fort for a very long time, even against overwhelming odds.

"It is old too." said Ajax. "A thousand years old or more in its oldest form. Everyone who owns it tends to change something or add to it."

When we approached the fort, we could see how the pool of water at the heart of the oasis curved across the front of the fortifications above it. There wasn't an inch of shoreline that was out of range of the archers and war machines we could see on the walls. Drake's Fort crouched above the water of the oasis like a sleeping dragon: as long as the dragon slept, you could have all the water you wanted. But wake the dragon, and you could go whistle for your water.

We moved off to the west side of the pool, away from the dwellings of the oasis people. There were several places where other travelers had built fires, and even a bit of firewood tucked away into a dry place beneath a shelf on a stone plinth carved with the sigils of the Minos. It was getting on towards sundown, and Ajax decided to make an early camp so we'd have a good night's sleep behind us when we started out at dawn the next day. We unsaddled the mules and I started to make camp while Ajax filled the water skins. After the mules had cooled off a bit, I'd take them down to the pool and get them watered and fed. Maybe I'd check and see if I couldn't find a merchant on the other side of the oasis that might have some fresh feed for them. Some carrots or an apple or two would be good; they were a good team of mules and they deserved it.

I'd unpacked and gotten a fire going by the time Ajax returned. He told me to wash up while he started preparing a meal, since we might be having a visit from someone from the fort. That made sense: any new arrivals at the oasis would be looked over carefully, and the watchers would see that Ajax was wearing iron. He might have important news from the north and the garrison commander would want to know it as soon as possible. Sure enough, a messenger from the fort approached our fire not long after we had finished eating. It was a man, neither young nor old, with a shaven head and a chin beard who wore an oddly patterned vest over a plain linen shirt and kilt. He barely glanced at me, but bowed to Ajax and said:

"Greetings, Lord. Kephtenes, Servant of the Minos, asks that you give him the honor of speaking to him, at your earliest convenience."

Ajax tugged at his beard and replied:

"Kephtenes? Hah! What a pleasant surprise! I have not seen your master in years and it will be a pleasure to speak with him again. As to a convenient time, now is as good a time as any. I will return with you to the fort."

The servant bowed to Ajax again, this time more deeply, and stepped back.

Ajax rose to his feet and touched my arm, saying:

"This is a stroke of luck. Kephtenes may be able to do us a favor, and I would like to speak to him again in any case. I don't expect any trouble, but keep your eyes open. I should be back shortly."

He hitched his sword belt into place and nodding to the servant, strode off towards the fort. I did the dishes and got the mules squared away with some fresh tubers I'd bartered from an old man of the oasis people for a couple of the hides we'd taken on our journey south. I checked my blades and was about to start practicing when I was distracted by my first glimpse of a Lycia knight. It was dusk and the setting of the Sun had taken the edge off the heat, when I saw the patrol coming up the track that lead southwest into the High Marches. There were two men on foot, trackers by the looks of them, and a trio of lancers, lean men in leather armor on fast-looking horses, but it was their leader who drew my eyes. He was a big man and he sat on the biggest horse I'd ever seen until then, both wearing better armor than I did.

He was just as dusty as his men, but he sat spear-straight in his saddle as he trotted his horse up to the gate and dipped his lance to the guards in salute. They returned his salute and the patrol went on into the fort, but not before something in the way that horse moved rang a bell in the back of my head. "Warhorse" I thought. A mount that would fight for its rider, and I had a healthy respect for what the hooves and teeth of a horse or mule could do in a fight. How would I go about fighting such a foe: an armored warrior on an armored mount, fighting together as a team? It gave me something to ponder, as I practiced with my swords, and the shadows deepened into night.

Ajax returned a couple of hours later; I could hear him whistling through his teeth, so we weren't facing any trouble. I moved into the light of the fire for a moment, so he knew where I was, and then stepped back into the shadows. He came up to the camp and asked me:

"Any trouble?"

"No sir. Just thinking about that knight I saw after you left, the one who came in with that patrol."

"Ah, yes. The knights are formidable opponents in just about any kind of fight. You'll see more of them, although not as many as you would had our plans not changed. We've had a stroke of luck: Kephtenes needs to send a preliminary report to his superiors immediately and he has asked me to take that report to Byzantium for him. In return, we will be allowed passage on the ship that waits for him in the harbor at the Haven. I had hoped to get us permission to use the post road that runs from Seleucia to Attaleia; that would have saved us a day or two for time. But this ship will take a week or more off of our journey; you will miss seeing the cities of Seleucia, Cibyrrha and Attaleia, but we'll get to Byzantium much faster. Kephtenes will be staying here a while longer, as his work is only half finished. His report is important enough to him that he asked me to deliver it in person, and I agreed. He's a good man, and I'd guess that he's going to recommend that the fortifications here be improved and the size of the garrison increased, in order to counter a possible thrust by the Imperials south along the Thunderhead Mountains."

"It is good advice, and I think the Minos will act on it. He fought off the empire once, but I don't think he'll want a rematch where the empire can attack from the north and the east at the same time. Kephtenes is finishing his report now; we will pick it up from him tomorrow morning and be on our way. We'll be turning south once we ford the Kyphax River, then we'll ride along the west bank of the river until we reach the ferry at Last Haven. For now, let's get some sleep."

I slept soundly enough, and after a quick meal the next morning, we walked our mules around the western end of the waterhole and up to the gates of the fort. The same servant I had seen the night before was there waiting before the closed gates, as was his master. This was a taller, older man, who was also clad in a vest, shirt and kilt, but whose clothing was cut from much finer materials. He wore armbands, an odd-looking torc and a skullcap as well, all made of silver and all marked with the sigils of the Minos, the last of the Sea Kings and Lord of Thrace. He clasped arms with Ajax and smiled as he handed over an ivory scroll case, tightly bound and sealed with wax:

"Thank you again, my friend. I shall rest easier knowing that this travels in your hands."

Ajax smiled back at him.

"I'm glad I can help you, Kephtenes. But there is no need to thank me; you're offer of that ship to carry us to Byzantium places me in your debt. "

He tucked the scroll case away under his cloak, on the left side where it wouldn't interfere with a fast draw.

"This will not leave my possession until I can place it in the hands of the quartermaster of the Minos's fleet in Byzantium."

Kephtenes sighed and rubbed the back of his neck; he looked tired and his hands were stained with ink. He must have spent most of the night finishing the messages he'd just handed to Ajax.

"It will be his responsibility to gather the men and materials I will need to finish my work here, so he should be the first to read my report. He'll pass copies of it on to those others who will need to read it." He glanced at me, and then raised his eyebrows at Ajax.

The old man took the hint, and said: "Ah, where are my manners. Kephtenes, Servant of the Minos, this is Joren, son of Dono, my pupil."

I bowed to him, and he nodded to me:

"Pupil? You are a lucky student indeed, to have a teacher such as this. Hold, did you say Dono?...Your face... "

He blinked at me twice, slowly, and I realized that he was searching his memory the way another man might sift gravel through his fingers. He turned to Ajax:

"Dono, brother to the Lady Natyr?"

At Ajax's nod, he said:

"Then my offer of my ship to you serves more than one purpose, for when I left Byzantium, the Lady Natyr was in very poor health. Poor enough, that if you wish to speak with her, you had best make all the speed you can to Byzantium, to the temple of the Willow and the Maple. That is where she was resting, last I heard."

Ajax and I met each other's eyes, and he said: "Then we must be on our way. Fare you well, Kephtenes." He gripped the other man's shoulder in farewell and swung into the saddle. I lingered long enough to bow again, and say:

"Thank you for your aid, Lord."

He shook his head at me.

"I am no lord, just a servant of the Minos. But you are welcome, son of Dono. May your roads be opened before you."

I stepped up into my saddle, and with a last wave to the two men in the shadows of the gate, we were off.

225

Chapter XX: Last Haven and a Ship

WE RODE HARD ON THE TRAIL from Drake's Fort, south and west into the land known as the High Marches. It was the easternmost of the lands ruled by the Minos, and the eastern edge of Lycia, peopled by hardy folk who preferred the frontier to the more settled lands to the west. They were lead by the roughest kind of nobility: younger sons seeking to establish their own houses, retired adventurers who had made good, and former mercenary captains who had received grants of land along with their promotions. They called themselves the Marcher Barons, and they were a salty lot indeed if they could keep the Minos's law and order this close to the wildlands of Scythia and the Thunderhead Mountains. They ruled from hilltop manors and fortified steadings, and the swords and lances of their warbands were as much a part of Lycia's defenses as Drake's Fort itself. I didn't see much of these folk at that time; we were pushing the mules hard enough that I was starting to worry for them, but Ajax assured me they'd get a rest at the village of Eastridge. The two groups of riders we did see hailed us thinking that we carried urgent news.

"Where do you ride on lathered mules?"

"What is the news from Scythia? Is there word of a raid?"

Ajax stopped long enough to satisfy their curiosity:

"Nay, no ill news, and Scythia will be quiet for a time; the tribes have been beaten by the Empire. It is just that we must catch a ship at the Haven."

Then we were off again. There wasn't much left in the mules when we made Eastridge, but Ajax had planned on trading them for horses there anyway. We stopped just long enough to swap our loads and saddles onto a brace of horses, wash up and get a bite to eat. When we pulled out and headed for the Ford of the Kyphax, we still had a bit more than an hour of daylight left. Ajax planned on using that hour. Gesturing to the Thunderheads to our north, he said:

"I want to camp on the far side of the Kyphax, boy. I've seen too many storms come boiling out of those mountains to take any chances I don't have to. If we don't cross the ford tonight, a cloudburst upstream could raise the river high enough that we could lose a day or more waiting for it to fall again. So we push on; the road is good and it will be a clear night. Tonight, we make camp in the domains of the GothKarissa, the land of

Sword and Song."

As we rode towards the sunset, I wondered again about Ajax. He and the hostler who got our mules knew each other, I was sure of it. The four horses we rode were of better quality than I had expected, not pretty but with bottom, (by which I mean endurance) and fresh supplies had appeared, almost by magic. It was if everything had been set aside for our coming. That I doubted, but I would not have been surprised to learn that the old man who rode at my side was involved with those who strove to ignite resistance to the empire among the tribes of Khetar. Any rebel movement would need to have a means of moving information and money to where it was needed, and it looked as if Ajax was making use of that courier network to get us to Last Haven as soon as was possible. I wasn't going to argue; I had my own debt to settle with the imperials and if rebel horses and supplies got me to Byzantium before my aunt died, I would repay those rebels ten times over, if I lived long enough.

We pushed on, and once into the hills west of Eastridge, the road began to go downhill, into the vale of the Kyphax River. We rode west for as long as the light lasted, and then walked single-file with Ajax leading the way. By then, I could smell water. The sky was clear and still enough that the stars could light our way, made easier because of the white stones that had been laid to mark the road bed. After an hour's walk, we came to the Ford of the Kyphax. There hadn't been any rain recently so the ford was clearly marked and the water was so low, we'd barely get our knees wet, even on foot. Also, we wouldn't be camping completely alone; there was a merchant caravan encamped on the other side of the river. Ajax had me hail them to warn that we were crossing the ford, just in case their camp guards were the nervous type. We got a hail back in return, and an invitation to their fire. The offer of a hot meal after a full day (and then some) on the road sounded good to both of us, and we accepted.

As we walked towards the campfire, I noticed that some of the caravan guards seemed to recognize Ajax. This included the guard captain who spoke a few words to the leader of the caravan before we were introduced. The merchant was a Lord Merchant of Nabu by the name of Willem Whitestaff, and he was headed for Eastridge and the holds of the Marcher Barons with a full load of fine fabrics, tools and jewelry. He was eager for any news that Ajax might have about bandits, nomad raiders and the condition of the road ahead of him. He didn't ask me any questions, which meant I didn't have to say anything and could concentrate on cleaning my plate, twice. From what I overheard, I gathered that Willem had no plans to visit Drake's Fort this trip. He had no interest in the Scythian markets, and from what I could see, was doing just fine with the customers he already had. By the time he was finished talking with Ajax, he seemed to be greatly relieved; apparently there were a great many rumors running through Lycia about the frontier since the battle at Roaring Springs. We thanked him for his hospitality, and made our own camp a short distance from their tents. After tending to our horses, we fell into our bedrolls and slept like logs.

I had odd dreams that night; a strange scent tinged with salt seemed to fill them and I found myself running through forests in strange lands, my ears filled with the songs of strange birds. When I awoke, I could still smell that strange scent, it seemed to come from the south. When I mentioned this to Ajax while we broke camp, he stopped what he was doing and looked at me:

"That nose of yours is something, boy. What you smell is the sea."

We gave thanks to merchant Willem again and bade him farewell, then we headed southwest across country. The road continued due west some miles until it joined the Crown road that then swung south and lead to the ferry at Last Haven, but Ajax knew of a more direct path that cut straight to the road to the sea. We were in the Vale of the Kyphax, which descended to the coast in a series of shallow terraces thick with all kinds of game. The river itself ran on our left and, less than half a mile south of our night's camp, broke into a series of whitewater rapids that rioted down to the coastal plain. There the river widened and ran more placidly until it met the sea, but here it roared and crashed through the rocks in a narrow bed and filled the air with a shimmering mist. We walked or trotted our mounts for 2 or 3 miles along a track not much more than a deer path, and then hit the Crown road running south, wide enough for two wagons abreast, and our pace quickened.

The farther south we rode, the higher the cliffs that were the walls of the vale rose on either side of us. The Highlands of Lycia are separated from the coastal plains by an escarpment a thousand feet high or more, and the only easy paths through those cliffs are where the rivers of Lycia have cut paths to the sea. The Tareel, the Calthi, the Rython, the Oxblood, the twin rivers of Garlos and Gonthos, and the Kyphax have cut the only road beds that connect the ports of the coast to the cities of the highlands. We made good time, and we saw a number of travelers, more in just a few hours time than we had seen since we left Aleppo. The harbor at Last Haven did a thriving business with the eastern towns of the GothKarissa tribe, from Ragga in the south to White Herds in the north and with the farms that dotted the bottomlands of the Kyphax valley. It looked to be a land at peace. Ajax said that there had been a pack of bandits known as the Skull and Bag Gang that had raided the length of the vale at one time, but they had been put down years ago. As we rode south, the smell of the sea grew stronger; the river widened and I saw why the only road to the Haven was on the west bank: the cliffs on the east side of the river often came right down to the water's edge, in one place for more than a mile. Last Haven lay at the foot of those cliffs, where the river met the sea. It must have been a lonely place before the Minos opened the seas to travel again. East of Haven, there was only the salt marshes and the desolate coast of Scythia, to the south lay the sea, and to the north the cliffs that towered a thousand feet above the coastal plain. Ajax said that there were rumors of smugglers' trails that lead up those cliffs and then north to the High Marches, but no roads worth the name. With the only way in being the ferry to the west, Haven would have seemed to have been on the very edge of the known world.

Even before the coming of the Minos, it had been home to those who were seen as misfits and outcasts, who either could not find, or did not want a place in normal society. It had a strange history and some strange traditions to go along with it; I asked Ajax if we would be staying in the city while waiting for the ship to leave. Maybe I could look around a bit. His answer was as much a warning as anything else:

"I doubt it, Joren. When the ship's captain sees this scroll case and reads the note Kephtenes wrote for him, he'll want to leave as soon as he's able, and we should get there in time to catch the tide. Not that you're quite ready to go wandering the streets of Haven yet, or that Haven would want you to."

I looked a question at him.

"Haven has been a place of sanctuary since at least sometime before the Fall, some say since before the Dawning. In that time, people have gone to ground there from many places, not just the rest of Thrace. Although it is laid out like a western city, there are temples and shrines to many different gods to be found there, along with their worshippers. I serve Wurrunk and you have sworn yourself to Tarhunt; there are quite a few folks who think that the Lord of Death and the King of the Gods are a little too single-minded for civilized society. Not to mention that you will find more thieves and more kinds of thieves in Haven than in almost any other city you will ever visit. I wouldn't be surprised to learn that a great many of the people in Haven have had a price on their heads at one time or another. And since Wurrunki often work as bounty hunters, I tend to make people like that a bit nervous. I know that whenever I'm in Last Haven I can feel I'm being watched, and I can almost hear them wishing I would leave."

"Like in Adari.", I said.

He nodded.

"Just like in Adari. I want you to have a lot more training under your belt before you go drawing a blade in a city of more than 5000 people, very few of whom are going to be happy to see you in the first place."

Well, that made sense, and the mention of training got me thinking of something else. During our ride south, Ajax had told me that he had made arrangements with those who led the temple of Wurrunk in Byzantium for my training. For a full year, I was going to get the best training from some of the finest warriors in the world; all I had to do was get to Byzantium, get to the Great House of Death and...pass the tests of the temple examiners. Teachers that good weren't going to waste their time on just anyone, I was going to have to prove to them that I was worth their time and effort. I couldn't count on being Ajax's pupil to make things easier for me; each of the examiners was sworn to test me fairly as to my abilities, and at least one of them was likely to be an unfriend to Ajax, and would gladly dismiss me if I didn't make the grade. There would be six tests; if I failed even one, I was out. Ajax didn't seem to be worried about the tests at all, which was good, because I was starting to obsess about them. He just said:

"Loricon and I have been at loggerheads for years; when he hears that I have brought a pupil of mine to be tested, he will make sure that he is one of the examiners. If there is anyway that he can fail you and stay within the bounds of his oath, he will. So let's just make sure that you can handle whatever he throws at you."

We pushed the horses hard, harder than we would have if we had planned on keeping them. There wouldn't be room for them on the ship though, so Ajax was going to sell them while I unloaded our belongings and kept an eye on them. We had good luck and good weather, and with two hours of daylight to spare, we rode up to the mooring of the wide, flat bottomed ferryboat just as its crew were getting ready to cast off. I paid the ferryman and we began the river crossing with the smell of the sea and the shore heavy in the thick air of the coast, and with the seagulls wheeling and crying overhead the whole way across.

Chapter XXI: The Pride of the Waves

I WOULDN'T SET FOOT IN LAST HAVEN ITSELF for years yet, but my first glimpse of the city left an impression. It wasn't just that it was the biggest city I'd ever seen up until that time, it was the way it was built, all right angles and stone walls, more like Drake's Fort than Melid or Gazian. Also, just walking from the ferry to the downriver side of the quay where the deep water ships were moored, I could feel what Ajax had spoken of, the sense of being watched. It was if something or someone had fled to Haven to hide, and that it watched constantly to see if it had been followed. We strode up to the dock where a long galley whose single mast flew the Minos's banner was tied up, and where a single spearman stood guard, watching us approach.

Ajax showed the soldier the scroll case he carried and said:

"I have a message for your captain."

The man's eyes widened at the sight of the seal pressed into the wax on the scroll case, and lifting a small brass horn, blew three notes, two short and one long. A dozen or so men came running across the wharf to the ship, while more than a score came from the ship itself in answer to the horn's call. They were burned brown by the Sun and had the heavy muscles and deep chests of oarsmen, but there wasn't a single slave among them. They were free men and each wore a weapon of some kind; a picked crew who could fight as well as row in the Minos's service. They were lead by a tall lean man in a pleated headdress whose breastplate and greaves had been enameled a bright blue. He wore a short, heavy blade at his side, and rubbed a hook-shaped scar on his left cheek as he looked us over with hard brown eyes in a face weathered by wind and sun.

"You have a message for me, Attar?" he said to Ajax, with a slight bow.

Ajax bowed back and handed the man a piece of parchment tied with a rawhide thong.

"I do, Captain. From Kephtenes, Servant of the Minos at Drake's Fort. I am to place this scroll case into the hands of the Quartermaster of the Minos's Fleet in Byzantium, as soon as you can get me there."

The ship's captain read through the message twice, looked at Ajax standing there in his iron armor, with a sword on either hip, and then at me. He nodded. "Welcome aboard."

He turned to the men behind him and started barking orders:

"All hands, make ready to sail! Kroton! Take some men and turn out

231

the dives in the Haven. To catch the tides, we leave here in one hour. Anyone not on board then will be left behind. Go."

He turned back to us: "Put your gear on the deck in the stern, portside of the steering oar."

Ajax pointed me at the horses and said:

"Thank you, Captain. We'll try to stay out of your way."

"I would appreciate that, Attar." And he didn't say another word to us until we were a good ten miles at sea.

I went to unpack the horses and put our belongings on the spot on the ship's deck which the captain had assigned to us, and I was slinging a saddle bag over one shoulder when the wind shifted and I caught the full scent of Last Haven for the first time. It was like a physical blow that rocked me back on my heels. It wasn't just the smell of so many people living so close together, with their food and their garbage and their sweat, but the smell of fires and frying fish, of incense and wines; and underneath it all, the smell of magic. Not just one kind of magic, but many, all woven together. There was the smell of bright sunlight and cool deep shadows, of sawn wood and hammered metal, of green growing things and that sharp smell the air has when lightning strikes nearby. Then there were the other smells: stenches of things gone rotten, of poison and of sickness and of blood. And underneath it all, behind everything else, there was the scent of something very, very old, and of something else that was very, very dead.

It wasn't until Ajax touched my shoulder that I realized I had fallen to my knees. So many things I smelled....I realized that I was starting to feel sick. He helped me to my feet, and asked:

"What is it, Joren? You're face is turning green."

I swallowed hard and managed to blurt out: "That city stinks so strong I can almost taste it." before I staggered to the edge of the dock and inhaled deeply, filling my lungs with the clean smell of the sea.

I did NOT want to puke my guts out before we even set foot on board the ship; that was exactly the wrong kind of first impression to make on its captain and crew. After a few moments, I got my stomach under control and took two of the saddle bags from Ajax to carry along with my weapons and my bedroll. Then we boarded the Minos's ship, and I tried to put all thoughts of Last Haven behind me. The ship's name was Pride of the Waves, and her prow was carved with the image of a girl holding a crown in one out-stretched hand. It smelled of tar, paint and lubricants: grease (for the oar ports) and weak beer (for the crew). Ajax and I moved to the rear of the ship, dodging crewmen scrambling to finish preparations for departure, and set our things on the deck at the stern, with the steering oar on our right. As we watched the captain and his crew ready their ship to put to sea, Ajax had some words of advice for me:

"Remember something, Joren. The sea is dangerous place, and it can change from placid to stormy in minutes, not to mention the threat of pirates, shoals or sea monsters. That means there must be only one voice giving orders in emergencies, or you will have chaos. There can be only one captain of a ship at sea and when that captain gives an order, it has to be obeyed, or the ship and the lives of all aboard her may be at risk. So when this captain tells you to do something, don't look at me, either do what he says or draw your sword. Defiance of a captain on his own ship is called mutiny, and only fire is worse than a mutiny at sea. At the very least, it will be considered a challenge to the death, and more often than not, the crew of the ship is more than happy to help the captain throw you overboard. At worst…well, I've seen mutiny split a ship's crew down the middle and set them at each other's throats. Most died."

I looked at him.

"If he asks you to do something, you will do it. He's unlikely to ask you to do anything you don't want to do, unless he has a very good reason. So I will obey him too: I want to see my aunt, and he will take me to her as quickly as he is able."

Ajax nodded to me, and we went back to watching the ship's crew at work. What we left unsaid was what every man on that ship knew: Ajax was an Attar of Wurrunk. If he did decide to draw his sword in defiance of this captain, he could probably kill every man on this ship with or without my help, and then go walking down the quay and book passage on another ship. No one in their right mind was going to tell Ajax to mop the deck.

I, on the other hand, might be considered fair game. I shrugged to myself; it was probably just as well. I'd get bored with nothing to do, although Ajax would no doubt want me to practice once the ship was at sea and we wouldn't be in anyone's way. That was fine, but I wanted to know more about ships and how they worked. Maybe if I kept my eyes open, I could learn enough that I wouldn't be completely useless the next time I traveled by sea. So I watched the organized bustle of the crew as closely as I could, and kept out of their way.

As near as I could tell, we upped anchor just about one hour from the time of our arrival. I noticed that the man the captain called Kroton had returned with his men and a dozen or so others, some of whom did not look well at all. Kroton didn't seem too happy as he made his report, but the captain just nodded once and took his place at the steering oar. Among other things, the crew had cleared the deck and hoisted a broad blue sail marked with a yellow trident to catch the wind blowing from the north. The captain, whose name we learned was Resostris, had his own task to perform. It was his duty to complete the ceremony that asked the gods to bless our voyage and bring us safely to our destination. Needless to say, the captain was left undisturbed until this task was completed. Ajax leaned against the rail and tugged on his beard while he hummed a tune to himself.

"It seems to me that I've heard of this captain before; he has a reputation for reliability, and his ship is said to be one of the fastest in all the Narrow Sea. We could have done worse."

It has been a long time since that day, but I still remember the feel of the wind at our back, and the sparkling dance of the waves and how lightly our ship seemed to skim across the waters. As we left the shelter of the harbor, the ship began to pitch and roll a bit due to the waves that came marching in from the south. I had to hold onto things until I became accustomed to the movement of the deck beneath me, but before long, I could keep my footing and I went back to watching the crew at work. I soon noticed that they were watching us right back, me especially. There seemed to be an anticipatory air about them, like they were waiting for me to do something entertaining. I mentioned this to Ajax, and I could see he was himself amused.

"You're not sick.", he said to me.

"No, I feel much better now, thank you."

"Heh. No, I mean you're not seasick; they're waiting to see you puke your guts up over the side of the ship. The movement of the ship often does that to people who've never been to sea before. But it doesn't bother you at all, does it?"

"No, sir. It kind of feels like I'm in a tall tree when the wind blows, but different."

I bounced up and down on the balls of my feet a couple of times to see if that made any difference. Nope.

"I'm hungry."

"JUST like your father."

The speed of our passage, the smell of the sea and feel of the wind thrilled me and before I knew it, the day had gone and night had come. Arinniti sank in the west and the heavens were lit by the stars and planets above before the captain spoke to us again. He left the steering oar to Kroton, and then walked to where Ajax and I were sparring. We stopped and I bowed to him as he approached. He bowed to Ajax and said:

"You have been to sea before, Attar?"

Ajax answered: "I have, but not the boy."

Resostris nodded. "I'm short one oarsman who spent the night in a drinking house my men could not find before we left the Haven. This might be a problem; if we don't catch the tide in the Darkling Strait just right, we will need all of the help we can get."

"Ah. Then, with your permission, I'll spend sometime teaching the boy how to handle an oar. That way, when the time comes, we can both pitch in."

"Thank you, Attar. Use this last bench on the portside when you practice; I will let my crew know what you are about before I go to sleep. As to our journey, we should make good time with this following wind. Soon, we will pass between the harbor lights of South Temple to the west and Sayedra to the east. From there, it will be a straight sail of fifty miles till we pass Salenis, where we will be able to see the light of the Pharos at Kition. Then, we will turn west and head for the Great Pharos outside the Narrow Sea. Once we pass Phaselus, we will be close to the mouth of the Strait. With luck, we should be able to ride flood tide all the way through. Good night to you."

We bade him good night, and settled into our bedrolls. At first, I couldn't sleep, but soon enough the sounds of the ship around me sounded less and less like the creak of ropes and timbers and the flap of a sail and more and more like the breath and movements of a living thing. Then I fell so deeply asleep that Ajax had to shake me awake an hour after sunrise. We ate a hot meal for breakfast, to my surprise. The Minos's ships used a cunning little stove made of brass and clay, shielded with sand in a box. There was one at either end of the ship, enough to provide hot porridge to go with some day-old bread from the Haven. Good enough for me. Then Ajax and I got to the business of teaching me to use an oar. We had made the turn west before dawn, and were now just southwest of the village of Phasilus at the southern tip of Lycia. It was 40 miles or more to the Darkling Strait, more than enough time to teach me the basics; at least I would be of some use if needed, and not just baggage. I sat on the inside of the oar bench, with Ajax to my left, and I was surprised at how light the oar felt; it was not only counterweighted, but finely balanced, and I saw that some skill had gone into the making of it.

We weren't getting the full force of the wind anymore, but the sail was catching enough that the captain left it up and had half a bank of oarsmen at work on either side of the ship. This left us with enough elbow room that I wouldn't foul anyone else when I screwed up. We were facing the stern of the ship, but I didn't pay any attention to the captain at his steering oar, I listened to Ajax and watched every move he made. He showed me how to hold the oar; how to brace my foot on the oar step set into the deck and how to pull. It wasn't just how strongly you pulled the oar, but also how well you could keep time with everyone else. Everyone had to pull together, or one oar would foul others and the ship wouldn't be going anywhere.

"Find the rhythm that the others are rowing to and match it. Feel it in your head and match your breathing to it, and then row, not before."

I waited then, listening, feeling the ship move as the crew pulled stroke after stroke, and when I was ready, I looked at Ajax and nodded. He nodded back and said

"Now... pull."

I pulled, and felt the oar catch the water.

I pulled again, and felt the power of the waves that caught at the oar.

I pulled a third time and felt the ship itself move through the water, and that I was a part of it. I had never felt anything like it. Ajax grinned when he saw the look on my face.

"Heh. More to it than just that, boy." So there was, much more.

Ajax showed me how to hold the oar so as to not get it in the teeth or the ribs if the oar blade caught a rogue wave; how to unship the oar and hold it so that the butt was on the deck and the blade pointed at the sky, and then how to ship the oar back out the port as smoothly and as quickly as possible. I wondered at this until he explained that it was a common tactic in naval battles to attempt an oar rake on an opposing ship. The attacker would try to run his vessel down the side of the enemy ship and ram not the ship itself, but the oars on one side. The goal was to cripple the enemy by breaking oars and also disabling as many of the crew as possible; the force of another ship striking an oar could throw a man clear across the deck of the ship and smash arms, legs and ribs like kindling. We practiced until Ajax was satisfied, and then he bade me rest for a while and oil my weapons and my harness, since sea salt doesn't treat either kindly. While I was tending to this, my mind wandered a bit, as it usually did, to thoughts of Belkara. I could feel her, off to the north of me, and I wondered what she was doing. I missed her, I was worried about her and I very much wanted to see her face again. Maybe I could find a mirror when we got to Byzantium, like the one Aunt Syara used to have. Hmm. Mirrors cost money though, and as much as I liked to watch Bel, what I really wanted to do was HOLD her. Well, thinking of that got me thinking of other things, and that got me on my feet ready to ask Ajax to spar with me, to do something, anything to burn off some of this energy and take my mind off of Bel. As luck would have it....

"The Darkling Strait is not far off, Attar."

It was Resostris, and he didn't seem too thrilled with the prospect. Ajax rose to his feet and nodded to the captain; I bowed.

"Trouble, Captain?" Ajax asked.

"Not exactly, Attar. At least not yet, but I didn't get as much help from the wind as I had hoped, and we may have to row for it if we wish to be far enough north of the other end of the strait before the tide turns. I think it was wise of you to show him how to use that oar; we may need every strong back we have if we don't want to spend half a day waiting to get the tide right. The Servant of the Minos said to get you to Byzantium as quickly as possible, and I mean to do just that."

He turned to give orders to his crew, and Ajax and I stepped back against the rail to watch. The sail was furled and lashed tight, and everything on deck that might come loose in a heavy sea was tied down as well. I went and checked our waterskins; I thought we might need water if we were going to be spending a lot of time at the oars and I was able to fill them from one of the water casks below deck. As I finished, the older man who was both chief cook and sailmaker for the ship asked me to give him a hand. His name was Ahiram, and together we rolled a big black drum up the steps and over to the stern of the ship, to the right of the steering oar. Ahiram tied the drum into place by running a length of rope through leather hoops on the drum and three brass rings set into the deck. It turned out he was the drumsman for the ship as well, and he showed me the small wooden mallets padded with leather that he would use to sound the beat to which we would row.

I returned to where Ajax waited by the rail to the captain's left; we could see the soaring tower of the Great Pharos clearly now, and the smoke from the fire burning at its summit four hundred and fifty feet above the waves. You could see the light from the Great Pharos at night from a distance of one hundred miles and all waters within that distance were calmed by the powers harnessed by the Minos when this, the first Great Lighthouse was built. That had been more than thirty years ago, and the other cities that ringed the Great Sea had followed suit; within ten years, there was a chain of Pharos Lighthouses stretching from Gades on the Outer Ocean to Kition on Alashiya. Waters that had been unnavigable for more than five centuries were once again open to trade, and ports that had withered away since the Breaking bloomed once again. Twenty five years ago, Byzantium had been a provincial capital with a population of just less than twenty thousand people, little more than the administrative center of the lands ruled by the Minos. Now it was the greatest port in the known world, its population swollen to more than one hundred thousand souls.

The waters of the Narrow Sea had been protected from the ravages of the Breaking, and the cities along its coasts had maintained their fleets to move people and cargoes along its 200 mile length. When the Great Lighthouses had calmed the seas, the Minos had been able to expand his influence more quickly than anyone else. That influence had brought trade back to Byzantium, and with it, wealth and power. It had also brought the attention of the Empire, which desired an outlet to the Sea and of course a taste of all that wealth. The Minos was going to need all of that power and more, if he was going to keep Thrace from becoming an Imperial province.

I turned when Ajax touched my shoulder; he wanted me to know something else about the entrance to the Narrow Sea. He told me that we would actually pass over a town when we entered the Darkling Strait, a stronghold of the mer-folk who lived in these waters.

"There is another world beneath the ocean's waves, Joren. When at sea, don't ever make the mistake of forgetting the powers that rule that world."

I leaned over the side and peered intently into the water, hoping for a glimpse of one of the mer-folk or some fabulous sea creature, but before I could do more than begin to guess at the shapes that moved in the waters around our ship, the roar of Kroton's voice drew my attention back to more important matters.

"All Hands! To your benches!"

The Darkling Strait was dead ahead. It was called the Darkling Strait not because darklings lived there, but because it had been a favorite spot for the war galleys of the Lord of Shadows to ambush ships of the Sea Lords during the many hostilities between the two powers before the Breaking. Anyone unused to the tremendous power of the tides in the strait would be at a serious disadvantage in a fight, and the navy of Kasku the Wise had used that advantage whenever they could. We were close enough by now that even I could feel the difference; the current of the waters rushing in to fill the shallows of the Narrow Sea had the ship in its grasp and we began to pick up speed. Soon, I could see whitecaps, and realized that the flow of the waters through the strait was more like the flow of a great river than the pull of the tide you might find off of any beach. As we entered the throat of the strait, Kroton took a place at the prow of the ship to keep watch for anything that might drift across our path. The main channel of the strait was deep enough that shoals weren't a threat, but unlucky ships had wrecked in the Darkling Strait before, and a floating hulk would be a deadly menace to a ship moving at speed through these waters. As a wise man once said, "A collision at sea can ruin your entire day".

Resostris had taken the steering oar, with Ahiram at his side, to keep the ship on the proper heading. The rest of us had taken our places on the benches; our oars were needed from time to time to keep the ship from drifting broadside to the current, but the real work was ahead of us. Ajax had told me that we probably needed to be north and west of Tillat, the village on the northwest corner of Sharpstone Island, if we were to be beyond the reach of the currents in the Darkling Strait when the tide turned. That meant a lot of rowing. As we waited on our oars, all I could think of was: "I don't want to look like a idiot in front of these men." That probably should have been the least of my worries right then, considering that if the ship wrecked, I'd be swimming, not rowing. But I was still very young, and the last thing I wanted to be was dead weight or worse, a hindrance. I might never see any of them again, neither the quietly competent crew nor old Ahiram nor the silent, watchful Resostris, but their scorn would gnaw at me for days.

I wouldn't have to worry about scorn from Ajax though; if I screwed up, he'd just rent a boat and have me row it from one end of Byzantium harbor to the other until he was satisfied I knew what I was doing. That might not be all that bad, at least I'd get plenty of practice...

"All Hands!!!"

Well, that was quick. Looking around me, I realized that I'd been in a funk, and more time had passed than I had thought. We were nearing the eastern end of the strait, and it was time.

"Oars Ready!" I gripped the oar and stretched and exchanged a glance with Ajax.

"Pull!" And it began.

"Pull!" And the drum beat.

"Pull!" Breathe, boy.

"Pull!" Feel the grain of the wood beneath your hands.

"Pull!" Feel the water move across the blade of your oar.

"Pull!" Feel the stroke of the other oars around you.

"Pull!" Feel the ship move through the water around you.

"Pull!" Feel the ship move with each oar stroke, like the slow beat of a heron's wing.

"Pull" Feel that you and your oar are part of living thing, this ship, that has two score hearts and four score arms and Pull!

After a while, Kroton stopped calling the stroke, and we pulled our oars just to the beat of the drum. Time went by.

Was it hot? No, I had been at Roaring Springs, I knew what real heat was.

Did my hands bleed?

Did my shoulders burn?

Baby. Keep pulling.

More time went by.

After a while more, I began to get angry.

I was a man of the Taurus Hills, and the last prince of the Mabirshan. I had met enemies blade to blade and put them down, and I'd be damned if I'd let a pack of tar-stained wharf rats see me falter. I'd show them, I'll pull this oar until the bottom drops out of this stupid ship....

"HOLD OARS!"

Ajax and I stopped as one, and we all looked to the captain, breathing slow, deep breaths. The captain stood at the steering oar, with one had raised in the signal that had prompted Kroton's order to hold oars. He nodded once to himself as he looked off to the north, and said:

"Well enough. Shake that sail out, let everyone who sees it know that we sail in the service of the Minos himself. Then get some food into their bellies."

"Aye, Captain. OARS IN!"

As we pulled the oar in and prepared to stow it, Ajax spoke to me in a quiet voice:

"All right, take three deep breaths and get your broadsword. We're going to spar a little to loosen up those muscles."

"Yes, sir."

My arms felt numb and the muscles in my back and legs were burning, but I knew better to say no. Ajax knew what he was about, and I always like to practice with any sword: it calms me down and I always seemed to learn something new when I sparred with Ajax. I took those deep breaths and, drawing my broadsword, turned to face my teacher.

He had his bronze broadsword out and we nodded to each other. Then he came in on me, one hand behind his back, flicking his blade at me in that way he had, almost like it was a rapier. I countered and countered again, tried a cut that went nowhere and realized the old man was backing me against the railing. I forgot all about my muscles and being tired, and focused on the swordsman and the blades in front of me. He went easy on me, I know it. But when he raised his left hand and spoke "Hold" to end the bout, I still felt like an idiot and an exhausted idiot at that. From my point of view, it felt as if he had been chasing me around the deck for a quarter of an hour. But then I noticed that everyone who wasn't at work was gaping at us, at *me*. Ahiram was leaning on his drum, laughing, and the captain himself seemed to be holding back a grin.

"Attar", he said, "There is no need for you to intimidate my crew in such a manner."

Ajax sheathed his sword and smiled at Resostris.

"Why, whatever do you mean, Captain?"

"Attar, please. YOU look old enough to be Ahiram's father, and your "pupil" (here he looked me right in the eyes for the first time) looks barely old enough to grow whiskers, yet the two of you row any number of miles through the currents of the Darkling Strait, and then put on an exhibition worthy of a Great House's fencing master."

Huh? Us?

"Forgive me, Captain. I just wanted to help the boy make a good first impression."

"Hah! Well, consider the impression made."

Then he went below deck, looking suspiciously as if he was choking back laughter. Ahiram didn't bother trying to hide his grin, and asked me if I could give him a hand stowing the drum now that we were done with it.

I grinned right back at him. "Of course, Sir."

"I've never been a Sir, lad. Ahiram is good enough for me."

"I'd be glad to, Ahiram."

We rolled the drum back into place and, after wiping it dry with an old cloth, replaced the canvas cover that would keep it clean and dry until it was needed again. Then I went and had some of the food being passed around; it was venison, with onions and the last of the bread. It tasted wonderful, and even the weak beer tasted good, although not as good as our own beer at home. When the meal was done, twenty men took their place on the oar benches and began rowing with a long slow stroke that they kept up for hours. After two or three hours, they switched places with the rest of the ship's oarsmen, and this pattern was repeated until we reached our destination. We were well into the waters of the Narrow Sea proper; the wind had little strength here. Only magic and long oars pulled by strong arms could move a ship with any speed over these waters, and Ajax thought our ship was using both. Resostris had turned the ship more to the west to follow the traditional path to Byzantium and the wind died away to the barest of breezes. Despite this, the ship still seemed to almost skim across the waves. We made excellent time, passing east of the Salt Horse Islands and out into the central part of the Narrow Sea. That night, I slept so soundly that Ajax says someone headed for the night soil pot in the stern actually tripped over me, and all I did was roll over and snore deeper. I had dreams, but all I remember of them is Belkara laughing at me. The best kind of dreams, those.

While I slept, the ship sailed on and more than lived up to her reputation. During the night, we turned northwest and sailed past the isle holding the City of Starlight, the Minos's own palace. We were following the old channel used by deep-water ships since the beginning of Time, and it lead us past the swamps around Fog Island to the northeast of us and Sanctuary Island with its many altars to our west. When the Sun rose in the east, we could see the dark bulk of the Shadowlands looming to the north beyond the swamps, while ahead the waves were dotted with countless sails: we were approaching the great harbor of Byzantium, at the mouth of the Lycus River, and it seemed like all the ships in the world called it home. There were deep-laden barges and flat-bottomed sculls, fishing boats of all descriptions, merchant vessels of every size and even a number of warships. Their bronze rams gleamed in the sunlight, and their decks were crowded with soldiers armed with javelins and clad in leather armor. Almost all of the warships were part of the Minos's fleet, but there was one great trireme that flew a broad pennant quartered in bright colors that Ajax said were those of the Duke of Marsalia, on the southern coast of Neustria. I would see that flag again.

Although the multitude of brightly colored flags and the scent and sounds of the harbor were fascinating, what draws the eye of anyone entering the harbor of Byzantium is the statue of Great Byzan herself. It towers more than 150 feet above the waters of the harbor, with the top of her head level with the top of the tallest building on the Acropolis, within the walls of the Old City, the oldest part of Byzantium. The statue rises just to the north of the Degirman Gate (or Harbor Gate), and is carved from one huge piece of translucent green stone. That stone must be very hard, because the details of the statue are seemingly untouched by time or weather despite the passage of more than a thousand years. The tines of her trident, the scales of her armor, the immortal beauty of her face are as sharply cut in the stone as if those who had wrought this likeness has just put aside hammer and chisel.

At the left hand of Byzan's statue is that of her loyal handmaid, Tawara, holding an infant in her arms (for Tawara is the patron of nursemaids) and followed by a flock of her faithful geese. From time to time, the statues of Tawara and her geese have moved, as have almost all of the statues in Byzantium, when great events or great magics have altered the fate of the city or its people. Of all of the statues in the city, only the great statue of Byzan herself has never moved, from the founding of the city to this day. Prophecies say that if her statue ever does move, then the city of Byzantium itself will fall, or change beyond recognition.

The first of the warships that spotted us had someone sound a long horn call that was repeated by others off ahead of us, until their echoes had spread across the entire harbor and up into the city above it. Every oarsman took his place at his bench as if summoned on deck by that same horn call, and at Kroton's count, began to row with a will. The brazen horns of the warships had warned that a ship on the Minos's business approached, and the merchant ships in the harbor would clear a lane for us, temporarily at least. Resostris meant to make the best speed possible given this opportunity, because it was his duty and because no captain worth the title would pass up the chance to flaunt his ship's lines and speed before such an audience. Ajax and I were not asked to take an oar: we carried the words of Minos's message, rowing here was beneath us. Not to mention the fact that Resostris had no intention of giving a greenhorn like me the chance to screw up and make his ship a laughingstock in the middle of one of the busiest harbors in the world.

We stood to the captain's left and rear, with our belongings packed and slung over our shoulders, and me with a freshly cut onion to sniff. The array of odors that assaulted my nose when we approached the city had set my stomach to churning until the clean bite of the onion drowned them out. I looked pretty stupid with tears running down my face, but better that than making a grand entrance into Byzantium harbor hanging over the side rail while I puked my guts out. Resostris had the steering oar and, although more than one voice from the vessels that we passed called his ship's name or his own in salute, his eyes never left the waters ahead of us. He guided us past the massive remains of the Dragon Shrine (which dated back to the height of the Dragon Empire) that rose on our left and on into the northwestern corner of the harbor; then north past the tower of Daedalus into the passage between the city and the island that holds Aruna's Fort and on into the mouth of the Lycus river. Our ship then rounded Tarhunt's Hill and sped past the Riverside port and on to the beach near the temple of Lycus, god of the river. In doing so, we passed over the great chain that had been laid across the river to keep invaders from passing up the river and striking at the Minos's shipyards. It hung slack in peace time, and I gaped in awe at its massive links, each thicker than a man's arm. As we approached the temple, we could see half a dozen hulls in different stages of construction: new ships being built by the order of the Minos.

Then Resostris leaned hard on his steering oar as the portside oarsmen dipped their oars and the starboard oarsmen ran their oars in and the ship turned towards the beach in so tight an arc I would not have believed it possible if someone had told me of it. The prow of the ship grounded at right angles to the beach, and with less of a jolt than I had expected. There were shouts and cheers of admiration from the work crews and guards on the beach; it seemed that Ajax and I were not the only ones concerned with making a good impression.

Ajax turned to Resostris with a smile. "Thank you, Captain."

He bowed in reply.

"There is no need to thank me, Attar. You carry the word of the Minos, and I am in his service. Fare you well."

"Fare you well" said Ajax, speaking loud enough to be heard by the entire crew. He then leapt over the rail to the sand below. After bowing to Resostris and touching my sword hilt in salute, I followed him.

Chapter XXII: The City of Byzantium

WE RAN STRAIGHT INLAND, up the beach towards a flat-roofed stone building that I learned was a customs house. There were three guards on duty there, armed with spear and shield, clad in bronze ringmail. Ajax showed them the ivory message case with its seal and said:

"I carry a message for the Quartermaster of the Minos's Fleet. Where may I find him?"

The oldest of the three saluted with his spear and then pointed to a large pavilion a hundred or so yards upstream from us.

"He and the Mistress of the Harbor are there, Attar."

Ajax nodded and we started north at a trot. The pavilion pointed out to us was green with bright yellow stripes, open-sided but partitioned so that there were a couple of inner rooms for privacy. It was at least forty yards long and twenty yards deep, with canvas curtains that could be unrolled and fastened into place to keep out the weather if need be. There were fifty or so guards in and around the pavilion and at least a dozen scribes, as well as the personal attendants of the two dignitaries who were tending to the business of adding to the Minos's navy and helping to run one of the biggest ports in the world.

We were noticed; that tends to happen when one of you is an Attar of Wurrunk in iron armor, and we were met by a detachment of guards led by an officer who appeared to be a nobleman of some sort. His chain mail and bright blue cloak certainly looked expensive enough for one of the nobility, as did the scabbards of his dagger and rapier. He looked to be five years or so older than me, but his bow to Ajax and the way he moved made me take a closer look at him. He might look like a popinjay in that cloak, but I think he knew how to handle that rapier.

"May I help you, Attar?"

Ajax nodded to him courteously enough, but his eyes were on the big man in the brown tunic behind the table in the pavilion:

"I have a message for the Lord Quartermaster from Kephtenes at Drake's Fort."

That brought the big man out from behind his table:

"From Kephtenes? For me?"

"From his hand to yours, Lord Quartermaster."

Lord Telos looked more like one of his shipwrights than a lord of

Cilicia; very little of his bulk was fat and he had the deft, callused hands of a carpenter rather than a courtier. He looked to be somewhere between forty and fifty years of age, with thinning brown hair and dark eyes in a broad, flat face. Those eyes didn't seem to miss much, flicking over the scroll case, then Ajax and then me.

"What else do you bring from the East? Ill news?"

"Nay, Lord. Little news and none of it ill since the Empire beat the tribes at Roaring Springs."

"Then it can wait." said Telos, as he cracked the seal on the scroll case, and opened it.

There was a low laugh from within the pavilion, and our eyes were drawn to the small, slender woman who sat motionless in the wide high-backed chair to the left of the Quartermaster's cluttered work table.

"Good News can take its own time. It is the Bad News that we need to hear at once."

The Lady Asri, Mistress of the Harbor of Byzantium, was dressed in fine linen with a shawl covering her head and shoulders. Her clothing was different shades of brown in color, with repeating images in yellow and green thread: the serpent and the goose, traditional symbols of power and authority in Thrace. She was attended by two servants and half a dozen guards, all women, all armed, which was also traditional. She appeared to be older than Telos by at least a decade, and she was taking a good look at Ajax and I.

"Well, this is going to play bloody hell with my schedule. But Kephtenes is no fool; if he says he needs it, then he needs it." said Telos. He finished the first scroll and handed it to the Lady Asri. She held it at arm's length to read it while Telos began to read the second scroll.

"He seems to want a great deal, but as you say, Kephtenes is no fool." She read through the second and third scrolls after Telos was finished, reading them even faster than he had. "You will need stonemasons and bricklayers as well, and at least one person who knows something about plumbing."

"Yenda." The taller of her two servants stepped forward and bowed.

"Send messages to each of those guild houses, ask them to each send a representative to us here, today, on the Minos's business."

Yenda saluted her lady and went to the youngest of the scribes seated in the rear of the pavilion, who was soon scratching away industriously. The Lady Asri turned her fine-boned face to gaze at me for a moment and then closed her eyes. Lord Telos took all three scrolls and gave them to the oldest of the scribes present.

"I want six copies of each scroll, at once." Then he turned to Ajax. "Do you have any other business with me, Attar?"

"No, Lord. My delivery of the message was an exchange of favors with Kephtenes. He loaned me his ship, and I carried his message to you."

Telos nodded once to Ajax and said: "Well enough then. And thank you." Then he turned back to the table and his work.

Ajax turned towards the Lady Asri, but before he could speak, she opened her eyes and asked him the same question: "Do you have any business with me, Attar of Wurrunk?"

He bowed to her and said:

"Yes Lady, I do. We need to speak with the Lady Natyr as soon as possible. I believe she will want to speak with us."

"The Lady Natyr? Ah." She nodded once at me. She was old enough to remember my father, and it seemed as if my face and the mention of my aunt's name had jogged her memory.

"Then you must leave now. My woman Dangi will escort you to the city gates, so you will not be delayed. Fare you well, Attar."

The remaining servant bowed to her mistress and motioned us to follow her. We bowed and gave the Mistress of the Harbor our thanks, and followed her servant at a brisk walk. She lead us south, up off of the beach, past warehouses and wagon yards all thronged with sailors, merchants and travelers of a score of nations, to the road that lead to the River Gate. This was the road that went through Portside, and the gate it lead to stood wide open to anyone who cared to walk through.

Portside wasn't much more than a shanty town built to service and house the foreigners and outcastes that lived and worked in the port, and provide temporary lodgings for anyone just traveling through Byzantium. Portside sprawled off to either side of the street in a confusing tangle of alleys and side streets that didn't seem to have any kind of organizing principle at all. Ajax told me that nine tenths of Portside had burned to the ground at one time or another in the past forty years and that new buildings had been thrown up according to immediate needs, not according to any master plan. The result was chaos, but all of that ended when you reached the River Gate, sometimes called the Gate of Eugenios or the Northwest Gate of Byzantium. This was the gate just north of Enki's Hill, a key element in the city's defenses and there was nothing haphazard about those defenses at all.

The wind shifted to the east and I caught the smell of smoke and not hearth smoke either. Off to the east and south there was a column of black smoke that had to be a building on fire, and not a small one. I took another sniff from the onion I had under my cloak, as the stench of Portside began to overwhelm the relatively clean smells of the harbor, and took a closer look at the gates ahead of me. They were big, not just tall but massive, built from whole tree trunks that had then been faced with thick bronze plates to armor them against attacks by fire and ram, and there was magic on them too, I could smell it.

There were a dozen guards at the gate keeping an eye on traffic going both ways and occasionally checking packs and wagons, with at least a score more on the walls above. The guards at street level were Axe Sisters, sworn to the service of Tisiphone the Avenger; some wielded axe and shield, others carried poleaxes that could shear through the best armor. The guards on the walls were probably armed the same way, and with javelins, throwing axes and crossbows for good measure. Dangi strode forward until she was about ten paces from the guard captain, a tall, lean woman with graying hair and an iron axe. She then stopped and holding her hands palm out at shoulder height, spoke loudly and clearly:

"I serve the Mistress of the Harbor; My Lady Asri has commanded that I escort these males to the city gates, so that you may know that they have urgent business in the city."

The guard captain drew herself to attention and replied: "I have heard your message; give my regards to the Mistress of the Harbor."

Dangi nodded and then, after bowing deeply to Ajax, turned and left. The guard captain had recognized Ajax, and greeted him amiably enough:

"Welcome back to Byzantium, Attar. Do you require an escort to your destination?"

Ajax stepped close enough to her that his words couldn't be easily overheard:

"Not if the Lady Natyr is still to be found at the Temple of the Willow and the Maple."

Her eyes narrowed, and after a glance at me, she answered loudly enough for all of her people to hear:

"Well enough. You may pass. May Byzan speed you on your way."

We nodded our thanks and moved along. I know Byzantium much better now than I did then, so I know what path we took to our goal, but for me that day, our journey through the city was utterly confusing. There were so many colors and odors, so many houses, all made of stone or brick and many bigger than the biggest barn I'd ever seen. There was running water that came out of pipes and every street was floored with cobblestones. But there were so many people, men, women, children, merchants, tradesmen, soldiers, servants, priestesses, more people than I had ever imagined, all living in this one place. I stuck to Ajax like a burr; Byzantium scared the hell out of me.

I remember we walked uphill for a while, and we turned south; somewhere along the line, we passed through another gate whose guards were watchful enough, but who were not checking everyone who entered or left. The nature of the crowds changed a bit, they weren't as thick, and there seemed to be more money and less noise, so to speak. Then there were more temples, a lot of temples in fact. We turned right, which meant west, and eventually stopped at the intersection of two streets (Willow and Maple streets, I later learned) and entered the grounds of an old temple built of brown and grey stone, surrounded by a low stone wall. It was well shaded by the trees on the streets that gave the temple its name, and you had to get right up to the temple doors before you could see all the guards who were packed shoulder to shoulder in the antechamber. Well, either my aunt had visitors, or we were going to have a fight to commemorate our first day in Byzantium.

They were visitors. Actually, they were the entourage of Dilfara the Weaver, the Brown Earth Queen herself. A score of Axe Sisters, a handful of mercenary swordsmen, three scribes and the queen's two youngest children made for quite a mob when combined with the guards and staff of the temple itself. Ajax strode forward and they moved out of his way, the Axe Sisters reluctantly, but the mercenaries gave him a salute and backed away. He was met by a woman who was the chief priestess of this temple, to whom he bowed and said:

"We have urgent business with the Lady Natyr. Family business."

The priestess looked at Ajax and then at me, and her eyes went wide. Her voice rang loud enough to silence the crowd and echo through the temple:

"Back, all of you! Clear that stairway!"

She led us to a broad flight of stairs that went down, and we followed her down the steps and two turns and more steps until we had to have been well below ground level. That's when I remembered that temples of the Earth are often built so that least half of the temple's area would be below ground. I caught some unusual scents: oil from the lamps that lit the main corridor, perfume, incense, a strong smell of snake, and underneath it all, the cold throb of magic. There were three cross corridors between us and our goal, and none of them were lit; still I caught the gleam of a flicker of light off of polished bronze and heard the slither of what should have been a huge snake. I couldn't see the snake's shape clearly in the shadows, but I'd never heard of a snake carrying an axe before. That is when I decided to just keep my eyes to the front, and not worry about the shadows here.

The corridor ended in what looked to be a large room, more brightly lit than the corridor by several lamps; as we approached the elderly woman who was standing in front of the door to that room, I could hear another woman's voice, a deep strong voice with a laugh hiding in it:

"So, Natyr. When you get to the Underworld, I want you to clear a space for us, and arrange a party. I want it ready when I get there: good wine, singing, dancing...you know the kind of men I like."

I heard a faint whisper, what might have been the echo of a very dry laugh, and then the woman standing watch in the corridor spoke:

"Isarla! How dare you! The Queen is not to be disturbed for ANY reason, was I not clear enough in that? Who is that...you dare bring HIM here?"

"Dare? Watch your words, Renatha, I am the priestess of this temple, not you. I bring these men here and now in accordance with the Lady Natyr's wishes. Her nephew is come, as she said he would."

The older woman looked at me and gasped, covering her mouth with one hand and backed away from me. Then that same deep voice came again as a tall woman clad in brown and gold stepped out of the inner chamber.

"Peace, Isarla. Renatha's temper is short on my account. But what do you mean, 'The Lady Natyr's nephew?' How can you be sure he is..."

Then Ajax moved to one side so that she could see me and even in that dim light I could see the blood leave her face.

"Dono's son."

Her voice changed as she said those last words, and she came two hesitant steps towards me, with her right hand out as if to touch my face, but she didn't. Then we all stood there, speechless, motionless, as I stood up straight and looked the first queen I had ever met right in the eyes. Dilfara the Weaver at that time was well past fifty years of age, but not yet really touched by those years. Most of her hair that I could see was still dark, and she had beautiful eyes, with a strong straight nose and a firm chin. She had broad shoulders and strong-looking hands, and she smelled of roses and soap. The rings and bracelets on her fingers and arms were copper and they gleamed with their own light. "Magic" I thought to myself, and then I realized that she wore copper armor under her outer robes, and a broad bladed axe swung from her belt. The Brown Earth Queen didn't seem to be the type who took chances that she didn't have to, if she went armed for battle even here beneath a temple of the Earth itself. I realized two other things as well. First, I didn't just look like my father, I looked *exactly* like my father. The resemblance was so strong that it shocked people who had known him as a young man. Second, what Ajax had told me before, the rumor that Dilfara might have cared for my father in their youth? Well, it wasn't a rumor; my father had been dead for ten years, and it had been thirty years since she had last spoken to him, but I could see the sight of my face pulling at her heart. I'm not sure how long we stood like that, until the silence was broken by footsteps behind me and then a girl's voice:

"Mother? What is it? What's wrong?"

It was the youngest of Dilfara's daughters, with her mother's dark eyes and shining dark hair that hung in the five braids that were the style of her house. Drawn down the stairwell by the sound of voices raised in anger, and alarmed by the utter silence that had followed, she had come forward to stand with her mother. Dilfara jerked as if she had been falling asleep and barked an order without her eyes ever leaving my face.

"Go back up stairs, Gwyntarla. Now. I command it."

Her daughter stopped in her tracks and then saluted her, hands at her side, palms down.

"I hear and obey, Queen and Mother."

She turned and bolted up the steps without another word. That was the first sight I had of your Grandmother Gwyn. The queen then spoke to me:

"My past, my mistakes are mine alone. I'll be damned before I let them swallow any of my children."

Too late. But I had no idea what our future held, so I just stood there and blinked at her, not having the slightest idea what to say.

"And you have no idea what I'm talking about, do you boy?" She gave a deep sigh, and turned towards the door way behind her:

"He is here, Natyr. I'm sending him in. Farewell, my sister."

"The rest of you, come with me. You too, Attar; I need to speak with you."

Ajax bowed to her. "But of course, Queen Dilfara."

He gave my shoulder a firm clasp of encouragement and then he followed Dilfara to the stairs, as did Islara and Renatha. I noticed that the

Lady Renatha kept as far from me as the corridor would permit and had been eyeing me as if I was likely to bite or stab her if she turned her back to me. It seemed that not everyone was happy to see my father's face in Byzantium again. I'd have to talk to Ajax about that; my father's enemies might decide to be my enemies as well. Enough; I was stalling. I took a deep breath and stepped up to the doorway, and hesitated. The woman in that room was my last blood relative left alive in the world. She was old, powerful, proud and sick; and she had laid a curse on my father for defying her. What the hell was I supposed to say to her? A woman's voice came from within the room then, weak, breathy, a sick woman's voice, but I had the feeling she knew exactly what was going through my mind.

"Enter, Joren, son of my brother Dono. You are welcome here."

I took a deep breath and then three quick steps into the room, and I turned to my left to face the side of the room where that voice had come from. As I crossed the threshold into the room, I felt as if I had touched something, just for an instant, but it parted before me. I realized that I had crossed the boundary of a Warding, and then the sight of my aunt and the smells of that room hit me. In health, my aunt would have been a few inches shorter than me, with dark hair and dark eyes; physically, she was the image of her mother, the Lady Mirani. But she had been sick, very sick, for a very long time. Her hair had gone completely white, and she wasn't much more than skin and bones; the bones sharp and fragile-looking underneath skin gone mottled and wax-like. Only the eyes were unchanged, and they burned at me with the intensity of her will. That is what I remember most of that night: her eyes and the strength of her will, not the shrunken body or the bony face or the claw-like hands. That and the myriad odors that filled that room like a fog. So many different scents: the smell of sickness and the medicines that tried to fight it, the smell of perfume and incense, the scents of lamp oil and hot wax, of linen and leather and lace, and underneath them all, the smell of death and of magic. That I could smell death was no surprise, because even I could tell that my aunt was holding it at arm's length by the sheer force of her will. But the smell of magic had me puzzled, because it didn't seem to have a source. It seemed to pulse through the room in slow, cold waves; I couldn't figure out where it was coming from until I caught a glimpse of the markings on the floor and walls where they were not covered by hangings or thrown rugs. Then it hit me, and I felt a prickle of fear: this wasn't just my aunt's sickroom, it was her Place of Power, the sanctum that she had returned to year after year to practice and experiment with different types of

252

ceremony and enchantment. The magic that I could smell was hers, her power, laid into the walls and floor like coats of paint, and it would obey only her command.

The sound of someone weeping alerted me to the fact that there were people other than my aunt and myself in the room. My attention had been drawn so completely by my aunt that I had not noticed the people standing in the shadows against the far wall. There were three of them, two women and a man, all of them more than seventy years of age by their looks, and they were staring at me. The two women looked to be sisters, and it was they who were crying. My aunt introduced them:

"These women are Valena and Varsene; they were nursemaids to your father and I, and have served me ever since. I would count it as a personal favor, nephew, if you would let them touch you."

These women had helped to care for my father as a child? They were not servants, they were family. I bowed to them, and kissed each of them on the cheek. They cried harder, and touched my hands and my face, repeating my father's name over and over. I looked past them at the old man who then stepped forward. What little hair he had was white and his faded grey eyes never left my face as he clasped my hand and spoke a few words in a language I did not understand, not then anyway. My aunt translated for me:

"Raven's Blood indeed, old friend."

Then she spoke directly to me: "This is Joris, who was sworn to the service of your grandfather. He taught your father how to ride and how to hold a sword."

I bowed to him, and he touched my shoulder and smiled at me, unable to say anything else. I turned back to my aunt, to find her staring at my face as well.

"That face of yours is your father's and your grandfather's before him as well, on back in our blood for years uncounted. Every generation of our family has had one boy who has worn that face; the color of the hair and eyes may change, height and weight, even the heaviness of the bones beneath may differ, but the face is always the same. Usually, the one who wears that face is the one who wields Oathtaker. Not always, sometimes a woman of our family would take up the Lady, but she prefers men."

"The Lady? Is that what I should call...her?", I asked.

"Yes, Oathtaker is female, and would be offended if you were dim enough to refer to her as 'IT'. I will tell you what I can of her, but she will have to tell you her secrets herself. We got along well enough, but she was

253

very much taken with your father." Natyr paused for a moment and closed her eyes. "As were many women."

I was smart enough to keep my mouth shut and wait, and after a short pause, my aunt went on.

"I will answer all of your questions as best I can; that information is your birthright, as is the house and the monies you will inherit upon my death. You are the last of us, boy, and it is you who must go on. In return, I ask a great favor of you, nephew."

"Call me Joren, Aunt Natyr." A great favor; it would be difficult to deny her a favor, she was the last of my kin and on her death bed. Would she want me to marry someone? That would be a problem, considering how it was between Bel and me. Would she want me to kill someone? Actually, that might not be a problem at all, especially if she wanted Imperial scalps.

"What kind of favor?", I asked.

"Joren. I want you to let me give you a Gift."

A Gift? I could hear the emphasis in her voice; she wasn't talking about a new belt knife or a pair of boots. "What kind of gift?"

"An enchantment, a magic worked into your skin, so that you may carry it where ever you go, and never lose it. I have Power and more than a little skill in these things. I can give you aid that will bolster you against those you must face no matter what path you set your foot upon."

A chill ran through me. If I agreed to this, she would have to touch me. It would be her hands against my bare skin, and nothing would be able to protect me against any spell she might choose to cast upon me. I had no doubt of her power, and if she meant me harm, this would be the perfect opportunity. I was the son of the man she had cursed, only to have the curse rebound upon her. This would be her last chance to make someone pay. She could turn me to stone, or into a serpent; I had heard of such things happening to those who displeased the priestesses of the Earth. Whatever her intentions, for good or ill, this would take hours, and at the end of that time, I would be changed forever. I looked into the eyes of that terrible old woman, and asked her one question.

"Why?"

Her gaze never wavered as she answered, and I wondered if she was speaking only to me.

"Why? "

"So that I may give, where so often I have sought only to take."

"So that I may build, where too often I have destroyed."

"So that I may bless, where once I cursed."

"So that I might be...forgiven."

I did not sense any malice in her; Wurrunk's gift was silent, and I sensed only the resolve of someone who had come to terms with both her life and her death, and who wanted to do one last thing to make a difference. For an instant, I felt my father beside me; she spoke to him as well, across the years and past the Veil of Death. She was right about how useful such an enchantment would be; I would need the gift that she offered, if I attempted the path I had chosen. I took a deep breath.

"Of course, Aunt Natyr. I welcome your gift. What must I do?"

Joris, Valena and Varsene all let their breath out at once in relief. I looked over at them, to see both of the women smiling broadly at me; the old man nodded once to me when I met his eye. Good, I had made the right choice. I turned back to my Aunt and realized she had tears running down her face. She blinked at me and frowned:

"You're not afraid of me at all, are you, boy?"

"No, Aunt Natyr." I realized that I wasn't, that she was my own flesh and blood, and even with what I knew of my uncle Ketil, I couldn't be afraid of her.

"Huh. Well, we have to start now, I don't have much time. Luckily, I have everything ready. Take off your tunic and your shirt; I must see what has already been done, so I can determine how to add to it."

Joris went and doused all of the torches, so that only the candles and two braziers gave off light, a warm golden light that seemed to pulse in time with my aunt's breathing. He then brought in ewers of water, and two of wine, and then left closing the door behind him. My aunt said that he would sit guard for us, but he could not be in the room without interfering with her magic. The two women helped my aunt sit forward, and then made her comfortable, propping her up with velvet cushions, and wrapping what had to be a spider silk shawl about her shoulders. They then brought over two side tables, one with pots of dye and tinctures, some smaller than a thimble. On the other table was an array of needles, sharp gleaming lengths of copper most of them, but the last three, the ones closest to my aunt, were iron. Iron needles? I was stunned.

"You were expecting me."

It was not a question, it was obvious that preparations had been made for this ritual well ahead of time. My aunt answered me rather absently, as the women fussed over her.

"I had a dream you would come; that all I had to do was hold on a little longer, and you would come. And you did. Dreams have always spoken very clearly to those of my mother's clan. Sometimes they foretell terrible things, sometimes wonderful things or commonplace things, but they always come true."

She touched the needles in the tray very lightly with her fingers and they began to glow. She looked up into my face then, and spoke directly to me.

"I believe that someone learned this about our family, and used this knowledge to lead your father to his death. I had Joris look into this, and he found that several merchants had been making inquiries into the history of the great families among the A'as scholars at the Great Library. A couple of them seemed to be very interested in our House. This was a number of years ago, just before you were born, and both men were imperials. Unfortunately, they had already returned to the Empire before I could speak to them. Talk to Joris when you get the chance; he will tell you all that we learned. Now let me take a look at you."

I straightened up and held still. I was going to get another tattoo; or I should say, have something added to my tattoo. It wasn't going to be fun, but I knew what to expect; Aunt Syara had done it twice, adding to the tattoo given me by my mother soon after I was born. Everyone gets marked, I know, but mine was different: it was hidden, invisible to the naked eye. Not invisible to my aunt Natyr of course, she murmured the words of a spell and for an instant, her eyes gleamed with a coppery light. She hummed gently to herself and she examined my chest, and I heard her say absently:

"Wise to hide it, I think. Yes, and what is this? Hmmm. Four of them...And where did she learn that? Very neat, yes, I like that..."

She touched me lightly over my heart with one hand, and then slumped in her chair with a deep sigh. I was a bit alarmed, as was Varsene.

"What is it, Aunt?"

"Nothing. Nothing that I can change now. I wish...I wish I had gotten to know them, your mother and your great aunt Syara. I think your mother was foresighted; she did something I did not expect to see, and it was masterfully done. Your father's hand is visible too, he helped her, but the overall design is hers. And the enhancements done by your Aunt Syara were extremely skillful; she used a technique I have never seen before. I should like to have just sat and talked to them." She sighed again.

"Two more regrets to add to the pile that is already so high I cannot see over it."

"Enough." She leaned over and picked up the first needle and dipped it into a pot that smelled of oak gall. The needle smoked as she held it up to inspect it.

"Ready your questions, Joren my nephew. We begin."

I took a deep breath; getting marked wasn't exactly pleasant, but I'd had it done before. I asked my first question:

"What did Joris mean, when he said 'Raven's Blood'?"

"The sign of your grandfather Robard's house was a raven with outstretched wings. That was the emblem on his banner and also his war name. He told me that it was an old tradition in his family to never harm a raven in any way. If you should ever go west of the lands ruled by the Minos, do not ever strike at a raven unless it attacks you, never eat the meat or the eggs of a raven, and never wear their feathers. It would be unlucky."

It was good to know that. Different lands have different traditions; I would never think of harming a raven here in Thrace or Issuria. The raven was one of the animals associated with Wurrunk, the other being the wolf. In Scythia, it was different; there, the raven is the servant of Pirwa the Trickster, and men avoid them whenever possible. The more I thought about this, the more I liked the idea of having the raven as the emblem of my house. Since I was caught in a feud with the children of Lupak Wolf Father, I couldn't use the symbol of the wolf, but the raven would have meaning for those who followed Wurrunk. A raven emblem would allow me to acknowledge Wurrunk's Gift, but would have no obvious tie to the Black Oak of the House of the Mabirshan, so I wouldn't be raising a red flag that might attract the attention of the Empire. Who knew, it might even bring me luck. I'd have to be careful in Scythia though. You don't want to make the Trickster jealous.

I asked my aunt other questions as she worked and the hours slipped by. About my grandfather and my grandmother, and about Oathtaker, the sword my grandfather had passed onto my father, and which was now held by Othar Inkson. I think that is when I started to feel intimidated. I wasn't overawed by the hard old woman who was working her will and magic into my very flesh, I wasn't overly impressed by the fact that all of this was happening in the depths of a temple of the earth that was older than most nations, and it didn't really bother me that the most powerful empire on the continent wanted to turn me into a puppet and that every wolf in the world wanted to turn me into dinner. I think I was just too young and too stupid for all of that to register. No, what was making me feel small,

257

inadequate and outclassed was that sword.

It was old, older than the collective memory of my family and that went back centuries. It had many names, each name a link to the history that it had helped to shape: Blade of Truth, Death of Lies, Scythe of Shadows, Bane's Fang, The Shackle, and there were others. It had power, and my aunt told me how to awaken that power to its fullest extent, and the price that would be paid in doing so. It was bound to Truth: if you told a lie while the sword was in your hand, it would turn and strike you down. If you swore an oath on Oathtaker, and broke the oath, you died. Not even the sages of the Sea Lords had found a way around that magic, which was why they called it The Shackle. It was alive, not a spirit or ghost bound to a man-made tool, but a living thing in and of itself, with its own mind, its own memories and its own plans. And sometimes the eyes of the woman's face in the sword's hilt would open and be lit by the purple fire of wild summer lightning, and when that happened, even the sword's wielder had to beware.

That sword was my responsibility, mine alone. My father's bloodline was bound to that sword in ways that no one really understood, and my aunt Natyr and I were the only ones left. Even if I tried to forget about the sword and do something else, anything else with my life, I would sooner or later be driven to seek it out. That had happened to others before me. That part of it really wasn't going to be a problem, I pretty much thought about Oathtaker every day. That and killing Othar Inkson; I just wasn't ready to handle either of them yet. Ajax had some plans he had discussed with me, about training at the Great Temple of Wurrunk here in Byzantium, and Aunt Natyr nodded in agreement when I told her of them.

"If Ajax says you need this time for training, do it. He and I have never gotten along (Varsene's and Valena's eyes grew wide indeed when she said this), but as a teacher in those matters you will never find anyone better, and I doubt if you will ever find his equal."

After a time, she wiped her hands and motioned me to a curtained alcove at the other end of the room.

"You have been standing for hours, and I must rest a bit; go and refresh yourself there and get something to drink. I will have Joris bring you something to eat, and then you will tell us about the girl on the other end of that life bond."

"You can see my life bond, Aunt Natyr?"

"See it? Boy, if it were any stronger, we could hang laundry from it. Now go."

I did as she suggested, realizing that if she could see my tattoo, well of course she could see the life bond. Idiot. I needed to wash my face and neck to wake up; my aunt's room was heated by braziers for her comfort, but it was putting me to sleep. When I returned, I felt much better and quite up to tackling the plate of grilled fish and spicy noodles that Joris had just laid out on a small table to the left of my aunt's bed. My aunt was sipping green tea with honey, and watching Valena and Varsene pull a heavy cloth from the frame of a large mirror to the right of the door. The mirror's frame was of beaten copper, but there seemed to be something wrong with the glass: it didn't reflect an image of the room, just bands of colors that pulsed across the glass in a slow rhythm. Then I got close enough to smell the magic wafting out from it. So, it was a scrying mirror then. I stuffed down some food while the sisters folded the cloth and my aunt finished her tea. When she was done, I looked at her and said: "Now?"

"You have used your bond to give you visions of her before? Good. Yes. I want to see her first, and then ask you a few questions. You've played havoc you know; looking over a prospective bride for a male of the family is exactly the kind of thing women like us would love to spend three or four seasons doing to the exclusion of all else. It was quite rude of you to just appear out of nowhere with a bride already selected and lifebonded to boot."

"I'm sorry, Aunt Natyr."

"And pigs have wings, nephew. Go ahead and start; we should be able to get a glimpse of her in any case, but if there is a mirror in the room with her, then this glass will look at her through her mirror. We won't have much time though, no more than ten slow breaths without a mirror like this one at the other end."

I closed my eyes and pictured my heart's desire: her eyes, her smile, the curve of her lips…, then I took a deep breath and let it out, frosting the length of the mirror's surface with it. The mirror went dark, and I spoke her name.

"Belkara."

With the sound of her name still echoing in the room, the mirror cleared and we were looking into a room. But it wasn't a clouded or distant room, it was if the mirror had become a doorway, and we were looking into a room on the other side of this wall. Bel was there, asleep at a table with her head pillowed in her bare forearms. I heard my aunt's breath hiss between her teeth and Joris muffle an exclamation; this didn't seem normal, if you can call using a magic mirror normal. Then the scents struck me: leather and lye soap, hickory smoke and horses, the oil she used on her weapons and the scent of the girl I loved. How could a mirror carry odors across such a distance?

The mirror on the other end of the link looked to be on a shelf or table close to where Bel was sleeping. She was wearing a brown tunic and her shortsword, with her broadsword slung over the back of her chair. She looked to have doing her accounts: there was a smudge of ink on her nose and another on her chin, and there were a number of scrolls on the table in front of her. She looked wonderful. I went on staring at her like an idiot until it struck me that I had been looking into the mirror for a lot longer than ten slow breaths. I couldn't just let her sleep like that, she'd get a crick in her neck. I called to her softly:

"Belkara! Bel, go to bed, you'll be stiff as a board if you spend the night there."

She stirred and lifted her head from her arms. And I heard her voice:

"Mmmm? Oh. Guess you're right, Jo."

She stood up and, lifting her arms, gripped a rafter and stretched. And I forgot all about those ink smudges. Then her eyes came all the way open and she turned towards her mirror, towards me.

"Joren! Is that you?"

Her face lit up with that smile and she stepped towards me, and her hip bumped into the table. The view in the mirror jerked, and then spun dizzily. I heard her voice say "Son of a b...!" and then the mirror before me went dark. I was going to have to pay for that other mirror, but at least I had seen her again, and knew that she was well. I turned back to the room, to find everyone staring at my aunt. Joris and Valena (her hand over her mouth) were silent, but Varsene was stammering at my aunt:

"She...she heard his voice!?"

My aunt made an impatient gesture with one hand.

"WE heard HER voice. That should not be possible!"

Natyr turned and shot a hard glance at me.

"Nephew, you do not really know how to use a mirror like that, nor do you need to. All you do is consciously open the link and the life bond attempts to use the easiest way available to reach the one you are bonded to. That is to be expected, but this...." She shook her head, more to herself than at me.

"Your bond to Belkara is stronger than any I have ever seen." She mused on that for a while, and then looked at me. She folded her hands in her lap in an oddly formal stance and said:

"I approve of this girl as your prospective bride. Not that my opinion matters as much as a plate of beans, since you have a life bond with her, but I like the look of her."

This unleashed a flood of words from the others:

"So tall! Is she an only child?" said Valena.

"Muscles in those forearms." This from Joris.

"Where was that room?" asked Varsene.

"That must have been her room at her family's ranch. She works it with her uncle, Barlen. Her parents were killed in the war; I never heard of any siblings." I replied.

"Raised on a ranch, then." She turned to my aunt: "She'll be a worker, she will get things done."

My aunt's eyes gleamed as she asked her own question:

"What was she doing at that table? There was ink on her hands and face; does she write you letters?"

"No, Aunt Natyr, we do not think that would be safe. I think that she was settling accounts, she does much of the bargaining for her clan when they drive to market."

"So, she not only can read and write, but she can work with numbers and she knows how to bargain. Better and better, and yes," she nodded here to Joris. "She is not just some pretty, helpless thing fit only to be an ornament or a brood mare. Hmm. Has she borne you a child? She did not look to be pregnant."

I could feel my face burning as I answered: "No, Aunt Natyr. We talked of this and decided to wait until our lives were more settled before we risked having children."

The four of them just stared at me for a moment.

"Two more regrets, I think.", said my aunt.

"How old are you?" said Varsene.

"Ajax says I'm sixteen." I replied. I didn't understand the question, though.

She just shook her head, but her sister spoke up, moving her fingers as if there were fabric between them. "She will need a gown. We will make her a dress, brown and green, I think, for that hair and those eyes. Or should we make it brown and grey?"

"Brown and grey" said my aunt. "Grey for the bond to Wurrunk."

The two sisters looked at each other.

"By your command, Lady."

I didn't understand this at all; Bel and I weren't sworn to Wurrunk. Not then.

"It is not a bond that can be ignored, and his father helped prepare him for it. Speaking of which, Joren, it is time we finished my gift. I do not have much time left."

I bowed to her. Joris cleared away the food and resumed his post outside the door. Varsene and Valena rearranged my aunt's tools and needles on either hand and drew back. My aunt took a deep breath and picked up an iron needle, which began to glow.

She motioned me closer and said: "Come, let us finish this."

She used each of the three iron needles in turn, and when she was finished with each, I noticed a slowing and a fading of the magic pulsing through the room. She took a little time to rest before using each of the last two needles, and we spoke for a little while each time. She gave me good advice about a number of things, and I told her that I had resolved to give the estate I would inherit from her into the care of Joris, Vorsene and Valena, that they might live in comfort, which they had earned. I wouldn't need to live in the house my grandfather had built; if I passed the entrance tests, I would be spending the next year in training in the Great House of Death, one of the largest temples to Wurrunk in the world. Ajax and I had discussed this at some length. I would spend a year in training and in practice before I took formal possession of my inheritance. I would be better prepared for trouble when that year was done, and in the meantime we would plan on how to get Belkara out of the reach of the Imperial Empire. We would also keep watch to see if anyone came sniffing around Byzantium for me. It would be nice, for once, to see trouble coming before it got to me.

When my aunt had finished the last part of her enchantment, the room no longer smelled of cold, throbbing magic; it was just the bedroom of a very tired, very sick woman. My aunt pressed her hands together over my heart and spoke three short sharp words, and each word jolted me like a blow. Then she fell back into her chair, her eyes glittering with triumph. "Done! And well done.", she said.

The two sisters hustled forward to fuss over her. I spoke then:

"Aunt Natyr?" She looked up at me.

"May I kiss you?" Both Varsene and Valena stepped back and looked at me, speechless.

My aunt seemed surprised, but took a deep breath and said: "Yes, of course, Joren."

I bowed to her, and kissed her hands, her forehead and then carefully put my arms around her and kissed her cheek. She felt so horribly light and fragile, and I was very much aware that she had held on for so long with so much pain, just to see me, and that this was the first time anyone of her own family had so much as touched her in more than a quarter of a century.

I leaned back and she blinked at me with her hands on my arms, and smiled and said to me:

"Well. I..." and then she died. She slumped backward and the lines of pain began to smooth away. Varsene called for Joris and then she and her sister took my aunt's left arm and hand in their hands and Joris came in and fell to one knee and took her right hand in his and they wept quietly. It was over now. No more pain, no more waiting. I stepped back to give them their time with her.

"Good bye, Aunt Natyr. Thank you."

Chapter XXIII: The Great House of Death

I DID NOT STAY TO ATTEND the public portion of my aunt's funeral services; Aunt Natyr had recommended that I keep out of sight as much as possible until I was accepted for schooling at the Temple of Wurrunk, and I had agreed. The final part of the funeral services were not open to anyone who was not a sworn servant of the Earth goddesses, and so was closed to me in any case. Before I left, I made a point of speaking to Joris, Varsene and Valena, who wanted to know when they would see me again. I promised I would visit them as soon as I could; Ajax said that I would have time off from my training to visit them on occasion, and I wanted to know anything they could tell me of my father and his family.

Before Ajax and I left to seek entry into Wurrunk's temple in Byzantium, I was summoned to speak again with Dilfara the Weaver; it seemed that she was the executor of my aunt's will. We were given a private audience as she was being prepared for her part in my aunt's funerary services; we found Queen Dilfara swathed in mourning robes and seated in a small quiet room that looked out over a well-tended garden. Her head was uncovered and her servants were fussing with her hair and her face paint in preparation for the ceremony to come. She had been looking out the window when I entered, and when she turned her face towards me, I bowed and waited. After a glance at Ajax, she looked me in the eye and said:

"Joren, you are the sole heir of your Aunt Natyr; with her death, you inherit your family's house and a considerable amount of wealth. You may not directly handle the monies you have inherited until you reach the age of 18, but you may take possession of the house immediately.   As executor, I will disburse any funds you might need to keep the house up and running until you reach your majority."

I thanked her and said that I intended to follow my aunt's advice and leave the use of the house and the inherited monies in the hands of the House of the Brown Earth, with the provision that my aunt's servants be allowed to leave out the rest of their lives in my house, which was more truly their home than mine. I owed them that much, at least.

She nodded in agreement, and then stood up, her hands clenched at her sides, and said:

"There has never been anyone, not the fathers of my children, not my own mother, who was closer to me than your Aunt Natyr. It tore at my heart to see her so sick, in so much pain for so long. And yet, in death, she smiles, and looks more at peace than...than I have seen her in a very long time. Her servants said that you were responsible for this?"

I didn't really know what to say.

"She was my father's sister, Great Queen, the last of my own flesh and blood. "

That wasn't really an answer, but it seemed to satisfy Queen Dilfara. She closed her eyes and sighed deeply, and then nodded at me.

"I wish you well, son of Dono. You may send word to me through any of the servants of my House, if you should need to speak with me again before your 18th birthday."

She turned her face back to the window and the garden beyond in dismissal, so we bowed and left. Ajax said that he had told the Queen our plans for my training at the temple of Wurrunk and of my intention to keep out of sight of the imperials here in Byzantium, and anyone else who might have had a grudge against my father and recognize me as his son. She had not objected, and agreed to contact Ajax if she heard of any news of the White Sun Empire that might concern me. We gathered our packs and set off across the city again, this time north and a little east, until we crossed Great Kings Road, just east of the Column of the Celts, and traveled through Northside to reach the entrance to the Great House of Death.

The Temple of Wurrunk in Byzantium City was more than just a simple building; it was a walled compound that contained a barn, a smithy and other buildings in addition to the temple proper, which faced south, and which was built of the same dark grey stone as the city walls. There were quite a few people coming and going, and even more clustered together practicing or just talking, and what struck me first were the colors of their clothing. It seemed that every hue of the rainbow was here and in so many different fabrics that I didn't have a name for half of them.

The array of colors in the feathers, sashes, tabards and cloaks of the crowd was bewildering, and I began to understand what Ajax had said about there being more than one kind of Wurrunki. These people were nothing like the Kothmir tribesmen among whom I had spent all of my life that I could remember.

There were two people waiting for us just outside the main gate. One was an older man of average height but with very broad shoulders, clad in plain grey clothing with a heavy leather apron and a wide work belt hung with many tools, some of which were iron. He smelled of weapon oil and smoke and hot metal. His companion was a woman, taller than he by half a head, who smelled of wax and ink and cedar wood and who leaned upon a tall staff of white ash. She looked to be about the same age as him and wore grey and brown, which matched her hair. They both wore iron blades, and they eyed me curiously. Ajax introduced us:

"This is Dangmag Three Hammers, Master of the Armory, and Rostaka the Brown, most learned of all the sword sages of the House of Death in Byzantium."

I bowed to them deeply, tongue-tied.

"This is my student, Joren."

Dangmag bade me welcome and then raised an eyebrow at Ajax.

"It has been quite some time since you last brought a student to our House."

Rostaka grinned at me and Ajax, suddenly looking 10 years younger, and said:

"Welcome, Joren. I don't know what this old vagabond has told you, (here she thumped Ajax lightly on the shin with her staff) but no one may bring anything that is magic into the House without it first being inspected. He told Dangmag and I that you had inherited a sword that we would find interesting. May we see it?"

"Of course, Lady. I have an amulet as well."

I had realized two things while she spoke: first, that staff was magic, it smelled of rainwater and the sharp odor that follows the strike of lightning bolts. Second, they were friends, the three of them, old friends by the look of things. I unbuckled my uncle Farad's broadsword and handed it to her, and then took the leather bag from around my neck and took out the medallion that the darkling Azzhka had gifted to my aunt in the walnut grove in Nesa, all those years ago. Rostaka raised her eyebrows at the sword as she passed it to Dangmag, and then draped a bit of cloth over her hand before she accepted the medallion from me. She hummed to herself as she examined it and said:

"Now where have I seen serpents like that before? Hmm...."

She nodded at me and went on:

"Your sword and medallion will be returned to you no later than sunset tomorrow, and in any case, before you leave the temple grounds."

In case I flubbed my testing and got booted out the front gate, is what she meant. She closed her hand around the medallion and turned

266

expectantly towards Dangmag. He was peering intently at the hilt of my sword, while turning the sword slowly in his big, callused hands. Ajax and Rostaka spoke to him at the same instant:

"Well?", they chorused.

Dangmag sighed and said to Ajax:

"I've never seen a sword quite like this. At first, I thought it was of Tyrian make, but I was wrong." He shot Ajax an exasperated look. "There, happy?"

Ajax grinned at him and said: "Yes; and I'll be even happier once you pay me."

Dangmag dug two silver pieces out of one of the pouches hanging from his belt and handed them over to my teacher.

"You know, you have become a rather obnoxious old man, Ajax."

"So I've been told." Ajax breathed on both coins and then began buffing them with the edge of his cloak. Dangmag snorted and turned to me:

"He hasn't rubbed off on you, has he, boy?"

"Sir?"

"Never mind; if he's been teaching you this long, it's probably too late anyway. We'll see you both tomorrow."

I bowed to them and, with a nod and a wave, they turned and walked up to the temple doors and went on inside. Ajax and I picked up our packs and entered the gate, where Ajax turned to point out the small golden bell in its recess cut into the inward side of the keystone in the gate's arch. Had I attempted to bring anything magical into the temple grounds without giving it into the hands of those guardians on duty, or if any enemy or outsider attempted to enter, that bell would have rung, and an instant later, all of the bells in the temple would have chimed in. He said that sometimes the bell would also toll for a passing: two chimes, one for when the dead left this world and another for when they entered the Land of the Dead. We walked into the temple courtyard, with the stable and smithy on our left, close to the gates, and the hiring hall and barracks ahead of us and to the right. The courtyard seemed alive with color; not just of the cloaks and tabards of the men and women who were beginning to fill it, but also with the banners and pennants of more than a score of noble and merchant houses.

Any mercenary company or merchant venture that was looking for guards had a banner hung by the door of the Hiring Hall; any noble family whose members or guards were being trained at the Great House of Death had their colors hung on either side of the temple doors for all to see. The smells were overwhelming: oil and leather, manure and liniment, expensive perfumes and cheap soaps, onions, garlic, charcoal, beer and underneath them all was the smell of magic and power that poured out of the temple doors like a ground fog. Ajax noticed me turning green and headed for the hiring hall at a trot.

"We'll get you bedded down in the Common room for good six hours; you won't be able to be tested until after the evening meal in any case, and you need as much sleep as you can get after the night you just had."

I grunted my agreement; it was late morning when we entered the temple grounds and I had not slept at all since we had left the ship. If I didn't get some sleep, I wasn't going to be passing any tests at all. The hiring hall's common room was a place where down-at-heel warriors could find a place to sleep and something to eat while they looked for work. We entered the north door of the hall and found a corner of the common room that was clear and clean, and I tugged off my boots, wrapped myself in my cloak and was snoring on my bedroll before I could here Ajax say any more than: "Rest now…"

I awoke just at sunset, and hungry enough to chew boot leather. Ajax laughed at me and threw me a piece of sausage and a bit of bread, and some water to wash it down. Anything more, he said, and I might not be as fast on my feet as I would need to be. I packed up my bedroll, washed my hands, face and neck in one of the basins by the north door and followed Ajax outside.

We walked past the two-storied barracks building, where I might be sleeping for the next year. IF I was both good and lucky, that is. Between the barracks and the stone building that contained the kitchen and dining hall was a long, level area that had been set up as a practice range; it was a good 60 feet wide and ran the length of the barracks. A woman of average height, clad in dark brown and black, was setting torches to light the targets. Ajax introduced her as Urika Smoke Eyes, the first examiner. I bowed to her and she nodded back; she smelled of lilacs and beeswax.

"Bow, javelin, axe…" she said, raising one eyebrow.

"Javelin."

"Well enough. Take three javelins and put them as close to the center of the middle target as you can." She waved towards the closest set of targets, to my left.

I picked three javelins from the rack and hefted them; they felt right, like the one who had made them had known what he or she was doing. I thought of my mother then, and how I had chosen the javelin as a weapon in her memory, and how I would want her to be proud of me if she had been here. Then I walked up to the mark and threw the javelins one after the other at the target. It wasn't hard, the target wasn't moving and the light wasn't bad at all, so they pretty much went where I wanted them to go. Urika pursed her lips and walked up to the target and tried to slide her finger between the shafts of the javelins clustered at the target's center. She could do it, but only just. She looked back at Ajax and said "Pass."

He smiled and said, "Thank you, Urika."

She looked at me as I bowed my thanks. "Can you shoot a bow too?"

"Yes, Lady. But I prefer the javelin."

She shrugged and pulled the javelins from the target, and I heard her place them back in the weapon rack and then her footsteps followed us to the entrance of the stone long stone building they called the Temple Hall. There was an older man there, seated next to a pile of weapons and a couple of shields. He was under average height, with broad shoulders, a full head of grey hair and very bright blue eyes; he smelled of beer and lye soap and leather. He stood up as we approached, and he spoke to me, ignoring Ajax.

"I am Broddi the Short", he said, and then he drew his dagger and came at me.

I drew my own knife and easily evaded an obvious lunge and then barely blocked three very quick jabs. I parried a hard thrust and backed away and to the left from a series of cuts that looked to be a setup for an overhand left to my jaw (most fighters are more than happy to grapple, throw or just slug you one if they have a hand free and you get distracted). I was right; I parried the last slash and skipped back away from his fist, and he said "HOLD!"

I froze. He sheathed his knife and said,

"Not bad; let's see how you do with sword and shield."

He tossed me a practice shortsword, with no edge and a blunt point, and when I was sheathing my knife, he spun and threw a round shield at me like a discus.

I clapped it out of the air and readied it. Broddi readied his own sword and shield and then he rushed me, running almost on tiptoe and I started sweating. I braced myself so the impact of his shield on mine didn't throw me and his sword came darting at me, over and around his shield. I barely managed to block or parry his thrusts and then he locked shields with me, pushing to throw me back, stamping and kicking at my instep and ankles. I managed to keep him from mashing my toes with his hobnailed sandals and threw him off, and as he went backwards he brought his shield rim up and I missed having my teeth loosened by no more than an inch. He grinned at me when his trick failed, and signaled a halt.

"Fast. I like that. He passes.", he said, nodding to Ajax.

"Catch your breath for a bit, lad. You don't want to rush this.", said Ajax.

A woman's voice came out of the shadows inside the Hall doors then, almost in echo of Ajax's words:

"Yes. Rest, boy. I don't like people having excuses when they fight me."

She stepped out of the shadows then, above average in height, clad in grey with black gloves and boots. She had graying red hair cut short, and clear blue eyes and she smelled of cedar and of lemon. She carried a rapier that was longer than most, and there was something about the way she moved that alarmed me. She waited until my breathing had steadied and then drew her sword:

"I am Herva, called the Needle."

Uh oh. She motioned for me to draw my own rapier; no blunted weapons this time. I drew and she came at me then, and I realized what had alarmed me: she was nigh as fast as I was. I had always been the fastest person I knew, and while other boys had been bigger and stronger, I was tough enough to last as long as most and fast enough to keep out of their way until I had read their pattern and could take advantage of it. But that wasn't possible with Herva; she was almost as fast as I was and that long rapier of hers just kept coming at me. I never really got a chance to attack; right off she hit me with a high slash and a low thrust, then I found myself in two wickedly tight binds that I just barely broke out of. Then I was backing and parrying madly, but the point of that damn rapier always seemed to be in my face. There was blood on my left hand and on my right arm from cuts I didn't remember getting and then she did something I had never seen before and turned a parry of one of my high cuts into a flat swing from right to left and nicked my chin.

I managed to backup half a step and recover, and she signaled a stop. She looked at me while she fished a scrap of cloth from her belt and cleaned my blood off her blade, and I realized she was breathing as hard as I was.

"You were right, Broddi. He is fast. He passes."

Urika's eyebrows went up at that. "Passes? He's bleeding in three different places. You touched him at will."

Herva sheathed her rapier and shook her head at the other woman:

"No, I did not. I tried to disarm him twice and failed. That's when I lost my temper a bit. He should be bleeding in nine or ten places, not just three. "

She looked over at Ajax.

"I always wondered what one of your pupils would be like, Old Man. This should be interesting."

Ajax's face was expressionless, but he nodded to me once in approval. Me, I was just happy she hadn't nailed my ears to the bloody temple doors. He healed my scratches and helped me clean up the blood a bit, and then we stood and waited for the next examiner. And waited. And then, we waited a little more. Finally, the sound of footsteps and voices from the temple signaled the arrival of the next examiner, and many others as well. I was to have an audience for this test. One glance at the man who lead them and I knew this had to be Loricon. He was tall, taller than anyone else present, and dressed in a mix of yellow and red that brought to mind a leaping flame. He smelled of perfume and an eager sort of hate; he had long black hair he wore in a thick braid, and eyes so dark they looked black. Other than a quick glance at me, those eyes never seemed to leave Ajax. It was if he and Ajax were the only ones present, and I could not only smell, but feel the hate radiating off him like heat from furnace. The crowd following him fanned out around us and I realized that this test had been the subject of some discussion. There were not only followers of Wurrunk from the temple itself, but members of the nobility, free mercenaries, guardsmen for some of the merchant houses and more than a hundred men and women who wore the grey shoulder sash of students. There was a group of these last who wore armbands of red and yellow and who stood in a block behind Loricon: his current class of students and assistants plus a few personal servants and hangers-on. Henchmen, in other words.

Loricon carried a broadsword, although I learned later that he was a master of at least five different weapons, and there was something familiar about the way he held it. He turned his attention to me and said:

"I am Loricon. Begin."

So Loricon didn't want to waste time on blunted weapons either. He came in fast with two high cuts that I deflected and then struck not at me, but at my sword, and with enough force to knock it from my hand if I had not seen it coming. That was when I realized that I had seen Loricon's technique before, that Ajax had been using it whenever we had sparred with broadswords on the journey to Byzantium. I backed up and tried to look for an opening while I parried a thrust that came right at the bridge of my nose; I was faster by a bit, but he had the advantages of reach, strength, skill and about 20 years or so of experience. I tried a cut in return and got a light wound in my left arm for my trouble and I back away. Then he touched my left arm again at the shoulder and I felt the sleeve start to come loose; he had cut the stitches in my shirt. And then he touched me at the hip and my belt came loose. I pulled it free and tossed it aside and leapt to the side to avoid being backed against a pillar by the doors, and he slashed my breeches at the right hip and my pants started to come undone. He was making a fool of me, and from the lazy smile he gave Ajax, he wasn't even giving it his full attention. That's when I started to get mad.

He came in high again, going for my right shoulder, and without thinking it all the way through, I did what Herva had done to me: I turned a parry of his first cut into a slash of my own from left to right and because he wasn't really paying attention to me, I caught him. I didn't draw blood, but I managed to do something that might have been worse: I cut his sleeve, and a jeweled stud that had held the fabric tight to his wrist fell free and bounced across the flagstones. There was a gasp and the shuffling of feet and the whole crowd went silent; as I said, we had drawn an audience for this test. Then Broddi's harsh laugh echoed across the courtyard.

I was looking Loricon in the face when Broddi laughed, and I saw his eyes change, and I knew I was going to bleed for what I had just done. I began backing away, but it was too late. Loricon came at me in a blistering whirlwind of an attack that drew blood from four different places and ended in a hard thrust that, had it landed, would have torn open my face from the left side of my mouth to my left ear. The only reason I parried it was because Ajax had used exactly this attack in our practice bouts; as it was, it slit open my left ear and the force of the blow sent me tumbling across the temple flagstones. I started to scramble to my feet when I heard at least two blades being drawn, and Herva's voice shouted "HOLD!".

I was on one hand and one knee; there was a pair of boots next to my right hand and they belonged to Ajax, as did one of the swords that had been drawn. He was staring over my shoulder into Loricon's face, and he held his sword at his side, point down, waiting. Loricon was a pace behind me, his sword pointed at me, but his eyes were locked on Ajax, and his hate was something I could almost touch. Then Herva's voice rang out:

"You volunteered for this duty, Loricon, so you know as well as I that when a candidate is knocked to the ground, the test is done, and the examiner must render his judgement. What do you say, does the candidate Joren pass or fail?"

Loricon straightened and sheathed his sword with a flourish. His face was expressionless now, and when he spoke his voice was emotionless, completely without inflection.

"This candidate passes the test."

Then he spun on his heel and walked out of the temple, without a glance at me. More than a score of those who had gathered to watch the bout followed after him, after one of them had stooped to retrieve the stud I had cut from his sleeve. The rest of the crowd broke their silence once Loricon left the temple, and from the snatches of conversation I could hear while Ajax got me patched up, few if any had expected me to pass this fourth test:

"Didn't expect THAT…"

"Very, very fast…

"…lucky he didn't lose an ear or worse…

"Slippery little hill weasel, isn't he?"

"First student Old Ajax has brought to the temple in three decades…"

"Pay me."

"He'd better be fast, he's gone and made an enemy of someone who has founded his own sword school…"

So now Loricon and those who followed him were my enemies? Well, if they were Ajax's enemies, they would have been mine too, sooner or later. After I had caught my breath, Urika, Herva and Broddi walked up to Ajax. I bowed to them and stepped back. Broddi the Short nodded to me and then turned to Ajax with a laugh:

"I don't know what you're up to, old man, but I like it already!"

Ajax grinned at him, and bowed in thanks to Herva.

"Thank you for helping to keep that under control. Loricon and I have our differences, but we need to be keep them just between us. I will do better in the future."

"You are welcome, but it is not you who worries me."

She turned to me.

"You, boy. YOU are the one who worries me. From now on, practice any moves you learn from me BEFORE you use them in a fight, real or otherwise. A heartbeat slower on that lateral, and he would have taken your hand off at the wrist."

I bowed to her. "Yes, Lady."

Broddi started cracking his knuckles and mused aloud:

"Hmm. That's four tests down and two to go. Does anyone know who the last two examiners are?"

Four tests and two? I thought that there were seven tests...then it hit me: I had passed the first test when I had killed in the fight at Long Ear Springs. The Lords of the House of Death would not accept just anyone for this kind of training.

Urika nodded: "I saw the duty roster: the Shepherd and...His Grace."

She winced a bit as she said the last name. I didn't understand, but Broddi's eyes lit up.

"What! First he tweaks Loricon Longshanks, and now he gets to bandy words with Arkell the Proud? Is there time enough for me to grab something to eat and drink before the show starts?"

Herva glared at Broddi to no effect whatsoever. "Ass. This is no joke."

She turned to Ajax and lowered her voice so that no one farther than a few feet away could hear her.

"Whitebeard, don't you think you are pushing this a bit? You know what Arkell is like."

Ajax shrugged at her, hands spread, palms out, in a gesture that was both exasperated and resigned.

"I know, I know. But he is the best teacher here for the greatsword, and that is exactly what Joren needs: to learn from the best. I couldn't think of any painless way to do this, so I decided to go for fast instead."

"I get it; like ripping a bandage off of a crusted wound, instead of slowly peeling it off, right? What? What did I say?"

This was Broddi again, and it earned him glares from both women and another grin from Ajax. The first didn't seem to faze him any more than the second. He glanced at me.

"Joren, isn't it? Are you any good with your greatsword?"

"It's my favorite, Sir." I answered.

Broddi did not say anything in reply, just bobbed his eyebrows at Urika and jingled his coin pouch. She pursed her lips in thought, and said:

"Put me down for fifty silver. I think it a good investment!" This last statement was in reply to a hard look from Herva, who folded her arms in disgust and proceeded to ignore both of them.

Me, I didn't like the sounds of this at all. I'd already made one enemy, and I could deal with that, but I'd rather not take instruction from someone who had an active dislike for me. As I was thinking this, I noticed a man who had stepped out of the shadows and was standing silently a few feet away, close enough to be noticed, but not close enough to intrude. He was about six feet in height, with short black hair and a goatee streaked with silver, and he was missing his right hand from about two inches above the wrist. He was dressed in grey and white, and wore a shortsword in an oddly slanted scabbard; he smelled of ink, and sadness. He noticed me looking at him and smiled as he raised his left hand towards me:

"Are you injured? Can I help?"

Then he stepped forward and began to gesture in those movements that marked the beginning of a spell. But not a spell of healing. I stepped back from him, and as I did so, Ajax, Herva and Urike all moved out of his way and turned to watch me. So, the fifth test had begun.

He shrugged at me. "No? A pity."

This must be the one Urika had called the Shepherd. I had no idea how he had earned that name, and I didn't waste anytime wondering about it then, because his hand was moving in the pattern of another spell. I watched closely and then relaxed as he drew closer. This spell I knew.

"Will you let me cast this spell on you?" and he leaned forward with the index finger of his hand pointed right between my eyes, all the while his own eyes searched my face. I waited and he touched me and he cast the first level of the spell that can protect against physical damage. He nodded at me, and then his hand began to move again but slower this time, with broader gestures. I couldn't tell what the spell was constructed to do, but suddenly I realized that it was a ceremonial spell, one which would take an hour or more to complete.

"What of this one?"

Well, he was the examiner, and if he wanted to take hours to finish the test, that is what we were going to do. I drew myself to attention, and said:

"My time is yours, Shepherd. I will wait as long as you like to finish the ceremony."

"Hah! Well, we really don't need to do that."

He looked at me for a moment, rubbing his chin in thought. Then he nodded to himself.

"What about this one?"

His hand began to move in a way completely different from the three spells that had gone before; they were harder, less fluid and somehow... wrong. The hair on the back of my neck stood on end as I began to smell something that was cold and bottomless and...HUNGRY. I realized that I was backing away from the Shepherd, and that my hand was on a sword hilt and that I couldn't let him finish that spell, not if it was aimed at me. It must have shown on my face, because the Shepherd stopped casting the spell. He had followed me step for step and now stood less than an arm's length from me, his head down and his eyes staring into my face. He made no attempt to guard himself; if I had drawn and struck at him, I could have cut him down. He couldn't have cared less.

"What was it about that spell that was different? Why did you back away from me that time, when the other spells bothered you not at all? Tell me!"

"It smelled hungry to me."

He straightened in surprise, and I saw an expression of excitement, almost a fierce sort of joy cross his face, and I realized that he was the type of person to whom a good puzzle was worth as much as a gold coin.

"Explain!"

So I told him, with Herva and Urika listening at first, but soon Broddi and some others joined them. I told them how I had joined forces with the old shaman who had been the last of the Forsaken, those Lupaku outlawed by the Empire for the destruction of the Mabirshan tribe. I told them how I had worn the flayed, living hide of werewolf in a night-long race to save a handful of children from imperial chains and to exact vengeance against their captors. I told them how ever after my sense of smell has been much keener than it had been before, and that I can smell emotions and magic and power.

The Shepherd turned to Ajax when I was done, and said:

"Does he exaggerate?"

"No, Magan. I've never been able to determine just how keen his nose is, but his sense of smell is many times more sensitive than any normal man. I am certain he can smell magic, although he often has trouble putting the sensation into words."

"Excellent! He passes this test." The Shepherd turned then to me.

"I am Magan One Hand, called the Shepherd because it is my duty to keep order amongst those students who are not enrolled by a Great House or noble family. If you pass the last test, we shall see much of each other. Tell me, do you seek training here as a Guardian, to protect those in your charge from assassins?"

"Yes, Lord." Ajax and I had spoken of the possible paths I could take in my training.

"Why?"

"Because my mother and sisters were murdered by stealth and my father was poisoned by those who feared to face him blade to blade."

He nodded, more to himself than to me.

"Then you have come to the right place. We have much to teach anyone who seeks to learn the way of the Guardian, but for one of your abilities, our library and its storehouse of poisons will provide invaluable training. If you pass the last test, that is. Good Luck."

As he spoke those last words, he gestured again, and I felt the spell I had let him cast on me fall away.

"Thank you, Shepherd."

Why did I sense an unspoken "you're going to need it" at the end of his last sentence? I saw Broddi slip away, probably to place his bets; Ajax, Urika and Herva had their heads together in low-voiced conversation, and suddenly, I could feel my heart pounding in my chest. It was starting to get to me and I could not afford that, could not risk losing my edge at the very end. I took three deep breaths, and centered myself. Patience, determination, focus; I would need them all for this last test. I very much wanted to make a good showing with the two-handed sword. And maybe, just maybe, I could avoid pissing off the last examiner.

"What the hell are you people dithering here for? Move aside, or I'll pitch the whole bloody lot of you into the street!"

Or, maybe not.

The man who came gliding down the stairs from the upper floor of the temple hall was of medium height, but was broader of shoulder than anyone else I had yet seen. He was clad in silver and black clothing that looked to be just as expensive as that worn by Loricon, but his manner somehow managed to be even more arrogant. He was very fair, with icy blue eyes and hair so blonde that it looked white in the torch light. He smelled of perfume and ice and iron. Behind him came a file of a dozen young men and women, all wearing the grey sashes or grey tunics and carrying bronze greatswords: his students. They were lead by a youth who could not have been more than a year my senior, but who towered over his teacher by at least a foot. Ajax stepped out in front of this procession and nodded to the swordsman in black and silver; the people crowding the temple hall backed off and quieted down to hear their words.

"Arkell, called the Proud, I have a new student for you."

Arkell barely glanced at Ajax.

"No, you do not, Whitebeard. I only accept new students at the beginning of the year. Your student will have to wait until after the Winter Solstice, and then pass the entry requirements, just like anyone else."

My stomach sank. Not to even begin training until next spring? That was the better part of a year away; we couldn't afford to wait that long. Ajax felt the same way.

"But this student is here, now, and he needs to learn from the best teacher he can find. He knows much; he won't be an impediment to your class, but he needs to learn more. I've taught him all I can. Now, he needs a teacher like you. Test him and see for yourself; he will be worth your time."

Arkell turned to face the older man, and I realized that he neither liked nor disliked my teacher, he just had his own way of doing things. He couldn't care less what anyone else thought of him, but he very definitely did NOT care for someone telling him what he had to do, and in front of an audience, no less.

"I don't make exceptions for anyone, Ajax; and there is no way this boy could know enough to fit into a class that I have been instructing for more than a season. Find someone else to test and teach him, you old fool, or you can both come back at the start of the New Year."

Before Ajax could respond, Herva spoke up:

"Arkell, did you even LOOK at the duty roster for today?"

"Eh? Roster?" Arkell's eyes narrowed at Herva, but then he turned to look at Ajax.

Herva went on.

"Ajax brought an applicant for special training, and that means that six examiners are required to test him. If he fails any of the tests, then he is rejected. There were four volunteers as examiners and you and Broddi were chosen to fill the last two slots. The applicant has passed five of the six tests; you are the last. Since you never protested your assignment as examiner, I assume you are prepared to test the applicant now."

Arkell nodded once to Ajax. "You arranged this."

He turned back to Herva.

"If my memory serves me, examiners do not have to test the applicant themselves, they can simply set a task for the applicant and then pass or fail them based on their performance of that task. Correct?"

Oh, wonderful.

Herva stared at him a moment and then said: "Yes, you are correct."

"I thought so."

Arkell turned to the hulking youth behind him and motioned at me with one hand.

"Impetui, give this hill brat a beating."

Impetui is a colloquial Latium term, usually used as an endearment; roughly, it means "my little rash one". The big young man who Arkell had spoken to grinned in satisfaction and pulled the sheath from his greatsword, and then I drew mine and leapt at him in a single motion. Only Ajax and perhaps Herva really knew how fast I could move; Impetui and the rest of the crowd were a bit shocked. I had been on my best behavior up until now; my examiners were known warriors all and I was just a bit intimidated by them and my surroundings. But I wasn't intimidated by Impetui; he was just another student like me and I gave vent to all of my worry and frustration when I threw myself at him. Besides, no one has ever GIVEN me a beating; I have fought for every single one I ever had.

He barely got his blade up in time to parry my first blow, and then I was at him with a flurry of cuts and slashes that drove him back a half dozen paces, until his back was right against the wall. Then he rallied and came at me; he wasn't bad, and his advantages in height and weight began to tell. He pushed me back three paces and then we stood toe to toe and crossed blades in a whirling clamor that drew everyone in earshot running to see who was fighting. This went on for a bit; he kept on trying to disarm me by locking our sword guards together and then throwing his weight against my arm, but I always slipped free and he gave it up after I almost broke his nose with my pommel. That is when Impetui snarled something at me, and I gathered it was at this point that he overwhelmed the other students by either outlasting them or by beating them down by main strength. I smiled at him, and began to attack faster. He went white around the mouth and tried to redouble his efforts, but I had him. I had found his pattern, it was *there*, and I could...

"HOLD!"

Arkell's voice froze both of us where we stood. He stalked up to us, and after a check of Impetui's stance, nodded to him and motioned him back with a flick of his left hand. Then he looked at me, at the way I held myself, the way I positioned my feet and the way I held my sword. He stood where Impetui had stood, and looked down the blade of my sword into my eyes. Then he nodded.

"The applicant passes."

There was a bit of an uproar then, with everyone talking at once, either commenting on the fight or on Arkell and Ajax or settling their wagers or all three at once. Arkell ignored them all and strode right up to Ajax, and waited until everyone quieted down. Then he spoke to directly to Ajax, just as loudly as he had when he called him a fool.

"I was wrong." Herva's jaw dropped.

"You were right. I accept him."

He turned to me. "You, what is your name?"

"Joren, Lord."

"Very well, Joren. If you wish to learn from me, come to the upper hall tomorrow one hour after the end of the evening meal. We meet there every night, and until I say otherwise, you share the class lead with Impetui."

He nodded to me once, and then turned to his students:

"Class is dismissed."

Then he walked away without looking or speaking to anyone else, through a door that I later learned lead to the rooms of some of the acolytes who lived here on the temple grounds. Then Ajax put his hands on my shoulders and shook me once in congratulation.

"Well done, Joren. Very well done. That was risky, but I think that it was the only thing that could have persuaded Arkell to teach you. Make no mistake though, regardless of what happened here tonight, he will hold nothing back in his instruction. None of your new teachers will, it is not our way. But enough from me; my time as your teacher is done. From now on, you will learn from the best."

I straightened and looked him in the eye:

"I have already learned from the best, sir. I will show them that your time spent on me was not wasted."

Broddi came up to Ajax in time to hear this last from me. He laughed and said:

"You've already shown people quite a lot, boy. How are you fixed for coin by the way? I've won a lot of money betting on you tonight, and it's only fair that I share some of my winnings with you. No? What about you, Ajax? Let me buy you dinner and enough ale to wash it down."

The old man stretched and rubbed the back of his neck; I could feel how tense he was. This had meant a lot to him, more than I had realized.

"I will not say no to that, Broddi and thank you. Let me show Joren where he'll be sleeping for the next year first though. Join us for a meal, Herva? Urika?"

Herva was watching Broddi pour more than a dozen gold coins into Urika's hands. She sighed resignedly, and said:

"Of course, Whitebeard; I have some questions for you anyway. As for you Joren, you are welcome here. You're a quick study and you should learn a great deal in your time with us. I only hope that you don't pick up some bad habits from anyone along the way."

She glanced at Broddi pointedly when she said this, but he was oblivious. She pulled her cloak around her, nodded once more at me and walked off towards the temple gates. Urika joined her and Broddi followed them after giving Ajax another grin and me a slap on the shoulder in congratulation. We picked up our packs and turned to find Magan One-Hand standing before us, with what looked like a grey cloak draped over his right arm. He held it out to me, and I realized it was a tunic, the same as those worn by some of the students who had followed Arkell the Proud, but marked with the sigils of Wurrunk: Death and Truth.

"Welcome, Joren. You have been accepted into the service of this House of Death as a both a student and a...guest. Wear this tunic whenever you are on duty or on the business of the temple; it will identify you as a servant of Wurrunk's House to the City Watch, to the guards of the queens, and to the people of Byzantium. It is a tradition here that those who wear the grey tunic may be called upon to aid the City Watch in the performance of its duties, when the need arises. Now, if you will follow me, I will show you where you will be sleeping from now on, and also where you can get some food, since I could hear your stomach rumbling from across the room."

I bowed to him; "Thank you, Shepherd."

I WAS hungry; those tests had done a wonderful job of sharpening my appetite and I was looking forward to my first real meal since we had left Aleppo.

We followed Magan out of the Hall and turned north to a smaller building that lay between the Hall and the Temple itself. It looked to be a combination of storage and sleeping quarters that might have been built at the same time as the Temple Hall. Both buildings were solidly built with deep foundations and thick walls on the first floor, with high, narrow windows. Like all of the older buildings that I had seen in the city so far, they seemed to have been built to last through rough times. I learned later that in the past, different armies had held different sections of the city against one another for seasons at a time (as would happen again years after I left the city, when the Empire aided the Red Queen in her attempt to seize Byzantium).

The shepherd opened a door in the far end of this smaller building and told me to stow my gear under one of the three empty beds I saw. Then he and Ajax walked me over to the entrance of the Great Temple itself to swear me in. If I was to train for a year in Wurrunk's House, then I would need to bind myself to Wurrunk's service. It was the least of all the oaths accepted by his followers, but no oath should be taken lightly and it would be enough to mark me as one in the Death god's service and to gain the benefit of the magic protecting the temple and its grounds. Magan stood in front of the temple doors and drew his sword; as Shepherd, it was his duty to administer the oath, while Ajax stood behind me and to my left, as my sponsor. The sword was a very fine broadsword: two feet of razor edged iron that glowed with its own light. He held his sword out to me, hilt up, and I raised my right hand (palm out) and clasped the sword blade with my left. I closed my fingers around the cold iron with no more pressure than a gentle breath and then sealed the oath with a few drops of my blood and my own magic, freely given. When we were finished, I felt something change, and then it seemed as if I was at the center of an expanding blossom of silver light. It spread out to the walls of the compound and everything, even the two men before me, looked different somehow. Then I heard that voice again, that same quiet voice I had heard before in Wurrunk's shrine in the Temple of Tarhunt in Melid, and it said:

"Welcome."

Magan's eyes widened; he had heard the voice too. He glanced at Ajax and seemed about to say something, but thought better of it. He then pointed me to the door in the back of the Temple Hall.

"You should be able to find something to eat in the kitchen. Cook will set you up; he is expecting you. I will see you in an hour or two, after you have had a chance to eat and settle in. In the meantime, I wonder if I might join you while you eat, Ajax. I have a few questions; about Joren and about Khetar, and the battle fought at Roaring Springs."

"Of course, Magan. You are more than welcome."

Then Ajax turned and looked at me. I straightened up and looking him in the eye, nodded to him. He nodded once in reply, and I realized that he was proud of me. Then he spoke one word to me, exactly the way he did at the start of practice:

"Begin!"

I watched the two of them walk out into the great courtyard, and it struck me that almost everything Ajax and my aunt had taught me had been aimed at preparing me for this moment. From now on, it was my responsibility to learn what I would need to know in order to become the man I wanted to be, and to build the life I wanted Belkara and I to have.

Time to begin.

Chapter XXIV: The Cook and His Pies

I HEADED OVER TO THE KITCHEN through the doorway that Magan had pointed out. It was a big kitchen; during a muster, it might have to feed a thousand or more fighters. But once I got past the smells of the spices on the shelves near the door, I could tell that something was wrong. Something was burning, or rather, about to burn. I ran to the long ovens against the north wall of the room; they held trays of pies, five rows of ten each, all different kinds and all about to burn. I glanced around the room and spotted the cooling racks on the eastern wall; this was going to be close.

I slid open the oven doors and began moving the pie trays to the racks, the trays with the pies closest to burning first. I didn't see any gloves, but a couple of clean, wet clothes worked just fine. I had to be careful because of the heat and the overwhelming aromas fogging the room, but I got it done; Aunt Syara would have been proud of me. I stepped back from the cooling racks, closed the oven doors with a careful foot and turned to find three men who stood in the wide doors that lead to the hall staring at me. I'd been so focused on getting the pies out of the oven that I had not noticed them. Two of them were average height and build, one a few years older than me and the other was twice my age or a little older. The third man was past middle age, six feet or more tall with wide shoulders, short grey hair and a big belly. He motioned the other two men back into the hall to finish whatever they had been working on, and went to check his pies. I could tell when he sniffed at them that they were HIS pies. He checked all of them, and then turned to me:

"You kept my pies from burning! How did you know to do that?"

"I have a very keen sense of smell, Sir; and also my aunt made enough pies that I knew what to do."

"Ah! Your aunt was a baker? Good for her, and lucky for me. I would have been fit to be tied if those pies had burned. It would not have been just the waste either; I have found that few things make trouble faster with a group of fighters than bad food. You must be the new Lamb. Now, you look hungry, yes? Yes. Then sit and I will feed you."

He had me sit down at a table over by the steps leading to the cellar, and brought over a plate, a bowl and a mug. He told me where to find a fork and spoon, then brought out the food. There was fresh baked bread with little jars of honey and jelly, spicy snapping turtle soup, baked fish and a dish made of yellow noodles, carrots, green beans and sliced beets topped with melted cheese. The scent of all that food reminded me that I really WAS hungry and I stuffed myself.

That was how I met Gultar the Fat, or as just about everyone who lived within the walls of the Great House of Death called him, Cook. While I ate, he asked me questions; not about weapons or fighting, but about my Aunt Syara and her kitchen and what she had liked to cook. When I had finished eating and downed the last of the weak beer I had been given to drink, I offered to give him a hand cleaning up. He looked me over and accepted. I was introduced to Hendorl and Kamil (his two assistants) and pitched in.

We had gotten the dishes and the ovens done, and were working on mopping the floors when Magan came in through the front door. He was looking over what was written on a long piece of parchment when he spotted me.

"Ah, Joren! I was hoping that I would find you here. I was just going over the work list for tomorrow and…"

"Magan."

Cook had stepped into the doorway to the kitchen, and when he had Magan's attention, he just pointed at me with his right index finger. Magan's eyebrows went up, then he smiled and nodded at Cook. He turned to me and said:

"All right then. When you are not needed for ceremony support or a rotating duty, you will see Cook about work in the kitchen. When you are finished here, I suggest you get to sleep early; we will be up by the time the Sun rises."

That was good advice and I took it.

Cook was one of the mysteries of the Great House of Death. He was Quartermaster as well as Cook, and all purchasing of food, potables and any type of supply went through his capable hands. He was also one of my teachers; he and Magan were the ones who taught me to distinguish between the different types of poisons whose samples were stored in the Temple library, as well as basic training in how to deal with a victim of poisoning. Gultar was on good terms with everyone, and was special friends with Magan and Dangmag, but he was the only person in Byzantium who could sit and share a glass of wine with Arkell the Proud. Often it was more than one glass and they would argue about wine, or food, or horses. For whatever reason, Arkell considered Gultar to be his equal, and that led me to think that in another time and place, Gultar had been someone of consequence. Here and now however, he was just Cook, and that seemed to suit him just fine. He was a good man and a good teacher; he taught me how to make pies and how to plan; both skills have served me well ever since.

Chapter XXV: The Smith and the Sage

THE HOUSE OF A'AS IN BYZANTIUM is one of the greatest libraries in the world, and has been a gathering place of knowledge (and of those who seek it) since at least the beginning of Time. It is presently located on the eastern side of the Old City, where many of Byzantium's countless temples are to be found. When I first heard from Ajax of the size and contents of the Great Library, my mind simply could not grasp what he told me. It was one of the many things that I saw in Byzantium that was just beyond my own (very) limited experience. It has literally hundreds of thousands of books, mainly scrolls of vellum and papyrus, but there are stone and metal tablets from many lands and in many languages. Each year, more books are added to the Great Library, and as it has grown it has spilled over to include more than one building, with more than one method used to organize its contents. That was a problem for me, since there was a scroll in the Great Library that I had to find, a book mentioned in Aunt Syara's last letter to me that contained a great many things I needed to know. Trying to find a single scroll that I had never seen before in the mazes of the Great Library would be like looking for the proverbial needle in a haystack.

The scroll I was looking for was the Book of Mabirh, which had been written by a son of Queen Mabirh the Tall, founder of the Mabirshan Tribe (and my many-times removed grandmother). That son had been called Narden the Wanderer and he had sought knowledge, rather than war, power or wealth; that path had eventually led him to Byzantium. He had died here, in his old age, while perusing the treasures of the Great Library. Apparently, he had left a treasure of his own behind when he died, and I needed to talk to someone who could help me find it. My first morning in the Great House of Death had been a continuous whirl of movement and instruction, and I was glad when the mid-day meal gave me a chance to sit and catch my breath. I had just finished eating when Ajax walked past me and motioned for me to follow him.

"Let's go see what the Smith and the Sage have to say about your amulet and that sword. And don't forget to ask Rostaka about your family's book."

"Yes, Sir."

We walked out of the barracks to find Rostaka and Dangmag waiting for us.

They smiled at me cheerfully: "Hello, Joren."

It came out as an unintentional chorus, and they each turned to give the other an exasperated look. I swallowed a laugh, but Ajax didn't even try to hide his amusement. He turned to me and said:

"They finish each other's sentences too."

"Ajax!"

"Ill-mannered old scalawag..."

"As we...I was saying, we have your possessions for you, and congratulations on passing your tests."

"Thank you, Sage."

She turned to look at the Smith, who bowed and said:

"Ladies first."

"Thank you, Dangmag. Joren, your medallion is very old and very valuable. The crystal is magic and can be used to store power needed to cast spells, but be warned that you must attune it to your will before you can use this magic, and that can be dangerous. But that is not all."

I was stunned; this type of magic item was worth more than its weight in gold, hundreds of times over in fact. Then I remembered what the darkling Azzhka had said those years ago when my aunt had healed her mother and the others in her party: 'My heart itself will balance the scales'. Treasure though this was, it had meant less to her than her mother's life and well-being. I think Aunt Syara had known full well how precious this gift was, and had passed it on to me, knowing how I would need it. Rostaka had wrapped the medallion in a soft cloth; she placed it in my hands, and then touched my shoulder to get my attention.

"That medallion is at least 1,000 years old, and there is an enchantment on it that has nothing to do with the crystal. It is some kind of summoning spell, but it requires two components to be complete. One is seawater, the medallion must be immersed in the sea itself, a mere bowl of seawater won't be enough. I was unable to determine what the other component is, but when that is provided while the medallion is covered by seawater, the enchantment on the medallion will call...something."

Ajax rubbed his chin and spoke: "An elemental summoning spell? For undines?"

Water elementals? That could be very useful, but I did not know much about water magic. That sort of thing had never interested me. Rostaka went on:

"Maybe, but that enchantment isn't like any elemental summoning spell I've ever seen. Also, it is different in that it isn't a matrix, it is a one-use proposition that doesn't require any power to fuel it, just those two components. You might think of it as an incomplete ceremony: provide the two missing components and it will go off. I would be very careful if you intend to experiment with this, Joren. Magic this old can be extremely dangerous."

I thanked her and told her that I had no intention of experimenting with the medallion at all, it was just too useful to me exactly the way it was. Then it was Dangmag's turn; he stepped forward with my uncle Farad's sword in his hands.

"This sword is a puzzle; it is only bronze, but whoever forged it used tools that I do not have and spells that I do not know. No one in the temple has ever seen a sword quite like this, and it does not match any of the blade or hilt patterns recorded in the temple library. The next step would be to check the sword patterns listed in the Great Library of A'as itself, but that might take weeks or even seasons. I do know this: the enchantment on the sword is tied to the blood, to the family of whoever the sword was made for. This was your uncle's sword?"

I remembered how my aunt had handled the sword, sometimes drawing it and testing the edge with a far-away look in her eyes.

"I think perhaps, that it had belonged to both of them."

"That would explain why the magic of the sword is awake for you. Draw the sword and hold it out to us"

I drew the broadsword and held it at arm's length, with the flat of the blade across my palms. All three of them laid their fingertips on the sword's blade and held their breath. After a moment, they took their hands away and looked at each other.

"Power. There is an immense amount of power behind the enchantment." said Ajax.

"Patience. It seems content to wait until it is needed." said Rostaka.

Dangmag nodded in agreement.

"It may sound strange, but it seems that the primary focus of the sword's makers was to forge a tool to aid your aunt and uncle, not to kill. The sword does hold a keen edge (I had never had to sharpen it), but when I was looking for the maker's mark on the tang of the hilt, I scratched the sword with one of my etching tools. It repaired itself, and I think it might try to heal its wielder." Dangmag said, and then he shrugged.

"This is guesswork, but I think your aunt and uncle helped to forge this blade and it is tied to their family, their flesh and blood. What do you feel when you hold that sword, boy?"

"I can feel an echo of my own heartbeat, almost as if the sword had a pulse of its own, and it never feels cold." It also reminded me, very strongly of Aunt Syara, her voice and her touch, but I did not speak of that.

"Then the sword accepts you as your aunt's heir, and its magic will work for you. But I think that when the power fueling the sword's magic is spent, the sword itself might break into pieces. After all, it IS only bronze."

Rostaka had been thinking while Dangmag had been talking, and now she asked a question of Ajax:

"Do you have any idea where Farad and Syara might have gotten that sword?"

"I've been thinking about that; I knew Farad as a boy, but there was a period of about 10 years before they settled down where they were not in Khetar at all. No one knows where they went, but there was no word of them during that time and they did not speak of it afterwards. Not to me at any rate."

"Nor to me." I said when they turned and looked at me.

"Ah, well. Time will tell.", Rostaka said.

Ajax nudged me with an elbow. Oh, right.

"Your pardon, Sage, but could you help me find a book in the Great Library?"

"A book? Well, the Great Library certainly has a great many of those; only the Minos's own library is said to match it. Now, what kind of book, exactly?"

I told them then of the book left behind by Narden the Wanderer, its title and its provenance. Rostaka's eyes lit up.

"A first person account of the founding of one of the tribes of Khetar? During the opening of Issuria? Joren, that sounds fascinating! I know half a dozen scholars who would be greatly interested in such a book, and one of them has to have heard of it. There will be minor fees involved in tracking the scroll's location and having it retrieved when you want to read it, but I doubt if they'll amount to more than a few pieces of silver. I will be glad to help you find your family's scroll, but I have a favor to ask of my own, in return. May I read the Book of Mabirh, once it is found?"

"But of course, Sage. It would be the least I can do to thank you for your help in this matter."

"Then I will begin the process of searching the Great Library's catalog systems, all three of them. I'll let you know when I hear something definite, but it may take some time."

Dangmag spoke up:

"Why don't you see if you can find a match for that sword's pattern while you are at it, if you are going to be diving into the Great Big Pile of Books. I took a rubbing of the sword's markings and here is a list of its attributes and a sketch to compare to any illustrations you might find. You can bill me for the fees."

"Bill you? You pay in advance, like always."

"Ajax, she doesn't trust me!"

"Don't get me involved in this."

"Trust? I KNOW you, Dangmag. The last time I gave you credit, that idiot Broddi talked you into backing one of his schemes, and I had to help the two of you clean out a pirate lair before I got my money back. Not this time!"

I wanted to hear more about the pirates, but Ajax was already pushing me towards the temple doors.

"Speaking of time, I think it is time we went about our own business."

I thanked them again, and we parted ways. I had to get back to my chores.

Chapter XXVI: The House of the Raven

THE FIRST AFTERNOON THAT I HAD FREE, I went to pay a visit to my aunt's servants and to see the house my grandfather had built. It was at the corner of Sixth Street and Mercy, in a good enough part of Byzantium, south and a bit east of the walled area of the Old City that contains the Acropolis. This meant a walk across the north and east sides of town, through an area that was seeing some new construction and a bit of reconstruction as well. One of the tenements that had been thrown up to house the tide of immigrants that had swept into the city from the countryside twenty years ago had caught fire the day I had arrived in Byzantium. Its burned-out shell was due to be torn down. It wasn't that long a walk, I would just have to watch my footing on the way back that night. It took me a bit to find the right section of the street, but I spotted the house right away; not many residences have a double wall protecting them. On closer inspection, it definitely had the look of a house built by a man of military experience.

My grandfather Robard had quite a bit of money when he rode into town, and he had not hesitated to pour some of it into that house. It was all of stone, not unheard of in Byzantium, but expensive. The outer walls and those of the house itself were thicker than normal, with the outer face of the wall on the street sloped so that it provided no cover at all to fire coming from anyone atop the inner wall or the protected roof of the house itself. There were few windows visible from this side of the house, and those were all long slits, but most houses in Byzantium get their light from the central courtyard anyway. I was spotted by someone, probably one of Queen Dilfara's people, but it was Joris who came out of the house to meet me.

"Welcome, Joren! Welcome to the house of the Lady Natyr, your aunt and of your grandparents before her, that now is yours. Be thrice welcome, son of Dono!"

He wasn't speaking just to me; there were people gawking at me up and down the street and there were at least a dozen men and women in Dilfara's colors along the walls or crowding the entrance to get a look at me. I thanked him and shook his hand, then reached into my tunic to get the pouch filled with grain that I needed for the homecoming ritual. Grain is the source of Thrace's wealth and Byzantium's too, so Halki, god of grain is important here, as is his wife, Tawara. She is the goddess of midwives and Byzan's faithful servant. In many ways, Byzantium is Tawara's city as well, and every residence has one or more geese, the symbols of that goddess, and her messengers. The people of Byzantium have been saved more than once by flocks of geese over the centuries, and feeding the house goose was not just tradition, but a perfectly reasonable sign of respect. Grain wasn't the only thing I had in the pouch; there are others who live in the homes of the people of Byzantium, and not all of them run on two legs, or any legs at all. As I was pulling the pouch free, the sack tied to my belt with a couple of rawhide thongs began to jerk and move. Good, the rat was awake.

As I was pulling the mouth of the pouch open, I could hear some of Dilfara's people talking about me. It wasn't that my hearing was supernaturally good, it's just that they didn't care if I heard them or not. Mostly, it was talk about me being a runt (Joris was taller) or just being a foreigner, and it had an edge to it. I was a stranger, I wasn't from around here and I was the son of the man who had defied a woman they had respected and obeyed for years. They resented me, and they really didn't like the fact that I was taking possession of the home that had been denied the Lady Natyr. The depth of their resentment told me something about how they had felt about my aunt; fear had not been the only emotion felt for the Lady Natyr by those who followed the Brown Earth Queen, there had been admiration and pride in her accomplishments too. All this I could understand, but there was another voice amongst that crowd, a kind of voice that I had heard before, with the hungry, hard-edged tones of the bully.

"He has no right and no place here, and if he steps out of line, he'll be heading someplace else, in pieces if need be."

Well, well; it looked like some the hostility I could scent from this bunch was going to be right out in the open from the start. Good, that might make it easier to deal with. At least, that is what I was thinking when it was all taken out of my hands, literally. Joren had just placed his hand on my back to support me, in more ways than one, when everyone was startled by an emphatic "Honk!". There was a goose at the top of the short flight of steps that came down from the doors of the house. It honked again to make sure it had everyone's attention, then marched down the walk to where I was standing at the edge of the street.

She was a good-sized bird, mostly grey and white, with a touch of black on the head and the wingtips. She walked right up to me, and then spread her wings and cocked her head to look at me. I had just managed to get my mouth closed when Joris told me:

"Pick her up, boy."

I hesitated for just an instant and then carefully bent over and got my left arm underneath her; she wasn't the biggest goose I would ever see, but big enough: a blow from one of those wings could break a man's arm. She muttered at me while I lifted her up, and then laid one wing on my chest and wrapped the other around my shoulders, for all the world as if she was shielding me. I froze and she began her examination of me.

She poked her bill into my ear and ran it through my hair, laid her head along my cheek and rubbed it under my chin, all the while sounding as if she was talking to herself. She examined the folds of my cloak and peered down my tunic, and then lifted her head and turned it so she was looking at me out of her right eye, from a distance of only three or four inches. What did I see in that eye? Something...not just a domesticated bird, but something else...something that had been waiting for me. Then she stuffed her head down into the sack and started eating. There were six different grains in there; she seemed to like the brown rice the best, but she eat it all. The grain, that is; she was careful to leave the egg clusters, the bugs and beetle grubs behind.

When she was done, she stretched and shook herself, and then pointed her head at the house doors and honked twice; time to go. I took my time heading up the walk to the house; I had to be careful with my balance and I did NOT want to make a bad impression by dropping the house goose or falling on my face. The goose didn't seem to mind; she never seemed to stop moving her head, taking in everyone on the street, the wind moving through the trees, the sound of a child singing from the next house down. Until we reached the top of the steps before the doors to the house, that is. Then she stared at one of the women on the left side of the porch, where the bully's voice had come from earlier, and she began to hiss. It was surprisingly loud in the sudden silence, and it seemed to have a lot of force behind it; it sounded like steam that had been pent up a long time. She kept this up until we had passed through the doors and entered the long passage that lead to the courtyard of the house, all the while keeping her head turned towards the one who had offended her.

The crowd outside erupted in spirited (although muffled) conversations as soon as we were out of sight, but I heard the voice of an older woman say quite clearly:

"Pack, Druva. You're leaving. Today."

No one wanted to risk Tawara's disfavor, and that would be the least consequence of offending a house goose in her own home. I could smell the inner court before I entered it: mostly dust, leather, oil (for weapons and harness) and cheap beer, but behind that was the scent of running water, of green leaves and back of it all, something delightful cooking. The courtyard was a bright place, and not just because I entered it from a dark corridor. Varsene and Valena were there, and their obvious delight in seeing me warmed my heart. They both nodded to the goose, who dipped her head to each in reply, and then honked peremptorily; her pool was in sight and she wanted to go cool off. I walked carefully across the courtyard with the image of a raven with outstretched wings laid into its cobbles, and set the goose gently on the rim of the pool built against the eastern wall of the yard. It was shaded by two trees, (one a silver maple, the other some type of willow) and was fed by steady trickle of water from an earthen pipe. She hopped right into the water and proceeded to shower herself with flicks of her wings, sighing to herself with pleasure. I settled myself on the poolside, wondering what I was to do with the contents of those two sacks when something very small and light jumped onto the top of my head. I froze, and it soon hopped onto my right shoulder and began moving down my arm with short, quick movements. It was a dark green lizard, no bigger than my hand, with jewel-bright eyes and a yellow underbelly. It had reached my elbow when I felt a tug on my left sleeve; another lizard, this one the size of duskcat kit, had climbed onto my other arm while I was distracted. This one was dark grey above and orange below, with eyes that moved independently of each other. It kept one eye on me while it walked down the length of my arm, to where I was holding the offering sack open with both hands. The smaller lizard on my right ran up to the sack to peer into it and promptly fell in, which was followed by a busy series of crunching noises. The other lizard dove in after it, and the two of them proceeded to clean the burlap sack of every single egg mass, grub and bug I shoveled into it earlier that day.

When they were done, they leisurely climbed out; the larger of the two taking two twigs laden with insect eggs into the maple tree and up out of sight. Feeding his family, no doubt. The smaller lizard, its belly bulging, climbed up my arm just far enough to wrap his prehensile tail around my wrist and sink his tiny claws into my bracer. In the space of two breaths it was fast asleep. Then I caught the scent of a snake, and I knew who the rat was for. Snakes are sacred in Thrace, as indeed they are any place where the Earth temples have influence; they are the traditional guardians of the Earth, and the average person considers themselves lucky if their house is blessed by the presence of one. This snake came with a rustling sound out from under the stonework on the far side of the pool, a black snake and a big one. All reptiles grow as long as they live, and I'm sure that there were bigger snakes in Byzantium, but this was the biggest snake I had ever seen out in daylight up until then, a full ten feet long from snout to tail tip. It reared up to look me in the eye, more than three feet of its length off the ground, and then it waited, tongue flickering. The rat in the other sack had gone motionless when it had caught the snake's smell; I gently untied that sack from my belt, careful not to disturb the lizard asleep on my arm, and threw it off towards the center of the courtyard. The rat shot out of the bag and hit the ground running when it landed, but not fast enough; that black snake struck so fast and hard, I heard the rat's back break when the blow landed.

The snake picked the rat up in its jaws and brought it back to the pool, where it began the process of swallowing the body after casually laying a few lazy coils across my boots. It did not even have to distend its jaws to get the rat to fit; that was handy, so to speak. Things settled down a bit then; the house goose dozed with her head under one wing, the lizard was just about comatose and even the snake went still after stretching part of its length in the bright sunlight. I sat there for a while, relaxing bit by bit, looking at the white and red painted walls of the courtyard around me, the old flower beds and the lampposts that would light an evening's gathering or hold birdcages to fill the place with song during the day.

It had been a bright place full of life once; although the house had been used mainly as a combination storehouse and barracks for the last thirty years, you could see where it could be that way again. It would take time and work though, which I did not have to spare just now. The heat began to make me drowsy; normally that makes me get up and start practicing to clear my head. But I felt no urgency to be up and moving; I felt a curious sense of being welcome here, in this place. After a time, I went to sleep too.

"Joren."

I opened my eyes to find Valene smiling at me; the house goose was standing on the edge of the pool looking at us expectantly, but the lizard and the snake were nowhere in sight. Odd, I should have felt and heard them leave; they should have roused me from any normal nap. I stood up and took the arm that she offered me.

"It is time for the evening meal. Will you join us, my Dear?"

This last was addressed to the goose, who hopped down and lead us into the door in the southern wall of the courtyard's southeast corner. This lead into what was once the kitchen, which was now also dining hall and common room for my aunt's servants while they began the process of turning the House of the Raven back into a home. There were four places set for the meal, along with a plate and bowl by the door to the old hall for the goose. Valene and Varsena invoked the blessing of the Earth goddesses in unison, and then we sat down to the meal.

The house goose had grain and a rice cake smeared with bean paste; I had beans and onions with mutton, a dish that the sisters said had been one of my father's favorites, and I could see why. Joris joined us then; he had spent most of that day overseeing the movement of the last of my aunt's belongings from the temple where she had passed back here to her home. We ate our meal together and then had a wonderful dessert of rice pudding with brown spice. Once the goose had finished her meal, she went to Varsena, and was pulled up into her lap to be petted and to have some rice pudding of her own. Then the two sisters and Joris each told me a story of my family. Each story was a memory of my father, or my aunt Natyr and or of their parents; each told to me that I might see them with my heart where I could not with my eyes, and each one felt like a precious gem dropped into palm of my hand. I did not want them to stop, but they were tired and I knew I would come back. The Shepherd had said that six hours out of every two weeks was mine to spend as I wished. I would spend that time here, with these three who had known and loved my flesh and blood, and I would have the memories of my family that I wanted so dearly.

Valene and Varsena each kissed me on the brow goodnight, and Joris (and the house goose) walked me down to the bottom of the steps before the great doors of the house. Joris clasped hands with me:

"Until I see you again, son of Dono."

"Good night, Joris, and thank you. Good night, my Dear."

The house goose honked gently at me twice, and then turned to Joris, who picked her up, smiled at me and then walked back into the house. The Brown Earth guards on watch took all of this in without saying a word. I looked at their leader, a middle-aged woman with two axes in her belt; she just looked back at me, so I nodded to her and walked out to Sixth Street.

I took my time walking back to the Great House of Death; I did not have to be back until the last bell before midnight, and Byzantium after nightfall was a world unto itself. The city wasn't asleep by any means, what with one or more ceremonies at the temples in the Old City, the movement of those going to and from their jobs, and people just out seeing friends or family. As I picked my way past the burnt out tenement going north, I could hear laughter, children singing, people calling out to a child, a wife, a father. So many people, so many scents and sounds, I was only just starting to get used to it. One good thing, the streets were surprisingly clean (all things considered), something I had noticed even in Northside. I was crossing a small square south of Upelluri's Temple when I found out why. I caught the sound of many hooves on the cobblestones, and was struck by an overpowering stench of pig. A herd of pigs? Here? Pigs are often sacred to the cults of the Earth, but they will eat anything and I was the only person in sight. There was an obelisk in the center of the square commemorating Phidalia, the founder of the city of Byzantium, and I went up it like a scalded cat.

The sound of hooves came closer along with what sounded like a bloody BELL, and a score, no, two score pigs came streaming into the square from the east. They were led by a red boar with a collar of black leather with a silver bell hung from it; he squealed when he caught my scent and began to circle the obelisk. Soon I had dozen pigs surrounding my perch while the others spread out and snaffled up anything remotely edible from the gutters and alleys nearby. That red boar came right up to the base of my obelisk to get my scent good and proper, and then gave what sounded suspiciously like an amused series of snorts, which were echoed by the pigs around him and drew the attention of the others.

Wonderful. First night out on my own, and I get treed by forty sacred pigs, one of whom was almost better dressed than I was. I was so glad I was alone.

After having a good laugh at me, the red boar turn his snout west and lead the whole herd out of the square towards the River Gate; probably headed down to the slaughterhouses to raid the offal piles. I gave them a good five minutes before I climbed down from my perch and bloody well ran the rest of the way back to the temple of Wurrunk. By the time I made it through the temple gates (with 20 minutes to spare), I had come to a conclusion that I have not changed in all the years since:

Cities are strange.

Chapter XXVII: The Shepherd and His Lambs

THE LAMBS WAS A SARCASTIC NAME given to those students who trained at the House of Death, but who could not afford to pay for their training. So when they weren't training, they worked for the temple: cooking, cleaning, doing laundry or running errands and such. There were six Lambs while I was in training at the Great House of Death in Byzantium: myself, Impetui, Alusad, Rig, Grali and Pelessa. Impetui, Rig and Grali were sworn to Wurrunk's service, but Alusad, and I were sworn to Tarhunt and Pelessa had dyed her hair red and taken up the path of Rundas. Grali, Pelessa and I had been formally sponsored by Herva, Urika and Ajax, respectively. The others had been recommended by someone in the cult of Wurrunk with an eye for talent, either here in Byzantium or some other city. It didn't really matter how we got here, we were all Lambs just the same. Some of the students sent by the Great Houses or the merchant families might look down on us, but no one was stupid enough to say anything out loud; each Lamb had passed the same battery of tests to get accepted for training. That was good enough for the disciples and priests of Wurrunk, and everyone else could go hang.

We all bunked together in the same room, roughly the same distance from the kitchen, the forge, and the stables. It wasn't much, but it had running water at either end, so Grali and Pelessa had some privacy behind a tapestry that hung from the ceiling to the floor at the east end. We boys slept in two sturdy bunk beds at the west end, where the door was. We got along, with one exception. The six of us getting along wasn't surprising; no one wanted to cause trouble and risk being dismissed from training, it was such a golden opportunity. The one exception was me and Impetui, of course, but I'll get to that in a bit.

We each had our talents: I was the best with the two-handed sword, Impetui was best with sword and shield, and both of us were tied with Alusad with a blade in either hand. Grali was the best with a rapier and Pelessa was the best (and very fast) with a bow. Rig wasn't the best with any one weapon, but he was very good with all of them, and was a wrestler as well. We had our own special skills when it came to magic as well; Impetui and Rig were the best when it came to casting spells on weapons, Alusad was the best at casting spells at opponents and Pelessa and I were the best at healing. Impetui and Alusad were the tallest and I was the shortest; Rig was the oldest at twenty, with Pelessa and I the youngest at sixteen. We were an odd bunch, but we got things done. Part of that was because we wanted this, we wanted to be here, but a big part of it was because of our Shepherd.

Magan One-Hand didn't have the presence that Loricon or Arkell or even Broddi had, but he didn't miss a trick. He never seemed to sleep much; he never went to bed before we did, but he was always up, dressed and ready to go when we crawled out of our bunks in the morning. He had a quiet sense of humor and was unfailingly polite to everyone in such a way as that everybody responded in kind. Not even Arkell was rude to him, and I began to see why Ajax and my aunt had drilled my manners into me. Good manners can sometimes prevent misunderstandings or even keep a tense situation from exploding into violence.

Behind his formal manners, we could each tell that our welfare was Magan's primary concern. That wasn't what we had expected coming to Wurrunk's House, but it was good to know, and we responded to him in our own way. Magan was also one of our teachers; he knew a great deal about magic, all kinds of magic. He had trained for years to overcome the loss of his right hand of course, but he also had an intense interest in (and a natural aptitude for) the magic arts. He knew quite a bit about the magics used by Wurrunk's enemies, and had a special interest in the magic of the northern tribes of Scythia and beyond. Rostaka later told me that Magan's reputation was such that he was known and respected even in the Great Library, and had been called upon to consult with A'as researchers on more than one occasion.

Magan also helped Gultar with my study of poisons, and taught me the rudiments of treating someone who had been poisoned. Rostaka sometimes helped them. Gultar also paired with Dangmag to teach us the basics of supplying, moving and caring for large numbers of fighters. I was reminded that this Great House, this city, and all of the cities of Thrace lived under the dominion of the Minos, a ruler very much in need of armies, not just bands of armed men and women.

We had other teachers: Loricon taught the broadsword to Rig, Grali, Pelessa and Alusad, but not to Impetui or myself. Herva taught the rapier to everyone but Rig and Impetui, so I think it was a matter of matching the instructor to the student's abilities (not that anyone was surprised that I never had Loricon as a teacher, for anything). Then we had Urika when we were taught just about anything that dealt with throwing or shooting. She could throw with either hand, whether it was knives, darts, axes or javelins. She was very good with a crossbow and with any bow I ever saw her pick up. Arkell taught the two handed sword of course, and both he and Broddi taught us wrestling and boxing, which was also a good way to loosen up before sword lessons. Broddi taught short blades and shield work; he was the one who showed us the sword style that Loricon had developed, what the fighters of Byzantium were starting to call the Striking Adder style. It was a technique developed for dueling, and it emphasized balance and speed above all else. It required the use of a shortsword or dagger, and had the combatants standing facing each other within arm's length with blades sheathed. When the signal to fight was given, the duelists were to draw their blades and strike; no shields or parrying weapons allowed. Impetui and I were the best of us six at it, but we took care not to let Loricon find that out.

All of my teachers were alike in one thing, just as Ajax had said when I had passed my tests: they held nothing back, it was not their way. When they taught, they poured everything into us: tricks and techniques, stories and history, stance and posture, attitude, everything. It was the kind of training a warrior dreamed of and we soaked it up like rain on dry cropland. There were other weapon masters in the temple; some taught, some did not. Not everyone is cut out to be a teacher, and others like Ajax had prior obligations. He was in and out of Byzantium continuously the rest of that year, but I began to hear rumors immediately.

I was the first student sponsored by Ajax in more than 30 years, and the last student of Ajax's before me had been my father; when he had broken publicly with my aunt Natyr, it had appeared to some that Ajax had deliberately entered into the political game being played between the Great Houses. Getting dragged into THAT particular morass was something the Cult of Wurrunk wished to avoid if at all possible, and a great deal of time and effort had been put into allaying the fears of the different factions in the city. Now the Great Houses of Byzantium have very long memories, and a number of powerful people had taken note when Ajax had returned with the heir to Natyr's estate. A decision was made to keep Ajax out of sight as much as was possible, so he was on call as an envoy, diplomat and advisor; this meant that he was constantly traveling: Khetar, the elf forest of Paristri, the volcano country of Nikopolis, Lycia, even the court of the Minos himself. I never saw him more than two or three times a season, and he never spent more than one night at a time in the rooms set aside for him the temple.

After his return from his first trip, to Cibyrrha in Lycia, Ajax made a point of spending some time with me to see how I was settling in. We were standing on the docks between the base of the great statue of Byzan and the temple of Daedalus, looking east towards the Lycean coast; I remember that we had spoken of Belkara, and of the Empire's advance into Scythia and the fall of the city of Carchemish to the empire. Then Ajax turned to look at the city behind us, and glanced back at me. I knew that look, it meant I was going to be tested.

"Since Byzantium is to be your home for a time, you need to learn more about her. Now, it would take more than one lifetime to learn everything there is to know about Byzan's City, but a good place to start is to learn Byzantium's limits. I want you to run around the city, going south, then west, then north and then around to the east to return to me here as soon as you can."

He folded his arms and grinned at me; I was to start now. I grinned back at him and started running. I had missed the old man, more than I had realized. I started south past the feet of the Great Statue, weaving my way through the dockside traffic of one of the busiest ports in the world. This section of the docks was where the fishing fleets put in and it seemed that the women of every household in Byzantium, great and small, were here to take their pick from the bounty of the Narrow Sea. South of there the waters deepened, and the big ships that docked here were from lands I had only heard of. From Egypt to the south and east, and from Gadir to the west, and all the points in between, the cargo ships came to Byzantium. They came for the beer and the bright fabrics, they came for the myriad goods that flowed into Byzantium from all the nations that called the Minos friend or lived under his rule, but most of all, they came for the grain. With its multiple harvests every year, Thrace fed more than one nation, and the grain shipments were measured in tons and ships instead of in bushels and sacks.

There were merchants of every kind. I saw a tall Egyptian in green robes and a sphinx headdress checking a list near a shipment of wine and silks that was being unloaded; the yellow ibis shapes embroidered on his perfumed robes moved by themselves.

I saw a merchant of Nabu from Khetar showing his son the sigils of the different merchant families while the old woman in the gilded litter next to him flicked her quill back and forth between half a dozen journals and account books. Her armed bearers watched everyone and took turns fanning the flies away from their mistress. Beyond them a Gadiran captain escorted his lady past two matrons of different Thracian Houses who were arguing over the services of a fomorian porter. Byzantium has a very long history with the darklings of the Shadow Lands, and often employs them for heavy labor.

There are not that many around during the day, and they take care to keep out of the Sun's light whenever possible, but their services are in demand because of their great strength. Once the Sun would set, the fomorians would take up the tasks of loading and unloading the ships dockside. Made up of humans during the day and darklings at night, the longshore gangs could move cargoes into and out of the port at any time. Indeed, short of a major holy day, a big storm or open war, the docks of Byzantium never really slept.

Kak had told me of humans and darklings working side by side like this while he was teaching me the darkling language; when I had expressed my surprise, he told me that in years past almost all of the great cities had been a mix of human and one or more of the Longaevi, the older peoples. If the city had been under the influence of the Court of Light, then the Aos Si were elves, brownies and pixies; if under the influence of the Court of Darkness, then the Aos Si were fomorians and goblins, with the occasional small giant here and there. Before the coming of the Minos, Byzantium had paid homage to one of the Daoine Si of the Court of Darkness: Kasku the Wise, called the Lord of Shadows, because he could pull darkness about himself and his followers like a cloak.

He had ruled all of Thrace, Lycia and down into the Achaian lands from his stronghold in the Shadowlands to the north and east of Byzantium, since before Time began. He had been old, wise and powerful, and it had availed him naught before the Minos, master of magic and intrigue. The Minos had landed at Starfall in the year 300 MK, in the only ship to survive the Breaking of the World (although no one knows where the ship was in the three centuries after that cataclysm), and then proceeded to dismantle the domain of the Lord of Shadows in no more than a year. Kasku himself had been struck down with a sword of meteoric iron, and the lands he had once ruled now payed homage to the Minos on his throne of silver and pearl. From that day forward, the darklings of Thrace had begun to drift apart from the humans, but not just because of politics. It was iron, Kak said, cold iron that burns elf and darkling alike as if it were a hot brand. Even the great ones of the Courts of Light and Darkness can be slain by iron weapons; just the presence of iron over time can cause the lesser Longaevi to wither and die. As time has passed, men have begun to use iron more and more, and this has driven a wedge between them and the elder peoples. Most goblins could not bear to enter cities like Byzantium any more.

South of the grain ships, the waters were deepest at the Great Piers, which had been built to service the great warships of the Dragon Empire; but it had been more than 600 years since a Dragon ship had been seen in any harbor. I ran past them and then swung west and crossed the road to the Tower of Sergius just north of the market at the Forum of Bacchus. I turned northwest and ran along the road that runs between the city walls and the Caenopolis, the great necropolis of Byzantium and then on to the north. There are no gates in the walls in that stretch, and the road was a bit crowded until I reached the Gate of the Twins near the new temple to Telepinu. I continued on past the old guard tower and kept the walls built by the Minos on my right as I ran on through Portside, and kept going until I hit the Lycus River itself. I swam north and east until I reached the southern end of the Chain, then ran along the Riverside docks to Tarhunt's Hill, where the temples of Tarhunt and Wurrunk stood. I rounded the north side of the hill to see Hatepuna's Seat on its marshy island to the east; then I continued south east and then south along the beach. There were dozens of ships pulled up on to the sand for repair or repainting, and I could see the roof of Upelluri's Temple off to the west.

I continued south to the wharves near the Harbor Plaza, and then ran past the square with the great temple to Nabu behind it and then on by the temple to Daedalus. There were more people out and about now, and I had to take care not to run into anyone as I continued south to where Ajax waited for me. I could swear he had not moved at all, except to turn north to watch for my return. I stopped in front of him to catch my breath, and Ajax handed me a water bag; when I had a chance to quench the thirst I had built running, he grinned at me again and stood with his hands clasped behind his back. I knew what that meant: He wanted to hear what I had to say about the lesson.

"What did you learn during your run?"

I thought for a bit, looking over my shoulder at the great city behind me, and then I spoke:

"You must first learn the limits of a thing, if you wish to understand it."

"Hmm. Let us head back, and while we walk, you can tell me what you have done to put Dangmag in such a frenzy."

The stocky swordsmith was in a frenzy because of what he was calling "Samelir's Knell", the ringing sound that had reverberated across his smithy the very first time I had set foot in it. At that same instant, every single thing in the smithy that was enchanted for swordsmithing or marked with Samelir's sigils (Samelir Redhammer was Wurrunk's loyal follower and the patron of those who crafted weapons for Wurrunk's cult) had been limned with a silvery light that had faded after a moment or two. I had thought Dangmag was going to have a stroke. His eyes had gone wide with shock, and then he had bellowed at me like a startled bull:

"What the hell is it with you, boy? Does EVERYTHING get more complicated when you're involved?"

Well, what exactly could I say in reply to that? Complement him on how perceptive he was? He would have boxed my ears, and I would have deserved it. Dangmag had then booted me out of his smithy and told me not to return unless I had Ajax with me.

We found Dangmag sitting by himself in his smithy; I thought at first he was dozing, with his eyes closed and his hands open palms up on his knees. Then I caught the whiff of magic, of power that was more than mortal, and I realized he was meditating after having performed a ritual of some kind. He stood up when we crossed the threshold and there was no drowsiness or hesitation about him. He glanced at me first, but then he directed his attention at Ajax, and his hands clenched into fists. Ajax looked back at him and said with a shrug:

"What?"

"'What?' he says. Ajax, I respect you as much as anyone living, and I love you like you were kin, but things HAPPEN around you, Old Man!"

Dangmag took a deep breath and unclenched his hands; he looked Ajax right in the eye and asked:

"Did you plan this?"

Ajax burst out laughing.

"Plan WHAT, old friend? I have no idea what you are talking about, truly."

Dangmag described what had happened the first time I stepped across the threshold of the smithy, and then had me verify it.

"Nothing happened just now though, right?" Ajax asked.

"No, although I could feel Joren enter the room with you; I can feel everyone who enters the shrine, but he's different. It is as if he has his own echo. Did the same thing happen the first time he entered Samelir's place in Hattusha?"

"I have no idea. He went missing in the night but no one noticed his empty bed until breakfast. Ashart was the one who found him; Joren was already in the smithy, spinning one of the grinding wheels when the workers came in to start the day's tasks."

Dangmag looked at me narrowly.

"Those doors would have been locked. How did you get through them?"

"I can't remember, Master Smith. I don't remember anything from the time before Aunt Syara touched me and woke me up."

"After Hattusha fell.", said Ajax.

"Eight years ago…wait, you're sixteen; you mean you cannot remember anything or anyone from the first eight years of your life?"

"No, Master Smith."

His look softened and he and Ajax put a hand on my shoulders at the same time, for a moment.

"I am sorry, Joren. I did not mean to yell at you when Samelir sounded his Knell, it is just that I have so many questions. Fewer than you, I am sure, but they puzzle me: What marked you in such a way, and why? How is that even possible? How did you get through those locked doors to the smithy in Hattusha? And Ajax says that you have never cut yourself, ever."

Ajax rubbed his chin;

"Good questions, all of them. Good enough for you to perform a divination and ask Samelir one of those questions yourself?"

Dangmag nodded, never taking his eyes from me.

"I finished a short while ago. His answer was very clear: IF HE WOULD LEARN, TEACH HIM."

So the scent of magic I had caught was that of a divination, a ritual question, and it had been answered. Wait…TEACH HIM? …teach ME???

"Teach me how to make swords?" The words pulled themselves out of my mouth, almost as a shout. My hands started ache and itch, and all I could think of was making swords of my own, to serve and protect my friends and my kin.

"Ah!" Dangmag's eyes searched my face and his own expression brightened.

"You want this! Then I'll teach you what I can, in the time that you have. I have spent two score years serving Samelir, I'm not about to defy him now. I know, I know; you have other obligations. That is understood. But if you are as smart as I think you are, and you can learn the basics, you will leave here knowing enough to learn from other smiths and teach yourself in time."

"That is a big part of being a swordsmith: learning new designs, experimenting and testing your own ideas. First, we'll find out what you know; Ajax says you can sharpen most anything, we will test that. Then I'll show you all of my tools and what they are for. Then the forge and the fire, how to use the billows to give the fire breath to burn the hotter. Then we will look at the ore and the metals, and when I am satisfied that you won't set the average village on fire, I will show you the simple things. How to make a horseshoe or a nail, how to patch a pot … I'll let you in on a secret, boy: a good smith is never bored, and almost always welcome anywhere he goes."

He rubbed his big, callused hands together in anticipation: "I'll have to talk to Gultar and the Shepherd to work out your schedule, but yes, Joren: I will teach you how to make swords!"

He taught me more than that of course. Just by being around him while he worked, I began to pick up his work habits, the best practices and the little tricks that he had learned that had helped to earn him the title and place of Master Smith in Byzantium's Great House of Death. To be organized and to be ready when something goes wrong (and sooner or later, something always does), to be thorough and to be complete in your work, and to take pride in a job well done, but never to be satisfied with less than that.

There were a few things that each of us Lambs knew that was unique to us. Alusad was the best rider by far, and could get horses to obey his commands. Grali was not only the best dancer, but could walk on her hands or along the length of a rope strung between rooftops with no more effort than you or I walking down a street. Rig could outdrink even Impetui; in fact, the Shepherd was not sure if it was possible to get Rig drunk at all, and thought that he was probably immune to many poisons. Me, I had my sense of smell and I could cut arrows. It turned out that there was no one at the House of Death who was better at arrow cutting than Ajax, and he had spent years teaching me what he knew. There was literally no one here who could teach me anything more about this skill. Now, it was up to me to find my own way of refining and perfecting a very uncommon ability; that meant lots of practice, and practice in this case meant people throwing and shooting things at me. The Lambs were happy to help, and would give me the exhilarating experience of having half a dozen very capable people try to hit me with real weapons, all at the same time. Urika would often join us for those sessions; she and Pelessa would work as a team and push me to my limits, and that is when it began to happen, just as Ajax had told me it would.

Time would slow, and I could SEE the movement of each arrow or dagger through the air; I knew where it had come from and where it would go: I knew which missiles were threats and which ones would miss. I could judge which arrow could be deflected and which could be ignored and which ones had to be stopped or cut. I worked best with a blade in each hand, but I could do it with just one sword or with a stick or a fan instead of a sword. Did I get hurt? From time to time, but that was true of all of us, in all of our lessons; we trained with real weapons most of the time, and mistakes and accidents happen. We followed training rules to minimize the bloodshed; and I was given fair warning and a moment's notice before the Lambs would open fire on me for a training session. Unlike the time Broddi managed to involve everyone in the East dining hall in the same wager, and two hundred people started whipping food, plates and articles of clothing at me when the bell sounded to end the evening meal. I thought Cook was going to wring his neck.

Of all the Lambs, only Grali developed any real skill at arrow cutting; she said it was like dancing. That was how she was able to match her movements to the motion of the missiles. Everyone comes at these things their own way, from their own point of view. It is a good thing too, because I dance like a three-legged cow.

Chapter XXVIII: The Mirror and the Door

NOT LONG AFTER I STARTED PRACTICING arrow cutting with the help of Urika and the Lambs, Impetui and I were doing some chores around the great courtyard and the entrance to the temple. Dueling was as popular as it had been during my father's time, and the great courtyard of the Temple of Wurrunk was a favorite spot to meet an opponent. Cleaning up after the throngs who had come to see the duels (and their horses) and polishing the brass were things that had to be done every day, and that day, it was our names that had come up on the roster.

It was not hard work, just boring, but it had to be done every day or it got away from you. For example, the brass fittings of the temple's great doors showed every touch of the hand, and since they could be seen by anyone who even looked inside the courtyard, had to be polished to a shine every morning and again just after the midday meal. We also had to clean and polish the Duelist's Mirror; a mirror that had been a gift to the temple a decade or so before I arrived. It was one of the biggest mirrors I have ever seen, even bigger than Aunt Natyr's mirror, a yard wide and as tall as Impetuii and set in an ornate brass frame.

It had obviously been meant for the Great Hall or perhaps the inner rooms of the temple's chief priest, but to the followers of Wurrunk it was practically worthless. They had not thrown it away or scrapped it (it was a GIFT you see), but instead had just placed it off to one side of the vestibule just inside the temple doors and promptly forgotten about it. Or would have, if some of the duelists had not started primping themselves in it. Some idiot started talk that it was good luck to give yourself a last look in that mirror before a fight, and the next thing you know, every feather-wit in the city was doing it. Of course, they had to touch the brass frame to adjust it so it was just right, and to touch the glass while they were admiring themselves; all of which meant we had to polish the bloody thing as well. It did not take long for all of us to develop a very strong dislike for that stupid mirror.

Well, we had gotten our chores done, and had cleaned ourselves up and put everything away in the little storeroom in the first sub-basement of the temple, when we realized that we could not hear anyone else. It was completely silent, the kind of silence that tells you that you are alone, and there is no one around to tell on you, or to talk you out of doing something stupid. That is when Impetui and I looked into each other's eyes and decided to kill each other.

We had always despised one another, right from the very beginning of that first fight; it was a completely illogical dislike, and those can be the most enduring. Also, I think that Impetui did not like that I could cut arrows and he could not (and I, of course, had been rubbing it in). We were dressed in practice armor but our weapons were real, rounded points and unsharpened edges and all. We were wielding our favorites: Impetui with sword and shield, I with my two-handed sword; then we went at each other like wolves fighting over a lamb.

We did not say anything; we did not need to, and we both needed our breath for fighting. He had the advantage of a longer reach and greater strength, but I was quite a bit faster and neither one of us had ever been able to push the other to exhaustion. I do not know how long we fought, but then there was an opening and I struck. It was a hard, perfect thrust, the kind that punches through armor to shatter bone or burst organs, and I had caught him right over the heart. At that same instant, his sword came down across the top of my head and we both went down.

Everything was black and pulsing red, but I managed to get to my feet and I realized I was in another Place. It was a small room, and I do not remember what I was wearing or what I had in my hands. There were only two things in the room, and they drew my attention completely. On the right, there was a mirror, and it was the same damn mirror I had just finished polishing before our fight. It could hold nothing of interest for me, and I did not even glance into it to see what it might reflect. I turned instead to the only other thing in that room: a door that stood half open. Through the door, I could smell green, growing things and clean water; I could see trees whose leaves moved in the wind and a path that lead to what looked like a road. THAT interested me. I put my hand on the door ring to pull the door open, and I heard a voice say "DONE!".

Then I was back in the sub-basement in the Temple of Wurrunk, on my hands and knees with blood running from my nose and ears. Impetui was there on the floor too, coughing up blood. We both stopped bleeding and looked at each other. We spoke the same words at the same time:

"I had a vision..."

"I was in a room with a door and mirror..."

"I choose the door, and I heard a voice say..."

"Done!"

We both knew whose voice had spoken that word. You do not start a fight to the death in Wurrunk's temple and expect it to go unnoticed, or not to have consequences. We cleaned up the blood and went about our business; I have never mentioned that fight to anyone until now, and I do not believe Impetui has either. We still do not like each other, but we have never tried to kill each other since that day; that choice was made. From time to time, Impetui and I have fought as a team; when we do, we are a force to be reckoned with. In part, that is because we know each other very well. That may have been what Wurrunk wanted all along.

Hmm? Who would have won the fight had it actually been to the death?

Why I would have, of course: my skull is impenetrable.

Ask your grandmothers, they'll tell you.

One day at the end of Earth Season, Rostaka found me in the kitchen just before the noon meal and told me that a researcher in the Great Library had found the Book of Mabirh, as I had requested, and that we could go examine it the afternoon of the next day. I checked with Cook and the Shepherd to be sure I was cleared to go, and was told that Rostaka had arranged this time away from my chores on her own authority. The next day, after helping to clean the tables and mop the floor, I joined Rostaka at the gate to the Temple grounds and we headed into the city. Our route took us due south past the beautiful Temple of Dreams, dedicated to Upelluri the Lord of Dreams, on down past the walls of the Acropolis, then east to Mangana Square. Originally, the Library had been the House and temple of A'as, and was managed by one of his sons, Thokorion the Scribe. In the centuries since Time began, the Library has grown immensely in size and spilled over to include all of the buildings that take up the south side of that square; Thokorion is still said to be in residence as the chief Librarian, and it is now called the Great Library of A'as.

Rostaka lead the way to a large building on the eastern side of Mangana Square, a three story structure with a gleaming copper dome called the Eastern Preserve. There seemed to be a fair number of people about, most moving into or between the buildings that made up the Great Library, but there were also some who strolled along the cobbled paths that wound about the Library grounds and at least two groups of a dozen or more each who were engaged in spirited debate. Rostaka had said we were to be met by the sage who had found the book for me, one Philoctetes of Chalcedon, a city to the south in Thrace, on the border of Achaea. I spotted him right away, not because of his appearance but because of his behavior. He started bouncing on the balls of his feet the moment he laid eyes on us, literally jittering with excitement. Philoctetes was a middle-aged man clad in a rather plain tunic of brown and red; he was of average height, mostly bald and possessed of the nasty squint and the ink-stained fingers common to many of the sages who lived or worked in the Great Library.

He shook our hands and led us through the brazen outer doors of the Eastern Preserve into a foyer, babbling all the while about how delighted he was to see us and what a great opportunity it was to read the words of a founder of one of Khetar's tribes...and that was all I heard because then he opened the inner wooden doors of the library and a tidal wave of scent washed over us and almost drove me to my knees. I caught the scent of the cherry and maple wood of the inner doors and the shelves beyond them, the perfumes and sweat of those who had passed through the building, the papyrus and parchment, the woven tapestries and leather hangings, and the myriad whiffs of magic that came from the many magical scrolls and tablets stored here, and behind it all a single spell that seemed to be everywhere. It had an odd feel to it, almost cold to the touch and very powerful; I realized that I could not smell mold or mildew, and that this must be a spell of preservation, to help keep the knowledge stored here safe over time. Then the dust hit me and I started sneezing my head off.

Philoctetes smacked himself on the forehead and fished a white and pink square of fabric out of his pocket; when he placed this against my nose, the sneezing stopped and I was able to blink the tears from my eyes and see where we were going. Rostaka patted me on the back and apologized for not warning me about the dust; those who spent a lot of time in the different sections of the Great Library got used to it, and she had not realized that it would affect me so violently. I must say that the spell on that little piece of cloth did what it was supposed to do; my nose stopped running and just tingled the rest of the time we were in the library, and it didn't hinder my sense of smell at all. Philoctetes lead us off to the eastern side of the library, to a brightly lit room with wide windows where an elderly woman clad in the robes of a librarian waited with an odd-looking wooden rack. It had a handle that allowed it to be carried conveniently and it held a large scroll case. The rack itself was marked in at least three different places with letters, numbers and symbols that made no sense to me at all. The librarian nodded politely to Philoctetes and then spoke to Rostaka:

"The storage and usage fee for this scroll is 36 silver pieces for today. If you require additional time, another 36 silvers will be due at sunset, which will allow you to peruse the scroll until sunrise. Please remember that is against the law to attempt to damage or change this scroll in any way, or to attempt to remove it from the Library."

I nodded to show I understood, and Rostaka said: "We understand, Librarian." She counted 36 silver pieces into the old woman's hand, and then the librarian bowed to us and left the room. There were two tables in the room, along with a number of chairs; we placed the scroll case on the table in front of the windows and looked it over. It was crafted from black oak wood, and had black oak leaves carved into each of the sides. That made sense; the black oak was the sigil of my mother's house, the royal line of the Mabirshan tribe. Embedded into the top of the case was a square piece of bark cut from a black oak, and that was all; no lock or hinge was to be seen. Rostaka looked at Philoctetes, who cleared his throat and said:

"Ah, there are no explicit instructions as to how to open the scroll case in any of the sources I found; the only reference is in Nardan's own words when he deposited the scroll with the library: 'Those of my blood can open this case'. I can make a number of conjectures, but I don't really KNOW how to open it."

That was alright, I knew. I could smell blood, old blood on the piece of bark on the case; the blood of every member of my family that had opened the case and read the Book of Mabirh. Easy enough, and obvious when you thought about it. I nicked my left thumb with my belt knife and smeared the piece of bark with my blood. The bark absorbed the blood completely and remained dry, and I realized that the cut on my thumb had been healed. There was a pause the length of two heartbeats and then with a faint click, the wooden case shifted and the top slid free, partially revealing three scrolls within. Rostaka and Philoctetes murmured in appreciation of the simplicity and effectiveness of Nardan's work, but I was speechless. The scents that billowed out of the box were aromas I could not remember ever smelling before, but somehow I knew I had. I felt tears start to stream down my face for no good reason and all I could do was grip the edge of the table and cry. Philoctetes could not understand my reaction, but Rostaka knew enough to realize that I needed some time alone. They moved to the other side of the room, and I sat there trembling for a few moments until the tears stopped and I was able to get hold of myself.

I lifted the first of the scrolls, which were numbered, and I felt it grow warm in my hands: more magic. I opened the scroll, and looked it over. It was filled with neat lines of printed characters in a dark brown ink, nothing fancy; yet it held many of the answers I had been looking for since my memories began. I took a deep breath and thought "Focus; you need to remember EVERYTHING you see." I exhaled and froze, for when my breath blew across the scroll, blood red letters flared into life in the left margin.

"Greetings, O My Kin. These words are written in ink distilled from my own blood, and only one who has that same blood flowing in their veins will be able to waken my words into life with their very breath. In this way do I pass unto you the secrets of our family and our House; note them well, for they will soon fade."

Indeed, I could see that the first words at the top of the margin had already begun to fade; I began reading, committing every word in the margin of the scroll to memory, and then moving on to the other scrolls in sequence. I soon realized why the smell of the box and its contents had affected me so deeply: the scrolls had been written in the Queenshall in Oak Rest and the box was made of wood from the Black Oak Throne, the huge black oak tree around which the Queenshall was built and which formed the royal throne. I had been laid upon an arm of that throne the day I was born, and the bark and sap of that tree were ingredients in the ink used to mark me when I was given my first tattoo by my parents. The scents I smelled wafting from the black oak box were the scents of safety, of welcome, of family, of…home. They were the scents of the home I would never remember, and l started crying again. There was more information, much more and so much of it made no sense to me, not then anyway. After memorizing the red notes in the margin of the last scroll, I went back to the first scroll and read the entire book from the beginning as Nardan advised.

'When I saw the smoke from the bridge, I knew. My husband, my rock, the father of my children, was dead…'

I realized that these were not Nardan's memories of the events that lead to the founding of the Mabirshan tribe, but a copy of the words written by his mother, Queen Mabirh herself, during the Opening of Issuria. The original book probably had been kept by my mother's family as an heirloom, and so would have been lost when the Lupaku sacked the Queenshall. I continued reading, and the history and lore of my mother's tribe poured into my lap. I read of how she had gathered friends, neighbors and her 16 children and lead them north out of Lycea into the haunted wildlands of Issuria; of how she had seen a Dragon and bandied words with the infamous Black Wyrm.

I learned of the great power harnessed by Mabirh to raise the cyclopean walls of Oak Rest, the stronghold of the Mabirshan, and of the deeds she performed to earn the name of Queen Stonehand from the darklings of Stygia, the great darkling realm to the north of Issuria. I learned of the birth of the Oath Hounds and their bond to my mother's family, and of the perils that claimed the lives of many of Mabirh's followers, including two of her own children, before they were able to build a safe holding in their new homeland.

As I finished reading each scroll, I passed them onto Rostaka and Philoctetes to examine, having first ensured that none of the blood notes in the margins of the scrolls were visible. Rostaka made few comments, being absorbed in reading the book, but Philoctetes was ecstatic. Not only was this first-hand account of the settlement of Issuria exactly the subject he had specialized in for the last twenty years of his life, but the facts gleaned from the book dovetailed perfectly with his own theories. The book of Mabirh was the evidence he had been looking for, and with it, his professional reputation was secure. With Rostaka's help as both scribe and witness, Philoctetes was able to copy the bulk of the book's content before Arinniti set and the aged librarian returned. I returned the scrolls to the black oak box and placed the lid atop it; the wood shifted beneath my fingers and with a soft click, the box was sealed again. The librarian checked my actions against a list that she read from a small scroll, nodded in satisfaction and placed that scroll in the carrying rack with the wooden box.

She then had Rostaka and Philoctetes pay a small fee for the copy they had made and leave their marks in two different types of wax on a document that was placed on top of the black oak box. She then lifted the carrying rack, bowed to us, and left. As did we.

Before we parted, I thanked Philoctetes again for his help; he bowed deeply to me, saying that the pleasure was his, and that he wished me well. Then he was off to his chambers to peruse his new treasure at his leisure; Rostaka said that he would probably present his findings in a verbal presentation to his peers, in addition to publishing his own book sometime in the future. Other than this, we were both silent on our walk back to the House of Death. At the gate to the temple grounds, I turned to thank Rostaka for her aid and found her staring intently at me.

"You found what you needed, did you not? It was there, in those scrolls, just not visible to my eyes or the eyes of any prying stranger, eh?"

I nodded in reply, but she raised a hand to stop me before I could speak.

"Your secrets are your own, Joren. But let me offer some advice: before you act on the knowledge you have gained today, be sure that you are ready. I have the feeling that more than one life will depend on it."

"Thank you, Sage, for both your help and your advice. I will remember your words."

I bowed to her, and then ran for the kitchen. It was my turn to do the pots. Later that night, I lay awake while the others slept, pondering what I had learned. My memory had not failed me, I could remember every word from the book as if it were laid out on a table before me. I finally had answers to many (if not all) of the questions that had puzzled me for as long as I could remember, and clues that might allow me to answer others. I remembered the words my father had spoken when he had appeared to me at Ishara's Needles: "He has hidden them too deep…". I think I knew now what my uncle Ketil had done, and I cursed him anew.

That was not all; among the secrets I had read in the Book of Mabirh, there was one that would allow one of my mother's family to pass into the Queenshall from the outside without being seen by anyone who was not of our blood. Othar Inkson had my father's sword and ruled the old Mabirshan lands from Oak Rest; before I pried Oathtaker from his dead fingers, he would render me an accounting of my father's death. The problem was that he wasn't a simple mercenary or tribal warrior, he was a decorated officer of the White Sun's Army, and no teenager who could barely shave was going to waltz into his home and strike him down. Rostaka was right, I had to be ready before I acted; knowledge alone would not be enough, I had to have the skill and the power to see it through or it was all going to end in a bloody mess. It might end in blood anyway, but I had been aware of that possibility from the beginning. Well, if I wanted to improve my skills, learn new ones and get better at what I was and what I wanted to be, there was no better place to start than here and now, in the Great House of Death in Byzantium.

So be it.

Chapter XXIX: Master Arkell

MY ADDITION TO THE GROUP OF STUDENTS then training at the Great House of Death had a more than one effect. The first was to add an element of competition that had not been present before. By making Impetui and I co-equals in leading the two handed sword class, Arkell the Proud had deliberately set us against each other. Once we realized that we could not kill one another, we had settled into a sort of bristling, stiff-legged competition, which was about as close as friendly competition as we could get. We pushed each other every chance we got, and that meant we got better. One day at sword and shield practice, Impetui got in a solid blow with his shield and threw me half way across the room. Broddi had called "Hold" and stopped the class. He then walked up to Impetui and tapped him on the chest.

"Good."

Impetui had drawn himself up and then bowed in response. When a master of weapons makes a point of complimenting you in front of a crowd, you acknowledge it. Broddi had then continued:

"You were getting lazy, relying so much on your size and your strength. But when facing someone who is that much faster (pointing a thumb at me), lazy gets you dead."

As the two of us got better, we pushed the rest of the students as well, either directly (if we were in the same class) or indirectly (by example and reputation). None of the students who attended classes in the House of Death wanted to be ranked last in anything, let alone their favorite weapon, and our desire to excel proved contagious. Soon after that particular incident, I overheard a bit of conversation between the Shepherd and the Cook indicated that all of this was working out better than they had anticipated. Then the other shoe dropped.

Ten weeks to the day after my entry into the Great House of Death, we were preparing for our evening class with Lord Arkell. I found my balance in my place on the practice mat and recited the words I used to put myself in the right frame of mind since Ajax had started teaching me in earnest.

Posture. Balance. Focus. I am the weapon.

After stretching and warming up a bit, we usually had a few moments of wrestling to put us on our toes. Most of the time, we would wrestle in pairs, but sometimes we would go at Lord Arkell one or two at a time.

We were free to rush him as a group of course, if we were willing to accept the consequences. This was true of all of the classes: any student could directly challenge the instructor if they so wished, but if they did so, they had no reason to complain when the instructor put them in their place (typically a bed in the infirmary). The instructors themselves did not mind; after all, there are few things any teacher likes better than a good example.

That day, we were trying our luck against Lord Arkell, with the goal not of throwing him, but just in an attempt to move him. Arkell was not the tallest of those who dwelt in the House of Death, but he was definitely the broadest, with very wide shoulders and extremely long arms corded with muscle. Wrestling him was like wrestling a stone pillar, except that this pillar was capable of throwing you the length of the room.

I remember feeling remarkably good that day, at my best, ready for anything and so I decided to try my luck. On this occasion, Rig had come at Arkell from the side and wrapped both arms around his waist; Arkell had countered this by picking Rig up and holding him off of the floor with one arm, which meant that Rig could not get any traction and could not exert any real force. Arkell had then proceeded to fend off the rushes of a number of students while wearing Rig like a strange, student-colored garment.

I waited until he was looking the other way (I thought) and then I threw myself at his left leg in an attempt to knock him off balance. My aim was good, but Arkell had seen me coming; he pivoted and added a considerable amount of force and lift to me as I went by him. If I had not run into Impetui's belt buckle, I would have gone right out the flipping window. Impetui grunted once, picked me up with one hand, shook me a couple of times and then pushed me off to one side with an exasperated "Get off."

I never saw Impetui wrestle Lord Arkell, he always stayed on the sidelines with Rig or one of the bigger students as opponents. The other students told me that Impetui had wrestled Arkell on one occasion before I had joined the class, and had actually managed to push Arkell three or four feet across the floor while they grappled. Then Arkell had picked Impetui up and slammed his full length down on to the practice mat, then picked him up again by the shoulder and hip, lifted Impetui over his head and dropped him onto the mat. Impetui had not challenged Lord Arkell at wrestling again.

That evening I could not seem to do anything wrong, despite having the imprint of Impetui's belt buckle on my forehead. Impetui has always maintained it was BECAUSE I had that imprint, but I have never had unusual luck the other times that happened, so it had to be something else. I think now that it was just that everything that Ajax and Arkell had been teaching me finally clicked into place, and I fully understood what I could do with my greatsword. It felt like it was literally an extension of my body and will, and I just seemed to float through Arkell's lesson. I think he noticed, and chose me for an exhibition bout to illustrate the lesson to the class, and to put me in my place if I had not been paying attention. It didn't bother me at all; we saluted each other and began. It was as if I was one of the professional dancers that performed in the Great Square, one flowing movement after the other, all of a single piece. Everything felt so perfect that I almost did not hear the scrapping noise when my blade ground against something at the end of my attack.

That was when I realized that no one in the room but Lord Arkell was moving or even breathing. He was looking at his breastplate, running one finger along a gouge in his armor that ran right across his chest from right to left, two hand spans above the waist. Now, like all of the instructors, Arkell was wearing a separate set of practice armor that was kept painted or enameled to show every touch or blow. If a student managed to touch his teacher through luck or skill, the teacher wanted to know it so they would know what was going right (or wrong) in a class.

I had seen a few marks on Lord Arkell's armor in the past, scrapes on the vambraces on his forearms from demonstrating a defense or blocking blows that might have hurt a student (a beginner with a sword can be a threat to everything around them), but I had never seen a single mark on his breastplate, no one had. Until now. Had we been using sharpened blades, that would have been a serious wound, perhaps a fatal one, and I had done it. He looked up at me, and I felt a thrill of fear as I realized that from the first day I had met him until now, Lord Arkell had never been fully awake. He was wide awake now, and every bit of his attention focused on me. He looked at me with those blazing eyes and said:

"Do that again."

Then he came at me, not like a practice bout but like he really wanted to kill me. I parried, skipped back away from his next attack, parried, parried and realized he was backing me into a corner. I dodged behind two other students who froze in their tracks and ran out the door. I crossed the landing and put one hand on the balustrade to vault over it and landed on a table in the dining hall, scattering plates, dishes and assorted vegetables amongst a couple of startled guardsmen who come off duty for a late dinner. I leapt to the floor and turned to make my apologies, only to see Lord Arkell leap THROUGH the bloody doorway, across the landing and over the balustrade in a single bound to bring his sword down on the table as he landed. His blow shattered the heavy planks of the table like kindling, and he roared at me:

"AGAIN!"

My leap onto that table had startled everyone in the dining hall into an uproar, but Arkell's blow that broke the table shocked them into silence, all except Cook, who called out in a questioning voice:

"Arkell?"

Arkell ignored everyone but me and glided forward. One of the guardsmen was too slow getting out of the way; my teacher picked him up by his harness and tossed him to one side, then kicked the wreckage of the table out of the way and came at me again. I parried, and started throwing things (a chair, food, anything) and backed away. He slapped the chair aside, dodged the food and kept coming. I tried a couple of attacks that went nowhere and did a back flip over a table. He threw the table to one side with one hand and parried my attacks without even slowing down, and he just kept coming.

"AGAIN!"

I could hear other people talking, shouting and of course, laying bets.

"What the hell started this..."

"It must be about a woman."

"...finally had enough of his sass..."

"When was the last time a Lord killed one of the students?"

"Four years ago, that whole thing with the mule..."

"One gold wheel says that Lord Arkell kills that uppity little hill weasel!"

Uppity? That had to be one of Loricon's followers; if I lived through this, I was going to show him uppity...

I had let myself get distracted, and Arkell cut me off from the door to the outside, forcing me into the hall where the student ceremonies and competitions were staged. It could hold hundreds and soon everyone who had heard the ruckus, along with other teachers, the other students in Arkell's class, and the other Lambs had poured into the hall behind us. All the other doors lead outside and were kept locked and bolted; there was no way I could force one of them open before Arkell would have been on top of me, so I realized I had to stand and fight.

I realized too that I did not want to run anymore, that I wanted to make an end and go out fighting with a sword in my hand. I spun in the center of the room to face Arkell; he looked at me, ignoring the crowd that had spread out to surround us, and nodded once. Then we leapt at each other. That feeling of not being able to do anything wrong was still with me; I had never been faster or surer with a blade before that night, and it did not matter worth a damn. I could not touch him, but it was not that he was as fast as me, it was that he could read me so that he could see me coming and managed to block each one, a grin spreading across his face wider and wider with each attack. But at the same time, he could not touch me, and for more than two full minutes I went toe to toe with an Agent of Wurrunk with his chosen weapon and held my own. Then one of his attacks came in too hard on my sword when it was an inch or two out of position and the sturdy bronze blade of my sword snapped clean in two, leaving me holding the hilt and a hand's length of blade. Well, half a sword in my hand, anyway. I looked up at Arkell dazedly, and he laughed in my face. Then he twisted and threw his practice sword straight up into one of the rafters, sinking the blunted tip inches deep into the sturdy oak beam. He placed a hand on either of my shoulders and said for all to hear:

"Very Good!"

"Tth...thank you, Lord Arkell." I stammered.

He was not going to kill me after all. Well, that was good.

"Master Arkell to you, boy."

He strode on out of the room into the dining hall, roaring for Gultor to bring him wine. I stopped in my tracks. Master? For one of Arkell's stature to allow me to call him Master meant that he accepted me as his Pupil, somewhat in the same way a master craftsmen would accept an apprentice. It meant that I would be at his beck and call, of course, but it also meant that he would teach me what the average swordsman could not learn, his techniques, his secrets. It also meant that...

"Impetui, you are now class second; Joren is now class lead."

I did not think that was going to go over very well, but Impetui just said "Yes, Lord.", and stared at me with no expression at all. Then Arkell ordered everyone in our class to sit at an empty table in a corner of the dining hall while he continued his argument with Cook. Arkell wanted ale for all of us and wine for himself; Cook told him he would be lucky to get weak beer for us and watered vinegar for himself for breaking the furniture. Arkell finally won the argument by threatening to go rummaging through the pantry on his own. Gultor just threw up his hands and stormed off, with Arkell roaring after him:

"Make sure that is the yellow wine from Hellas, not any of this local grape juice! And bring a goblet for yourself!"

He turned to us and the second half of the night's lesson began.

"Did all of you see what Joren did upstairs? How we fought in the exhibition hall? Tell me!"

He started walking us through both fights step by step. Gultor joined us a few moments later with Grali and Pelessa, carrying tankards of ale and a big green bottle of wine with two goblets. Arkell uncorked the wine and filled Gultor's goblet first, then his own. They both drank and Arkell made sure that Cook got a good look at the scrape I had made on his armor. Cook ran a finger along the edge of the mark and gave me a keen glance; he did not say much the rest of the evening, but he kept an eye on both myself and on Arkell, who finished the wine after Gultor had a second cup. After Arkell dismissed the class, but before I went off to do my evening chores, he had me walk with him to the entrance of the Temple itself. There, he drew his broadsword and cut himself by lightly clasping the blade in his left hand. He then placed that hand over my heart, and held up his sword by the crosspiece towards the lamps that flickered in the heart of the temple, the lamps that lit the altar of Wurrunk. Those lamps seemed to burn the brighter as he spoke the words of an oath to the God of Death:

"Hear me, Lord of Swords and War…

There, before the temple of his god and everyone who was in earshot, lord, acolyte, student or just a down-at-heel mercenary who was passing by, Arkell the Proud swore his oath to me as my Master. He swore never to lie to me, to never use my skills solely for his own ends, and to teach me all that he could in the time he was allotted. As he finished, I felt...*something*, and I realized that there was now a link of some kind between us. He did not ask any oath in return from me; at the time, I thought this was because I was already sworn to Wurrunk's service. Then we walked to the entrance to his quarters; we did not speak until we reached his door:

"That night I tested you against Impetui for entrance into my class, I came here to my rooms after I spoke to Ajax. What do they say I did after that?", he asked me.

I hesitated; repeating gossip to a servant of the god of Death can have any number of consequences, most of them violent. He laughed at me.

322

"They say I got drunk, they say I went whoring, they say I threw a fit and wrecked the place. I know, I have heard the gossip; but do you know what I really did? I went to the statue of Wurrunk beside my bed, and I got down on my knees and I thanked my god for answering my prayer, the same prayer that every real teacher says at least once in their lives: For the gods to send them a pupil who can be greater than the master."

I just stared at him with my mouth open. Greater than him? He placed one hand on my shoulder and went on:

"I never saw your father fight, he was before my time. But I have read accounts of his duels and competition matches; he was brilliant. You can be that good, or better. Better than your father, better than me, better than anyone who has wielded the greatsword in a hundred years, IF you are willing to put the work necessary into it, and IF you live. Good night, Pupil."

"Good night, Master Arkell."

That night, I had a dream that I was back at Ishara's Needles, and I saw my father again. He was laughing, not at me, but in a satisfied sort of way. He nodded at me and then I woke up. So, I was headed in the right direction, I just needed to keep myself focused. I was going to be as much of a weapon and a fighter as I needed to be, to make my way along the Path of Kings.

Chapter XXX: Aiding the Watch

BYZANTIUM WAS SO VERY DIFFERENT from a village like Nesa that it might as well have been another world. One difference was the feeling of age; Byzantium had seen the beginning of Time, and a great many changes since then, and all of that had left its mark on the city. While running errands around the city, I realized that the gleaming walls built around Byzantium by the Minos were built on top of the remains of at least two other walls, two sets of defenses that had protected the city in the past. Both walls had been leveled by war or disaster, to the point where not one stone remained above ground. Another difference was the myriad temples and shrines that dotted the city, each with its own power and its own magic; Thrace was sometimes called the Land of a Thousand Temples for good reason. But theirs was not the only magic to be found in Byzantium; with the growth of trade, the city population had grown as well, and some of the new residents were from foreign lands and they brought the worship of their gods or ancestors with them. Then there were other gods, who would have been foreign in any land; we crossed paths with one of them on a cool, grey morning at the end of winter.

There were four of us running together that day: Pelessa, Rig, Impetui and I. We had stood at attention with swords raised as part of a ceremony at the Gate of the Twins when the Sun rose that morning, and we were headed back to the House of Death when a fight fell right into our laps. We moving north up a street a couple of blocks west of the Old City with Impetui and I in the lead, when we heard muffled shouts coming from a townhouse on our right. It was the kind of house a lesser noble might have built a hundred years ago, but it hadn't been kept up. Then the wind shifted and I caught the scent of blood; I started to turn to my right (Pelessa and I were on the left side, Impetui and Rig were on the right) when a door slammed open and two bloody figures staggered out. They fell over a low stone wall and slid a dozen feet down a weedy slope almost right to our feet.

It was a woman and a fomorian and they were both bleeding; the woman had been shot in the back with a crossbow and the darkling, not much more than a girl, was missing her left arm at the elbow and looked as if she had been beaten. I slung my shield over my back and was moving to help them when Impetui and I realized that the young darkling woman was a healer, a priestess of Brighid the Serene! There was a muffled curse from that open door, and we looked up to see two armed men in the doorway, one with a crossbow. I caught the scents of old blood, rotting meat and the stomach-twisting stench of something that had nothing to do with humanity at all, and then Impetui was snarling at me:

"Keep them alive!"

That is when he and Rig rushed the men in the doorway. The one with the crossbow fired a bolt at women on the ground, but Impetui blocked it with his shield before he leapt over the stone wall. Pelessa started blowing her whistle while I threw myself onto my hands and knees, with my Aunt Syara's words echoing in my memory:

"Stop the bleeding first; if you can stop the bleeding, you have time."

I threw every ounce of magic and concentration I had into healing the wounds that I could see, the crudely bandaged stump first. As I spoke the words that triggered the spells, I realized that I was imitating my aunt's gestures and intonations from those times that I had watched her heal. I think it made a difference, because none of my spells failed. I had just healed a deep gash in the axe woman's right arm (she looked to have been in more than one fight) when something struck me in the back hard enough to knock me sprawling across their bodies. Someone had taken a shot at the priestess again and had hit the shield on my back; from the angle, that meant they had a marksman on the roof or the second floor. Pelessa had strung her bow to cover Impetui and Rig in case anyone had tried to flank them, and she spotted the shooter. I heard the deep thrum of her bow and she said:

"I see him, second floor."

Her second shot threaded the slats in a shutter on a second-story window and we heard a hoarse scream from within. Good; the fewer distractions I had, the better. I was going to have to get that bolt out of my one patient's back and that could get tricky. I shot a quick glance at the townhouse and saw that both Impetui and Rig were still on their feet and fighting, with the bodies of at least three opponents choking the doorway.

It looked like the men chasing the two wounded women had gotten reinforcements, but the survivors were more concerned with keeping our squad mates out of the building than they were with coming out and finishing off their victims themselves. I took a deep breath and laid my fingers on the shaft of the bolt, only to feel the axe woman stiffen in pain. I had been hoping she had fainted, but I could not afford to delay any longer. Given where she had been hit, I could not push the bolt through and break off the head, so I was going to have to pull it back out through the channel made by the original wound and hope that my healing spell would be powerful enough to both stop the bleeding and stabilize her condition. I plucked the bolt out with as smooth and as steady a motion as I could and then put all of my remaining magic into one last spell. It succeeded and the axe sister slumped with relief, only half conscious. I was not in much better shape myself; I literally could not cast another spell without passing out. If it had not been for the magic I had stored in the sea serpent amulet, one of those two women would have died. So I stayed where I was until I could catch my breath, shielding the wounded with my body, while Pelessa kept an eye out in case they managed to get a marksman on the roof, or try another shot from one of the windows.

Only a minute or two later, we heard the tramp of boots and the sound of whistles blown in answer to Pelessa's call for help. Two patrols of the City Watch had come to our aid, one from either end of the street. While two of the watch linked shields with me to provide cover for the wounded, the other six took a long look at the fight in the doorway and trotted to the other end of the townhouse to begin chopping their way through the barred doors there.

That forced the defenders to split their forces and that was all Impetui and Rig needed; they cut through the reduced numbers facing them and broke into the house, driving the panicked survivors before them with no chance to regroup. The remainder of our foes died beneath the axes of the City Watch. Both of our fellow Lambs emerged from the fight wounded but neither seriously; Pelessa was able to heal them both, while I sulked quietly in the background. A fight like this, more than a dozen enemies slain, and all I had done was heal people; I felt cheated, somehow. Of the thirteen dead, Impetui had killed four, Rig had accounted for three more and Pelessa had killed the one shooting from the second floor; the axes of the City Watch had claimed the other five. No one on our side had been killed or seriously wounded, and none of our foes had escaped; that pretty much counts as a victory in anyone's book. I was too young and stupid to realize just then that it would have been a hollow victory indeed if both of the wounded women had died.

The women of the City Watch were quite happy with us; the senior of the two patrol leaders made a point of getting our names when she thanked us. The axe sister that I had healed introduced herself before they bore her off in a stretcher; her name was Britha and she promised us all a good meal and round of drinks when she was on her feet again, and she kept that promise too. Then two more patrols arrived, and the Watch went over every square foot of that house from rooftop to the basement; there had been four women in the patrol that went into that house to rescue the priestess and only Britha had come out. We heard later that the townhouse was listed as belonging to a merchant from Athens, but looked to have been boarded up since at least the end of the previous year.

None of the dead were ever identified, and the only things of interest in the whole building were the two pits in the basement, and the choking stench that emanated from them. Those pits looked like they had been chewed, rather than dug and each was more than three feet across and at least a hundred feet deep with no ladder or handholds. I say "at least" because any attempt to explore deeper failed. Not only was the air itself was too foul to breathe, but it caused lanterns and torches to gutter out. The Watch eventually dumped barrels of quicklime into them and leveled the house, collapsing the pits and filling the basement with rubble. They never found any trace of the other three members of that patrol though.

Before we left, the priestess regained consciousness and asked to speak to whoever had healed her. She thanked us and declared herself in our debt; she was a bit surprised to hear me respond in her own language. I bowed to her and said:

"Daughter of Solace, there is no need to speak of debt to us, we are bound by oath to uphold the law and aid the Watch of Byzantium."

"Nonetheless, Child of Thunder, you and your companions have my gratitude; if ever you come to the Temple of Night, you will be repaid for your aid."

In time, each of us did indeed go to the Night Temple for aid (I was the first) and that priestess was as good as her word, changing each of our lives in a time of need. It just goes to show you, you never know where you'll wind up, when you take a morning walk in Byzantium. We were late getting back to the Temple, but Magan did not seem surprised. I guess he had already heard from someone on the City Watch. He had us clean up and, after checking Impetui and Rig over for any injuries that might have been missed, then sent us on to our morning classes. Our Shepherd Magan was a good teacher, but what I remembered, more than his lessons, even more than his good manners and his endless patience, was the air of sadness that followed him. He rarely smiled and I never heard him laugh. It seemed to me that he was waiting for someone, given the way he watched people enter a room, or searched the crowds that came to see the duels and the competitions. Pelessa put it another way, and one that hit closer to the truth:

"It is as if he is waiting for part of him to return, a piece of himself that has gone missing and left the rest of him to walk through life not really whole."

It turned out that we were both right, in a way.

Chapter XXXI: Cnut

I DO NOT LIKE TO DRINK ANY KIND OF INTOXICANT, and for a very good reason. I was taught by those who raised me that to drink, whether it was beer, ale or wine, was perfectly normal or even expected (when you were someone's guest), but to get drunk, to let the drink do the thinking was rude, foolish and in my case, just plain dangerous. I have a great deal of anger inside of me; so much so that I can almost put a name and a face to it, as if it were a separate person. Most of the time, I can keep this anger, this rage locked away down deep inside of me, behind a series of bolted doors so to speak. But when I get drunk (or on one occasion, when I received a blow to the head) all of those doors swing open, and the man built out of pain and rage comes out of his dark little room inside of me to look out of my eyes and move my feet along the path of his own desire. The stupid bastard has nearly gotten me killed every time it happens, and the first time was in Byzantium, on one of the feast days of the goddess Mycara, whose cult is one of those that know how to distill liquor from grain. They are not the only ones in Byzantium who can do this, but theirs is an infamously potent brew, as I can personally attest.

I was out with three other Lambs: Rig, Grali and Pelessa, and we were running an errand with Herva (called the Needle for her celebrated skill with the rapier). Many ceremonies have a place for Wurrunk in them, and often require the donation of a ritual component. In this case, Herva was the only one who needed to speak; all the rest of us had to do was to carry the 16 sword blades (4 each) to the gates of the Old City as part of a procession. In order to complete our part of the ceremony, each of us had to drink from the silver bowl offered to us by the priestess of Mycara until the bowl was empty. Each of us had to drink at least once, and we had to empty the bowl or the ceremony would fail. Failure was not an option, and for one reason or another, I wound up drinking more than my share of that potent elixir.

I didn't really believe the stories I had heard of the potency of the distilled wines, and I drank more than was wise (or safe, for that matter). It was a clear, cool amber in color but it burned like fire going down. It seemed to just sit there in a cold puddle in my stomach, or at least it did until Herva dismissed us for the evening (the ceremony having concluded just after sunset). She had recommended that we eat before we began the procession, but I hadn't been hungry and decided to put it off until we got back. That was a mistake. The distilled liquor made from the best of the last rye crop went right into my blood from my empty stomach and the last clear memory I had was of Pelessa saying that she and the others were going to watch the dancing in the Great Square for a time, and that they would see me back at the barracks. Then, all I can remember for a time was the sensation of running, and laughing.

When I came to my senses, I was still laughing, but I stopped when I realized I was hiding in some ornamental bushes with my sword drawn. There was no blood on the blade, so I probably hadn't done anything too stupid, but I had no idea WHERE I was. I felt a bit numb, as if I was not entirely in control of myself, my senses or my reflexes. I did not like that at all, and tried to focus on my surroundings. The bushes and the grass were well tended, with a trimmed hedge behind me and a flagstone walkway leading to an arch in a freshly painted wooden fence in front of me. I could smell incense, perfume and good food, but underneath it all was the scent of blood. I went as still as I could and tried to feel what my other senses could tell me. It was quiet. I could even hear the music coming from the dance at the Great Square, but there was something wrong; everything seemed to be red. I tried blinking, but it had no effect. Red paint, red flagstones, even the light coming from around the corner of the building to my right was red...then I recognized the sigils painted and carved into the wood and stone of my surroundings. It was not my eyesight playing a drunken trick on me, everything WAS red, because I was in one of the famous Painted Gardens of the Empire of the White Sun. That meant I had to be smack in the middle of the grounds of the Imperial Embassy. How the bloody HELL did I get here?

There was a peace between the Minos and the White Empress at present, but it was an uneasy peace. Just a few years ago, the Empire had launched a two-pronged invasion into Thrace. The eastern thrust had ravaged Lycea, and the main thrust south into Thrace proper had only been stopped by the titanic magics unleashed by the Minos in the Falling Mountains battle. Since then, both sides had maintained stiffly formal relations; trade and travelers still passed between the Thrace and the Empire, but the Imperials were not popular with the people of Byzantium and the Imperial Embassy resembled a fortified compound more than a diplomat's residence.

It was protected by walls, guards and magic; how in the world had I gotten in without starting a fight or raising an alarm? That is when I heard the cursing; someone was swearing slowly and horribly, in a low voice just above a whisper, a voice tinged with exhaustion and despair. It was coming from beyond the archway, and I followed it. That is where I found the blood trail I'd been scenting; someone had crawled, or more properly, dragged themselves around the corner on my right and through the archway and into the small hollow beyond with the marble fountain in its center. Up the slope on the far side was a gate in a brick wall, and beyond that I could see the outer wall of the embassy itself. There was someone laying on the ground in front of that gate, trying to reach the bolt that held it shut. It was a gaunt old man clad in rags and there was something wrong with his legs. As I watched, the cursing stopped and he thrust himself up awkwardly on his right hand and clawed desperately at the bolt with his left. His fingers just touched it but slipped off and he had to fall back to the ground. I heard him take a deep breath, and then the swearing started again, and he glared at the bolt while he gathered his strength to try again.

I wasn't sure how long he'd been doing this, but it looked like he was willing to keep at it all night; me, I thought we both had better places to be when Arinniti rose. I started down into and across the hollow and he froze as I came up behind him. He turned his head slowly to look at me, and I looked into his eyes while I reached over and pulled the bolt back. He had cold, grey eyes, with white hair cropped short and a face weathered dark by sun and wind. He had scrapped his fingertips raw and his bony frame bore the marks of torture, but he didn't look like a broken man, and he had other, older scars as well. His eyes darted from the unbolted door to me and then to my sword, and then he nodded to me.

"My name is Cnut." he said.

"My name is Joren."

Then I turned to look at his legs, and I was the one who started to swear.

"All that and more, boy.", I heard him mutter under his breath.

They had hobbled him by taking a metal rod as thick as my index finger and driving it through both of his legs, from left to right, a hand span above the knees. Then they had put bolts through the outer ends of the rod so he couldn't pull or push the rod free. The rod was slick with his blood, but it looked odd, and I could smell magic. Damn the imperials! Well, I couldn't just leave him there like that and the thought of breaking a spoke in the Empire's wheel, even a small one, was an attractive one. I took my sword in a two-handed grip and told him:

"This is really going to hurt."

He took a grip on the doorjamb with both of his hands and told me to do what I had to do. I took a deep breath and pulled the edge of my sword across the rod in a long, drawing cut, turning as I cut so I could put my weight into it. I ended up cutting at a slight angle, but that may have been for the best. I felt the blade catch at first, but then it sheared through the softer metal of the rod, and I saw a flicker of yellow light when I cut it in two. Cnut had screamed through his clenched teeth when I made the cut, and had then gone limp. It looked like he had fainted, which was good considering what I had to do next. I was going to have to get my sword blade between the bolts in the ends of the rod and Cnut's legs before I'd have a good enough grip to pull the rod halves out.

Then I heard voices…damn it, I was going to have to rush things and that meant more pain for the old man, but there was no help for it. Those voices were coming closer and they didn't sound like Khetarites or native Thracians. I slid my sword edge between the bolt and his left leg and pried the rod out a bit; it was less than a half inch of purchase but it was enough. I ripped the first half of the rod out and then tapped the end of the other with the flat of my blade to push it out the other side; I pulled the second half of the rod free just as I heard more than one person enter the hollow behind me. I turned to face them with my blade at the ready, but I was still a bit unsteady on my feet. There were two of them, one a burly man in armor of middle height who was armed with a mace and who wore the insignia of one of the lower non-commissioned ranks of the imperial army. The other was taller than most, an officer armed with shield and scimitar, with a broad leather baldric that had a row of silver badges or buckles adorning it. I had never seen those before, but I had heard of them; imperial nobility often hosted competitions to celebrate weddings or honor their ancestors or patrons, and the winners of those contests would receive a silver trinket of some kind and a purse filled with silver coins. This man had five of them, marking him as a swordsman of no little ability.

I didn't know much of Teuton then, but I did know the word for kill; the officer pointed his sword at me and gave the order to the other man, never once taking his eyes from Cnut. His companion grinned and came for me; I don't know if he thought I was harmless because of my youth or because I probably reeked of strong drink, but he was wide open and I took him in the throat with a thrust at full extension. He went down, and that officer was on top of me in the blink of an eye. I don't know if I could have taken him sober, but half-drunk as I was, I didn't have a chance. He kept his shield moving and his footwork was superb; I drew my dagger and backed up and to the left to make him jump or trip over his companion's body, but he slipped to one side and came in. I realized he was maneuvering me up against the fountain, but I couldn't think fast enough to evade him. I held him off for a bit and then I was half a second too slow shifting back from a parry; he stepped in and hammered me with his shield. The blow spun me half around and left me off balance, with my right arm numb to the shoulder. I was wide open for a strike to the neck or the armpit, and all I could do was watch his sword swing back …and then he went to one knee, screaming in surprise and pain.

Cnut had crawled up behind him unnoticed and rammed one half of that metal rod through his left calf.

"Hurts, don't it?", he said.

The imperial twisted, trying to thrust his scimitar into Cnut's face while he braced himself with his shield, but I managed to slash his forearm with my dagger and then fell on top of him. I had dropped my sword when he shield-bashed me, so I tried wrestling the imperial for his; he almost caught me in the mouth with the pommel, but I realized that he was more afraid of Cnut than he was of me. Why? Why was he so afraid of a brutalized old man? I found myself thinking that this wasn't at all what I had thought it would be when I had dreamed of avenging my father. This wasn't battle or even a duel; it was a desperate, murderous scramble in the dark, with no holds barred and survival the only prize.

I pried the sword out of his hand, but he got an elbow into my face and pushed me away; then he started yelling his head off to attract attention. His yell changed to a scream of raw fear when Cnut grabbed his sword arm and put his mouth against the wound my dagger had made. He flailed his arm wildly to throw the old man off of him, shouting "Pirwani!".

Pirwa? I had freed a bound TRICKSTER??? Then a frenzied kick from a hobnailed sandal threw me back against the fountain. My head connected with the stone curb surrounding the fountain's pool and all I saw was red stars, and then blackness, and then…nothing. I woke up feeling nauseous, and with what felt like a nice big lump on the left side of my forehead. It was hard to think, but I could smell blood, some of it my own, and I realized that my feet were not touching the ground. I was being held up off the ground by someone, with one hand, at arm's length.

"That can't be comfortable", I thought.

The man holding me up was really quite big; not just broad shouldered, but thick through the chest and his arms and legs were like tree trunks. He had coarse grey hair down to his shoulders, and very cold grey eyes, and he was chewing on something. He winked at me and spat out a shiny object that clinked when it hit one of the flagstones surrounding the fountain. I peered over and saw it to be a silver belt buckle. A silver buckle? I looked around for the bodies of the imperial officer and his servant; there was plenty of blood, but no bodies. Where was the old man I had freed? I looked up at the man dangling me from one hand with no more effort than if I were a new-born kitten. He nodded back at me and said in an encouraging tone:

"Come on. You can do it."

It was him, Cnut. The starved and tortured old man, more than half dead, was now this hulking bruiser. He had eaten the imperials and in doing so had healed himself and regained not just health and strength, but youth and had even grown into the bargain. Shapechanger, Trickster…

Monster.

"You are Cnut."

"Got it in one! I knew you could do it. You are from the Kothmir lands, aren't you, sonny?"

I just blinked at him in reply.

"Well, I never liked them anyway. You know, I owe you three debts: my life, my liberty and my fondest desire, because I've been praying for the chance to kill that sadistic imperial bastard and his Nurrian partner for weeks. It would be truly bad luck for me to kill you now, the kind of bad that really hurts. But you know what, boy?"

He ran one finger down the side of my face, on the side that hurt; it came away red with my blood. He leaned in then, and smiled at me: he stank of blood, of boar, of belt leather and of a strange pulsing magic that was so alive it almost felt like heat. He grinned at me with his big, square, yellow teeth and said:

"I've been sore before."

He laughed and licked my blood off his finger like a child liking the juice of a ripe fruit. Then just for an instant, his eyes flickered green instead of grey and he staggered, almost dropping me. He gaped at me and said:

"You are going to marry my granddaughter!"

What? I was going to do WHAT???

He threw me into the fountain, and I think I heard a crash of something wooden breaking.

I splashed to my feet, dripping water and blood, my head spinning, screaming:

"I am going to marry WHO??????"

I was alone. My weapons were lying on the ground nearby and I grabbed them. The gate to the north was still open, but except for the tracks, the bloodstains and the big hole in the fence to the south where the archway had been, there was no sign that anyone else had ever been here tonight. The smell of boar was strong in the air and then someone beyond that gap in the fence started screaming something in Teuton, the common language of the Empire, and someone else joined them. What sounded like a fight broke out and a horn started blowing; this was a golden opportunity to get the hell out of there before anyone else showed up, and I took it.

I closed the gate behind me, slipped over the embassy wall and into some bushes, and then took a look around. Every guard in sight was running INTO the embassy. I could smell blood and smoke, and it looked the sounds of fighting was starting to draw a crowd. I jumped a hedge when no one was looking my way, and then darted into an alley before I looked back. All hell had broken loose in the imperial grounds; there were at least two buildings on fire, a bunch of people rushing about and I could hear a drum sounding where the horn had gone silent. What sounded like wall collapsed off to the south, and then I heard a deep voice chanting something in a language I didn't know.

I had a feeling that meant magic, big magic, and I was right. A spell powerful enough to stand my hair on end snuffed out one burning building, and the smell of it turned my stomach upside down. I threw up, and then started running north through the alleys and side streets. My memories are a bit confused after that point; I remember being sick again, and have a hazy memory of meeting (or running past) people who were alarmed and/or disgusted by my appearance.

Then I think there were some darklings who laughed at me, then it all went black. I woke up just before dawn to find myself face down in the garbage dump behind the Babylonian eatery at Fifth and Jepip, with no memory of how I got there. I continued north, stopping by the rubble of that burned out tenement to bring up what was left in my stomach (it felt like my boots). I noticed that they had leveled the ruin and were going to have to clean out the rubble before they could build anything else. Then I heard a woman's voice call:

"Father?"

Great, just great. Half drunk, sick as a dog and now someone's father was likely to put a crossbow bolt into me for frightening his daughter. I lurched to my feet and headed back to the barracks, praying that I wouldn't run into anyone who would recognize me. As I stumbled past the old Stormwall between the northern end of the Acropolis and Tarhunt's Hill, and on up the road leading to the Great House of Death, I made myself two promises: one, I was never, ever going to drink distilled liquor again and two, I HAD to talk to Bel about her grandparents.

There were all kinds of rumors running around the city the next day about the fire in the Imperial compound. Some said that it had been a raid of some kind, Khetarite exiles or even some Zarab Adar darklings from the Shadow Lands. Others said that imperial sorcery had gone awry or that something had escaped the ambassador's menagerie. Whatever it was, it had managed to lose its pursuers sometime before dawn when a very large herd of pigs somehow got in the way of the imperial troops. In addition to the damage done by the fires, there was now a hole in the southern wall of the imperial compound you could drive a wagon through. Not to mention the dead: more than half a dozen killed or missing, including a Nurrian merchant who had been pinned to a door with a silver rod driven through his chest. From what little I could remember of the night before, he had apparently been more than just a merchant.

I didn't see any more of Cnut, not then anyway. There was a reward of 10,000 silver pieces posted by the Imperials for someone meeting his description, but it was never collected. When I discussed this the next time I spoke to Belkara, she told me that all of her grandparents had been dead for years, and neither of her grandfathers had resembled the description I gave her of Cnut at any time in their lives. I must not have heard him correctly, or he was wrong or just lying. Lying was the most likely reason, but I decided to avoid the distilled wines in the future nonetheless. I've managed to succeed at that, mostly; but every time I've failed, it hasn't ended well. That wasn't all, though.

My sword, the sword I got from Aunt Syara, the one that never had to be sharpened? There was a dull part of one edge now, down near the hilt, that couldn't be honed away. It was just an inch or so of rounded metal, like it had been forged that way. That was the part of the edge I had laid against the metal rod in Cnut's leg when I had begun to cut through it. It had been too dark, and the rod too slick with his blood for me to realize it, but that rod had to have been of silver, purified runic silver, the kind used in enchantments. All the stories about what happened in the embassy that night agreed that an imperial merchant (Nurria is the imperial god of trade) had been impaled with a rod of silver, nailed right to a door. I could not forget that flash of red light when I had cut through that rod. What exactly had I done that night?

I had loosed a bound Trickster, one of such power that, after devouring those who had tormented him, had torn his way through and out of a fortified compound with all of the casual havoc of a wild boar tearing through a chicken coop. I knew, KNEW in my bones this was going to come back to me, because he had said "I owe you three debts". If Cnut had just wanted to escape, he could have gone north through the gate and over the wall, like I did. Instead, he had gone the other way, to wreak the last part of his vengeance, to leave a red trail of fire and ruin behind him...and to lead them away from me. I had this sick feeling that what I had done that night was just the beginning of a chain of events that I couldn't foresee or control, but somehow was going to end up right back in my lap sooner or later. And that was just the first time that drinking distilled liquor complicated my life. Not to mention the fact that it was a hell of a way to meet one of your In-laws.

It might seem odd, but I never talked to anyone about my life bond with Belkara while I was at the Great House of Death. I am sure that all of the Lords and teachers knew, Ajax was sure to have told them, but I never mentioned it to any of the Lambs or the other students. My link to Bel was mine, and I was reluctant to share her with anyone outside my family. Inside the family was different. Every two weeks I went to the House of the Raven to learn more about my father and his family and every time I visited, I looked into my aunt's mirror. Or, as I was told, my grandmother's mirror. My father's mother Mirani had been a woman of power in her own right, and the mirror responded to me the way it did partly because I was her own flesh and blood. That meant that, if I had the talent and the time, I could eventually use the mirror as my Aunt Natyr had, to see across great distances. As it was, I could use only a fraction of the mirror's potential and I used all of that to look at Belkara. Sometimes I just watched Bel sleeping or working; I did not want to wake her or break her concentration. But often we talked, even if it was only for a moment or two, and I was able to introduce her to Varsene, Valene and Joris. They were delighted with each other, and Belkara was touched by their concern for the two of us and especially with the dress the sisters were making for her. You just do not see dresses like that back in the hills, and they were making it by hand, stitch by stitch. I did eventually invite all of the Lambs to the House of the Raven, and I used the mirror to introduce them to Bel, but that was not until later, after the end of the year, not long before my time at the Great House of Death ended. But my story is not there, yet.

My time as Pupil to Master Arkell was not quite what I had expected it would be. Not that he did not teach me, he did. In fact he taught me everything he could about the two handed sword: every trick, style and technique he had seen and more, he showed those he had developed himself. Then there were the movements he had never taught anyone else, because they simply had not been good enough to learn them. It was not what he taught me that was unexpected, it was who HE was. For of all of the Lords, acolytes and teachers in the Great House of Death, even including Ajax, Lord Arkell was the one I was most like in personality. At first, I thought that it was just because he was just so good with the greatsword. He was teaching me what I wanted desperately to know, and I was such a quick learner, I just figured "Well of course we would get along." But I soon noticed the way that other people looked at us when we would discuss swords and fighting. Even the other Lambs would give me the blank stare from time to time and say:

"Alright, back up. You are not speaking in whole sentences, you know."

Then Lord Arkell and I caught Magan and Cook laughing about something (I think it was a comment on the way we could both curdle milk by looking at it). They both stopped when they saw us notice and walked away whistling, very nonchalant. Lord Arkell looked after them and said:

"Hmm. Joren, we need to talk about a few things."

I thought we had been talking about things, but maybe this would be something new, like the way some swords from the distant east had a single edge and a chisel point to punch through armor. We went up to the room where Arkell taught his classes. It was unused at that time of the afternoon, and when he sat me down on the window sill so I could see his face and eyes while we talked, I knew he wanted me to take this seriously.

"We do not have much of a sense of humor, you and I."

I tensed up right away; I mentioned before that Corlan had been the only person I met who thought I was funny, I am just not that type. Most people thought I did not have any sense of humor at all, which was not true. I do, it just is not like what other people laugh at. Lord Arkell noticed me hunching up a bit and went on.

"That can make life...awkward for us and those around us. It means that we do not understand a large part of what people say, and it is very easy for others to misunderstand us. With us, misunderstanding can lead to violence very quickly. You must always be polite, and it might be better if you kept to the background when in large groups of people or with people who do not know you. You do that a lot now, and your manners are surprisingly good. Was that Ajax's doing?"

"Yes, but mainly my Aunt Syara. She insisted on it, saying that it was beneath me to act otherwise."

"Your aunt? Your mother's sister?"

"My great aunt actually, my maternal grandmother's sister."

"The Elder of your family then."

He looked at me for a moment or two and then went on.

"Joren, there are many things about you and your past that I do not know, and that is as it should be. Your secrets are your own and you should not share them with anyone, including me, or they will not be secrets for long. But it seems to me that much of what I see in you, your manners, your training and other things, are part of a deliberate plan and a good one. I know for a fact that you have more self-control than I did at your age. That probably means that you will not kill as many people as I did before I was twenty...no, that was not a challenge."

Oh.

"I think your Aunt Syara was a very intelligent woman, and I will do what I can to put a decent edge on the blade she burnished so brightly. Your manners are good, but we will hone them; when you deal with princes and kings, you must speak their language and know what they expect from the world, and something about how to mingle with them."

I blinked at him in surprise; my plans for my House and my people was known only to myself and Ajax, but Lord Arkell seemed to have seen this in me fairly clearly. Was I that transparent to everyone? I had not said anything aloud, but Arkell smiled and shook his head at me. I sighed with relief; he knew, but it was not obvious and he would not tell anyone. Wait, how did I know that from a simple shake of his head? My Sword Master continued:

"Unfortunately, this means you must learn how to dance."

Oh Dear Gods No.

"No whining, it is not manly."

He spoke to me for at least 10 minutes to no effect whatsoever and then gave up, pulling at his hair in frustration. It was not that I could not dance; after all, dancing is just timed movement and that is what combat is all about. It was just that I did not see any point in dancing; it served no purpose, it did not interest me and it made me feel like everyone was staring at me. Why bother? Master Arkell was looking out over the courtyard and grinding his teeth when he froze, and then suddenly bellowed out the window:

"Herva! I need you!"

I peered out the window to see Herva and Grali (and about fifty other people) staring up at us in amazement. Disciples of Wurrunk simply do not run around yelling for other people to help them; for Master Arkell (with his reputation for poised arrogance) to do so was simply unheard of. I think it was that, more than anything else that persuaded Herva to enter the Hall and come up the steps to the practice room: she just had to know what the hell was going on. Herva strode into the room with one hand on her rapier hilt, and Grali just a two steps behind her. She was clad in her usual grey and black, with iron chainmail underneath her grey tabard; her scents were cedar and lemon, with the lemon growing stronger if she was in a temper. I could barely smell the cedar at all today as Herva flicked a quick glance at me and then glared at Master Arkell:

"WHAT?"

"Help me. Joren must learn how to dance, and I cannot explain why in a way that he understands."

Herva's brows rose in surprise: Arkell the Proud asking for help? Then she blinked as she realized that this was no joke; Arkell was literally at his wit's end in a matter concerning his Pupil, and he was asking for her help. She looked at her own Pupil, as she unfastened her long black cloak, then Herva passed that cloak to Grali and turned to face Master Arkell. She curtseyed to him, and then held out her hand to him. He swept her a bow and then took her hand, and they began to dance. It was a slow, stately sort of dance, which I later learned was a favorite in the ducal courts of Lycea. While they danced, Herva spoke to me (as I was the only one present who had yet to learn this particular lesson):

"Wherever people gather, they dance; sometimes it is with music and motion, sometimes it is with wit and words, but the dance goes on nonetheless. Dancing can be a way to express emotions, to show your respect for someone, or it can be camouflage."

Camouflage? Like what you would use to make it more difficult for the game to see you when you were out hunting?

"You seek to follow the path of the Guardian, do you not? Then you should know that when watching large groups of people, it is more difficult to see someone who is part of the dance, and easier to spot someone who is not. Only those who know the dance will able to spot an assassin who seeks to use the dance to hide their approach. Such a one will be wary of any who stand out from the crowd, and a guardian who has been spotted will be easier to distract or neutralize."

Hmmm.

"Assassins are such a conceited lot; they consider themselves to be the highest order of predator, masters of the hunt and the kill. I think you will find there are few things more satisfying than to have such a killer turn to strike their selected target, only to find you in their way."

Herva and Master Arkell brought their dance to a graceful end, and then burst into laughter. They were not laughing at me, but at a shared memory mostly, and a little, I think, at how well they danced together. Their laughs were different in that they were male and female, but underneath that their laughter was very much the same, with an odd echo as if someone had drawn a sword in an adjacent room. I thought about what Herva had said, and what Master Arkell had been trying to tell me before they had joined us. Then I turned towards Grali, only to find her staring back at me, her chin propped on one hand and her eyes alight with laughter. She met my eyes and said:

"You know, it is almost like I can actually SEE the light breaking through the darkness inside that thick skull of yours…"

"Aw, shut up and dance with me!"

So with Grali's help, I learned to dance. But I still felt like a three legged cow.

Chapter XXXII: Feralda

ONE NIGHT TOWARDS THE END OF WINTER, I was heading back to the Great House of Death from a visit with my family at the House of the Raven. I had begun to speak of Joris, Varlene and Vasene as my family, and I liked the sound and the feel of it. I was loaded with packages; in addition to the treats the twins would give me to share with the other Lambs, I was also carrying parcels I had been sent to get for Dangmag, Rostaka and Master Arkell. Dangmag's package was sealed with magic and surprisingly heavy; it felt like it had sand in it, but heavier than sand you would pick up on the beach. Metal filings, probably. Rostaka's box contained supplies for a scholar, but what supplies! They were from Babylon and points east: inks that glittered, feathers for quills that rippled with an iridescent sheen, and parchment so fine and pure that it seemed to glow of its own light. For Master Arkell, there was what appeared to be a simple letter, until you noticed that the seal shimmered with the sigils of the god A'as. It was from Thokorion the Librarian, a son of A'as, who had managed his father's Great Library in Byzantium since before Time began. Dangmag's and Rostaka's packages had been ordered through Pyramid Imports, and I had taken possession of them after showing the appropriate receipts at Pyramid's warehouse off of the Great Square. I had signed in blood to take responsibility for Master Arkell's letter, but I had been warned of that ahead of time. Dangmag's box smelled old and hot, Rostaka's smelled of sandalwood and jasmine and another scent that I would later learn was dragon scale. Master Arkell's letter had multiple scents that were oddly intertwined: apples and hot wax, barley and cold seawater...and I realized that I was scenting the layers of a spell, and an intricate one at that.

I was very careful with those parcels as I trudged north towards Tarhunt's Hill; it was not just the obvious value of them, but the fact that three people I admired trusted me with them, and I was not going to let anything happen to them. I was running a bit late when I came to the empty lot where the burned tenement had been, and decided to stay on the street to the west of the lot and not risk crossing it. The light was better on the street and the odds of a quick grab by a street thief or me tripping over my own feet were correspondingly lower. I remember wondering why the lot was still empty; space was at a premium in this part of the city, and they should have been half way finished on whatever was to replace the old tenement.

A group of five or six people a bit older than me turned into the street ahead and came south towards me; I moved out of their way and shifted my cargo so I had a good grip on everything. They went on by with barely a glance at me and I heard a woman's voice call: "Father?"

I turned to look back, but none of the group behind me were responding, or even acting like they had heard her call. It sounded like she was out in that empty lot, where I could see that the construction crew had dug down to the foundations of the old building. The result was a crisscross of shadows and trenches that could hide anything, definitely no place to be running around loaded with these packages. Then the wind shifted, and I caught the scent of death. It was not the smell of something recently dead, but old dead, bones and rotting leather dead, and I felt the hair on the back of my neck stand on end.

"Father?"

There was that voice again, sounding a little clearer, but I could not smell anything living in the shadows where that voice came from. I decided that I needed to get me and my load of valuables back to Wurrunk's Temple just as soon as I could, and I started running. I did not even look back, after the first ten or twelve times. Later that night, about an hour or so before dawn, I had a dream, the good kind. I was back in Nesa, in my Aunt Syara's house, and she was baking something, walnut and apple pie. She was talking to me as she worked, like she often did; when she turned to me and said:

"You look JUST like your father!"

That not only woke me up, but brought me sitting bolt upright with enough noise to wake up Impetui. He looked over at me:

"Hoofbeats?"

"No, it was a good dream, my Aunt was talking to me."

"Well, say hello to her for me and go back to sleep. The Shepherd is going to be down here in an hour."

He rolled over and went back to sleep. I laid back and thought about what had pulled me out of that dream. First, I realized that I had heard that voice calling for her father every time I had passed that lot at night. Second, the voice was calling out using the Khetarite word for father, not the Thracian. Third, the voice sounded like my Aunt Syara. Then I went back to sleep, because I decided I had to go back to that empty lot at night, and find out just what was going on. I always sleep better once I have made up my mind.

I decided to visit the construction site my next free night; I had always heard the voice calling "Father" at night, and something told me that I would want privacy for this. I timed my walk so that I reached the place around midnight, and found it deserted except for a young woman who looked to be an apprentice of some kind; she was walking briskly west and left the plaza with no more than a glance at me. She wore a tool belt and carried a parcel; I caught a whiff of wax, of linseed oil and of cherry and walnut wood shavings: a woodworker's helper then. Then I was alone.

The construction workers had marked the boundaries of the site with sawhorses and rough planks to prevent anyone from stumbling into the work area in the dark. The only light came from the stars and a slow-burning lantern next to the painted sign that bore the builder's name (it warned that the area was still under construction and to keep out). I took a deep breath, wiped my hands on my tunic and then checked to see if each of my weapons was loose in the sheath. It was when I touched the hilt of my sword that I felt it: magic, pounding like a drum through the sword that had belonged to Aunt Syara and her husband Farad. I had never noticed this before, but I realized that I had never had the need to touch the sword whenever I passed this way those other times. That was warning enough for me; I drew the sword and then dithered as to whether to take the lantern. I decided not to: if the lantern went out or was dropped, I would be blind until my night vision recovered; besides, a moving light might attract attention. I closed my eyes and took in the scents of the place with one deep breath: the smell of turned earth was the strongest, but there were others as well. I could smell the scents of the small creatures that live in the soil, worms, insects and rodents. I could smell paint and sawn wood, mortar dust and stale beer, even the smoke from the fire that had consumed the building weeks ago, and I could smell that other scent that I had sensed before.

Underneath all the other scents was the smell of something dead, years dead, and it had been human while it lived. Then the sword in my hand pulsed even stronger and I heard the woman's voice call "Father?" again. The voice seemed stronger than the other times I had heard it, closer...and it was coming out of the shadowed pit in front of me. I couldn't scent anything living in there that was bigger than a field mouse, certainly nothing big enough to speak aloud. Nothing living. Because of the great heat of the fire, the workers had not only removed the rubble and burned wreckage right down to the foundations, but checked and strengthened those foundations as they needed to do before any new structure could be built on this spot again. They just had no idea that they were opening a grave.

Now, if someone was telling this story to me, this is the point where I would say 'Surely this young fool isn't stupid enough to actually go down into that pit, is he?'.

Well, leaving aside the fact that I have been exactly that stupid when necessary, I would like to say in my defense that I did not feel any fear at all at the time. In fact, an idea was starting to form in my mind based on what I knew of my Aunt Syara's family and of the sword in my hand. It was pulsing steadily now, like the heart of some living thing, as I felt my way down the ramp that lead into the pit. Besides, I was sixteen; death was something that happened to other people. Aunt Syara had borne two children: a son, Toran, who had died in the same landslide that had claimed his father's life, and a daughter, Feralda. She had disappeared here in Byzantium twenty years ago without a trace, not even a whisper or a rumor from anyone about her since. Now, Dangmag had said that this sword was tied to Farad and Syara, and that its primary purpose was to aid them and those of their blood. Maybe I was meant to have the sword in order to find out what had happened to my cousin Feralda, and perhaps to bring her peace. I owed it to Aunt Syara to try, and besides, you don't turn your back on family.

That lantern left by the workers didn't illuminate the old foundations much at all; in fact, once you were below ground, it seemed to make things worse, to make the shadows seem deeper and darker. I was working my way over to where I had heard that voice, over towards the northwest corner of the lot, when I heard a rather disturbing noise. It sounded very much like something had been pulled (or pulled itself) out of the dense soil and clay of the bottom and sides of the pit. I stopped; I could hear something coming closer, something that didn't seem to be hindered by the darkness at all. I started to wonder if maybe this wasn't such a good idea after all (see what I mean: stupid), when I heard a hiss, very close, and that woman's voice spoke again:

"That is my father's sword, but you are NOT my father!"

Then I heard the unmistakable sound of a weapon being drawn. Oh, Tarhunt. I closed my eyes for a second and then held the sword out towards the sound of that voice, hilt first, saying:

"I am not your father, but if this is his sword, then I am your kinsman. My name is Joren, son of your cousin Tiresth by her husband Danu, and I was raised by your mother, Syara. She gave me this blade when I came of age; take it now, as is your birth right."

Then I held my breath, waiting.

Something moved in the shadows, a deeper darkness in the shape of a person, but...less so, the way a scarecrow in rags is less than the shape of living flesh and blood. A claw-like hand clad in a rotting leather glove reached for the hilt of the sword, and when it touched it, the power I felt throbbing in the blade rose in pitch until it was almost music. As it did, something grabbed at the darkness filling the pit and pulled those shadows inwards to the sword and the woman who held it.

I remembered Ajax's words after touching the sword with the others: 'Great power', he had said. Power enough to build a physical form for a woman twenty years dead out of the shadows in her grave. The construction pit was no longer dark, but lit with a dim grey light from the stars, and before me stood a woman nearly six feet tall, hooded and cloaked with studded leather armor, who blinked at me and the sword in her hand before she motioned me backwards and up.

"Up and into the light." She said, and I realized she wanted to see my face. When we had climbed the ramp into the light of the lantern, she peered at me intently and I returned her gaze. She looked a lot like her mother, and suddenly, desperately, I had a question I wanted to ask her. She spoke first:

"You look like him, just like him, but...Tiresth had a little girl and was expecting another when last I saw her." She looked me in the eye (she had grey eyes, like her mother) and asked: "How long?"

"Twenty years.", I said.

"Twenty years! " She put her hands to her face and then looked at them and herself, sweeping her cloak out away from her body. She laughed (it was a good laugh, like her mother's) and said:

"Well, I must say I'm remarkably well-preserved for a woman who's been dead twenty years. Ah! So THEY are the ones who killed me!"

She was looking down at her chest and I suddenly realized that two of what I had thought were metal studs in her breastplate of hardened leather were actually the tips of crossbow bolts. She had been shot in the back twice and then her body dumped into the foundations of what had then been a soon-to-be new building. Whoever they were, they were pretty good with those crossbows; either bolt would have been lethal, they were a finger's breadth apart in the center of her chest.

"They?" I said out loud.

346

"Karm and Dulo, henchmen for my betroth...my former betrothed, Partheneo. That was probably part of why he had them kill me; I was rather vocal about breaking the engagement. That and the fact that I had..." She suddenly put a hand to her neck.

"Damn. They took my locket. If Partheneo has my locket...."

She pursed her lips and looked at me: "We're going to need some help."

I nodded agreement. "And I need to get my other swords."

"Ah...yes. If we're going to storm a fortified house defended by half a dozen hardened killers, we'll need more than a ghost and a boy armed with nothing but a sword and a belt knife between them. Where do we go to get the rest of your weapons?"

"Not too far; the Great House of Death."

"Perfect! That's where I was headed when the twins bushwhacked me. There is someone there I need to see. Let's go."

Before we set off, Feralda had me break off the ends of the bolts sticking out of her back; the sight of them would have aroused the attention of anyone we met, and they were ruining the fall of her cloak in any case. She sheathed her sword (there was no sign of the weapon she had drawn on me at the construction site) and took my arm for our walk to Wurrunk's temple, but I noticed she never took her other hand from the broadsword's hilt. Then we were off. Feralda seemed keenly interested in our surroundings as we walked along; she said that the city had just started its growth spurt when she had last walked these streets. It was so much more full of people, energy and life that it fascinated her. She had questions for me as well, about her family and especially her mother. I was trying to find the words for a question of my own when we came to the main gate of the House of Death. That gate was always open in times of peace and there is rarely anyone on guard; the gate has more than one type of magical defense, and Wurrunk's followers can feel the approach of any enemy. Besides, if anyone really wants to start a fight with cult of the god of War, they are welcome to do so anytime they want. I stopped and looked up at the keystone of the gate.

"There is a bell there, and I'm pretty sure it is going to ring if you step through the gate. Maybe you should wait here." I said.

She seemed to be peering at something that I couldn't see.

"That gateway is a threshold in more than one sense. I can see...magic. There is a spell, maybe more than one that links to that bell." She drew her sword, and turned to me: "I cannot just stand here, Joren. I am about to ask for aid in battle from the followers of the god of Death, and Wurrunk has no use for cowards."

True. I nodded to her and walked around to her left side and offered my hand. She smiled, took my hand, took a deep breath and we stepped through the gate together. The bell rang, but only once, with a light, clear note, then stopped. It should have rung again when the bell swung back, but I could see that the bell had stopped moving, frozen after striking the clapper the one time. I heard footsteps and more than a score of people came pouring out of the barracks and the temple itself in answer to the sound of the bell. They were led by Master Arkell and Gultar the Cook, along with a dozen or more initiates of the temple, as well as Magan with the other Lambs. Grali was off running an errand to one of the temples at Seuthopolis with Herva, but Impetui, Alusad, Rig and Pelessa were right behind Magan. Arkell drew his broadsword and pointed it at my cousin; the runes forged into its iron blade began to glow.

"You are dead, and you should not be here." He said to my companion. My teacher turned to me and said: "Explain."

I bowed to him. "Master, this is ...", but Magan finished the introduction for me by blurting out "Feralda!" Everyone turned to look at him, and then my cousin's laughter rippled across the courtyard.

"Hello, Magan. You are looking well."

He was speechless; all he could do was stare at her helplessly, and I suddenly understood what people meant when they said that someone looked at you with their heart in their eyes.

"I approve of the beard, Magan; that salt and pepper thing works for you."

She smiled happily at him and I realized that she cared for him too. Then I heard Gultar speaking to Arkell in a puzzled tone.

"How can a ghost have a physical body? How is it she was able to pass the Threshold? Then there is the bell: that was no alarm, it sounded like the first note of a passing bell!"

Arkell nodded. "For someone who has died, but not yet entered the Realm of the Dead. That sword is why she is looks as she did in life; I can feel the power pouring out of it and into her."

Feralda heard this exchange as well; she took a deep breath and said:

"Your pardon, Lord, but I believe that part of the reason why I was allowed through the gate was because I was coming here when I was murdered."

"You were coming here!" Magan looked as if he'd been struck a body blow.

"I broke off my betrothal to Partheneo; it seems someone made me a better offer. But there is more."

She would have said more right then, but Arkell spoke up, and when a Disciple of Wurrunk speaks, you pay attention.

"Ah! That is why you were able to cross the Threshold; you have business with the God of Death and Truth. Speak, Woman. Wurrunk will hear you."

Arkell set the point of his sword on the ground and clasping both hands on its hilt, spoke three words in the tongue of swords. As he did, all of those sworn to Wurrunk drew a sword and waited. He had cast a spell, and I knew which one it was. Wurrunki magic can reveal lies when they were spoken; if anything Feralda said was a falsehood, every member of Wurrunk's cult would literally see the lie taint the air around her. She composed herself and made her request a formal plea for aid:

"I ask Wurrunk for succor in three things:

First, that Vengeance be delivered to those who killed me by stealth." Here, she touched the tips of the crossbow bolts that protruded from her chest armor. I heard the crowd stir as they realized that she had been shot down from behind.

"Second, that the Truth might be revealed after twenty years of lies."

"Third, that Justice might be done for one of Wurrunk's Own."

She turned to meet the Shepherd's eyes:

"Parthenio has your hand, Magan. He's got it nailed to a black wood board with slivers of ivory stained with blood, and there were little red candles sitting on each fingertip. If I had to guess, I'd say he has it in my old strongbox, the one I sealed with my mother's locket, because the twins took the locket when they killed me."

Gultar turned to Magan: "He keeps your severed hand as a trophy? Is there a blood feud between your clans?"

"No, until this night I would have said we were friends, although we have drifted apart. Ivory stained with blood...Lord, Partheneo spent time with the Skula as a hostage when he was a youth. If he learned more from them than their speech, he could use my hand to do many things. This much I know he has done: he has used magic to hide the presence of my own hand from me when I had to have been ten yards of it. If he can do that, he can hide a great many other things from just about anyone."

Arkell spoke then: "Who is this Partheneo?"

349

"A companion of our younger days when we walked the Adventurer's Path from the Tiber River to the edge of the ruins of Ur. Now, he runs the Boar's Head tavern in Portside, with a small shipping business he operates out of the back."

"Partheneo and how many others?"

"Partheneo, Karm, Dulo, Asran behind the bar, Willem and Moros...six in all.

"Then hear Wurrunk's Judgement in this matter: Woman, you have spoken the truth, and your cause is just! Six will go against six to see justice done. Magan will go to reclaim what is his. Joren, what is Feralda to you?"

"She was... is my kinswoman. Her mother was my great aunt who raised me.

"Then you are bound by blood to aid her. Three more are needed to go with you."

He turned towards the Wurrunki initiates only to find that Alusad, Rig, Pelessa and Impetui had formed up behind Magan.

"I see. Do any of you four know where the Boar's Head tavern is?" Alusad was the first to raise his hand.

"Good. Alusad will take a message from me to the City Watch to report this matter. We are bound by oath to report criminal activity to the Watch and to aid them as we can, so Alusad will accompany the officers of the Watch to the tavern and provide assistance. You other three will go with Magan, Feralda and Joren. Prepare yourselves! Unless I am mistaken, you don't have much time.

He looked at Feralda as he spoke those last words, and she nodded in reply.

"I agree, Lord. It feels...I think I have until Arinniti comes through the Gates of Dawn, no longer."

Arkell turned to Magan: "You'll have a head start, but if you have not finished this by the time the Watch arrives with Alusad, you'll need them as backup. In any case, I will visit the Boar's Head myself tomorrow morning, and if necessary, I'll burn the tavern to the ground and bury Partheneo in its ashes."

If we had failed and all of us were dead, is what he meant.

"How much of a head start can you give me, exactly?", said Magan.

"As long as it will take me to write a formal request for an investigation of Partheneo, and to come up with some kind of reasonable explanation why the Temple's Lambs and their Shepherd are following a dead woman through the streets of Byzantium with drawn swords."

Gultar laughed. "In the middle of the night, no less. I want to read that one myself. I will give Magan a hand with his armor, and bring back ink and parchment for your message."

He slapped Magan on the back, who nodded to both of them.

"Thank you, I appreciate the help."

We scattered to grab our gear, with Gultar going off with Magan. I was already in armor, so all I had to do was get my greatsword and shortsword from our room, and grab a spare broadsword from the barracks. Even so, Pelessa was only minute or so behind me; the others took a bit longer, with Magan and Impetui arriving last. Arkell and Feralda were deep in conversation as I came up.

"...dead for twenty years? You should have gone onto the Land of the Dead long ago! Why do you remain? Is your thirst for vengeance that strong?"

She nodded at him; "Well, it certainly is not weak. But there is another reason: someone would not stop thinking of me, caring for me, and I could not just...leave. Also, it seems to me that I was meant to come here, that Magan and I are meant to set things right; we just got sidetracked for a while."

We fell into line as each of us arrived. I could see Gultar and Magan come out of the temple together, but Magan ran to join us while the cook seemed to be taking his time with the ink and parchment. He was laughing, but Magan was swearing beneath his breath; I caught something that sounded like 'too much for woman for me...' as he joined us. Impetui was not far behind, and if I did not speak up now, I might never get another chance. I took a deep breath, and blurted out the question that had been knotting my guts since I had seen the color of my cousin's eyes.

"Do you look like my mother?" I asked her. She gave me an odd look and I babbled on.

"I cannot remember them, not their faces, not their voices or the touch of their hands. I know that I look like my father, but...but what did my mother look like?

She looked into my eyes, and then touched my face; "Oh, Joren."

She pulled the hood back from her head and I heard Magan draw a ragged breath. The lanterns here gave more than enough light. "She was taller than me by a couple of inches, and her hair was a foot or so longer but other than that, we looked very much alike. Your father said he would

351

have taken us for sisters, had he met us both at the same time."

I stared hungrily at her, committing every feature to my memory. I had wanted to know what my mother looked like since the very first day I could remember, and now I knew. Part of the ache inside me, the pain that had been a part of me since my aunt had awakened me, went still and faded away. I smiled at her.

"Thank you, cousin. It matters a great deal to me."

"You are welcome, cousin."

Impetui came trotting up then, and Magan looked us over as we checked our gear.

"Are we ready? Let us be off then."

Arkell nodded to Magan and Feralda: "Fare you well." I think he was smiling.

"One last thing", my cousin said, as she raised her sword towards the temple: "Lord of Death, if it be your will, grant us your favor this night, that we may avenge an old wrong, and reveal the truth."

Nothing seemed to happen at first, but when we stepped through the temple gate into the city, Feralda's sword glowed with a silver light. We checked ours and the same was true of all of our blades. She turned to Magan and said:

"Huh. I didn't really expect this."

"He's not really cold and forbidding all the time, you know."

"Really?" She grinned at him and then took his right arm with her left.

"Tell me what you've been up to the last two decades, Magan. You are in much better shape than I expected; you kept your girlish figure and all."

Then we were off.

The streets were nearly deserted at that hour of the morning, and Magan and Feralda were sharp enough that the few people we saw never saw us. Magan was different, more...alive. It wasn't just that he was actually cheerful for the first time we had ever seen, it was something more. He and Feralda never got in each other's way, never bumped together, were always checking over each other's shoulders. They had been a team once, and now they were a team again; one-handed or not, Magan was whole again, where he had been incomplete without her. We were working our way south and west towards the western gate of the city when I heard Magan and Feralda whispering to each other. I wasn't trying to eavesdrop, but I couldn't help but overhear the last part:

"YOU kept me here, Magan. So don't do anything stupid and go running ahead without me, understand?"

"Yes, Ma'am."

Then she leaned into him and kissed him. Magic or not, living woman or unhoused shade, that sure sounded like two very real people kissing.

We reached the western gate and didn't even try to hide; it wouldn't have done any good, that gate is well-guarded day and night. Feralda had us form up behind her and march right on out, with her saluting the gate captain with her sword as we passed. That earned her a salute in return, and when I thought about it, seeing a woman lead the grey tunics of Wurrunk's Lambs out of the city wasn't that strange a sight, after all. Getting back in might be a different matter.

I could feel the difference the moment we left the city; we were now outside the walls built by the Minos atop the ruins of the ancient ramparts wrecked by the wars that swept Thrace after the Breaking. Out here, life was simpler and quite a bit wilder than in the city. I could smell the living things that thronged the night, and they could sense us. Death and the Dead had come to Portside, and every living thing could feel it. What insects and animals could not run went completely still, and the rest fled from us, spreading outward away from our party like the bow wave of a speeding ship.

The Boar's Head was a good half mile west of the city gates, just west and bit south of the old temple to Lycus, the river god. It was on the south side of the road and, from the lights in the windows and the smoke from the chimney, was open for business. When we were fifty yards or so from the tavern, Feralda stopped short and swore underneath her breath.

"Well, I did not expect this to be easy." She turned to Magan and broke the bad news:

"Partheneo's got some kind of warding up on the entire building, Magan. It doesn't affect people, obviously, but it looks pretty solid to me. There is something about it...I do not think that I can touch it."

"Ah. A slight complication. I won't be able to break his hold on my hand unless I can see it; that is the only way I'll be able to target it because I cannot sense it in any way."

"Well, I won't be able to open that strongbox and reveal your hand until I have my locket back. Once I have my locket back, I can find that strongbox no matter where he has hidden it. That means that you boys and girls are going to have to get into the tavern, deal with his henchmen and either drop the warding or get that locket out here to me. Got that?"

"Got it."

Impetui ran a finger down the length of his blade and put into words the question we were all thinking:

"You don't mind if this gets a bit messy, do you?", he said, looking at both of them

Feralda tapped the heads of the crossbow bolts sticking out of her chest and said:

"Messy? Oh no, not at all. Just try not to kill Partheneo; I would like to have a word with him myself."

Magan told us his plan, and gave us the layout of the tavern. We could not count on anyone being asleep; if Partheneo was running a smuggling ring, he and his henchmen might work all night and sleep all day. Parthenio himself might be anywhere, but would most likely be in the room he ran his business from (which was through a door behind the bar directly across from the front door), or at the bar itself. Karm and Dulo would most likely be in the right-hand corners of the room, where they could watch the doors. Impetui and I were to go through the front door first, fast and hard. Then Magan, and then Rig, then Pelessa, then Feralda (if or when we had dropped the wards). I KNOW that is what he said, he was very clear, he just wasn't very honest. He looked each of us in the eye and nodded:

"Right, on the count of three, ready? One…", and he bolted through the door of the tavern.

Our jaws dropped and then we leapt after him, but we were too late and two long steps behind him when there was the flash of a spell being cast. Right after that we heard the hard slap of the crossbows and saw the bolts hit him and throw him into the wall. Then we were into the taproom and on top of them. The few normal customers had thrown themselves to the floor or against the walls, so our enemies were out in the open. Karm and Dulo were reloading their crossbows and that takes time, even for the weapons that are dwarven-made.

We did not give them that time. I darted for the one on the left (Dulo from Magan's description); a man with a red tunic and pockmarked face threw a bench in front of me to slow me down, but I leapt high and brought my greatsword down with my landing and split Dulo's skull to the collar. I heard an arrow whistle across the room behind me just as I felt the blade catch in the bone, so I left it. Drawing my other swords, I spun towards the bar. The bald man behind the bar in the black apron was pulling a crossbow of his own from underneath but he was too slow; I knocked the crossbow aside with the tip of my broadsword and one of Pelessa's arrows took him in the throat and he went down. That is when

Partheneo opened the door to backroom with a mace in his hand to see what the commotion was. What he saw was a bloody shambles.

While I had taken care of Dulo, Impetui had rushed his brother Karm; the twin killers were tall, lean men clad in black and grey, Karm was the one with the scarred cheek. A big man in brown who was going to fat tried to get in the way, but Impetui was bigger and stronger; he threw the fat man off with his shield and took Karm's head from his shoulders with a hard, flat swing. The fat man swung at him with a sword of his own; Impetui blocked the attack and then caught his foe between neck and left shoulder with a blow so hard that he had to stand on the body to pull his blade free.

The man in the red tunic might have been thinking about knifing me in the back, but Pelessa put her first arrow into the bar next to him, and distracted him long enough for Rig to reach him. Rig dropped him with a blow to the belly with his broadaxe, and Pelessa put her second arrow into the man behind the bar. She drew and aimed her third arrow at Partheneo when he opened the door. It happened fast; less than a minute, certainly no more, and we had turned a sleepy taproom into a slaughterhouse with blood and brains splashed across half the room. The shock of seeing his world in a red ruin and the sight of a girl with a bow drawing a bead on his nose set him back on his heels long enough for me to leap over the bar. I wanted to come at him from the side so I was out of Pelessa's line of fire, and to keep him away from that third crossbow.

I snarled at him the way a darkling would, with my mouth open and he jerked away; that was when I caught a familiar scent: magic. The kind of magic I had smelled before among the Skula who had fought for the Empire at Roaring Springs. Parthenio smelled like a Skula tribesman!

"Partheneo, old friend. How have you been?" Magan's voice was rough with pain, but I could hear the satisfaction in it too.

"Magan? What the hell is going on?" I saw him work the thumb and ring finger of his left hand, turning it away from Magan's view, and I guessed that he was turning a ring on his finger so that only the band could be seen.

Magan looked at Rig and nodded at the left hand door post just inside the front door. Rig stepped up and started swinging his axe two-handed, at the third stroke there was a flash of magic and Rig staggered back, his right arm numb to the shoulder. He had broken the wand that supported the warding on the building though, and that enabled Feralda to enter.

She came gliding through the doorway with her hood pulled forward and her father's sword naked in her right hand, and all of the candles in the tavern began to burn brighter, their flames flaring a finger's length above the wick. She pulled her hood back and laughed into Partheneo's face:

"Hi Honey, I'm back. Did you miss me?"

Partheneo's eyes went wide with shock, and I think he barely noticed when I struck the mace from his hand. He staggered backwards, and then turned and ran for the backroom, screaming all the while:

"You are dead, DEAD!"

"For twenty years now, dear. But you have been in my thoughts the whole time."

When she reached me, Feralda placed her free hand on my shoulder and smiled at me.

"Left ring finger", I said.

Her grip tightened. "Thank you, kinsman, for everything."

Then she turned towards the back of the tavern. The remaining customers fled gibbering into the night as Partheneo slammed the door of the back room behind him. He had just managed to finish fumbling with the lock when she kicked the door in. He managed to scream once before she started swinging her father's sword and then she hacked him to pieces. Then I heard Pelessa's voice: "Joren!"

I turned to find her kneeling next to Magan, her hands red with his blood.

"I cannot stop the bleeding!"

I went to kneel beside Magan myself and I could see the wounds were bad. He had worn his best armor and had even managed to partially muffle one bolt with his cloak, but at such short-range, the crossbows had torn right through both. The wound in the left shoulder was bad enough, but the wound in the groin was mortal unless it was healed now. I put everything into a healing spell, only to have it fail.

I tried again as the sound of a rending crash came from the back of the tavern, and failed again. I think now that the magic Partheneo had used to enchant Magan's severed hand had in some way weakened our Shepherd, so that his wounds could not be healed by magic. By rushing into the tavern first, he had deliberately risked his life for ours, and now we were going to have to watch him die. Impetui said it first:

"Thank you, Shepherd."

He looked into each of our faces as we thanked him, and nodded once. I could hear the sound of many boots out in the street; Alusad had delivered Arkell's message to the city watch as promised. I heard Feralda come out of the back room, and turned to see her opening a silver box, with her sword tucked under one arm. Behind her I could see into the room where Partheneo had met his end; it was spattered with blood and there was a hole gaping in the back wall, as if something had torn itself out of the wall, bursting through the wood and plaster that had hidden it. Feralda's arms were red with blood to the elbow, but I could see that she had a ring in her left hand that must have belonged to Partheneo. She pulled a severed hand from the box, and then handed the box and the ring to me. I rose to my feet and stepped back as she knelt next to Magan. I did not want to touch that hand; it looked and felt...*wrong*. It had small red candles stuck to the ball of each finger and the thumb; the hand itself bore the sigils of Wurrunk on the palm and back, but they were twisted somehow. The candles reeked of blood and pain, and there were other marks cut into the hand that I did not know; the stench of magic that enshrouded it nearly turned my stomach. Later, Ajax and Rostaka said that Partheneo may have enchanted the hand so that it helped him hide the truth about himself and his activities not only from the authorities but from Magan and anyone who followed any deity with ties to the Truth.

Feralda sank to her knees beside Magan and placed his severed hand in his lap. She took his left hand in her right, and laid her sword so that it touched both of their legs; then she touched her forehead to his so she could look into his eyes and said to him:

"Now, we go together."

With those words, Feralda's sword shattered as if it were glass. In the same instant, every flame in the building, even in the fireplaces and the oven, went out like a single snuffed match. Later, I heard from Arkell that the bell at the gate of the House of Death sounded three times at what we think was that same moment. There was an uproar from Alusad and the axe-sisters of the city watch out in the street; when we called to them, they entered with their lanterns held high. They found the four of us gathered around the body of a man with one hand, a pile of bronze sand, and the bones of a woman twenty years dead.

Naturally, the captain of the city watch (a stocky woman with brown hair and deep set eyes that didn't seem to miss anything) wanted answers, and naturally, all of the other Lambs pointed at me. That was fair. I tried to explain, and even I thought I sounded crazy. It helped that the captain was holding Arkell's letter in her hand while I babbled. It helped even more when the women of her command took the tavern apart and began to find every sort of contraband they could think of, and a number of items that had obviously been stolen. Partheneo had been both a smuggler and a fence for stolen goods, and a very successful one based on the amount of silver coins found the chest in his personal rooms and another chest buried in the basement. It did seem odd that no one could remember Partheneo or any of his obviously dangerous henchmen ever being suspected of or even questioned about any serious crimes. Ever.

She let us go when Master Arkell arrived just after dawn, just as he said he would. She knew where to find us if she needed to, and if a Disciple of Wurrunk had approved this raid, then it was a matter for the queens to decide. She released the remains of Magan and Feralda to us as well; she had them wrapped in Magan's cloak, and placed on a litter carried by two of the city watch. Master Arkell said that he would escort them back to the temple. We all thanked the captain, and then Master Arkell ordered us to run the whole way back to the House of Death, to sharpen our appetites he said. It worked too; that breakfast of porridge (with honey and fresh baked bread) tasted pretty good, and we even got a few hours of sleep in, here and there, during the day. The funerary ceremony was held at dusk; the remains were cremated together and the ashes gathered into a single urn. Magan had been born in Byzantium, and there was a place set aside for that urn in his family's crypt in the Caenopolis, the great Necropolis of Byzantium.

Gultar acted as Shepherd from that point on, and he performed his duties with the same quiet efficiency that he brought to everything else he put his hand to, but we never forgot Magan, nor have I forgotten Feralda.

Fare you well, Kinswoman.

Chapter XXXIII: Marked with the Sign of Night

THINGS CHANGED WITH THE NEW YEAR. For one thing, the Lambs disbanded; the time allotted to each student was one year and everyone but me had started their time at the beginning of 610 MK. By the end of the first week of spring, Alusad, Rig and Impetui had said their farewells and left Byzantium. Alusad had returned to his family's lands near Hatnah, while Rig and Impetui were sent to Athens with Broddi. The temple of Wurrunk there was a bit short-handed due to a sickness that had come down the trade road from Dyracchium; what with the illness and the turmoil caused by the ascension of a new queen, they were expected to be gone for at least three seasons.

Grali and Pelessa gave up their grey tunics and put on other colors. Pelessa with Urika were tasked with training archers for the Minos's army. Herva, aided by Grali, had the daunting job of assuming those duties of Magan that fell within her abilities, including the formation of the next group of Lambs, tentatively scheduled for the beginning of fall. Due to the disruption caused by the Shepherd's passing, there had been a delay in gathering new candidates. Not that prospective Lambs were all that plentiful to begin with. Indeed, my class had been unusual for its size; normally, there were rarely more than three or four Lambs at any given time. By then I should have completed my own time as a Lamb, as I had started in summer. I was changing too; I had turned seventeen at Mid-Winter, and while I was no taller, I was putting on muscle. I was more certainof myself as well, more confident since I had proven I was competent not only in my weapon skills but also in performing my duties.

Then there were the new skills I was learning. Herva and Cook had continued with Magan's plans for my training in detecting poisons and extended my research into the halls of the Great Library itself. I had to take care with those poisons that could be inhaled, but by the end of spring, I could identify more than 300 different poisons by their smell. But what had me excited was that I was making swords now! Dangmag and Cook had tested my knowledge of ores and metals, of fire and the forge, and of the weapon smith's tools to their satisfaction before I was allowed to work the bellows and watch the smiths of Wurrunk's Temple at work. I had learned to watch the pattern of the metal as it was heated and hammered and cooled, and to judge the temperature of a blade by the color it glowed in the dark. I was tested in other ways as well. I really could sharpen any blade, and I quickly picked up the skill of polishing and sharpening blades of spell-wrought iron. I never cut myself by accident, even when Dangmag's apprentices tried to play some nasty tricks on me, and they soon stopped. I realized that they looked at me oddly and I remembered that Dangmag had said that I seemed to have my own echo in the smithy. The apprentices had all taken Samelir Redhammer as their patron just as Dangmag had, and they all sensed something different about me.

When he thought I was ready, Dangmag tested me by having me make a sword for myself. In his opinion, a real weapon smith will take the time and put in the effort to get a weapon done just right. If I would not do that for a weapon of my own, I would certainly never bother to get it right for anyone else, and so would not be worth teaching any further. It took me three tries before I crafted a blade that satisfied both of us, but it was worth it. It was very much like my Uncle Farad's sword that had served his family so well, but made for my hand and it felt just right. With this proof of my ability and focus, Dangmag decided to go a step further, and taught me the magic for forging iron. These were not the same as the spells for healing wounds or repairing tools, but rituals that could take days to complete. Those spells were not taught to anyone who just came in off the street, either. People had been killed for that kind of magic, more than once since Time began. It would have taken years as an apprentice to earn those spells, and it would be years before I was skilled enough to use them reliably, but I was given them as a gift because Some One thought I was going to need them.

I can still remember that day: every single man and woman sworn to Samelir in Byzantium crammed into the Temple smithy, the apprentices in the back, each touching their master, each smith touching Dangmag, Dangmag's callused hand on my forehead as he intoned the words of the spells. I realized that they were here as witnesses as well, for my part of this ceremony included an oath to keep this magic secret and safe. This I swore to do, and when he was done, Dangmag had given me all of the knowledge I needed to eventually become a sword smith. Eventually.

"It will take years, boy. Years to find or make your own tools, to build your own forge or find one that answers to you. Years of hot work with a hammer in your hand, trying, failing, learning. Maybe all the years in the rest of your life. Can you do that?"

I thought about that for a while: years working at a forge, making things, fixing things, forging swords for myself, my family, my friends. Maybe other things as well; I had sometimes wondered what shapes I might be able to pull and hammer metal into, while I worked in the heat of the forge.

"Yes, Master Smith. I can do that. It seems to me that there are worse ways to spend my life."

"Hmm. I think so too. Let's go get a drink and see what Cook has saved for our dinner."

I was still learning from Master Arkell, but along with the finer points of swordplay, I was learning how to teach. I had finished the past year at the head of my class, and had been offered a post as his assistant. After discussing the matter with Ajax, I had accepted. I needed to learn more from my master and Ajax thought teaching would be good for me. When I asked him why, he said:

"Patience."

Well, alright, if the Old Man wanted to be mysterious about it, fine. I just wished that he and Master Arkell would stop giving me THAT look and laughing at me with their mouths closed so much. I was seventeen now, not some brat in short pants. It turned out that I liked teaching. I liked seeing the other side of the lessons I had been taught the year before and I began to get a feel for the strengths and weaknesses of those I taught. Gradually, I also caught the knack of showing students how to use the first and overcome the second, at least as much as they were able, and then I began to realize what Ajax had meant when he said "Patience".

Hmm. Maybe my pants were a little too long at that.

After the 12th week of classes, Master Arkell informed me that I would be taking over as instructor until the end of the season, as he would be taking long leave to visit his family in Cibyrrha. He had received a formal-looking letter from his brother the Duke, and since there was temple business there that only a few of the Lords were qualified to handle, he was expected to be gone for three to four weeks. In his absence, I was in charge of the students who were taking instruction in the two handed sword. After a day and a night of absolute panic, I decided I might actually be able to do the job without embarrassing both my teachers and everyone else living in the Great House of Death. All in all, things were going fairly well: I was polishing my skill with my swords, crafting blades of my own, and planning a welcome for Bel when she finally made it to Byzantium. So naturally, that is when everything went to hell in a hand basket.

Late one day a week before the end of summer, I was walking back from making a delivery of sword blades to the Pyramid warehouse on Cat Island when I met two initiates of Wurrunk who were looking for me. Hadelor and Chala were both natives of Byzantium, but had been serving as caravan guards for the Princes of Adria for the past two years; they had only been staying at the temple barracks for a couple of weeks. I knew something was wrong right off; Chala was eyeing the street in both directions and both men reeked of onions. They must have been giving Cook a hand in the kitchen when they had been sent out to find me. Hadelor did the talking:

"Lord Ajax needs you; something is up. You will find him west of the city, past the first mile marker on the river road. You know, where the barley fields start."

"What is wrong?"

"Lord Ajax does not share his plans with me; I do know that there are initiates out looking for you all over the city. Let's go this way, it will be quicker."

We headed southwest through the well-to-do neighborhood near the Old City, then across the Lion's Road into a poorer section of Byzantium. After the first block, I realized that this was all wrong; there were no gates in the city walls between the Gate of the Twins and the Lion Gate, and both Hadelor and Chala would know that, they were born here.

"But they know I am a stranger." I thought to myself, someone who would not know their city as they did. The smell of onions was overpowering; was that to mask another scent, one that might give them away? I stopped to check left and right at the next intersection, we all did, and I used that to move a bit closer to Chala. We moved on down an alley too narrow to move more than two abreast through, and I caught the barest whiff of something else. There WAS something there, under the heavy odors of onion, leather and weapon oil...perfume. Loricon's perfume!

They were my enemies!

Some movement of mine gave me away, and when their intent changed, the Death God's Gift flared into life: "Death! Death at your side and at your back!" whispered that cold voice I had heard twice before, and I moved. Someone had told them about my sense of smell, but they had not been in Byzantium long enough to see me fight and they had no idea how fast I was. I spun to my left and grabbed Chala's arm as it came up and threw him head first into Hadelor, who had to check his striking adder attack or spit his companion.

362

I drew my new sword and caught Hadelor in the mouth with a hard thrust, and then pulled my return stroke down and to the right across Chala's neck as he turned towards me with a shortsword in one hand and a knife in the other. Bright blood spattered the grimy walls on either side of me, and I looked at the other people in the alley ahead and behind me. They backed away with hands spread wide; I wore the Grey Tunic and no one in their right mind steps between followers of the Death god in a street fight. I wiped my blade clean and pushed past the people behind me and started to retrace my steps, my mind reeling in shock. Then I found a place where I could put my back against a wall and see anyone coming at me and stopped.

Breathe. Focus. Think.

Loricon had made his move against Ajax. I had no idea where those two had aimed to take me, but their actions had turned lethal at the first hint that I was on to them. Whatever the game Loricon was playing, the stakes were Life and Death. Now, both Hadelor and Chala had been sworn to Wurrunk and would have avoided lying out of habit. I thought back over what Hadelor had said to me, and realized how carefully his words had been chosen.

I had to assume that Ajax needed me or needed help, he was indeed one mile west of the River Gate, and Loricon's henchmen were combing the city for me. He was said to have more than a hundred followers, both within and without the cult of Wurrunk; the Sun was setting now, and while I might be able to evade that many people at night for a time in a city this big, all Loricon would have to do would be to hire some darklings to find me, and that would shortly be the end of me. There was no place that I could get to in Byzantium that would be dark enough or secret enough to hide from darklings who had been set on my trail, not between sunset and sunrise. The only safe options were to ask for refuge in a temple or cower behind a queen's warband. Or I could go seek those who had taught me and fought alongside me for the past year, and find the old man who was the only grandfather I would ever know. I thought about that for a bit and came to the conclusion that I did not feel like cowering in a safe place, I wanted to know what the hell was going on and I wanted to find Ajax. He had told me that he was leaving Byzantium for Dyrrachium the next day on a ship that was docked seaside. Well, if I could make it to the Great House of Death, I could find out what was going on, grab his gear and go meet up with him to see what he wanted to do. I did not think about what I would do if he was dead; I had to find him first. I could think about killing people then, if I had to. Right now, I had to get back to the Temple of Wurrunk and I had to do it without throwing myself into the arms of the people who were scouring the city for me. Well, Loricon was not the only one who could turn to the darklings for help; I knew at least one Child of Darkness in Byzantium myself, and she owed me a favor.

I would head to a temple of Night (there was such a temple behind Tawara's Temple on the Great Square, which would be closest), and see if I could get word to the priestess of Brighid the Serene whose life I had helped to save. I would see if I could get the debt she had acknowledged repaid, or at least get some good advice from a neutral party along with some food. The Sun set as I approached the Night Temple, and I wondered how many more people would die before dawn. Turned out, it was even more than I had imagined.

There were only two guards in sight at the temple entrance; after all, there is more than one temple to the Goddess of Night in Byzantium and this was not the largest. One guard was a darkling, the other a human, both male, both clad in black, both wielding spears and maces; I could tell that the darkling had caught the scent of blood of the two men I had killed. For most temples, this would mean I would be prevented from entering until I had been ritually cleansed; darkness temples do not necessarily have this prohibition. For some darkling temples, it was almost expected that you would have blood on your hands. After I had requested an audience with a priestess of the Night, the darkling guard ordered a servant to carry a message into the temple proper, and made note that I came to the temple after killing someone. The human guard shifted his stance a bit after hearing this; he was not being aggressive, just careful.

After a few moments, an acolyte of Eresh appeared and bowed to me; she was young, a bit taller than me and pretty, with very fair skin but with eyes and hair that were as dark as...well, night. She smelled of soap, and fine linen and incense; she just said "Follow me", and turned around and walked back into the temple proper. So I did. It was very cool inside compared to the heat of summer that clung to the city streets, and I sighed in relief.

As we walked, I took the opportunity to enjoy the very fine tapestries that hung from the walls of the corridor leading to the center of the temple. They were exquisite, and depicted the birth of Eresh's son, Arma Arn, and his childhood. The chamber we soon entered was not very big; the ceiling was supported by four round pillars and the only adornment was the mosaics laid into the floor before the black stone altar. I was surprised how well lit it was by only eight candles, until I saw the mirrors of black glass that hung from the inner face of each pillar.

There were two full priestesses waiting for us, one about my height of middle years and the other as tall as the acolyte beside me, but older, much older. Both women smelled of perfume, the shorter priestess of cloves and the older of fir trees, balsam I thought, and I was struck with a very sharp image of the hills of Khetar, of home, and of magic. Power billowed outward from the altar and radiated from each of Eresh's priestesses. The shorter of the two spoke:

"You bear the Grey Tunic of Wurrunk's Servants; are you here on temple business?"

"No, Lady."

"Do you seek sanctuary then? Is that why you come to us with a man's life blood drying on your hands?

"Two men." Corrected the older priestess. "And not sanctuary. You do not seek a place to hide, but aid for the path you walk, eh, Son of Dono? Oh yes, I know that face: I saw your father win his first duel and taught your aunt some of the finer points of enchanting, many years ago."

"Ah!" breathed the young acolyte behind me. "The Lady Natyr's heir, her nephew!"

"Just so." The shorter priestess nodded at me. "You are owed a debt, young man: you healed one dear to us of wounds that would have taken her life, and then shielded her with your own body when her enemies struck at her again. We do not have troops to send marching with you through the streets, but what aid we can give, we will. Ask!"

The wave of relief that hit me was so intense my knees almost buckled. They would help!

"Daughters of the Night, I am hunted by enemies who walk Byzantium's streets. I must reach the Great House of Death without being noticed, and run from there to the first mile post west of the city. I do not seek aid to fight, but to avoid a fight that would sow chaos through the city's streets. The two men I slew sought to take me by trickery, and when that failed, drew blades on me."

"The shadows have whispered to us that there are pairs of swordsmen abroad in Byzantium, hunting someone. But who has the will and the means to throw a net of more than two score armed men across our city, all for one boy, who they are willing to kill if they cannot capture?"

"Loricon."

That one word from me started a chain reaction of thought that I could actually see flickering from one priestess to another as they spoke:

"Loricon!...

"Has moved against his enemy Ajax Whitebeard by seeking to take or kill the pupil of Arkell the Proud...

"This pupil serves Wurrunk but is not bound to him, and if slain could be brought back by certain powers...

"No healer akin to the Earth would do so without telling the Queens of the City of it...

"But the Empire has healers of their own who are that strong...

"The Empire has a price on Ajax's head and has designs on Lycea, where Arkell has close kin...

"Loricon has allied with the Empire of the White Sun...

"This could be the first step towards open war!"

"And no matter the outcome, our people will be the weaker for it."

Both women sighed deeply, and the eldest turned to the acolyte, who had been feverishly scribbling notes on her wax tablet:

"This goes to the Queens, now, this minute!"

That young woman turned and sped off without even a bow to her superiors, and as her footsteps faded in the distance, I realized that in coming to this temple of Night, I had literally put my words into the ears of the Queens Council. Who better than the followers of Eresh to see and hear what went on in Byzantium once the Sun had set? But if they were hand in glove with the Council of the Queens of the city, what would they do with me now? I looked back to find both priestesses watching me closely, and the eldest spoke as if she could hear me thinking:

"Our debts are our business, no one else's."

The shorter priestess gave a surprisingly deep laugh:

"Boy, if you wanted to walk unseen and unheard through the streets of Byzantium at night, you have come to the right place!"

"Yes, the right place at the right time; I wonder, was that just dumb luck, or a touch of the wit that made your aunt Natyr so formidable?"

This was the old priestess; she had come up to me, to straighten my tunic and place her hands lightly on my shoulders.

"If I was you, Lady, I would bet on dumb."

"Ha! Well, perhaps a touch of both. We shall see."

The other priestess had come up behind me and placed her fingertips lightly on my temples; I could see them both and myself clearly in one of the mirrors. They murmured a prayer to their goddess and I could feel the magic in the room surge outward from the altar and into them. The eyes

366

of the woman in front of me turned black and then that blackness spilled out over her face and down her arms onto me and I felt a cool rush of power, like the welcome cool brought by a clear night after a long hot day.

"Night's Cloak do we cast about you!"

"Night's Eyes do we lend you!"

"Walk unseen and unheard, until Byzantium's midnight bell has sounded!"

I thought I heard a third voice as well, whispering words in a shivery counterpoint. As they finished, the blackness that was the power of Night flowed up over my face; I could see it in the mirror! Where it flowed, my skin, my clothing, even my eyes turned black, a flat black without a shine or glint to it. My eyes felt odd for an instant, but I blinked and it passed; my sight had been bespelled as well. The shorter priestess explained:

"You will be unseen and unheard as long as you stay in the shadows; we gave you the ability to see in Darkness as well, otherwise you would be tripping over your own feet until you learned the trick of it. You will not have that much time; these spells will fall if you get into a fight or are touched by magic powerful enough, and in any case they will fade at midnight."

"More than enough time for what I have to do. Thank you, Ladies, and thank you, Mother Night."

I bowed towards the altar. "Your debt...."

"Still stands. Our Goddess has spoken to us; this will not be the last time you will have dealings with those who follow the Night. Also, her magic may have marked you in a way you do not yet understand. Good Luck, Joren of the House of the Raven."

They walked alongside me to the antechamber inside the front doors; it had been empty before, but now it was crowded. There were snakes large and small, human beggars, shadowy forms that did not look quite human, and the biggest goose I had seen in my life, all of them eyes and ears for the Goddess of Night. The acolyte came running into the room from a narrow corridor that lead north; she looked a bit winded and more than a bit worried. The older priestess stopped to speak to the acolyte briefly, just enough time for a few terse sentences and then she turned to me and gestured towards the temple doors:

"Hurry, boy. Loricon Longshanks has divided his forces; some are still looking for you, some have left the city going west, and the rest have joined with him and entered the Temple grounds of Wurrunk with bare swords. Strife now walks through the House of Death, and the city guard will do nothing. After all, what can normal folk do when the Lords of Death draw blades on each other?"

I bowed once again and ran from the temple, the crowd splitting in front of me, and then I headed east around the temple of Tawara and then north along the east edge of the Great Square. The world seemed strangely inverted: I could see into the deepest shadows, but found that I could not look directly at a torch or bright lamp. There was a light overcast of clouds blocking the starlight, and I found that I was indeed invisible if I stayed away from the bright areas around the lamps and doorways. This took a bit of getting used to, since people who could not see me would not know to give me room to walk by them or any warning if they decided to run through the space I was in.

Once I had adapted myself to the way my world had been twisted, I began to make good time. I passed at least two pairs of warriors who were looking for me (they were wearing Loricon's colors) and several more that might have been guards or just some toughs looking for a fight. I had gotten as far as the North Harbor road when I heard the ringing of a bell, not just any bell, but the golden bell in the gate to Wurrunk's Temple. It was ringing for a passing, then another and another and I knew it was ringing for followers of Wurrunk who were dying; Loricon had started a war inside the House of Death, and I had a horrible feeling that it was all because of me. That was not my only problem; I was being followed. They were behind me and on either side, but I thought they were starting to close in. I was right, they made their move at the Temple of Upelluri: a dozen fomorians, all of them armed. I might have guessed; Eresh's magic made me invisible to the eye, but darklings had their own ability to sense objects in the dark that had nothing to do with eyes or light. I had no idea how I appeared to them, but it had been odd enough to draw their attention. They apparently wanted to know what the hell I was doing running around their city like this, and I could not say I blamed them.

They had no armor to speak of, but they had maces, spears, a couple of clubs and each of them towered a foot or more over me. Five of them blocked me just before I reached the plaza in front of the temple, with half a dozen more coming in from the sides. There was something else coming up behind me too, something that made me want to put my back against a wall, someone who reeked of old blood, a hunger for vengeance and a boundless rage that could shake the city of Byzantium like an empty gourd were it unleashed. It had to be a follower of Zarab Adar, the darkling god of war! Whoever it was, they were not just an initiate but one so enrobed in the magic of his god that I could smell it from 100 yards away. The other darklings were right in front of me though, and the tallest of them tapped his spear butt on the cobblestones and spoke to me:

"Who are you to run through the shadows so freely, Black One? You are no Child of Darkness!"

Then the others spoke up as they got a clear scan of me:

"Human, he wears the Grey Tunic..."

"Blood on him, but not his..."

"He has been marked with the Sign of Night!"

"He is marked with more than that."

This last was from the Zarab Adar darkling coming up from the south; he had to be an acolyte at least with that much magic. He was not as tall as the darkling in front of me, but as broad as any of the others and heavily scarred. He was naked except for a loincloth and smelled of sea water; he must have swum ashore to avoid making an account of himself to the guards at the gates. That would not help him if he was still within the city when the Sun rose, but he might be able to elude the City Watch if all he did was look around. As it turned out, that was exactly why he was here.

"I came to scout the embassy of the White Sun, but I crossed a blood trail to the south and west. Someone hacked down a couple of those puny sword-loving slugs, and now the streets are full of them! That blood trail leads to you, Runt. Why did you kill those swordsmen? Do you hold my Dread Lord as your own?"

"I follow Tarhunt, King of the Gods! I have to reach the Great House of Death unhindered, and the priestesses of the Night Temple gave me Eresh's blessing to allow me to do so. It is a matter of life and death."

One of the other darklings, a male in his middle years, spoke up; he had been silent until now, and I realized he had been scanning my face intently:

"I know him; he is the heir of the House of the Raven, the one Kak spoke of."

The Zarab Adar acolyte glanced at the tall spear-wielding darkling.

"If the Goddess of Night wants him to get to the Great House of Death, then that is where he is going."

That worthy nodded back and spoke to the other darklings.

"Anhur, Baku, with me. Zauk, take word of this to the Temple of Night. The rest of you can get back to work. I will let you know what happens."

The scarred darkling went on: "We're going to deal with anyone who gets in the way, of course."

"Of course, but this is my city, we will try to talk some sense into them while the boy runs ahead."

"Talk? You city people are funny, but sure, you can talk to them. I will just make sure they do not try to go anywhere while you talk to them."

We started running north, keeping to the shadows. The guards at the Temple of the Dreamer could tell something was up, but could not get a good look at anyone from across the plaza, and we soon left them behind us. The rest of the run to the Stormwall gate was uneventful; the Stormwall marked the boundaries of Northside and its foundations dated back a thousand years. From there, I would be able see the gate of the House of Death. The ringing of the passing bell had slowed and then stopped by the time I reached the Stormwall, and while there were plenty of tracks (and blood), the area was deserted except for the body lying in the gate to the grounds to Wurrunk's Temple.

The fomorian with the spear looked around, shrugged and said to me:

"This is where we leave you, Child of Storm. Fare you well."

I thanked him; he and his two companions nodded to me and disappeared in the shadows to the south.

The scarred darkling leaned down to get a good look at my face.

"Kak's nephew, eh? Well, Kak Boneslitter has been a problem in the past for the followers of the Lord of Blood and Fear. Perhaps I will go deal with this problem.", he taunted.

"Perhaps you will. If somehow you manage to do that, then you will see me again."

He threw his head back and laughed at that, then we showed each other our teeth, darkling-fashion, and he was gone. Then I drew my sword and headed for the gate to the temple grounds. I did not know the man whose body lay under the golden bell, but he was wearing Loricon's colors, a wide sash around his waist. He had caught one of Pelessa's arrows in the throat, and my heart started to pound. How many of my friends were dead now because of Loricon? Because of me? I crossed the threshold beneath the bell and was greeted by a shout from Rostaka:

"JOREN!"

There were bodies everywhere it seemed, and people tending to some wounded and two groups of warriors with swords drawn, moving in good order. One group was headed by Dangmag, and seemed to be checking all of the outbuildings for holdouts. He had bandage around his head, but

370

otherwise looked to be in good shape; he gave me a wave of his hand and then kicked in the door of the stable, the fighters following him put their shields up and went on in. Rostaka lead the other group, which was checking the bodies near the gate for survivors; two of them went past me and dragged the body behind me in and off to one side.

Rostaka was unwounded and put a hand on my shoulder as she looked me over for injuries. I realized that she could see me just fine, shadows or not; perhaps it was because I was sworn to Wurrunk and therefore Night's magic had no power to hide me from Wurrunk's followers on their home ground. She breathed a sigh of relief when she was finished and gave me a gentle shake:

"I am glad to see you free and unharmed. You have killed tonight."

It was not a question. I nodded to her and explained, wanting to push past her, but afraid to see who had died here tonight.

"Hadelor and Chala; they tried to corner me in an alley near the Oak and Ivy temple and drew on me. After that, I... I was not sure what to do, so I went to the Temple of Night to ask for aid. The priestesses there gave me their blessing and let me run here unseen through the shadows. How bad is it?"

"Bad. I had not realized Loricon had so many men and women who would come when he called. But you...going to the Night Temple was a wise move; Eresh's Blessing is still on you, I can feel it, but it does not hide you from our sight, here. It will not last forever, but it should last a few hours more. What are your plans?"

"To get Ajax's gear, find him and get the both of us the hell away from here before anyone else is killed."

"Good plan, but I will go get Ajax's gear, you must talk to Cook and...say good bye. Joren, remember, NONE of this is your fault. Loricon has hated Ajax since before you were born; when someone offered him whatever it was he wanted so badly, HE choose this road, not you."

"Thank you, Sage."

She shook her head, and then gave me a push towards the temple while she headed for Ajax's quarters. There were some other bodies with Pelessa's shafts in them scattered about, but most of the dead where over between the Temple of Wurrunk and the center of the great courtyard. There was someone there crying; it was Pelessa, and she was kneeling with Urika's head in her lap.

Near them were three bodies, two clad in iron. One was Grali, who had been killed by a thrust to the neck. One was Herva, with Loricon's broadsword in deep under her ribs. Herva's left hand was on the blade of that sword, and her own rapier was lodged in Loricon's skull. Her thrust had taken him in the left eye, with a good foot of the needle sharp blade protruding from the back of his head. Loricon had other wounds as well: one arrow in the left leg, two more in the left arm, one of those in the elbow, all Urika's arrows. Urika's body did not have any wounds that I could see.

Pelessa lifted a tear-stained face to stammer:

"She told me to cover the gate, she…she told me not to shoot at him!"

So Loricon would not see her as a threat; Urika had been a real threat and he had killed her from a distance, with magic as he closed on Herva. Grali had been in the way and he had cut her down. Damn him.

"Joren."

It was Cook, sitting on the temple steps with his left arm in a sling and a bloody bandage around his left hand. I went to him and clasped his good hand; he was very pale and I realized he had lost a lot of blood. I explained what had happened to me and what I had done in as few words as possible. He nodded in approval:

"That was smart. Loricon came here just after dark, looking for you. He was pushed for time, something must have thrown his plans awry and he was not taking it well. He had stormed through the hall and barracks and then he saw me. He wanted you and demanded that I produce you; when I told him 'No', he almost took my arm off. That started a brawl right enough; everyone in the Hiring Hall and the smithy came charging out and pitched in, but it was when he went after Grali and Pelessa that…this happened."

He gestured at the bodies in the center of the courtyard.

"He wanted to get information from them, and Urika and Herva were not having any of that. Urika saw him coming and started shooting…I will have to send Pelessa home now, I think."

He shook his head to clear and then focused on me:

"Loricon's men lost heart when he fell; the ones who could, made it to the gate and got away just before you arrived. But they are not important now, they can be dealt with later. What worries me is your information, about Ajax and Loricon's henchmen trying to take you right out in the open. Loricon has wanted to kill Ajax for years; I would have bet a fortune that he would be crossing swords with him right now, instead he was here looking for you. Then there is the matter of sending scores of armed men into the streets of Byzantium in broad daylight...that could have been the work of one of your Aunt Natyr's old enemies, you do not make the kind of show of force in Byzantium without the backing of a Queen..."

"Or the Minos?"

I had started to wonder about that; in nearly 300 years, no one had come close to matching the skill, the determination and the legendary luck of the Sea-King when it came to the game of politics. What were the odds that something involving one of Byzantium's Queens, the Great House of Death and the Empire could boil over into open violence without attracting the attention or support of the Minos?

Gultor met my eyes: "I do not know."

The only thing worse that finding out that you are a piece in someone else's game is finding out that you are a piece in more game than one, and no one you trust knows what the hell is going on.

"I have got to get out of Byzantium!"

"Agreed; you cannot take the north or south roads, they will be patrolled."

"Ajax said something last night about a ship on the seaside docks?"

"That ship will be watched and might even be crewed by your enemies, if it is still there. Your best bet might be to meet up with Ajax and head west; see if you can make it across the border into the Illyrian lands. The empire and the queens have no power there, and you two have a good a chance as anyone I know of making it across country off the roads. I would stay out of the Caenopolis if you go west though; strange things can happen there, in times of strife."

Wandering around in biggest necropolis in the world had not really been in my plans, so I would make a point of taking his advice there. Then the golden bell rang twice, and I fell to one knee. Just for an instant, I felt the clasp of a familiar hand on my shoulder and I knew Master Arkell had died. I staggered to my feet and then helped Cook to his. Dangmag and Rostaka had come up carrying Ajax's gear, and they all asked the same question at the same time:

"Ajax?"

"No. Master Arkell."

Rostaka gasped: "Arkell? Joren, you must leave NOW! "

Dangmag started swearing and Cook closed his eyes briefly. I had learned that he and Master Arkell had been friends from their childhood. He sounded very tired when he opened them.

"Worse than I thought, and their reach is longer than I had imagined.

The Illyrian lands will not be far enough, boy."

He pulled the grey tunic that I had worn for the past year from my shoulders, then Rostaka and Dangmag slung the packs with Ajax's belongings over my shoulders.

Rostaka kissed me on the forehead:

"I will go to the House of the Raven and tell your family why you left without saying good bye."

Dangmag whispered while he shook me three times for emphasis:

"Practice, Practice, Practice."

Then Cook touched me on the face between my eyes and said:

"I release you from your service to Wurrunk. Fare you well, Joren, son of Dono."

I felt the link between me and the temple fall away, and the world changed with it, although I could still feel Night's magic swirling about me. It felt odd to be the outsider in the Great House of Death. I could not think of what to say, so I bowed to the three of them there in the darkness, and then I walked back to where Pelessa sat with Urika's body in her arms. I placed my hand on her back and wished her good luck, but I do not think she heard a word I said. Then I ran to the gate, and then out past the Stormwall and turned west; I loosened my sword in its scabbard as I took a good look around.

From the tracks and the blood trails, a number of Loricon's followers had gone this way as well, so I stuck to the shadows all the way to the River Gate. That gate was still open, as there was still a fair amount of traffic in and out of the city at this time of the evening. There were wagons moving freight to or from the shipyard, people on foot from the Lycus temple, and common folk headed home after working a long day in the city. I did not want to invite a half dozen crossbow bolts in the back trying to sneak past the gate guards, so I made sure that I was well within the area lighted by the lanterns at the gate and waited for someone to notice me.

All of the guards had seen me before, and I was often carrying parcels for one lord or another, so I did not seem that out of place. One guard jeered at me in a genial tone:

"What is this? They have you playing the mule at this hour?"

I brayed at her like a donkey in reply and got a laugh or a grin from them all. They waved me through and as I passed out into Portside, I heard someone behind me and to the left say:

"Was that him? The heir to the House of the Raven?..."

I picked up my pace a bit, and soon heard footsteps, five or six people, coming along behind me. Fifty yards from the city gates, I stepped into the shadows and the people following me stopped dead in their tracks, while I kept moving.

"Wait...where did he go?"

"He ducked inside that warehouse..."

"No, he went down that alley!"

"Quiet, you fools!"

That voice held enough authority to silence the lot of them. They were all silent for a time, while I kept moving. Then I heard that voice of command raised above other voices that were too low for me to make out:

"I said back to the city, now. We are not being paid enough for this!"

So, there had been at least one group waiting for me at the River Gate; they had thought better of trying to take or follow me, but would certainly pass word to their masters that I had left the city headed west. I kept moving, alternating walking and trotting, until I had traveled more than half the distance to the first mile marker. The road was empty of normal foot traffic this far out of the city; except for couriers on urgent business, I might not anyone at all on this road until just before dawn. That was when I smelled the horses and realized that there were mounts tethered on either side of the road up ahead of me. The sound of muffled cursing drew my attention, and I set down my packs behind a willow tree with 3 trunks and drew my greatsword. A moment later, someone stumbled onto the road from the woods on my right and began trotting west ahead of me. He was carrying a burden of some kind; if it had not been for the horses, I would have smelled him sweating a hundred yards off, that and the cheap beer, mutton, bee's wax, and...Loricon's perfume. One of Loricon's men carrying something, and in a hurry too. Then I heard a clatter as he tried to shift what he was carrying and realized he had dropped a quiver of arrows. Arrows? That is when I had a hunch as to what kind of trap Loricon had closed on Ajax. He was dithering as to pick up the dropped arrows or just keep going when I trotted past him and then turned to face him sword in hand, and Night's magic fell from me. It must have seemed as if I had appeared out of nowhere. He staggered backwards, then realized who I was:

"No! No, no, no....".

He dropped what he was carrying and drew a broadsword and a shortsword to parry with, but my first blow beat down his blade and opened a wound in his scalp. He started to backpedal when the blood ran down into his face, but I nicked his right wrist and he had to drop the broadsword. He tried to close with me then to grapple but he just was not fast enough, and I ran him through. I checked what he was carrying while I wiped my sword clean; both of the spells cast upon me by the priestesses of Night were gone, so I did most of my searching by hand and smell.

The scent of that perfume was all over him; he had applied it liberally, in imitation of the man he followed. That seemed a bit strange to me, but would certainly help me keep track of who Loricon's henchmen were. I had the feeling that Loricon's malice would outlive the man himself, and I was right. I have had to deal with more than one of the men who had followed Longshanks's commands that night in the years since, and his hate seemed to have marked all of them in some way. This man had been carrying six full quivers of arrows in addition to his own weapons; arrows...he had been sent back to get more arrows for the archers and there might be as many as six of them in the ambush. I grabbed one quiver and started running west. 'Please let me be in time', I thought. I was.

A breeze began to blow from the west, and I caught the scent of more horses (from north of the road) and then the reek of death well before I stumbled over the first body. It was right in front of the mile marker, and I could hear shouting and see the flicker of torches off to the south and west. I started picking my way through the trees and found more bodies, a lot more. I knew the style of the man who had taught me to use a sword, and I could see that Ajax Whitebeard had done the Death god's red work from the road back through the trees to the barley fields, dropping warrior after warrior as he retreated. He had lured them out into the fields that were sown with the second crop of the year, heavily irrigated against the heat of summer, and the muddy rows had slowed and hindered them. That should have been the end of him though; his attackers had brought torches and some sort of mage light, and six good archers to bring him down now that he was out in the open. However, they had not counted on his ability to cut arrows; either they did not know or had not believed the tales of his skill, and he had flicked their arrows aside as easily as he dropped the fighters who assailed him on foot. So they had sent one of their number back for more arrows and they would be expecting him. The archers had positioned themselves on shields that had been laid down to give them firm footing in the mud, and four of the six had put their bows aside and joined the melee fighters when their arrows had given out.

The remaining archers were down to one arrow apiece, and out in the fields, a dozen of Loricon's followers had survived long enough to finally close a half circle around Ajax Whitebeard. The old man was wounded in half a dozen places and was down to his broadsword and a dagger for weapons, his other blades having gotten stuck in men he had killed. I had come in time, but only just in time. I ran towards the archers, holding up the quiver, yelling "Arrows!". Both archers flicked a glance at me and I heard the far one mutter: "About time!".

The near archer started to draw, and then took another look at me, and realized too late that I was not the man they had sent back for their reloads. Then I was on him, too close to shoot and I caught him across the belly with my blade as I leapt past him and ran on towards the last archer. He saw me coming and fired, but I cut the arrow to my right; he was left-handed and I took him in the armpit when he dropped his bow and went for his sword. He screamed as he went down and not everyone in the field heard him. I remembered the words of the god of Death when he had given me his gift:

"I ask only that you not dishonor it."

So be it, I would give them fair warning; I picked up one of the discarded bows and shouted:

"I have twenty arrows and a bow, and I am going to shoot everyone in that field who is NOT Ajax Whitebeard!"

The men facing Ajax froze in their tracks; then I drew and fired in one smooth motion, and I have absolutely no idea where that arrow went. Focus, you idiot. My second shot went low and spitted one man through the buttocks; not fatal, but very painful (trust me) and he screamed like stuck pig, as he went down, hamstrung.

I had the range now; I put my third arrow into one man's ear and caught another man in the throat with my fourth shot, a tall man clothed in the Rhigos style, but rich enough for a Royal Husband. That was when Ajax killed a man wearing a silver torc, who had let himself be distracted by my arrows, and their nerve broke. The old man dropped another of his attackers who had turned to flee, and then began tending to his wounds. I dropped one more with arrows in the back before the remainder managed to reach the edge of the lighted area and make good their escape. I did a quick circuit of the area to be sure they had all fled, then I retrieved his other blades from the bodies they were stuck in and wiped them clean. Ajax looked pale and for the first time that I could remember, tired. He had lost a lot of blood, and it takes a special kind of magic to heal that. He put a hand on my shoulder and gave me a rueful smile; I could tell he was relieved to see me, and not just because I had been in the nick of time.

I started to tell him of the events in the city, but he stopped me with a raised hand and walked over to the man I had shot through the buttocks. He was the only one of the attackers still alive, and he was cursing desperately as he tried to pull my arrow from his flesh. He looked up at the man he had tried to trap and kill and asked:

"Mercy?"

Ajax looked him over for a moment and told him: "No.", then drove his sword point into the assassin's throat. He turned towards me, and began to sheath his blades as I handed them to him, one by one.

"You have bad news, and I did not want that one hearing it."

He sighed deeply then, and patted my arm.

"Help me back to the road, and then you can tell me how many of my friends have gone ahead."

I gave him my shoulder to lean on and it came to me that this was the first time I had ever been able to help him, this strange old man who had been my father's friend, and who had cared for me since before my earliest memories began. I realized too, that his manner towards me was different; I was no longer a boy to him, but a man, and he treated me as such. We made it back to the road, and he eased himself down on a flat rock next to the mile marker that bore a sigil of the Minos. There was no sign of anyone east or west on the road, so I told him what had happened from the time I had met the two men who had smelled so strongly of onions. He closed his eyes and sighed again when I told him of the deaths in Wurrunk's great courtyard, but he swore out loud when I told him I had felt Master Arkell die.

"Damn them, how did they arrange that? You and Gultar had it right; we have to get you away from Byzantium until we can figure out what the hell is going on and exactly who it is we are dealing with."

"We go west then?"

"No, we will do something they will not expect, I hope. There should be some horses around here; we will need two of them."

"Three, Sir. Rostaka gave me the packs you had in your room; they are just down the road a ways."

"Did she now? That is a relief, and yet another debt I am glad to owe her. Very well, get three horses. We will load the one, mount the others and ride like hell for Portside. There is someone I want you to meet."

Portside? We were going back to Byzantium? Well, I certainly had not expected us to go that way, so maybe we actually had a chance of doing what our enemies were not expecting. They seemed to have prepared for everything else, and it had almost cost us both our lives. I went for the horses. It did not take long to find them, and I was able to lead three good mounts back to Ajax in short order, but I had caught the scent of other horses, horses that had come with the others who had attacked Ajax, but who had left before I arrived, and at least one of their riders had been a woman who favored a very expensive perfume. Not quite what you would expect an assassin to wear. I mentioned this to the Old Man and he frowned, and then shook his head.

"This fight was meant by Loricon to be between us, not his followers. It was to be a show, a display of his skill and of my humiliation before an audience of his choice. I have no doubt that he would have invited his hangers-on to watch, but that kind of perfume suggests that real wealth, real power was here too. I was to meet someone from Bluewater a couple of miles up the road just before sunset; they were supposed to have information for the Council of Queens on what is going on among the tribes in Illyria. When they did not show, I headed back and ran into this crowd. If your attackers knew I would be here before the Sun even set, then we have to assume that my orders, the messenger, the information, everything, were all part of the trap. A trap that should have worked. I think something else happened, something they were not expecting, that disrupted all of their plans. Your refusal to be taken, and then the way you disappeared after you went to the Night Temple, drove them to the edge of panic. "

"There was someone else involved on the other side; I think that Loricon had promised you to that someone, and the possibility of you escaping was an outcome so unacceptable that he threw over his personal feud with me and stormed into the temple grounds to get you."

"His timetable must have been very tight; he was pushing his luck, and then he ran into Urika and Herva, and his luck ran out. But how did they kill Arkell? That could not have been easy, and they coordinated their attacks; both happened at the same time, on the same day, and a hundred miles apart."

He turned and looked at me, and I felt a chill as I realized he was afraid, afraid for me.

"There are at least two other players in this game; we do not know their goals, and their capabilities are...impressive. We are leaving Thrace, and with any luck, we will do it tonight. Mount up."

Chapter XXXIV: The One-Eyed Sea Serpent

LEAVING THRACE SOUNDED GOOD TO ME; I just wished my duties had included some riding in the past year. I had not sat on a mount since the day I first came to Byzantium, and I could tell I was going to be sore before we had finished this run. We did not meet anyone on the road back to Byzantium until we reached Portside and turned off down the street that lead to the wharf next to the Temple of Lycus. Ajax did not slow at all, but the drumming of our horses' hooves was enough to scatter the folk between us and the wharf. They yelled a number of things at us, of course, and I think it drew the attention of those who had been set to watch for us. It did not matter much either way; we had a boat to catch, and it was already underway. It had been moored right up against the temple of the river god, possibly on temple business, but was now moving out into the river. It was no shallow water vessel but a deep-water ship, high-prowed and broadwaisted, with a white sail striped with a blue so deep it looked black in the torchlight, and a figurehead of some kind of serpent.

Ajax galloped right down the length of the pier, his wide scarlet cloak flowing out in the wind behind him, and jerked his plunging mount back on its haunches at the last possible moment. He swung down out of the saddle, turned and in the same motion stepped off the pier, onto the gunwale of the passing ship and then onto its deck without breaking stride. Me? I jerked my mount to a halt, grabbed Ajax's packs from the third horse, threw them onto the deck of the ship and just barely managed to land on its deck with one last wild leap of my own. Luckily, neither I nor the packs had struck any of the crew who were using poles to move the ship out into the current, and I managed to roll out of their way and onto my feet without tangling myself too badly in my cloak. Ajax nodded approvingly at me and said:

"Follow me; I want you to meet an old friend of mine."

Old friend? The crew kept an eye on me as we walked towards the bow of the ship, but ignored Ajax; it was almost as if he was expected. There was a man in the bow of the ship watching us approach: not much above average height, but broad and heavily muscled, with a thick braid of hair gone mostly to grey. He wore armor that had been worked to look like the scales of some sea creature, and an air of command like a cloak.

He smelled of power, of cold, deep water and of apples (one of which he had just eaten). He spoke to Ajax as if he had just come up from below decks:

"Change your mind?"

"Yes, I think I will take your advice after all. A sea voyage seems to be just what I need to relax. This is Joren, son of Dono. Joren, this is Tormus, Lord and Captain of the One-Eyed Sea Serpent."

He looked at me and nodded; he had very dark eyes, and just for an instant I had the odd impression that he was not the only one looking at me out of them. Then he glanced at the growing commotion on the docks. There was a small group trying to control our horses, and a bunch of people along the pier shouting and shaking their fists at us. There were also at least two more groups with lanterns on the street out to the River road who were shouting at us, at the ship and at each other.

"Is that anything I should be concerned about?"

Ajax did not even look back.

"Eh? Oh, no, I would not think so."

Then the horns started blowing. I felt the ship lurch as we entered the current of the river, and Tormus turned and gave the Temple of Lycus an open handed salute. Then he roared one word:

"Oars!"

His crew slid their poles into their racks and shipped their oars, looking at their captain and starting to grin as they realized that every eye on shore was looking at them and their ship. A tall man with a shaved head wearing a green kilt was checking the benches and prodding the oarsmen:

"You lot look soft, and you smell like beer rags. You been ashore too long, but don't you worry none, Captain will sweat that right out of you."

"Tormus, how far would you say it is to the Chain?"

"Oh, more than half a mile in a straight line. Down Oars! "

The man in the green kilt started beating time on a drum in the stern of the ship, just as the bells at the River Gate started to ring.

"Pull!"

The One Eyed Sea Serpent began to pick up speed as the oarsmen found their rhythm, then the sail caught a stiffening breeze and the ship surged forward. Odd, she did not look to be that fast a ship. Ajax raised his eyebrows at Tormus in surprise:

"She feels different!"

"Aye, I had the barnacles scraped, some of the woodwork replaced, new rigging, new sail; she feels pretty, does my one-eyed girl! Let us see if she wants to run a bit."

There were other bells ringing, some from inside the city, and then we heard the deeper tone of the great brazen gong by the Chain. The Chain was strung between two fortified towers, and was meant to be raised to protect the vulnerable shipyards and the Lycus Temple in case of a raid that might penetrate as far as the Riverside port. If they were sounding that gong, then someone with enough political pull to order that alarm was willing to accept the consequences of rousing the entire city in the middle of the night. Someone really did not want us to leave Byzantium. I could hear the clanking of the mighty gears in the city-side tower as they started to raise the Chain. Ajax asked a question of Tormus, just like he might ask about the weather or a horse race:

"Do you think they will get the Chain up in time?"

Tormus answered him in much the same way:

"I hope not; I like Byzantium well enough, I would not want to hurt their shiny little chain."

He did not sound like he was joking. I looked at him, at the deck of the ship, at the sigils I could see carved into that deck, and I thought of the cold, deep current of power that I could sense growing from Tormus, like the currents that move through the great ocean deeps where the Sun's light does not reach. 'Lord and Captain", Ajax had said, and it came to me that he considered Tormus his equal.

Aruna.

Tormus was a servant of Aruna, Father Ocean, who the Sea Lords called Poseidon, and Sire of Monsters. The river gods of the world are the sons and grandsons of Aruna, and they flow to the sea for a reason. It might not be wise to attempt to bar one of Aruna's own from returning to the sea; not with the power of a river god behind him. I noticed that while Tormus had not moved, Ajax had placed himself up by the ship's figure head, and braced a boot against a block and taken a good grip on the gunwale to steady himself. That is when I walked back to the mainmast and carefully wrapped myself around it.

The Chain was coming up, and we could hear horns being blown on both the city's tower and the Kastellion, the northern tower on the Galatan shore, amid calls to turn back. I could see the thick links of the Chain starting to glow with magic; we were not going to make it...then the river itself rose behind the ship and I felt the ship rising, being lifted and we passed over the Chain on the crest of a surging wave that took the One-Eyed Sea Serpent half way across the Northside harbor before it subsided. Tormus and his crew roared with laughter, pointing and waving at the workgangs and sailors who were gaping at the sight from the docks and ships of the Byzantium's inner port; even Ajax was grinning. Me, I breathed half a dozen prayers before I let go of that mast.

There were shouts of "What ship?" coming from shore, because the light of the dockside lanterns did not carry that far out, and the man in the green kilt, whose name I learned was Gyffun, shouted back:

"The One-Eyed Sea Serpent! Remember the name, you scuts!"

From the lights and the sound of things, it seemed as if the whole city of Byzantium was in an uproar. While it did not look as if any ships were making to chase us, Tormus decided to make the most of his speed and the clear waters he could see ahead of him, and we rounded Tarhunt's Hill and headed out to sea. There was no pursuit.

While Ajax and Tormus conferred on where we were headed next, I sat down in a corner out of the way and thought about Master Arkell. Revenge was all I could think of at first, but then I began to wonder. Right from the day I accepted him as my Master and he swore his oath to teach me as his Pupil, he had poured every technique, every trick, every memory that might possibly be of use into me. Had he foreseen how short his time would be with me? Many years later, I heard of how he had died, of a centuries-old blood feud that had broken out anew, of how he had smashed the assassination attempt on his brother and tracked the surviving assassins to the one who had hired them. The trail had led to a fortified inn on the road to Bearford, and when the Sun rose the next morning, all that was left of that building was a smoking pile of rubble, leveled by a powerful magic. The sleuth hounds of Cibyrrha could find no trail leading away from the wreckage; Master Arkell, the assassins and their paymaster all were entombed together. That meant that there was no one left to answer any questions about a wider conspiracy; so maybe Master Arkell's death in Lycea had nothing to do with Loricon's plotting in Byzantium. Maybe, and maybe I would look into it myself one day. In the meantime, what I remembered most about him was his last words to me before he had taken ship for Cibyrrha:

"You can be greater than I!"

That was going to take some doing, Master.

Tormus and Ajax decided to head west after leaving the waters of the Narrow Sea, and sail to Venice, Adria's City near the mouths of the Padus River at the northern end of the Sea of Adria. This was beyond the lands of the Illyrian tribes, and hopefully beyond the reach of my enemies, known and unknown. Ajax and I could then travel overland along the caravan routes laid down by the Hermetic League and return to Thrace from the west. This would take a while, but maybe that was for the best; I needed things in Thrace to settle down a bit before I could risk coming back. I was going to have to tell Belkara that I might not be able to meet her as planned, and that she should be wary indeed if her path took her to Byzantium City before I found her.

We sailed through the Darkling Strait, past the Great Pharos and around the Islands of Marmara (famed for their marble quarries) without incident and with surprising speed. Tormus and his crew had a fine ship and the weather was perfect. Ajax had been right, a sea voyage seemed to be exactly what we needed.

Of course, that was when the storm hit us.

But rest now, Grandchild of mine; I will tell you that story in its own good time.

This ends the book Queen's Heir; the story of Joren's time in the lands of the West will be told in the book Raven's Blood, coming in 2017.

APPENDICES

Appendix A: Hittite Deities

A'as – god of wisdom, who the Mesopotamians call Enki
Alalus – primordial entity
Arinniti or **Arinna** – sun goddess, Consort of Tarhunt
Arma Arn – the Son of the goddess of Night
Aruna – god of the sea, whom the Achaeans call Poseidon
Aserdus – goddess of fertility and wife of Elkunirsa
Elkunirsa – creator god and husband of Aserdus
Ellel – god of oaths, who loves Ishara
Eresh – the goddess of Night
Halki – god of grain, sire of the grain goddesses
Hannahannah – mother goddess
Hanwasuit – goddess of sovereignty
Hapantali – pastoral goddess
Hasameli – god of metalworkers and craftsmen
Hatepuna – daughter of the sea, sister of Byzan
Huttellurra – collective of midwifery goddesses
Inar – god of woods and fields
Hutena – goddesses of fate
Inara – goddess of the wild animals of the steppe
Ishara – goddess of oaths and love
Istanu – a judge of the dead
Istustaya and **Papaya** – goddesses of destiny
Jarri – god of archers, "Lord of the Bow"
Kamrusepa – goddess of healing, medicine and magic
Kasku – the Wise, Lord of Shadows, son of Arma Arn
Khetar – founder of the kingdom of the Hittites, and its capital, Hattusha
Lupak – the god of wolves
Nabu – the god of trade
Pirwa – deity of uncertain nature, the Trickster
Rundas – god of the hunt and good fortune
Samelir – servant of Wurrunk, patron of swordsmiths
Sandas – lion god
Sarrumas – god of the mountains, Sire of all duskcats, brother to Sandas
Šauška – goddess of fertility and healing
Tarhunt – King of the Gods, God of Storms, Bringer of Rain, Lord of Thunder

Tawara – nursery goddess, friend and companion of Byzan

Telepinu – god of farming

Tillar – bull god, sire of the race of minotaurs, patron of berzerkers

Tuhus – son of Tillar, patron of the nomad chieftains

Upelluri – god of dreaming

Wurrunk Atte – god of war and swords, brother and ally of Tarhunt

Appendix B: The Longaevi

The Longaevi – the Elder Peoples, the Non-Human races

These are divided roughly into three groups:
The Court of Light, the Court of Darkness and the Twilight Host.
The Court of Light values Beauty above all else, and is mostly centered in the Elven Forests.
The Court of Darkness values Strength above all else, and has their centers of power in the dark places of the world such as the Shadowlands near Byzantium and the Kingdom of Stygia in the Pontine Mountains.
The Twilight Host consists of those races that do not align with either the Court of Light or Darkness, such as dwarves and brownies, and groups of creatures or individuals who do not fit in anywhere else. Dwarves and Brownies are unusual in that they are the only Longaevi who can handle cold iron.

Logaevi societies are divided into three classes: the Daoine Si, the Aos Si and the Ir Si.
The Daoine Si are the high nobility, the rulers and the most powerful of their kind. Some Daoine Si are thousands of years old and are so magically powerful that they are treated as deities or supernatural forces by lesser folk.
The Aos Si are the middle classes, and the leaders of most Longaevi communities. They are the chieftains, healers, merchants and captains of Longaevi society, and make up the bulk of the best warriors.
The Ir Si are the lower classes, the commoners of Longaevi society. They are the smallest and weakest of the Longaevi and the most vulnerable to the effects of iron, and are not be found in human cities anymore.
Servants of the Court of Light are called the Alfar, and consist of:
Aos Si – the elves, the centaurs and drayads.
Ir Si – pixies, fairies, fauns

Servants of the Court of Darkness are called Darklings, and consist of:
Aos Si – the fomorians, and lesser giants
Ir Si – goblins, satyrs, harpies

Appendix C: Darkling, Egyptian and Assyrian Deities

Darkling Deities

NOTE: It is often difficult to distinguish between Darkling rulers and Darkling gods, even for darklings. Many darkling gods have human followers.

Arma Arn – son of Eresh, goddess of night

Brighid the Serene – darkling goddess of healing and protection

Eresh – the goddess of night

Kasku – Kasku the Wise, Lord of Shadow, son of Arma Arn, ruler of Thrace who was deposed and slain by the Minos circa 300 MK.

Nyx – goddess of darkness, Mother of the Darkling Races

Zabab Adar – Darkling god of war, rival and enemy of Wurrunk; sometimes called the Bloodstained God. He is cruel, utterly ruthless and without mercy. His disciples are called Blooddrinkers.

Egyptian Deities

Horus – Egyptian god of the sky, war and hunting; referred to as the Avenging Son, the Hawk, the All-Seeing Eye. He is the son of Osiris and Isis

Sekhmet – Egyptian goddess of war, fire and dance. Sekhmet is depicted as a lioness and is seen as the protector of the Pharoahs.

Assyrian Deities

Erra – Assyrian demon or god who is the chief servant of Nergal, and the leader of his demonic slaves

Gibil – a demon or minor god of wild fire

Nergal – Assyrian god of death and the Underworld.

Appendix D: Deities and Heroes of the Empire of the White Sun

Sunna – the White Sun. Her banner is a white sun wheel on a red field. Only members of the Imperial family by birth may wear all white garments; priests, heroes and those who marry into the imperial family may wear yellow, all others are encouraged to wear red.

Bokar Sha – goddess of war, destroyer of external enemies

Eir – goddess of healing

Hel Blackwitch – goddess of intrigue, magic and death

Hoenir – god of silence, servitude and punishment

Loki – god of mischief, considered by many to be a face of the Trickster

Mimir – god of knowledge and wisdom

Njord – god of the sea

Sigurd Dragonsbane patron of generals and heroes, Conquering Son

Sjofn – goddess of love

Snotra – goddess of prudence and trade

Tyr Redhands – god of war, Champion of the White Sun

Vali – god of blood feuds and vengeance

Appendix E: Deities of Thrace

Thrace was ruled by the Lord of Shadows for more than 1600 years. He was one of the Daoine Si, a Great Lord of the Darkling races, who ruled both humans and darklings with an even hand. As a result, the deities of Thrace are a unique mix of human and darkling gods, with a sprinkling of heroes and lesser gods revered nowhere else.

Byzan – Patron goddess of Byzantium, daughter of Poseidon and Sauska. Greatly revered in Thrace, almost unknown elsewhere. A huge statue of her dominates the harbor of Byzantium. Her servants are snakes, pigs and in Byzantium, geese by way of Tawara.

Daedalus – a legendary architect who built the Hippodrome and crafted the Great Chain and other defenses of the city of Byzantium for the Minos. He is said to have helped the Minos build the Great Pharos, the first of the great Lighthouses, but has not been seen since. There are conflicting reports as to whether he was human or darkling.

Kasku the Wise, called the Lord of Shadows – A powerful Daoine Si and the ruler of Thrace from before Time began to 300 MK, when he was slain by the Minos. Kasku was said to be the son of Arma Arn and the grandson of Eresh, both of whom are considered to be gods by the darklings. Kasku ruled Thrace from his fortress in the Shadowlands, a rugged plateau to the north and east of Byzantium. That fortress is now a ruin, but the darklings of the Shadowlands pay tribute to the Minos and fight for him when he calls them.

Lycus – the god of the river Lycus, which flows into the harbor of Byzantium. He is the brother of Byzan and her steadfast ally.

Mycara – one of the grain goddesses, daughters of Sauska. Mycara's grain is rye, and her followers are famous for the liquor they distill from that grain.

Phidalia – Founder of the city of Byzantium before Time began; may have been human or darkling.

Posiedon – called Aruna by the Hittites, this is the god of the sea and the father of both Byzan and Lycus. He is immensely powerful but unpredictable. He is also the god of horses and earthquakes.

Sauska – goddess of fertility and healing and often considered to represent the Earth itself. Sauska is the mother of the many grain goddesses and of Byzan herself.

Tawara – is the goddess of nursemaids, and is the great friend and companion of Byzan in all of her myths and stories from before Time began. Her symbol is the goose, and she is always drawn or carved with a goose following her or in her arms. She loves the city of Byzantium and its people, and time and again geese have been responsible for saving lives by warning of enemies or of disaster or by appearing out of nowhere during times of famine to feed the people of the city. Tawara is a popular goddess in Thrace and very much so in Byzantium, where geese are considered to be lucky.

Thokorion the Scribe – a son of A'as, the god of knowledge and wisdom. He founded the Great Library of Byzantium before Time began and is still in residence, although not just anyone can see him.

Appendix F: The Minos

Ruler of Thrace for the last three hundred years, this human wizard claims to be the last king of Crete, greatest of the Lords of the Sea before the Breaking of the World. No one knows for sure just how he escaped the ruin of Knossos where all of the other Sea Lords were destroyed, or where he was for the first three centuries after the Breaking; the Minos isn't saying. What is known is that in the year 300 MK, he and his followers landed at Starfall in a ship like no other, and then managed to inspire a revolt among the humans of Thrace against the Lord of Shadows. After a whirlwind campaign that lasted two years, Kasku, weakened by the chaos unleashed by the Breaking of the World, was defeated and slain with a sword of meteoric iron, and the Minos took his place.

Since then, his rule has been unshakeable. He built the Hippodrome, and has proven himself a master of politics and intrigue as well as magic. He has outwitted all attempts to dethrone him, and the power of his voice is legendary. In the battle of Falling Hills that stopped the Empire of the White Sun in its tracks, the Minos was said to have commanded a mountain to fall upon the lead elements of the imperial army, and it did. His arcane knowledge has begun to effect the world beyond the borders of Thrace as well. The Minos built the Great Pharos, the first of the magical lighthouses that have begun to calm the seas disturbed by the cataclysm of the Breaking, and commerce once again begins to link the nations of the world together for the first time in nearly six hundred years.

No matter who he really is or where he came from, he is the real power in Thrace now and the only real obstacle that the Empire of the White Sun faces. Never forget that while there are many kings and queens in Thrace, there is only one Minos.

Appendix G: Dragonkind

To the Hittites (and to most humans), anything that has scales and is not a snake is of Dragonkind, the descendants of Illuyanka, the Great Dragon defeated by Tarhunt before Time began. There are three general types of Dragonkind found in the world:

Mushusar

There are the greater dragons, each of which is worth an army of men in battle. There were said to be eleven Mushusar, each with their own name, but none of these monsters has been seen since the Fall of the Dragon Empire, and their names have been lost or forgotten.

Sirrushar

These were the dragons used by the Dragon Empire as mounts and as guard beasts. They are found today in swamps, river bottoms and in ruins that date back to the time of the Dragon Empire. A full grown sirrush can be as large as a big horse; they are cunning and have no fear of men, but luckily tend to be solitary in nature. They do not fly, but can swim quite well and can run as fast as most horses.

Dragonkin

This is a general term used to refer to any other scaled creature that is not a snake, from the great plant-eating Behemoths that graze along the banks of the Euphrates to the packs of Bladefeet that hunt the steppes and the plains of Scythia. All dragonkin can be dangerous, and while there are carvings, paintings and murals that depict all of the different races of dragonkind as domesticated animals, no one has been able to tame ANY of the scaled beasts in more than six hundred years.

Behemoths – long-necked plant eaters, huge but placid.
Three Horns – horned plant eaters almost as big as an elephant
Bladefeet – meat-eaters with a long claw on each foot; only grow to three feet in height but hunt in packs of up to a dozen beasts. Have no fear of men.

There are other breeds of Dragonkin, but these three are those most familiar to the Hittites.